YELLOW DOG

Martin Amis is the author of eighteen books, fiction
and non-fiction, including *London Fields*, *Money*, *The
Information*, *Experience*, *The War Against Cliché* and
Koba the Dread. He lives in London.

ALSO BY MARTIN AMIS

Fiction

The Rachel Papers
Dead Babies
Success
Other People
Money
Einstein's Monsters
London Fields
Time's Arrow
The Information
Night Train
Heavy Water

Non-fiction

Invasion of the Space Invaders
The Moronic Inferno
Visiting Mrs Nabokov
Experience
The War Against Cliché
Koba the Dread

Martin Amis

YELLOW DOG

V

VINTAGE

Published by Vintage 2004

2 4 6 8 10 9 7 5 3 1

Copyright © Martin Amis 2003

Martin Amis has asserted his right under the Copyright,
Designs and Patents Act 1988 to be identified as the
author of this work

First published in Great Britain in 2003 by
Jonathan Cape

Vintage
Random House, 20 Vauxhall Bridge Road,
London SW1V 2SA

Random House Australia (Pty) Limited
20 Alfred Street, Milsons Point, Sydney
New South Wales 2061, Australia

Random House New Zealand Limited
18 Poland Road, Glenfield,
Auckland 10, New Zealand

Random House (Pty) Limited
Endulini, 5A Jubilee Road, Parktown 2193,
South Africa

The Random House Group Limited Reg. No. 954009
www.randomhouse.co.uk/vintage

A CIP catalogue record for this book
is available from the British Library

ISBN 0 099 47042 X

Papers used by Random House are natural, recyclable
products made from wood grown in sustainable forests.
The manufacturing processes conform to the environ-
mental regulations of the country of origin

Printed and bound in Great Britain by
Bookmarque Ltd, Croydon, Surrey

To Isabel

CONTENTS

PART I

CHAPTER ONE

CHAPTER TWO

CHAPTER THREE

CHAPTER FOUR

CHAPTER FIVE

PART II

CHAPTER SIX

PART I

CHAPTER ONE

1. Renaissance Man

But I go to Hollywood but I go to hospital, but you are first but you are last, but he is tall but she is small, but you stay up but you go down, but we are rich but we are poor, but they find peace but they find . . .

Xan Meo went to Hollywood. And, minutes later, with urgent speed, and accompanied by choric howls of electrified distress, Xan Meo went to hospital. Male violence did it.

'I'm off out, me,' he told his American wife Russia.

'Ooh,' she said, pronouncing it like the French for *where*.

'Won't be long. I'll bath them. And I'll read to them too. Then I'll make dinner. Then I'll load the dishwasher. Then I'll give you a long backrub. Okay?'

'Can *I* come?' said Russia.

'I sort of wanted to be alone.'

'You mean you sort of wanted to be alone with your girl-friend.'

Xan knew that this was not a serious accusation. But he adopted an ill-used expression (a thickening of the forehead), and said, not for the first time, and truthfully so far as he knew, 'I've got no secrets from you, kid.'

'. . . Mm,' she said, and offered him her cheek.

'Don't you know the date?'

'Oh. Of course.'

The couple stood embracing in a high-ceilinged hallway. Now the husband with a movement of the arm caused his keys to sound in their pocket. His half-conscious intention was to signal an

3

impatience to be out. Xan would not publicly agree, but women naturally like to prolong routine departures. It is the obverse of their fondness for keeping people waiting. Men shouldn't mind this. Being kept waiting is a moderate reparation for their five million years in power . . . Now Xan sighed softly as the stairs above him softly creaked. A complex figure was descending, normal up to the waist, but two-headed and four-armed: Meo's baby daughter, Sophie, cleaving to the side of her Brazilian nanny, Imaculada. Behind them, at a distance both dreamy and self-sufficient, loomed the four-year-old: Billie.

Russia took the baby and said, 'Would you like a lovely yoghurt for your tea?'

'No!' said the baby.

'Would you like a bath with all your floaty toys?'

'No!' said the baby, and yawned: the first lower teeth like twin grains of rice.

'Billie. Do the monkeys for Daddy.'

'There were too many monkeys jumping on the bed. One fell down and broke his head. They took him to the doctor and the doctor said: *No more monkeys jumping on the BED*.'

Xan Meo gave his elder daughter due praise.

'Daddy'll read to you when he comes back,' said Russia.

'I was reading to her earlier,' he said. He had the front door open now. 'She made me read the same book five times.'

'Which book?'

'Which book? Christ. The one about those stupid chickens who think the sky is falling. Cocky Locky. Goosey Lucy. And they all copped it from the fox, didn't they, Billie.'

'Like the frogs,' said the girl, alluding to some other tale. 'The whole family died. The mummy. The daddy. The nanny. And all the trildren.'

'I'm off out.' He kissed Sophie's head (a faint circus smell); she responded by skidding a wet thumb across her cheek and into her mouth. And then he crouched to kiss Billie.

4

'It's Daddy's anniversary,' Russia explained. 'Where are you going,' she asked him finally, 'for your lost weekend?'

'That bar-type place on the canal. What's its name. Hollywood.'

'Goodbye, Daddy,' Billie called.

Leaving the house, he turned briefly to assess it – a customary means of assessing himself, assessing where he was positioned, where he was *placed*. It wasn't his style (we shall come to his style), but he might have put it this way:

If fine materials are what you like, then have a feel of that fleece there, on the extravagantly deep armchair (take as long as you like: don't stint yourself). In fact, if you have an interest in real estate or fine living generally, you could do worse than take a tour of the whole house. If, alternatively, German technology is your thing, then get you to my garage, just around the side there. *And so on. But it wasn't the money*. If you harbour an admiration for extreme womanly beauty, then feast your eyes on my wife – the mouth, the eyes, the aerodynamic cheekbones (and the light of high intelligence: he was very proud of her intelligence). Or, if your soul melts to the vivid ardour of unusually cute, healthy and well-behaved children, you would envy us our . . . *And so on. And he might have continued*: But then I am the dream husband: a fifty-fifty parent, a tender and punctual lover, a fine provider, an amusing companion, a versatile and unsqueamish handyman, a subtle and accurate cook, and a gifted masseur who, moreover (and despite opportunities best described as 'ample'), never fools around . . . The truth was that he knew what it was like, being a bad husband, a nightmare husband; he had tried it the first time; and it was murder.

Xan Meo walked down St George's Avenue and came to the main road (this was London, near the Zoo). In so doing he passed the garden flat, opposite, which he now seldom used. Were there any secrets there? he wondered. An old letter, maybe; an old photograph; vestiges of vanished women . . . Xan paused. If he turned right he would be heading for pram-torn Primrose Hill – itself pramlike, stately, Vicwardian, arching itself upwards in a posture of mild indignation. That route would have got him to Hollywood the long way round. If he turned left he would get there sooner and could stay there later. So he had a choice between the garden and the city. He chose the city. He turned left, and headed for Camden Town.

It was late afternoon, and late October. On this day, four years earlier, his decree nisi had been made absolute, and he had also given up smoking and drinking (and dope and coke. American pimps, he had recently learnt, called coke *girl*; and heroin *boy*). It had become Meo's habit to celebrate this date with two cocktails and four cigarettes and half an hour of writhing reminiscence. He was happy now – a delicate state: you could feel the tingle of its stress-equations. And he was steadily recuperating from his first marriage. But he knew he would never be over his divorce.

The rink of Britannia Junction: Parkway and Camden Lock and Camden High Street, the dozen black frames of the traffic lights, the slum of cars. Certain sights had to be got out of the way: that heap – no, that stack – of dogshit; that avalanche of vomit; that drunk on the pavement with a face like a baboon's rear; that old chancer who had clearly been incredibly beaten up in the last five or six hours – and, just as incredibly, the eyes that lurked among those knucklestamps and bootprints harboured no grievance, sought no redress . . .

Xan Meo looked at the women, or more particularly the girls, the young girls. Typically she wore nine-inch bricks and wigwam flares; her midriff revealed a band of offwhite underpants and a navel traumatised by *bijouterie*; she had her car-keys in one cheek and her door-keys in the other, a plough in her nose and an anchor in her chin; and her earwax was all over her hair, as if via some inner conduit. But aside from that – what? The secret purpose of fashion, on the street, the harlequinade, fashion in its anarcho-bohemian form, is to thwart the lust of your elders. Well, it's worked, thought Meo. I don't dig you. He thought too of the menpleasers of twenty-five years ago, their stockings, garterbelts, cleavages, perfumes. Girls were now breaking with all that. (And maybe it went further, and they were signalling the retirement of physical beauty in the interests of the egalitarian.) Meo would not say that he disapproved of what he saw, though he found it alien. And when he saw two teenagers vigorously kissing – an unimaginable mesh of lip-rings and tongue-studs – he felt himself assent to it. See the young kissing and run it by your heart; if your heart rejects it, retreats from it, then that's age, that's time – fucking with you.

As he joined the long queue at the service store, for ciga-rettes, Meo recalled his penultimate infidelity (the ultimate infi-delity, of course, had been with Russia). In a hotel room in Manchester he methodically undressed a twenty-year-old conti-nuity girl. 'Let me help you out of those nasty hot clothes,' he said. Which was a line of his. But the line felt accurate: the damp-dog sloppy joe, the woollen tights, the rubber boots. He was seated on the armchair when she finally straightened up in front of him. There was her body, with its familar circles and half-circles, its divine symmetries, but it included something he had never seen before. He was face to face with a pubic buzzcut. Also: 'What's that doing there?' he asked. And she answered: 'It helps me have an orgasm' . . . Well, it didn't help *him* have an orgasm. Something else was hard where everything was meant to be soft: he seemed to be pestling himself – against a steel ingot. Plus a nice telltale welt (with her name and phone number on it) to take home to a wife who was, in any case, and with good reason, psychopathi-cally jealous (as was he). The continuity girl, then, had not been a continuity girl. Discontinuity, radical discontinuity, was what she had signalled. How clear did it need to be? *No more monkeys jumping on the bed*. He had been sleeping with Russia for four and a half years. Passion survived, but he knew it would dwindle; and he was prepared for that. Xan Meo was on his way to realising that, after a while, marriage is a sibling relationship – marked by occasional, and rather regrettable, episodes of incest.

Dusk was now falling; but the firmament was majestically bright; and the contrails of the more distant aeroplanes were like incandescent spermatozoa, sent out to fertilise the universe . . . On the street Meo stopped looking at the girls, and the girls, naturally, went on not looking at him. He had reached the age (he was forty-seven) where young women looked through you, beyond you, they looked through your ghost: a trite misfortune, perhaps, but definitely a point in your leavetaking, your journey to ghostdom. You whisper goodbye, goodbye – *God* be with you (because I won't be. I can't protect you). And yet this was not quite fully Meo's case, for he was a conspicuous man, and knew it, and liked it, on the whole. He owned a lot of physical space, tall, broad, full; his dark brown hair was no longer thick and wavy but it still covered a fair part of his head (the unguent that lent it extra mass and fixity was called Urban Therapeutic); and his eyes had rather more twinkle in them than you necessarily want to see. His face held a glow to it – a talented glow, certainly, but what kind of talent? At its weakest, its most ingratiating, Meo's face was that of a man who might step up to a microphone and give you a competently leering rendition of 'Pop Goes the Weasel'. His air seemed likely: plausible for the purpose at hand.

And, more than this, he was famous, and therefore in himself there was something specious and inflationary, something bigged-up. He was, however, *quietly* famous, as so many are now: many are famous (and even Meo could remember a time when hardly anybody was famous). Fame had so democratised itself that obscurity was felt as a deprivation or even a punishment. And people who weren't famous behaved famous. Indeed, in certain mental atmospheres it was possible to believe that the island he lived on contained sixty million superstars . . . Meo was, in fact, an actor, an actor who had gained sudden repute by warily diversifying into another field. And the world has a name for these people who can do more than one thing at the same time, these heroic multitaskers: it calls them Renaissance Men. The quiet glow of quiet fame, then, further illumined Xan Meo. Every five minutes someone would smile his way – because they thought they knew him. He returned such smiles.

The stroll to Hollywood continued – and we will stay with Meo's stroll, because it will be his last for some time. He stuck his head round the door of the High Street bookshop and complacently ascertained that his paperback (a debut collection of short stories entitled *Lucozade*) was still on the table marked Our Staff Recommends. Then, turning right up Delancey Street, he passed the café where Renaissance Man played rhythm guitar every second Wednesday with four old hippies who called themselves the Original Hard Edge. He cut left down Mornington Terrace – rather poorer, very much quieter: he could hear his own footfalls despite the thrashing trees he walked beneath and the submerged clangour of the rolling-stock deep down over the wall to his right. The weather was of the type that was still politely described as blustery. A ragged and bestial turbulence, in fact, a rodeo of wind – the earth trying to throw its riders. And in the street: garden furniture, twirling dustbins, bicycles and (increasingly) car doors thrown open into the path of the boost. Xan was too old for fashion, for cuts and styles; but his trousers, now, were alternately flared and drainpiped by the wind.

Up ahead he picked out a figure that reminded him, or reminded his body, of his first wife – his first wife as she was ten years ago. Pearl would not have had a cigarette in her mouth and a tabloid in her armpit, and nor would her clothes have been quite so brief, so taut, so woman-crammed; but the aggressive or at least sharply defiant stance, the arms disaffectedly folded, the lift of the chin that said that all excuses had now been considered and dismissed . . . She stood, waiting, in the shadow of a dun-coloured mediumrise. Behind her a male infant lingered, wiggling a stick among the exposed innards of a black plastic bag. As Meo turned to cross over the railtracks he heard her say,

'*Harrison! Move* your *fucking* arse!'

Yes, most regrettable, no doubt; but with his back safely turned Meo did not deny himself a wince of laughter. He was a good modern person; was a liberal, a feminist (indeed a gyno-crat: 'Give the girls a go,' he'd say. 'I know it's asking the earth. Still, *we're* no good. Give the girls a go'). But he still found things funny. The woman, after all, had made her meaning plain; and it couldn't be said that she had minced her words. No: Pearl would have put it differently . . . He could see the building now, with its variegated Christmas lights, its squirming barber's pole. Sometimes a descending aeroplane can sound a warning note: one did so, up above – an organ-chord, signalling its own doom.

He stopped and thought: that feeling again. And he sniffed the essential wrongness of the air, with its fucked-up undertaste, as if all the sequiturs had been vacuumed out of it. A yellowworld of faith and fear, and paltry ingenuity. And all of us just flying blind. Then he stepped forward.

Xan Meo went to Hollywood.

'Good evening.'

'All right?' said the barman, as if querying the mental health of someone who still said that: good evening.

'Yeah mate,' said Meo comfortably. 'And yourself?' This was the thing about him: he was big, he was calm, he was comfort-able. 'Where is everyone?'

'Football. England. They'll come steaming in here around eight.'

Meo, who would not be around for that, said, 'You want to get those uh, plasma screens in. They can watch it in here.'

'We don't want em to watch it here. They can watch it in the

Worm and Apple. Or the Turk's Head. And trash *that* when they lose.'

The cocktail menu had been chalked up on a blackboard above a display of bottles and siphons arranged and set-dressed to resemble downtown Los Angeles. Out-of-scale mannequins of selected moviestars lurched through its streets.

'I'll have a . . .' There was a drink called a Blowjob. There was a drink called a Boobjob. He thought: it's like those companies called FCUK and TUNC. Meo shrugged. It was not his intention, now, to ponder the obscenification of everyday life. He said, 'I'll have a Shithead. No, a *Dick*head. No. *Two* Dickheads.'

Holding a glass in either hand Xan went out into the paved garden overlooking the canal where, in recent months, on a west-facing bench, usually with Russia at his side, he had consumed many a pensive Club Soda, many a philosophical Virgin Mary. And how much more solemn – how much more august and royal – his thoughts would be, pondering Pearl, alone with his cigarettes and his Dickheads . . . Meo's first glance at the motionless green channel rather too studiously confronted him with a dead duck, head down with its feet sticking up like the arms of a pair of spectacles. Dead in the water, abjectly dead: he imagined he could smell it, over and above the elderly medicine of the canal. Like Lucky Ducky or Drakey Lakey, after Foxy Loxy was done.

Xan seemed to be alone in his garden. But then a dapper young man emerged from a Hollywood side-exit, with a mobile phone held to his ear; he seemed briskly bound for the street until he stopped dead and then seemed to grope his way sidewise and steady himself against the canal fencing a few feet away. He acknowledged Xan's nod with a flicker of his brow and then said clearly, 'So everything we said, all the vows we exchanged, now mean nothing. Because of Garth. And we both know that's just an infatuation . . . You say you love me but I think we have different conceptions of what love really means. To me, love is something sacred, almost ineffable. And now you're saying that all that, all that . . .' He moved off, and his voice was soon lost in the hum of the city. Yes, and that was part of it, the obscenification: loss of *pudeur*.

Like the dead duck, the worldline of Xan's first marriage, that attempted universe – dead also. His divorce had been so vicious that even the lawyers had panicked. It was as if the two of them had been trussed together with barbed wire, naked and face-to-face, and then thrown overboard. Your flailings down there, your kicking and clawing: there could be no morality. When Pearl had him arrested for the third time, and he stood at the door of his service flat listening to the charges, Xan knew that he had reached the end of a journey. He had reached the polar opposite of love – a condition far more intense than mere hatred. You want the loved one dead; you want her plane to come down, and never mind about the others on board – those four hundred saps and losers . . .

But they'd survived; they lived, didn't they? Xan reckoned that he and Pearl came out pretty well even. And, fantastically, they came out richer than they went in. It was the boys, the two sons, who lost, and it was to them that Xan Meo now raised his glass. 'I'm sorry,' he said out loud. 'I'm sorry. I'm sorry.' As if in recompense for the waterbird upended in the green canal, a sparrow, a feathered creature of the middle air, hopped on to the bench beside him and, with eerie docility, began to ventilate itself, allowing its wings to thrum and purr, six inches away.

The wind had departed – fled elsewhere. In the west a garish, indeed a porno sunset had established itself. It resembled a titanic firefighting operation, with ethereal engines, cranes, ladders, the spray and foam of hose and standpipe, and the genies of the firemen about their massive work of hell-containment, hell-control.

'Is that your "bird"?' said a voice.

Meo acknowledged the passing of his solitude. He looked to

his right: the sparrow was still agitating on the arm of the bench, testingly close to his second Dickhead. He looked up: his smiling questioner, a square-looking, almost cubic individual, stood about ten feet away in the weak dusk.

'Yeah, well it's all I can pull these days,' he answered.

The man took a step forward, his thumbs erect on either side of his navel. Recognised, thought Meo. Made.

'Are you *the*?'

Expecting that he would soon have a hand to shake, Xan got to his feet. The sparrow did not yet absent itself.

'Yes. I'm *the*.'

'Well I'm Mal.'

'. . . Hello there,' said Xan.

'Why'd you do it, son?'

At this point it became clear that Mal, despite his air of humorous regret, was a violent man.

Far more surprisingly, it became clear that Xan was a violent man too. That is to say, he suffered from no great deficit of familiarity as the changed forcefield took hold. Violence, triumphally outlandish and unreal, is an ancient category-error – except to the violent. The error having been made, both men would know that from here on in it was endocrinological: a question of gland-management.

'Why'd I do *what*?' said Meo, and took a step forward. He hoped still to avert it; but he would not be going second.

'Ooh.'

He pronounced it *où*, as Russia Meo had, so long ago. He went on, 'I *heard* you was a bit tasty.'

'Then you know what to expect,' he said as levelly as he could (there was an acidic presence in his mouth). 'If you have it with me.'

'You went and *named* him! And I mean *that*, to me, that is totally, to *me* –'

'Named who?'

Mal breathed in and bulged his eyes and loudly whispered, 'You'll remember this in pain, boy. *J-o-s-e-p-h A-n-d-r-e-w-s.*'

'Joseph Andrews?'

'Don't say it. You don't *say* it. You named him. You put him there – you placed him. In black and *white*.'

For the first time Meo thought that something *else* was wrong. The calculations going on inside him might be given as follows: my five inches equals his two stone, and zero real difference in the other thing (time lived). So: it would be close. And the guy seemed too blithe and hammy for close. He couldn't be *that* good: look at his suit, his shoes, his hair.

'You'll remember this in pain, boy.'

But there is another actor on our stage. But I go to Hollywood but I go to hospital. A man (for it is he, it is he, it is always he), a sinner, shitter, eater, breather, coming up fast on him from behind. Mal is violent, and Xan is violent, but in this third player's scowl and its nimbus you see an absence of everything that human beings have ever agreed about: all treaties, concordats, all under-standings. He is palely and coarsely bald. His eyebrows and eyelashes seem to have been lasered or even blowtorched off his face. And the steam pouring from his mouth as if from a spraycan, on this not intemperate evening, reached out to arm's length.

Xan heard no footsteps; what he heard was the swish, the shingly soft-shoe, of the hefted cosh. Then the sharp two-finger prod on his shoulder. It wasn't meant to happen like this. They expected him to turn, and he didn't turn – he half-turned, then veered and ducked. So the blow intended merely to break his cheek-bone or his jawbone was instead received by the cranium, that spacey bulge (in this instance still quite marriageably forested) where so many noble and delicate powers are so trustingly encased.

He crashed, he crunched to his knees, in obliterating defeat: his womanblood, his childblood, taken by his enemy. The physics of it sent his Dickhead twisting up and away. He heard the wet crack, the wet crack of his knees followed by the wet crack of the sliced glass. The world stopped turning, and started turning again – but the other way. Only now after a heartbeat did the sparrow rear up with the whirling of its wings: the little paparazzo of the sparrow.

The sky is falling!

Then the words '*Get* down' and a second, fervent blow.

The sky is falling, and I'm off to tell the . . .

Seemingly rigid now, like the statue of a fallen tyrant, he crashed sideways into the damp paving, and lay still.

2. Hal Nine

The King was not in his counting-house, counting out his money. He was in a drawing-room in the Place des Vosges, absorbing some very bad news. The equerry on the armchair opposite was called Brendan Urquhart-Gordon. Between them, lying on the low glass table, was a photograph, face-down, and a pair of tweezers. And the room was like a photograph: for several minutes now neither man had moved or spoken.

A vibration was needed to animate the scene, and it came: the ping of a tuning-fork, as one of the thousand facets in the icy chandelier minutely rearranged itself within that ton of glass.

Henry IX said, 'What a dreadful world we're living in, Bugger. I mean, it's such a ghastly, dreadful . . . world.'

'It is indeed, sir. May I suggest a brandy, sir.'

The King nodded. Urquhart-Gordon wielded the handbell. More vibrations: scandalously shrill. The servant, Love, appeared in the distant doorway. Urquhart-Gordon had nothing against Love, but he found it awkward using his name. Who would want a servant called Love?

'Two large Remy *reserve*, if you would, Love,' he called.

The Defender of the Faith – he actually headed the Church of

England (Episcopalian) and the Church of Scotland (Presbyterian) – went on: 'You know, Bugger, this shakes my personal belief. Doesn't it shake yours?'

'My personal belief was ever but a slender reed, sir.'

An unlikely expression, perhaps, coming from a man shaped like a cummerbund. Bald, dark, rosy, with Jewish brains (some said) from the mother's side.

'Shakes it to the core. These people really are the *limit*. No. Worse. I suppose it's all part of some ghastly "ring"?'

'That is possible, sir.'

'Why did . . . How could it be so arranged that such creatures play a part in God's *plen*?'

Love reentered and, as he approached, perhaps a dozen clocks, one after the other, began to chime the hour. An instinctively practical man, Urquhart-Gordon reflected that more work would have to be done on the modernisation of the King's short 'a'. In times of crisis, especially, it sounded almost prewar. Brendan's rosy cheeks were for a moment all the rosier as he recalled Henry's visit, as Prince of Wales, to the trade-union rest-house in Newbiggin-by-the-Sea, and the Prince at the piano singing 'My Old Man's a Dustman': 'My old men's a dustman, He wears a dustman's het, He wears cor-blimey trousers, And he lives in a council flet!' The Fourth Estate had not been slow to point out that the truth was otherwise: Henry's old man was Richard IV, and he lived in Buckingham Palace.

Feebly averting his face from the humours of the brandy balloons, Love continued towards them, and still had a fair way to go. It was five past six by the time he left the room.

'Forgive me, Bugger. My mind's a blenk. Delivered . . . ?'

'The photograph was hand-delivered to my rooms in St James's. In a plain white envelope.' This envelope Urquhart-Gordon now produced from his case. He handed the transparent zipper-wallet to Henry IX, who gave it a more than averagely puzzled squint. MR BRENDAN URQUHART-GORDON ESQUIRE, and, in the top right-hand corner, Private and Confidential. 'No accompanying note. Calligraphy and the redundant "Esquire" suggest an uncouth or foreign hand, or an attempt to have us believe as much. Protection will conceivably tell us more.'

Urquhart-Gordon studied the King's frown. Henry IX normally wore his thick fair hair swiped sideways across his brow. But now in the royal disarray his quiff had collapsed into a baffled fringe, making his eyes look even more beleaguered and inflamed. Henry IX frowned on at him, and in response to this Urquhart-Gordon shrugged and said,

'We await further communication.'

'Blickmail?'

'Well. I would say extortion. It seems reasonably clear that this is not the work of the media, in the usual sense. If it were, then we would be looking at that photograph in some German magazine.'

'Bugger!'

'I'm sorry, sir. Or on the Internet.'

With a bedraggled gesture Henry IX reached for the thing on the table. His hand wavered.

'Use the tweezers, sir, if you would. Turn it with the tweezers, sir.'

The King did so.

He had not seen his daughter naked for perhaps three or four years, and, over and above everything else, he was harrowed, he was bitterly moved, by how much woman was already in her, in his girlchild who still played with her dolls. This, together with the dreaminess, the harmlessness, of the face, caused her father to cover his eyes with his sleeve.

'Oh Bugger.'

'Oh Hotty.'

Urquhart-Gordon looked on. A fifteen-year-old girl in what was evidently a white bathtub, with her arms up on the side, her legs folded at an angle in six inches of water: Princess Victoria, in her costume of nudity, her catsuit of nudity, adumbrating womanhood. The conspicuous tan-lines – she seemed, further-more, to be wearing a spectral bikini – suggested summer. Urquhart-Gordon had checked the scrolled itineraries: all the Princess ever did, apparently, was go on holiday. But she had been back at boarding-school for six weeks and it was now almost November. Why, he wondered, had they waited? There was something about the Princess's expression that worried him, that additionally disquieted him: the elevation of the pupils . . . Brendan Urquhart-Gordon's nickname, by the way, derived from his initials, Henry IX's from his performance as Hotspur in a school production of *Henry IV, Part One*.

'Do you think,' the King said miserably, 'that the Princess and a uh, girlfriend might have been messing about with a camera, and uh . . .'

'No, sir. And I'm afraid it is highly unlikely that this is the extent of it.'

The King blinked at him. The King always made you spell it out.

'There must be more photographs of the Princess. In other . . . poses.'

'Bugger!'

'Forgive me, sir. That was unfortunate. The point is: look at the Princess's face, sir. That is the face of someone who *thinks she's alone*. We must take comfort from the fact that the Princess was and is quite unaware of this really unprecedented intrusion. Quite innocent of it.'

'Yes. Innocent of it. Innocent of it.'

'Sir, do I have your permission to activate John Oughtred?'

'You do. Not another soul, of course.'

Henry IX got to his feet, and so, therefore, did Urquhart-Gordon. They fell into step together, the one so sleek, the other so lean. When the great embrasure of the central window had at last been reached, the two men looked out through the lace, through its weft and warp. Floodlights, cranes, gantries, retractable ladders: the firefighters of the Fourth Estate. It was the eve of the second anniversary of the Queen's accident. The King was expected to make a statement in the morning before flying back to England and then on to his wife's bedside. For the Queen was not in the garden, eating bread and honey. She was attached to certain machines, in the Royal Inverness.

'Well, sir. The family motto.'

The family motto, impressed upon Henry IX by his father, Richard IV, and his grandfather, John II, was unofficial. In Latin it might perhaps have been *Prosequare*. In English it ran as follows: Get On With It.

'What have I got tomorrow? The Aids people or the cancer people?'

'Neither, sir. The lepers.'

'The *lepers*? . . . Oh yes of course.'

'It could be postponed, sir. I don't see how it was arranged in the first place, given the significance of the date.' And he invitingly added, 'With your permission, sir, I will be availing myself of the King's Flight in – two hours.'

'No, I'd better go ahead and do the lepers, now I'm here. Get on with it.'

Urquhart-Gordon knew the real purpose of Henry IX's visit to Paris. He was obliged to conceal his astonishment that, despite the nature of the current *crise*, the King evidently meant to go ahead with it (and despite the atrocious timing, the atrocious risk). Now his eyebrows arched as he made a series of fascinated deductions.

'And after the lepers – then what?'

'You should be in the air by noon, sir. There's the ceremony at Mansion House at two: your award from the Headway people.'

Again Henry IX blinked at him.

'The National Head Injuries Association, sir. Then you go north,' he said, and superfluously added, 'to see the Queen.'

'Yes, poor thing.'

'Sir. I have Oughtred on hold and will liaise with him tonight at St James's. We must avoid passivity in this matter.' He shook his head and added, 'We've got to find somewhere to begin.'

'Oh Bugger.'

Urquhart-Gordon had an impulse to reach out and smooth Henry IX's hair from his brow. But this would surprise the King's horror of being touched: touched by a man.

'I feel very sorry for you, Hotty. Truly I do.'

Soon after that the King went off to bathe, and Brendan sat on in the drawing-room. He removed his hornrims; and there were the tumid, vigilant brown eyes. Brendan had a secret: he was a republican. What he did here, what he had been doing for a quarter of a century, it was for love, all for love. Love for the King, and, later, love for the Princess.

When Victoria was four . . . The Englands were holidaying in Italy (some *castello* or *palazzo*), and she was brought in to say goodnight to the company – in robe, pyjamas and tasselled slippers, with her hair slicked back from the bath. She went to the cardtable and, on her easy tiptoe, kissed her parents, then exchanged particular farewells with two other members of the entourage, Chippy and Boy. Sitting somewhat apart, Brendan looked up from his book in rosy expectancy – as she wordlessly included him in the final transit of her eyes. Then she took her nanny's hand, and turned with her head bowed. And Brendan, startling himself, nearly cried out, in grief, in utter defeat – how can I feel so much when you feel so little? All the blood within him . . . Brendan knew himself to be perhaps unusually fond of the Princess. Was it an aesthetic passion merely? When he looked at her face he always felt he was wearing his most powerful reading-glasses – the way her flesh pushed out at him like the contours of a coin. But this would not explain his condition in the Italian ballroom as Victoria went to bed without wishing him goodnight: for instance, the sullenly mastered temptation to weep. 'Goodnight, Brendan,' she had said, the following evening; and he had felt gorgeously restored. It was love, but what kind of love? These days she was fifteen, and he was forty-five. He kept expecting it to go away. But it didn't go away.

Now Brendan looked again at the photograph of the Princess. He did so briefly and warily. He was wary for her, and wary for himself – for the information about himself it might give him. Of course the point was to serve her, to serve her always . . . Brendan marshalled his briefcase, preparing himself for the drive to Orly, the King's Flight to the City of London Airport, and the working supper with John Oughtred.

Eight o'clock was on its way to the Place des Vosges. Downstairs, in the alpine vault of the kitchen, the security detail frowned over its instant coffees – and its playing-cards, with their unfamiliar symbols, swords and coins from another universe. Upstairs, Love, with a white napkin draped over his forearm, was setting the table in a distant corner of the drawing-room. He was setting it for two. Fragrant from his toilet, the King felt his way from one piece of furniture to another. In this room everything you touched was either very hard or very soft, invaluably hard, invaluably soft.

The house belonged, of course, to Henry IX's especial friend, the Marquis de Mirabeau. Less well known was the fact that the Marquis maintained a further apartment in the Place des Vosges . . .

Now the clocks chimed, first in relay, then in unison.

'If you would, Love,' said the King.

Against the wall on the landing's carpeted plateau stood a chiffonier the size of a medieval fireplace. This now began to turn, to slide outwards on its humming axis. And in came He Zizhen, greatgranddaughter of concubines.

Love bade her welcome.

When the clocks chimed again He began to undress. This would take her some time. The King, already naked, lay helplessly on the *chaise-longue*, like a child about to be changed. As she removed her clothes He caressed him with them, and then with what the clothes contained. He touched him. He touched He. He was hard. He was soft. He touched him and he touched He.

There came a ping, a vibration, from the chandelier.

3. Clint Smoker

'The Duke of Clarence played Prince ChowMein last night, *writes* CLINT SMOKER,' wrote Clint Smoker. 'Yes, Prince Alf wokked out with his on-again off-again paramour, Lyn Noel, for a slap-up Chinese. But *sweet* turned to *sour* when photographers had the sauce to storm their private room. Wan tun a bit of privacy, the couple fled with the lads in hot pursuit – we'll cashew! What happened, back at Ken Pal? Did Alf lai chee? Did he oyster into his arms and give her a crispy duck? Or did he decide, yet again, to dumpLyn (after he'd had seconds)? Sea weedn't like that – so how about a kick in the arse, love, to szechuan your way?'

'What's this?' asked Margery, who was passing.

'Photocaption,' said Clint pitilessly, leaning sideways so she could see.

Clint Smoker's screen showed a tousled and grimacing Prince Alfred and a tearful and terrified Lyn Noel fighting their way through a ruck of photojournalists and policemen in steaming Soho traffic.

'That rain's not doing her hair much good,' said Margery, who now took her place in the next workstation along. A ruddy sixty-year-old, Margery was pretending to be a glamour model called Donna Strange. She was also pretending to have no clothes on.

'Yeah well it's the drowned-cat look,' said Clint.

An identikit modern uggy, Clint himself subscribed to the

look-like-shit look (as he had seen it called), with closely shaved head (this divulging many a Smoker welt and blemish), a double nostril-ring in the shape of a pair of handcuffs (the link-chain hung over his long upper lip and was explorable by the petri-dish of the Smoker tongue), and a startlingly realistic, almost *trompe-l'oeil* tattoo of a frayed noose round the Smoker neck (partly obscured, it is true, by a further rope of Smoker blubber). And yet this man, with a laptop in front of him, was a very fine journalist indeed. Clint's shoes also repaid inspection: two catamarans lashed in place by a network of cords and cleats.

'Dear Donna: I am a nineteen-year-old heiress with a slender waist, a shapely derrière, and bouncers as big as your bonce,' wrote Clint Smoker.

'Actually not a lot,' Margery was telling one of her phones. 'Heels, ankle bracelet, and that's it, apart from me thong.'

'Me passion', wrote Clint, and then went back to change that *e* to a *y*, 'is to dress up in the shortest mini I can find and then go round all the shoeshops with no knickers on. I wait till the lad is on his little seat in front of me. You should see the way they –'

He then said in his uncontrollably loud voice, 'Here, Marge, they do –'

'*Donna*,' said Marge, pressing the mouthpiece to her breast.

'They *do have* blokes serving in birds' shoeshops, don't they?'

She shrugged a nod and said, 'Do you darling? Well we all feel a bit fruity in the afternoons. It's the biorhythm.'

'. . . drool', wrote Clint, 'when I yank my –'

Supermaniam Singh poked his head round the door and said in estuary English, 'Oi. He's here.'

By the time Clint clumped into the conference room the publisher, Desmond Heaf, was leaning over the cover of yesterday's *Morning Lark* and sorrowfully saying,

'I mean, look at her. Clint: nice to see you, son. I mean, look at her. That's deformity, that is. Or obsessive surgery: Munchausen's. They're very unhappy people and they look it. See her *eyes*. If I've said it once I've said it a thousand times. Keep the bosoms within reasonable bounds: forty-four triple-F would do as a benchmark. I say it and I say it. They go down for a while but then they always creep back up again. And then we get *this*.'

'More centrally, Chief,' said Clint, 'it makes the paper too embarrassing to buy. I bet we're losing wankers.'

Even before the first issue had hit the streets, it was universal practice, at the *Morning Lark*, to refer to readers as wankers. This applied not only to specific features (Wankers' Letters, Our Wankers Ask the Questions, and so on), but also in phrases common to any newspapering concern, such as 'the wanker comes first' and 'the wanker's what it's all about' and 'is this of genuine interest to our wankers?' The staff had long stopped smiling when anybody said it.

'Well said, Clint,' said Heaf.

'We wouldn't be *losing* wankers,' said Supermaniam. 'You might find a blip on the *rate of increase* but we're not actually *losing* wankers.'

'Red herring,' boomed Clint. 'We're losing *potential* wankers.'

'I'll have Mackelyne track the figures,' said Heaf. 'Who keeps putting these bleeding great . . . dugongs in the paper anyway?'

No one spoke. For the *Lark* was run along cooperative lines. The selection of the scores of near-naked women who appeared daily in its pages was a matter of cheerfully generalised improvisation. Naturally the editorial staff was all-male. The only women to be found in the *Lark*'s offices were its tutelary glamour girls and the retirees who impersonated them on the hotlines.

'I don't know, Boss,' said Jeff Strite – Clint Smoker's only serious rival as the paper's star reporter. 'You get in a sort of daze after a bit. You go, you know, "Sling her in" without really thinking about it.'

Clint said judiciously (and loudly), 'Some blokes do think you can't have too much of a good thing, so there's an argument for the occasional bigger bird. We've got to attract the more specialised wanker without grossing out the rank and file. It's this simple: keep the dugongs off the front page.'

'Agreed?'

'Agreed.'

'Anyway, who are we to complain?' said Heaf. Normally the Publisher had the air of a small-town headmaster – and one harassed by logistical cares to the point of personal neglect (so frayed, so meagre). But now he freshened, and said in a gurgling voice, 'Gregory, be a good lad and make a start on the beverages, would you?'

Mackelyne had entered and taken his seat. They listened as he talked about the latest sales figures, the multimillion hits on the hardcore websites, the fact that the new sexlines had caused the collapse of the local telephone network, and the inevitability of the 192-page daily format. Then came the money numbers . . . At the *Lark*, all profits were shared, with certain steep differentials. But even young Gregory, who was little more than an office boy, had plans to buy a racehorse.

'Now,' said Heaf, a while later. 'What have we got for tomorrow? Clint.'

There always came this moment (and by now the empty bottles of champagne were ranked on the Publisher's desk, and the dusty air looked gaseous in the low sun, as if everyone had joined in one cooperative sneeze), this moment when the men of the *Morning Lark* tried to feel like journalists. There was of course hardly any news in the *Lark*, and no global cataclysm had yet had the power to push the pinup off the front page. Even the vast sports section did little more than print the main results; the rest consisted of girls climbing in and out of the kit of famous football clubs, girls chronicling their one-night stands with famous footballers, early and reckless photographs of models who were married to or living with famous footballers, and so on, plus a few odds and ends about adulterous golfers, satyromaniac jockeys, and rapist boxers. But current events of a certain kind were covered, usually on the lower half of pages two and four.

It was Jeff Strite who spoke. 'The Case of the Walthamstow Wanker,' he intoned. 'And I *don't* mean the Walthamstow Reader. It's an interesting story. And it ties in with our Death to Paedophiles campaign. There's this public swimming-pool, right? With a gallery? He's up there alone watching a school party of nine-year-olds. Then this old dear, you know, Mrs Mop appears. The geezer does a runner, falls down the stairs and smashes his head in. For why? His trousers are down around his *ankles.*'

'Because he was having a . . . ?'

'Exactly. Good headline too: Pervs Him Right.'

'Excellent. And I see we've decided to go ahead,' said Desmond Heaf, 'with Wankers' Wives.'

Back at his laptop Clint resumed work on the heiress with a passion for visiting shoeshops in short skirts. This contribution posed as a letter to the paper's agony aunt, or 'Ecstasy Aunt', whose daily double-page spread was pretty well entirely composed by staff writers. Long narratives of an exclusively and graphically sexual nature were followed by three or four words of encouragement or ridicule, supposedly from the pen of Donna Strange. Readers *did* write in; and once in a blue moon their letters received the hospitality of the *Lark*'s correspondence columns. These letters dramatised the eternal predicament of erotic prose. It wasn't that they were insufficiently salacious; rather, they were insufficiently universal – were, in fact, impenetrably solitary. And they were never from women . . . Then, with a heavy heart, Smoker flagged the new photosection alluded to by Desmond Heaf. It was to be called Readers'

Richards, 'Richard' being rhyming-slang (via Richard the Third) for bird, just as 'Bristols' (via Bristol City) was rhyming-slang for —

'Why'd you want those bloody handcuffs in your conk?' asked Margery, who was packing up. She was sixty; he was thirty: these facts had suddenly to be acknowledged.

'Reminds me I've got a nose.'

'Congratulations. Why'd you want reminding you've got a nose?' Especially *that* nose, she felt moved to add (Clint's nose was a considerable accumulation of flesh, but one uninfluenced by cartilage). 'And what's that *rope* in aid of?'

'I'll swing for you, Marge,' said Clint in a softer voice than usual. 'It's my *identity*. Now shut it.'

He was still muttering viciously to himself when five minutes later his mobile sounded: the knock of a truncheon on a cell door.

'Clint? And.'

And was Andrew New, one of the sempiternal figures in the Smoker universe, someone with whom he had formed the stoutest of bonds. And was Clint's pusher. And this call was out of the ordinary. And hardly ever rang Clint. Clint rang And.

'*And*, boy. Jesus, what's that racket? She having another go then?'

'Gaw, hark at this. "*Harrison! Will* you *get* your *fuck*ing arse into that bath!" Terrible it's been. "*And! And!* Come and it im!" *You* fucking it im! I hit im the last time. Sorry, mate. It's calming down a bit now. It's not as bad as what it sounds . . . Uh, Clint mate. I think I've got a news story.'

'Well you've come to the wrong place.'

'Yeah, but you must have contacts.'

'I'm tolerably well connected,' said Clint untruthfully (and loudly. People placed near him in restaurants used to ask for re-location. That was when he still went to restaurants with other people). 'Come on then. What is it?'

'You know that bloke got done last night. Xan Meo. The actor that plays the banjo or whatever the fuck it is. What do they call him.'

'Renaissance Man.'

'I was *there*, mate. Fact. I saw them do im! By the canal. I was down on the path where I keep me stash. He's just sitting out there having a drink and there's this two blokes on him. They didn't half fucking give him one. No. They give him two. I thought: that's him fucking telt. Then they give him another.'

Clint, at stool, had read about the attack in the *Evening Standard*. His interest was only mildly piqued.

And went on: 'Seemed it was like, you know, payback time. Seemed like he'd grassed someone up and it was payback time. They've give the name. Said he grassed up *Joseph Andrews* . . .'

'Well it's no use to me, mate. Unless there was any topless skirt involved. Are you going to the Old Bill with it?'

'That's no fucking use to me, is it? There ain't any *reward* or anything. No. I was going to flog it round the newspapers.'

'Uh, don't do that, mate.' Clint considered. 'It's not that big of a story. And you might get yourself . . . Let me put out a groper and I'll give you a call. What was the bloke's name again – the one that got grassed up?'

'"*Harrison! And! And!*"' And And said, 'Gaw, Jesus. Here we go. Joseph Andrews.'

Clint Smoker worked in a sick building. It should have had a thermometer poking out of its first-floor window like a barber's pole – not writhing, but trembling. In the 1970s it had ambitiously served as a finishing-school for young women hoping for pre-ferment in the public-relations industry. So many of the students suffered from eating disorders that the entire plumbing system surrendered to the ravages of gastric acid. This in turn caused a 'billowing fracture' which warped its ventilation systems. The air was turbid with emanations, spores, allergies. Everyone at the *Lark* was always sneezing, sniffing, coughing, yawning, retching.

They knew they felt sick, but didn't know they felt sick because they worked in a sick building: they thought they felt sick because of what they did in it all day long . . . Today the sick building gave off an olive glow; a thin rain had fallen, and its face seemed to be dotted with sweat.

He shouldered his way out of there with a cigarette in his mouth. Big man: see the way the automatic doors jerked away from him in fright. Massive, pale, the flesh with the rubbery look of cold pasta; but Clint wielded the unreasonable strength of heavy bones. He kept winning these ragged brawls he kept having, on roadsides, in laybys and forecourts, with their flailings and stumblings, their miskicks and airshots. Clint's brawls were about the Highway Code: heretical as opposed to canonical interpretations. And Clint was the Manichee.

'Can you spare some change, sir?' asked the man with the HOMELESS sign. He asked it ironically: he knew Clint, and he knew Clint never gave.

'Yes thanks. *You've* done well for yourself. Stay at it: keep that pavement warm.'

If you saw Clint's jeep in your rearview mirror you'd think that an Airbus was landing in your wake. He needed a big car because he spent at least four hours a day in it, furiously commuting from Foulness, near Southend, where he had a semi.

Now, Smoker lived alone. He had never found it easy to begin, let alone maintain, a fulfilling relationship with a woman. His penultimate girlfriend had ended the connection because, apart from Clint's other deficiencies, he was, she explained, 'crap in bed'. Her successor, when *she* ended the connection, put it rather differently but in the same number of words (and letters): he was, she said, 'a crap fuck'. That was a year ago. Clint Smoker: crap fuck. It did not enhance his sexual self-esteem. He thereafter relied on escort girls, entertained in various London hotels; and even these encounters were far from frictionless. The truth was that when it came to love, to the old old story (and face it, mate, he'd tell himself: see it foursquare), Clint Smoker had a little problem.

The Foulness semi. It was a ridiculous situation. He had the cash to relocate further in. But the yearlong deprivation of a feminine presence had reduced his place to a condition of untouchable sordor. It was a wonder he kept his person clean. (The bathroom was, in fact, the only non-unbelievable part of the house.) He couldn't muck it out. He couldn't sell it. He'd have to board it up and abandon it. The sordor exerted an influence, a paralysis, a *nostalgie* . . . And the house was also saturated with pornography in all its forms.

Clint hoisted himself up into the driving-seat of his black Avenger. He now weighed four tons and had a top speed of 160 miles per hour.

A short while ago Clint had received a communication from a young woman. It was not addressed to him but to the *Lark*'s Ecstasy Aunt. It began: 'dear donna: honestly, what's all the fuss about orgasms about? I've never had one and i don't want one.' Clint responded personally, to 'k' of Kentish Town, saying that he found her views 'most refreshing'. She'd e'd him back: dialogue. Ah, e-love, e-eros, e-amour; e-bimbo and e-toyboy; ah, e-wooing on the Web . . . What usually emerged (Clint found) was all vanity and shadow, inexistent, incorporeal: unreal mockery. But something told him that 'k' was a woman of substance.

Smoker's cleated clog plunged down on the accelerator. Only weeks out of the showroom, the Avenger already resembled the bedroom of the Foulness semi. It smelt of new car and old man. Clint was now shouting at the truck he wanted to overtake. He quite sincerely hoped that the crocodile of schoolchildren crossing that zebra up ahead wouldn't be there when he shot by.

Soon afterwards Homeless John went home, with his HOMELESS sign. His HOMELESS sign leant against the wardrobe while he slept. It leant against the table while Homeless John's mother made his breakfast.

'You love that sign, don't you?' she said.

'Looks nice. Most of the blokes write it down with a Biro on a scrap of cardboard. That's depressing, that is. They don't even take it home with them. Chuck it away and do a new one in the morning. Couldn't do that. My sign's like a breath of fresh air.'

It was true. Homeless John's HOMELESS sign was a gentrified HOMELESS sign. On the blond wood he had painted a yellow sun, a white moon and silvery stars; then, below, the word *homeless*, in capitals with double quotes: "HOMELESS".

'I wish you wouldn't, you know,' she said.

'It's just a summer job, Ma.'

'That sign.'

'What about my sign?'

'Everyone sees you come whistling down the street with your HOMELESS sign and your door-key. You sit here having your tea with your HOMELESS sign. It makes me feel this isn't a home.'

'I'll put *you* in a home in a minute. Don't be silly, Ma. Course this is home. The sign's just the tool of my trade. And it's why I'm a superstar out there: top boy. Made a *fortune* last week.'

'And I've heard them call you "Homeless" in the pub.'

He had an idea. His estimation of his sign, already very high, climbed a further notch. 'Look at the quote marks, Ma. It's saying I'm not "really" homeless.'

Homeless John's mother was adopting an expression of sorrowful entreaty. She tipped her head and told him: 'You *won't* stay out in the wet, *will* you, love.'

'Not me, Ma. I'll come home.'

Which he would do. With his sign held up high against the rain.

31

February 14 (9.05 a.m., Universal Time): 101 Heavy

At Heathrow Airport they loaded the corpse into the hold of Flight CigAir 101 – bound for Houston, Texas, USA. The corpse's name was Royce Traynor. On February 11 the old oiler had been walking down a street in Kensington when a roofslate the size of a broadsheet newspaper came scything down at him. He died in the ambulance, cradled in the arms of his wife of forty-three years, Reynolds. Reynolds now sat in a more attractive part of the aeroplane, in seat 2B. She was tearfully drinking her second Buck's Fizz and looking forward to the moment when the Captain would switch off the no-smoking sign.

Of the 399 passengers and crew on this ten-hour flight, Royce Traynor was the only one who would feel no erosion of his wellbeing.

CHAPTER TWO

1. The transfer to Trauma

Tender-yeared Billie Meo walked through Casualty with such fascination that the scored lino strained to feel the weight of her tread. Her slippers were landing heel-down, but there was a tiptoe in her somewhere – in the calves, perhaps. Russia Meo, when she took her daughter's hand, could feel the fractional levitation of inquisitive anxiety as, all around them, figures like distorted statues were being lowered, winched up, bent over, turned. And the noises, and the smell.

It was nine o'clock before Russia called the police and started ringing round the hospitals. It was nearly ten when she learnt that her husband had been admitted to St Mary's with a closed-head injury that was thought to be minor – as opposed to major. By that time Billie was altogether caught up in her mother's agitation, and Russia felt she didn't have a choice but to let her 'come with'. (The baby, Sophie, had been down for hours – pompously at peace, with her nose upturned.) Russia had trusted herself to take the car, though she already felt like a driver on a stretch of black ice: no grip on the road, and many futures vying to become her next reality. But that would be to get ahead of yourself, because the evening had become a tunnel, and there was only one possible future now – the one at the hospital. She was aware that her body was being internally tranquillised, that time had slowed on her behalf. Like Billie, she was in a state of hallucinogenic curiosity. She parked the car across the street beneath the other building, where she had given birth to both her girls. Then the Reception area, where families and parts of families sat in taciturn vigil, some groups erectly tensed, others in sprawling abandon, as if for a twelve-hour flight delay.

In hospital, she thought: no *the* or *a*. In court, in jail, in church. What did these institutions have in common? Something to do with the settling of fates . . . Billie had been in hospital only twice before: on the occasion of her birth, and, more recently, when it was discovered that she had consumed half a bottle of liquid paracatemol. That had also taken place at night. Billie was in fact concluding that hospital was what automatically happened if you succeeded in staying up very late.

They were now directed to Trauma.

'A head injury', said the Intensivist, 'entrains a sequence of events. We talk of the Three Injuries. The First Injury occurs in the first few seconds, the Second Injury in the first hour, the Third Injury in the first days or weeks or months. Your husband – Alex – has sustained the First Injury. It is my immediate task to prevent the Second and the Third. He lost consciousness, it seems, for about two or three minutes.'

'I thought anything over a minute . . .'

'Three minutes is not the end of the world. Although he couldn't remember his surname or his telephone number, he was lucid in the ambulance. His blood pressure was normal. The brain was not deprived of oxygen: the Second Injury. His respiration was found to be strong and regular. When there is irregular or depressed respiration in the presence of an adequate airway, the prognosis is invariably grave.'

Some doctors are diffident about the power they wield. Other doctors glitter with it. Dr Gandhi (satanically handsome, it seemed to Russia, but starting to bend in on himself as he reached the middle years) happened to be a doctor of the second kind. He was gratified, he was warmed, by how intently people listened to what he said, with their imploring eyes. They were right to do so, and it was natural to fear him, to love him: he was their interpreter of mortality. What he dispensed – what he withheld . . . Billie was in the adjacent playroom. Russia could hear her. The

34

child, too, seemed to be taking deep breaths and then holding them; she gasped and sighed as she married and severed the plastic Sticklebricks.

'Alex was reasonably lucid in the ambulance. By the time I examined him he was talking gibberish. I was not discouraged. He enjoyed obedient mobility and his eyes responded normally to light. Over the space of an hour his score on the Glasgow Scale rose from nine to fourteen, one short of the maximum. The X-ray revealed no fracture. Better still, the CT-scan revealed bruising but only minimal swelling. Which would have been the Third Injury. I administered a diuretic as a precaution. This de-hydrates and thus *shrinks* the brain,' said Dr Gandhi, reaching out his hand and clenching it. 'He is in Intensive Care. And asleep, and breathing normally, and fully monitored.'

'And that will be that?'

'. . . Madam, your husband's brain has been *accelerated*. The soft tissue has been impacted against its container: the skull. On the front underside of the brain there are bony ridges. What are they for! Nobody knows! To *punish* the head-injured, it would seem. As the brain accelerates it rips and tears on this – this *grater*. Nerve cells may be damaged, or at least temporarily stunned. The brain, we believe, attempts to restore the deficit, using surplus cells in a process of spontaneous reorganisation. This may take time. And there are a myriad possible side-effects. Headache, fatigue, poor concentration, poor balance, amnesia, emotional lability. Lability? Liable to change. Mrs Meo, which of these four words best describes your husband's temperament: serene, easy, irritable, difficult.'

'Oh, easy.'

'Expect a tendency, in the coming weeks, towards the diffi-cult. Would you and uh, Billie like to look in on your husband? He has been given a muscle-relaxant. I suggest you do not wake him. An hour ago my colleague tried to shine a light in his eyes. Alex was not best pleased!'

35

Intensive Care felt like a submarine or an elderly spaceship: dark compartments where important devices whirred and ticked – electrocardiograms, panting ventilators; the churning of life and death in shapes and shadows. Smiling, the charge nurse drew back the curtain. In they crept.

When she saw him Billie gave her characteristic groan of love – but there seemed to be grief in it now. Feeling a pain in her throat, Russia stooped hurriedly and lifted the child into her arms.

They had him at a steeper angle than she expected. The hefty white collar he wore and the way the sheets were puffed up round his neck made it impossible to avoid the thought that he was slowly emerging from the depths of a toilet bowl; and there were wires taped to his scalp.

'Why he not awake?'

'He's *asleep*,' she whispered sibilantly. 'He got an ouch and he's *asleep*.'

Suddenly his eyes opened and he was staring straight at her. She felt herself rock back: what was it? Accusation? Then focus was lost, and the lids sank slowly, obedient to a chemical torpor.

'Blow a kiss,' said Russia, 'to make it better.'

As she was walking back through Reception, with that light tread, that flat-heeled tiptoe, Billie looked up at her mother and said, with unreadable contentment,

'Daddy's different now.'

'Count down from one hundred in units of seven.'

'One hundred . . . Ninety-three. Eighty-six. Seventy-nine. Seventy-two. Sixty-five. Et cetera.'

'Good. What do a bird and an aeroplane have in common?'

'Wings. But birds don't crash.'

'Can you name the Prime Minister?'

Xan named him.

'Can you name the Royal Princess?'

Xan named her.

'I'm going to ask you to memorise three words for me. Will you do that? They are: dog, pink, reality . . . All right. What were they?'

'Pink. Cat. Reality.'

His condition felt like the twenty-first century: it was something you wanted to wake up from – snap out of. Now it was a dream within a dream. And both dreams were bad dreams.

That morning, with Russia present, Xan had been moved from the Intensive Care Unit to the Head Injury Ward. He had won (it seemed to him) insultingly excessive praise for slowly walking in a roughly straight line, for negotiating a flight of stairs depending only on the handrail, for ponderously combing his hair and cleaning his teeth, and for successfully getting into bed. The consumption of a fish finger, with full deployment of knife and fork, brought him further accolades. It was a dream and he couldn't wake up. But he *could* go to sleep, and he did so, dreamlessly.

In the afternoon everything became a little clearer. There were fourteen patients in the ward, and they had all of them been split in time. Their minds had gone backwards, while their bodies had floundered on into age. The dullest chores of body-maintenance, those that normally made you numb with inanition, were hereabouts hailed as *skills*. For example: voidance. An unassisted visit to the toilet could win a round of applause from the staff and from all the patients who knew how to clap. (And even Sophie, at ten months, knew how to clap: a tinny, ticky sound, to be sure, but she seldom actually missed.) Then, too, there were accomplishments that were even more basic than going to the toilet – like *not* going to the toilet when you weren't *in* the toilet. Aslant the next bed but one there lay a seventy-year-old who was being taught how to swallow. And there were others, at different points along different roads, trudging off in tracksuits to the woodshop or the physiotherapy pool. And there were two or three like himself, the uncrowned kings of Head Injury – virtuosos of toothbrush and hairbrush, crack urinators, adepts of the shoelace and the beltbuckle, silky eaters: Renaissance Men.

'Do you know what the en ee oh is?'

'Meo. Neo. No.'

'Near Earth Object. Have you seen a newspaper? It rather drove you off the front page, I'm afraid. It's coming on Valentine's Day. Don't worry. It'll be close, but it'll miss.'

Valentine's Day, he thought. Not a good day for this particular woman. The full orange lips against the downy pallor, the massed orange hair. And yet there was something . . .

'Could you write out a sentence for me? Any sentence.'

Xan was handed a pencil and pad. His interlocutor was a forty-year-old clinical psychologist called Tilda Quant. She was having a reasonably good time, partly because it made a change from cajoling an elderly into spelling the word *the*, but also because this patient was indeed in the newspapers, was in show business, was a mediated individual. Tilda wasn't succumbing to the old-style reverence for fame. This was something more subliminal and interactive. Partaking of his publicity, his exposure to general observation, her own publicity was minutely enhanced. For his part, Xan thought it tremendously significant, for reasons as yet unclear to him, that Tilda Quant was a woman. She said,

'"The quick red fox jumped over the lazy brown dog." Hm.'

'It's an exercise,' he said. 'Supposed to contain every letter in the alphabet.'

'Yes, you're a qwerty too. Qwerty? You know: qwerty uiop.'

'Oh yeah. I think I got it wrong though. The sentence. Don't see a vee in it. I could never remember that one. Even before.'

'. . . You say you don't remember it, the uh, violence.'

'I do. I do. It wasn't just the rough stuff in the last few months. The whole process was unbelievably violent. I'll tell you how I felt. I thought: If I could find some very old people to sit near to, then maybe for ten seconds nothing that bad would happen. Then I wouldn't feel so incredibly frail.'

She was looking at him with a new fascination. She said,
'What are you talking about?'

'My divorce.'

'Hah,' she said, taking notes. 'I'd call that your first dabble in cognitive dysfunction. An inappropriate response to a question that was clearly related to the *assault*.'

'The assault? No, I don't remember the assault.'

'Do you remember the three words I asked you to memorise?'

'. . . Cat. A colour: yellow or blue. Oh, and reality.'

Outside the sun was an hour above the horizon, still showing one thing to another: showing the other thing to this thing, and this thing to the other thing. He watched shadows move. They moved, it seemed to him, at the same speed as the minute-hand of the clock on the wall of the sister's office, behind her sheet of glass. This felt like a discovery: shadows moved at the speed of time . . . Xan kept thinking about his dead sister, Leda: he hadn't seen her for fifteen years, and when he went to the hospital she never woke up.

His wife came, with Billie and the baby, and Imaculada.

When the girls had gone Russia called for the screens to be drawn around his bed, which she then climbed into, wearing only her slip. The way she did this made him think of the phrase *petticoat government* . . . He responded palpably to her warmth, her breadth. This was a distant reassurance, but it soon joined the pulse of his headache, and was then lost in his exhaustion and nausea and the ambient grief of his wound. He wanted to submit to a body of moving water. He wanted to let the waves do it.

Russia had put her clothes back on and was about to leave. Xan seemed to be sleeping, but as she tugged at the plastic curtain he sat up straight and eagerly pointed to the young man in the next bed along (who seemed far from grateful for the attention), saying,

'This guy here – he's a hell of a shitter. Aren't you son. Not
. . . uh, overly brill at the eating and the talking. So far. But you
can't argue with shitting of that quality. Boy can he shit.'

Xan felt that no one seriously expected him to remember the
assault. When they asked him about it (the doctor, the clinical
psychologist, the easily satisfied plainclothesman), he told them
that he remembered nothing between going to Hollywood and
going to hospital. This is what he told his wife. And it wasn't
true. 'Well I'm Mal,' the man had said. Well I'm Mal.

Whoever hurt me, he thought (all day long), I will hurt. Hurt
more, hurt harder. Whoever hurt me, I will hurt, I will hurt.

2. Doing Beryl

Five foot eight in all directions (he was roughly the size of a toilet
stall), Mal Bale carefully poked a number into his mobile (it was
no bigger than a matchbox, and caused him to rely on the nail of
his little finger). He said to his employer,

'There should be two of me here. To body this fucking bloke?
You come back from the Gents and he's gangraping a waitress
– all by hisself . . . No, mate. No, I only rang for a moan. Actually
he's not that bad tonight, with his injury: slows him down a bit.
And the journalist's here now and he's gone a bit calmer . . .
Yeah? Thanks, mate. Appreciate it.'

Mal referred, in the first instance, to Ainsley Car, the
troubled Wales striker. One of the most talented footballers of
his generation, Car was now up to his armpits in decline; and
he was only twenty-five. It was three years since he had represented his country (and three months since he had represented
his club). The journalist in question was the *Morning Lark*'s
Clint Smoker.

Ninety-nine point nine per cent of the work of a professional bodyguard consisted of one activity: frowning. You frowned here, you frowned there. You frowned this way, that way. Got to be seen to be vigilant: got to keep frowning. Some mornings-after you'd wake up thinking: Fuck. Who nutted me last night? Like your brow was one big bruise. Only it wasn't the fighting. It was all the frowning . . . But Car was different. Normally a body-guard protected the client from the outside world. With Ainsley, you protected the outside world from the client. Mal Bale, who had been hired by Car's agent, stood at the bar of the Cocked Pinkie, rubbing his eyes like a child. He wouldn't be called upon to do a lot of frowning. He would be called upon to do a lot of gaping – as a prelude to more concerted action. It's weird, thought Mal. Ainsley's just about controllable till the six-o'clock person-ality change. Half a shandy down him and he's a different bloke. His eyes go.

There they sat in their booth, Ainsley and that Clint: talking business. Ainsley's fourth cocktail looked like a Knickerbocker Glory – with a child's umbrella sticking out of it. You've got to respect him as a player, Mal inwardly conceded. And Mal in his early days (a different epoch, really) had been a loyal supporter of his native West Ham: the punnet of sweet-and-sour pork on the overnight coach to Sunderland; the frenzied, lung-igniting sprints down the King's Road; the monotonous appearances at the magistrate's court in Cursitor Street. Then disillusionment had come to him, one Saturday at Upton Park. It was half-time, and they had these two mascots romping around in the corner where the kids all sit; they were plumply, almost spherically costumed, one as a pig, one as a lamb. Suddenly the pig gives the lamb a whack, and the lamb whacks him back. It was comical at first, with them flopping and floundering about. You thought it was part of the act – but it wasn't. The lamb's on his back, flailing like a flipped beetle, and the pig's doing him with the corner-flag, and you can hear the kids screaming, and there's blood on the fleece . . . Up until that moment Mal had considered himself nicely pumped for the post-match ruck; but he knew at once that it was now all over. *Over*. Something to do with violence and categories: he couldn't articulate it, but never again would he fight for fun. Mal had recently become a dad himself, which might have had something to do with it. He heard later that the lamb had been stuffing the pig's bird, in which case the lamb, Mal believed, definitely had it coming.

He consulted his watch (seven-fifteen). Darius, his relief, was due at ten.

'Over the past two years Ainsley Car and the *Morning Lark* have enjoyed a special relationship,' said Clint Smoker. 'Fact?'

Ainsley did not demur. During his years at the top he had opened his heart to a series of mass-circulation dailies about his benders and detox programmes, about the drunken car-crashes, the wrecked hotel rooms, the stomped starlets. But that was in the days when, with a drop of his shoulder and a swipe of his boot, Ainsley could hurt whole nations, and instantaneously exalt his own. And he couldn't do that any more. These days, even his delinquencies were crap.

'There comes a point in every athlete's life', said Smoker in his loud and apparently humourless voice, 'when he has to take off his shorts and consider the financial security of his family. You have reached that point – or so we at the *Lark* believe.'

No, he couldn't do it any more: on the park. In his early pomp, Ainsley was *all* footballer: even in his dinner-jacket, at an awards ceremony – if he turned round you'd expect to see his name and number stitched on to his back. Ginger-haired, small-eyed, open-mouthed. In the dialect of the tribe, he was tenacious (i.e., short) and combative (i.e., dirty); but he was indubitably in possession of a football brain. His *mind* wasn't cultured or educated – but his right foot was. Then it all went pear-shaped for the little fella. The aggression was still there;

it was the reflexes that had vanished. Usually, now, Ainsley was being stretchered off the field before the ball had left the centre circle: injured while attempting to inflict injury on an opponent (or a teammate, or the referee). The *Lark*'s most recent in-depth interview had concerned the 'moment of madness' at a pro-celeb charity match when, with the vibrations of the starting whistle just beginning to fade, Ainsley went clattering into the sixty-six-year-old ex-England winger, Sir Bobby Miles. They broke a leg each.

'I got *years* left in me, mate,' said Ainsley menacingly. 'You know where I keep me pace?' And twice he tapped his temple. 'Up here. I can still do a job out there. I can still do a job.'

'Let's have some realism, Ains. Never again will you pull on a Wales shirt. You're on a one-year with them slappers up in Teesside. And they won't renew. You'll have to drop down. In a couple of seasons they'll be kicking chunks out of you down in Scunthorpe.'

'I ain't a slapper, mate. And I ain't playing for . . . for fucking Scumforpe. You know who's enquiring after me? Only Juventus.'

'Juventus? They must be after your pasta recipes. Ains. Listen. You were, repeat were, the most exciting player it's been my privilege to watch. When you had it at your feet coming into the box – Jesus. You were something unbelievable. But it's gone, and that's what frustrates you. That's why you're always in hospital by half-time. You've got to believe that the *Lark* has your best interests at heart.'

'The people', said Ainsley, with bitter gratitude, 'will always love Ainsley Car. They love their Dodgem, mate. That stands. It *stands*.'

Resembling an all too obviously non-edible mushroom, Clint's tongue slid out of his mouth and licked the handcuffs dangling from his nose. He said, 'You're done, Ains. You're gone. You've *given*. It's that nagging brain injury called self-destruction. You're fat, mate. And you sweat. Look at your chest. It's like a wet-T-shirt competition. And that wedding-ring is getting smaller every week. Which brings me to my next point.' Then, his sadism more fully responding to the masochism it sensed in Car, he gestured at the waiter, saying, 'Raymond! Another drink for Tits.'

Smoker paused. He was, this night, experiencing an unfamiliar buoyancy – rather to the detriment, perhaps, of his diplomatic skills. In the inside pocket of his big boxy black suit there nestled an enticing e-mail from his cyberpal, 'k'. In response to Clint's query, 'What kind of a role do you think that sex plays in a healthy relationship?' she'd e'd: 'a minor 1. have we all gone stark raving mad? let's keep a sense of proportion, 4 God's sake. it should only happen last thing @ nite, as a n@ural prelude 2 sleep. none of these dreadful *sessions*. i find a few stiff drinks usually helps – don't u?' Reading this, Smoker became belatedly aware that his most durable and fulfilling relationships had all been with dipsomaniacs. To put it another way, he liked having sex with drunk women. There seemed to be three reasons for this. One: they go all stupid. Two: they sometimes black out (and you can have a *real* laugh with them then). Three: they usually don't remember if you fail. Takes the pressure off. Common sense.

'We at the *Lark* reckon you've got one mega story left in you. The challenge, now, is for us to maximise that story. We've discussed various ways you could make the world sit up and listen. And this is what we want you to consider. Doing Beryl.'

'Doing Beryl?'

'Doing Beryl. And having Donna.'

Beryl was Ainsley's childhood sweetheart. They had wed when they were both sixteen, and Ainsley had left her two weeks later, the day after his record transfer. In a ceremony largely brokered by the *Morning Lark*, the pair had recently remarried: the event was designed both to confirm and solidify Ainsley's triumph in his battle with alcohol. Central to the symbolism of the story was the fact that Beryl, remarkable in no other way, was spectacularly small. Ainsley himself was the shortest player in the Premier League – but he beetled over Beryl. Journalistically, it was felt that a tiny bride would shore up Ainsley's protective instincts and sense of responsibility, unlike the circus-horse blondes whom he was always brawling over, or brawling with, in various spielers and speakeasies.

'Follow me here,' elaborated Clint Smoker. 'You arrange for Beryl to meet you in your London hotel room at a certain time. Earlier in the day, at a piss-up arranged by us, you pull the top *Lark* model of your choice. Say Donna Strange. You take her back to your room, and you're giving her one when the missus walks in. Donna scarpers and you do Beryl.'

'Why do I do Beryl? Why doesn't Beryl do me?'

''Cause she's one inch tall. No. Come on. She's *bound* to give you a bit of stick.' Smoker put his head at a craven angle and said in a wheedling voice, '"You were giving that model one! You betrayed me with another bird!" All this. I mean, how much shit can you take? So then you do Beryl.'

Ainsley's open mouth opened further, thus deepening the pleat between his nose and his forehead.

Smoker said, 'I mean *every* paper'll cover that. And we'll have Donna's tits and arse all over pages one to five, Beryl's black eyes all over pages five to ten, plus an eight-page pullout soul-searcher from the man himself, Ainsley Car.'

'How much?'

Smoker said how much: a jolting sum.

'*All passengers to the rear of the plane!*' Ainsley suddenly hollered. '*Stam back! Don't no one go near! Fuck amfrax – this geezer's got hepatitis G an an an-grenade up his arse!* OH MY GOD! IT'S THE TOWER! *IT'S BIG BEN, IT'S OLD TOM, IT'S BUCK PAL!* NO! THE UMFINKABLE! *OH MY GOD, WE'RE ALL GONNA –*'

By this time several waiters had hurried through the silenced dining-room, and Mal Bale was there with his palms on Car's shoulders, pressing him back into his seat, and looking round about himself, and frowning.

There's no *hard men* any more, brooded Mal (this had recently become an urgent mental theme, following the matter with Xan Meo), as he made his way to the bar, two hours later: all they got now's *nutters*. Nutters on drugs. Take Snort: that bloke Snort.

When he reached the bar and its ring of drinkers, Mal turned. Darius had been prompt. At this point Darius was on his first cranberry juice, Smoker was on his third litre of mineral water (he feared for his driving licence) and Ainsley was on his ninth cocktail. A seven-foot Seventh Day Adventist, Darius looked to be having some success in forcefeeding Ainsley with bread rolls.

Take Snort. No bottle. After the Xan Meo business, Mal gave Snort his drink (four hundred in cash) and said, 'I'm never using you again, mate. All right?' And Snort just dropped his eyes. And then Mal said, 'So you're having that, are you? Just think, "I'll fuck up, I'll get me drink and I'll creep away"? You ought to take a pill called *pride*, son. You ought to take a pill called *pride*.' See: no bottle. Just nutters on drugs. And playacting, too. Snort says he's ex-SAS, but all the right dogs say they're ex-SAS.

Mal was now joined by Smoker of the *Lark*, who was looking at him oddly, as if pricing his suit.

Smoker meant to say it softly, but his voice wasn't equal to saying things softly. He said, 'You're a face, incha?'

The first thing Mal had to establish was whether he was being trifled with. He was barely aware of the existence of the *Morning Lark* (and would have been scandalised by its contents), but he knew Clint pretty well, through the Ainsley Car connection and because of that time when he, Mal, had famously bodied topless models for six months and given interviews to various news-papers, the *Lark* among them. Seemed like there wasn't much harm in the bloke. Relenting, Mal said,

'Don't know about *face*. I'm a bodyguard, mate.'

'But you put yourself about a bit, in your time. Let the *Lark* do this.'

'Yeah. Well. This and that. A pint of Star please, love. I could have progressed. But I didn't have the correct temperament.'

Clint quietly rolled his eyes and said, 'But you've run with these blokes. You said in print that you've run with these blokes.'

'Yeah, I've known a few in my time. Ah, lovely.'

'See if this name means anything to you.'

'Goo on en,' said Mal briskly, tipping his head back and intending to neck a good few swallows of his first drink of the night.

'Joseph Andrews.'

Mal emitted a sneeze of foam and dived forward with his face in his glass.

'Whoah,' said Clint, wiping the beer off his brow and pounding Mal's back with a heavy white hand. 'Yeah. See they did that bloke Xan Meo? Mate of mine witnessed it. Said they were settling a score for Joseph Andrews. Reckons he'll flog it round the newspapers.'

It's gone off, thought Mal. It's all gone off.

At midnight Ainsley Car called for his crutches.

Already ashore, Mal watched the troubled striker as he levered himself along the gangway, with Darius looming in his wake. Beyond them flowed the Thames and all its klieg-lit history. Above, the moist studs of the stars, the sweating stars, seized on to spacetime.

'Legless,' said Clint from behind.

'No, he'll be getting his second wind about now. Want to be off up the clubs.' Around eleven Ainsley had entered a quieter cycle, like a washing-machine. Any minute he'd be back to tumbling and fumbling and shuddering up and down. Mal looked at his watch and said, 'Time for the submarine.'

And you could hear him, Ainsley, as he laboured up the slope, in a low, fiercely rigid voice, going: '*All men in level five proceed at once to level four. All men in level four proceed at once to level three. All men in . . .*'

Discreetly the courtesy car drew near. Mal saw with regret that Ainsley's course would take him past, or over, the poor bastard who was sitting under a lamppost with his dog in his lap . . . And this homeless person was not in the position of Homeless John, who had somewhere nice to go home to; he was a genuine carpark and shop-doorway artist, a dustbin-worrier hunkering down for his third shelterless winter. The bitch had spaniel in her blood, and smooth-haired terrier; he stroked and muttered and otherwise communed with her. They looked closer than a couple: the impression given was one of intense participation in each other's being. It was almost as if the dog was his strength, his manhood, surfacing erect from his slumped body.

So Dodgem poles himself into the frame and says, 'Do you fancy fifty quid?'

'. . . Course I fancy fifty quid.'

Out comes the money-clip and he peels off the note.

'. . . Thanks very much.'

'Now. I want to ask you a favour, mate. Can you lend me fifty quid.'

'I'd rather not. To be honest.'

'*Honest?* You know what my dad said to me?'

'What?'

'Nothing! Cuzzy fucked off when I was one. But me *mum*. Me *mum* said charity begins at home. And you ain't got one. Now *ghiss it*,' said Ainsley. His voice was vibrating; his whole head was vibrating. 'Where's your *pride man* . . . ?'

'We . . . we weren't all born with a talent like yours. You're a god, you are.'

Ainsley now turned inexorably on Clint Smoker. 'I stood, mate. I stood. The National Amfem! The fucking *King's* there just above the dugout with tears in his eyes! With the grace of a

48

pamfer I've put Hugalu on his arse, nutmegged Straganza, and laid it off for Martin Arris! The Twin Towers explode! With love, mate, with love!'

'They can't take that away from you, Ains,' conceded Mal.

The dog looked up at the footballer with eyes of loving brown.

'Here,' he said. 'Take it, son. Go and get arseholed on Ainsley Car. *Everyone stand back! That's not a dog! It's a rabies bomb!* ALL PASSENGERS IN SEATS FIVE TO TEN PROCEED AT ONCE TO THE SECOND LEVEL OF THE SUBMARINE! *IT'S GOING OFF, IT'S GOING OFF!'*

Then, like two athletes genuinely committed to winning the three-legged race, Ainsley launched his desperate hurdle into the night, Darius following, first at a jog, then at a run, then at a sprint.

Clint remained, as did Mal. Mal was wondering what kind of mood Shinsala would be in when he got back to her flat. As he swung the car door shut, as he listened to the chirrup of the lock, would he feel the *excuse me* of fear in his chest? Not physical fear, of course, but fear. Was fear a mood?

'You could do it by maths,' said Clint. 'Divide his weekly wage by his IQ. Something like that.'

'Clint mate,' said Mal, winding up.

Smoker offered him a look of effusive contrition. In the last thirty minutes there had been a power-shift between the two men. Clint had tended, in his previous dealings with Mal, to regard him as an affable plonker obliged to earn a living with his fists. But male anger, male heat so easily translatable into male violence, had rearranged this view. Clint thought of himself as big and strong, and there were those ragged brawls of his that he always won. Still, Mal's violence was efficient, professionalised and above all righteous: it was something that Clint could never counter. At this moment Clint's fear felt to him like love – love for Mal Bale.

'Clint mate. Are you a cunt?'

'No, Mal. I'm not a cunt.'

49

'Now. What happens if you let me down.'

'Well, obviously the proverbial'll hit the fan, won't it. Obviously.'

'If you want to know how hard, give your boy Andy a call at the end of the week. All right?'

'Yeah mate. All the best then, Mal. Go easy. Take care, mate.'

Clint Smoker was laughing by the time he hoisted himself on to the flight deck of his black Avenger. Adrenalin: it's very good stuff. As he put his foot down (within minutes, consecutive thought would be entirely sacrificed to motorly concerns) Clint began to compose an e-mail in his head, beginning, 'What do you say to the hoary old chestnut, Does size matter?'

3. On the Royal Train

The King was not in his counting-house, counting out his money – and the Queen was not in the parlour, eating bread and honey . . .

Henry was coming south on the Royal Train. This train of his had an 'office' car, a conference car, a drawing-room car, a bedroom car, a dining-room car, a kitchen car, a staff car, a security car, and an observation car. The potentate was in the 'office' car, writing his daily letter to the Princess. Like nearly all the interiors he had ever known, it was a chamber of restless lines: absolutely nothing had been left in peace. Every plane was harassed with ornament; the walls were tiled with paintings and framed photographs, the flat surfaces infested with curios and bibelots; each panel of the ceiling insisted on its cloudscape, its putto, its madonna, its nude. Denied the freedom of vast dimension, the train was like the condition of being royal: it was always on at you and it never let you be.

There were frequent and durable and much-resented delays,

but the Royal Train was technically non-stop. At this stage only the King knew of the coming rendezvous, in a siding at Royston, near Cambridge, with Brendan Urquhart-Gordon, who claimed to bear both positive and negative news.

'My darling daughter,' the letter had begun . . . 'The Lepers', he now wrote, 'were rather a pain. Then the nightmare of the flight back. The turbulence over the Channel was, as always, pretty good hell. On landing, straight off to the Head Injury lot, which was a fair form of medieval torture. You have to hang round listening to people who can barely talk and say how wonderfully they're getting on. Then, in the afternoon, I went north, on the Train.'

He paused. Going north had been like a journey into organic depression, a journey into night and into winter. At first, merely the obese cauldrons of the power-stations adding their clouds to the huge grey. Then the sky turned fuzzily black, with bright seams. Every now and then the sun would appear, like a miner's helmet coming down a chimney. They met the night at three-fifteen. And finally the Kyle of Tongue, strapped on to its crag in the North Sea.

'There has, alas, been no change in Mummy's condition,' Henry wrote on, his elaborate calligraphy rendered even more tremulous by the careening wheels. 'I must say I now thoroughly dread these visits. What's so heartbreaking is that Mummy is quite unchanged, as serenely handsome as ever.' He broke off, and shuddered. 'The hairdresser still attends her once a day, they still do her nails once a week, and she is of course frequently "turned". If it weren't for the ghastly wheezing of the ventilator, one might expect her to open her eyes and say, with all the old joviality, "Oh Daddy, don't just sit there! Where's my pot of tea?" As I have often said, whilst there <u>have</u> been cases of people emerging from "PVS" after periods of several years, we must contine to steel ourselves for the worst.' The "team", my darling, may be reduced from three to two, but it's <u>still</u> a team, you and I, my dearest one. You and I. We Two.

'The presence of the media . . .'

He paused. And continued:

'. . . simultaneously cheapens and confuses one's sufferings. Of course I am moved, of course I am shaken. But must I display my wounds to the camera? And this is when they are at their most respectful! "Don't be afraid to shed a tear, Your Majesty"! It makes one want to <u>vom</u>. More and more viscerally do I feel that the media are base violators who poison everything they touch.'

He paused. How had Bugger put it? 'The Princess should be told', Urquhart-Gordon had said, 'that there may have been a breach of her privacy.' No, thought Henry: too early for that. And continued: 'It seems to me that we two ought to have a "peptalk" on this very subject, and on security in general; I will come on Saturday (5th), and we can have a lovely chat in that perfectly decent hotel.'

There followed a fantastic display of diminutives and endearments.

Henry then rang for Love.

At Royston they began to slow. Up ahead, in an almost invisibly fine mist, lay the siding where large-eyed Urquhart-Gordon now stood with a lone detective. And the black car, beyond, with its driver. The train was still moving when Brendan climbed aboard.

Henry IX said, 'Give me the bad first, that good may come of it.'

'The discouraging news, sir, is that the photograph is not, in fact, a photograph.' Brendan composed the sleek lines of his eager, clever face. 'It is a still.'

He had mentally set aside quite a few seconds for Henry to take this in. And the King's head actually idled on its base for a full half-minute before he murmured,

'From a film.'

'Well, yes, sir. From a film.'

Brendan heard Henry's sigh – long and searching, with a muted whimper at the end of it.

'From a DVD DigiCam 5000, to be precise, sir.'

'You know, Bugger: I hope this *comet* or whatever it is smeshes us all to smithereens.'

'It won't smash us, sir. If it hits it'll burn us.'

'Even better. Hellfire. It's no less than we deserve.'

Now Brendan contemplated his monarch. It seemed a nice question: in a life so straitened, so predetermined, so locked down – you'd have thought that there was no room at all for individual variance. But Henry was an established royal anomaly. Unlike his father, Richard IV, and his brother, the Duke of Clarence, and unlike so many other males in their line, Henry had piloted no jets or helicopters, commanded no icebreakers or minesweepers, drilled no troops, bunked in no submarines, simulated no fighter-evasion sorties, parachuted athwart no mountainsides. Nor did he share his house's enthusiasm for horticulture, music, hunting, practical jokes and eastern faiths. Henry had merely loafed his way through a geography degree at Oxford and then got on with his social life. Even before he acceded, of course, his diary was plagued with 'functions', and he continued to shirk and chuck as many as he could. But the minimum was already a very great deal. Brendan thought that half the secret of the royal existence lay in the fact that it was quite unbelievably boring. You became a man of action to counterbalance this; you sought danger, exertion, intense states. And you busied yourself with arcana, with obsessional crankery – anything that would fill your mind. Henry was defenceless. He simply endured it, all the boredom, like a daily dose of chemotherapy.

Unlike his numerical predecessor, that glittering Renaissance prince, who was interested in astronomy, theology, mathematics, military science, navigation, oratory, modern and ancient languages, cartography and poetry, Henry IX was interested in watching television – or in staying still while it was on. Two years earlier, Brendan would have said that the King, at fifty-one, was senescent with ennui. For some reason his preternatural indolence endeared him to the million, and he had always been popular, despite everything (the gaffes, the insensitivity, the fathomless ignorance). They liked his frown, his blink, his sandy mop. Nowadays his numbers had in fact slightly dipped from their usual 75 per cent. The public didn't want to see their king trudging down hospital corridors and having fiendishly strained conversations with turbaned community-leaders. They wanted to see him fast asleep at the races.

'I went to her bedroom,' said Henry vaguely. 'It's still a zoo of cuddly toys. She's still so *little*, Bugger . . .'

Brendan reached for and unlocked his steel briefcase. 'Sir, we're somewhat further for'ard than we were. We think we have the location.'

'The location?'

'See, sir.'

Again the photograph – with the body of the Princess whited out of it. Though he recognised the propriety of the excision, Henry suffered a moment of snowblind alarm. Where had she gone? Whited out, like a mummy, like a ghost.

'I thought we'd have to start by trawling through every bathroom in all the royal households, looking for that tub, that mirror, that basin, in that particular alignment. But Oughtred's people have rather brilliantly narrowed it down. Look, sir. To the Princess's left is a bar of soap in its dish.'

Brendan paused, giving Henry time to say,

'Are you telling me that this is the only royal bathroom with a cake of soap in it?'

'No, sir.' Brendan dipped into his case and was presently unscrolling what seemed to be a poster or a silkscreen: twenty by twenty, and glossy to the point of liquefaction, and *all* white.

'And what may I ask is this?'

'The bar of soap, sir. Or rather a detail from it: the crest.'

Henry stared into the swimming cream.

'It's rather worn down, sir, but you see the indentation. A lily. Three petals bound together. The fleur-de-lis. That's the brand the household uses at Cap d'Antibes. The Princess holidayed with you there for two weeks in August. And that, I submit, sir, was when her seclusion was surprised.'

'That's a pretty way of describing what I consider to be a capital crime, Bugger. Well then. Now what?'

Brendan had never seen it before: the King with a kingly air. He said, 'With your permission, Your Majesty, Oughtred and I fly to Nice tonight.'

'Given . . . Oh, poor darling.'

The two men listened to the train as it slowly rocked and knocked . . . Brendan considered. Victoria England, naturally, had already been the theme of many a national furore. The first of them erupted when she was seventeen days old: a sacked nanny claimed she had walked out because the Queen refused to practise 'demand' feeding. Six months later the country was similarly divided on the question of whether the Princess was ready to be weaned. And so on. Should she be allowed to ride a training-bike indoors without a crash-helmet? Should she be eating fast food on school outings? Should she have worn 'that' miniskirt at the ill-fated 'Dunsinane Disco'? It was at this stage (the Princess was eleven) that Brendan started to detect a half-conscious salacity in the native fixation. No, not salacity: something indecent, but innocently indecent. When she turned twelve there was a sudden crossfire of think-pieces on the arguable virtues of a) sanitary napkins, and b) riding sidesaddle – in which the Princess was of course never mentioned. You could feel it gathering, building; it was on the people's mind: Victoria poised between childhood and nubility. So much disquiet, concentrated on the precious membrane of the Princess . . . Brendan thought that the relationship between the English and the Englands was incestuous and narcissistic but essentially subliminal (*sub*: under;

limin-: threshold); down there all was obscure, sunless, moonless, starless.

'You'll see she gets this today, Bugger.'

Henry now stood and moved to his desk where, using an ivory shaving-brush and a silver saucer of water, he fixed the envelope containing his letter to the Princess, adding the Royal Seal with the ring on the third finger of his right hand.

Brendan gathered his things. First the blow-up, the grotesque enlargement, like a plastic tablecloth. Then the photograph itself. He was glad he couldn't see Victoria's face, with her pupils on the top left-hand corners of her eyes, which disquieted him so. He thought he knew what the Princess was doing. She was *listening*.

The sprawling map of the fleur-de-lis, now that was just a *detail*: the crest. Why, who knew? With a bar of soap that size, maybe you could wash all Fucktown clean . . .

Laterally the Royal Train moved across North London, continuing west.

Andy New saw it pass. He was down on the actual track (his fresh stashpoint), and he saw the curtained carriages, the crests and emblems. He thought: taxpayers' money! Not that And was much of a taxpayer . . .

And was a pusher: of drugs, and of pornography.

And And was an anarchist, a street-partyer, and a committed savager of junkfood restaurants during antiglobalisation riots. Two years earlier his common-law wife, Chelci, had presented him with a child: little Harrison.

Having vaulted the gate, he made his way up the back slope, meanwhile fielding a call from his older brother, Nigel. Nigel had been a bit savoury in his earlier days but now he was dead straight just like any other cunt.

Nigel: 'You're not still peddling that muck, are you?' And: 'The videos and that: course. Freedom of expression. But not *that* stuff.' Nigel: 'Because that's a no-no, that is.' And: 'Definitely no go.' Nigel: 'It's not on.' And: 'No soap whatso.' Nigel: 'I worry about you, And. On the train to Manchester.' The brothers had recently travelled to Manchester, to watch the match and see their dad. The City Hall wearing a green fishnet vest, and the cabbie's shortwave going Britannia Ridgeway, Rodger-Rodge, Oxnoble, Tango Three, Midland Dinsbury. Nigel: 'Us sitting on the floor between the compartments? Okay, there's nowhere else to sit. But I look at you and I think: He fucking loves it. Down there in the dirt with his can of lager.' And: 'What's this in aid of, Nige?' Nigel: 'I worry about you, And.' And: 'Well worry about your fucking taxes.'

As he came muttering up over the bridge a voice hailed him from behind:

'I say! Excuse me! Young man!'

Turning, And saw a compact gent of late-middle years, wearing a chalkstripe suit with its three jacket buttons fastened, dark glasses, and a black borsalino.

'Thank you, thank you. Now. I wonder if you could very kindly direct me to . . .'

With some difficulty he detached an envelope from his inside pocket. He smiled. 'How *are* you?' he asked heartily.

'All right. How are you?'

'I've never felt better in my life, thank you, and I'm thoroughly enjoying this spell of fine weather we're having.'

One of those accents: posher than the King.

'I'm looking for Mornington *Crescent*, do you see. Not Mornington Terrace, Mornington *Crescent* . . .'

Andy soon set him right.

'Ah. Thank you so much.'

At this point, with an elegant rotation of the wrist, the man in the suit removed his dark glasses – to reveal the strangest eyes And had ever seen. So bright yet so pale: Antarctic blue, with yellow haloes. For a moment Andy wondered where the bloke had left his guide dog.

'Tell me. Would you be Andrew New?'

'Who wants to know?'

'My name is *Semen Figner* . . .'

Pronouncing the name in a different voice: Slavic. And New saw that the blue eyes had foully darkened.

'Your woman is shit,' Semen Figner said normally. 'Your kid is shit.'

February 14 (10.41 a.m.): 101 Heavy

First Officer Nick Chopko: Hey, that's kind of cool . . .
Flight Engineer Hal Ward: Excuse me?
Chopko: See it? Second to go, runway right.
Captain John Macmanaman: . . . Well well. The old De Hav Comet.
   What? Nineteen fifty-five? Where's *that* going?
Ward: Croydon, maybe? The Aviation Museum?
Macmanaman: . . . This wait is going to eat into my retirement.
Chopko: Yeah. I *would* like to take off while I'm still quite young.

After the seventy-minute weather delay, CigAir 101 had pushed back from its stand and joined the queue on runway nine. Flight regulations insisted on a three-minute interval between ascents. But on this day, of course, all the transatlantic equipment had to be off the ground by eleven o'clock sharp. The tower decided on the Emergency Interval of 130 seconds. And the Captain coolly advised his passengers to prepare for some 'slipstream turbulence'; with slipstream turbulence, he might have gone on to say, the passenger will feel more like a mariner than an aeronaut, shouldering through heavy seas at 200 miles per hour.

Tower: One oh one heavy, you are cleared.
Macmanaman: Acknowledge.
Tower: Up and dirty.

At 10.53, 101 Heavy put its head down and went looking for the escape velocity. Reynolds Traynor was bolt upright in seat 2B. She had a cigarette in her mouth and the trigger of a lighter waiting beneath the print of her bent left thumb.

Chopko: V1 . . . V2. *Out* of here.

The instant the tyres left the tarmac the Captain extinguished the no-smoking sign.

A climbing plane normally welcomes the surge of a stiff headwind; but the headwind facing 101 Heavy, while no longer describable as a *storm*, was still, at forty-six knots, a *severe gale*. The Captain thus faced two immediate dangers, one grave, one merely very serious, with or without the slipstream turbulence and its 'funnelling' effect. The first danger was that the aircraft would go 'beneath the BUG', or the minimum flying speed, and submit to its own gravity load (resulting in a black box which consisted of a brief squall of obscenities). The second danger was that of 'nose-lift': here, the windforce meets the plane on its rising breast and renders it vulnerable to 'toppleback'. Nose-lift was what happened to 101 Heavy. Lighting a cigarette from its predecessor's trembling ember, Reynolds leaned into the aisle and looked aft. The inter-compartment curtains had fluttered up to head height. She was staring into a lift-shaft – but one thickly peopled. The women she could see wore contorted faces: bared teeth, incredulous scowls. As for the others, their brows were marked by the childish, the calflike frowns of men expecting death.

101 Heavy was twenty degrees from the horizontal (it felt more like twenty degrees from the vertical), and at maximum power, when it hit the torn air of the slipstream.

At this point the locks securing the coffin of Royce Traynor snapped free from their bracket. Falling end over end for thirty-five feet, Royce powerdived into a mosaic of wall-bolted mountain bikes. Wedged at an acute angle against the cargo door, he remained more or less upright when the plane steadied and continued a shallow climb to its cruising altitude.

'Isn't it great to be above the weather?' said the man in 2A. 'I'd like to *live* above the weather.'

'Yeah,' said Reynolds. 'But not today.'

'Not today.'

He was staring at her legs, very critically, or so it seemed to Reynolds, who *liked* her legs. Now he was staring at her feet.

'You shouldn't have worn heels,' he said. 'You could puncture the inflatable emergency-slide. Which might also serve as a liferaft. You're wearing tights.'

'. . . That's true.'

'You shouldn't have. They're partly synthetic, you know,' he said. 'They melt and cling when they burn.'

In the hold the corpse of Royce Traynor seemed to square itself.

It was ready.

CHAPTER THREE

1. The publicity of knowledge

For her next encounter with the Intensivist, Russia Meo wore the most expensive clothes in her possession. A customised Italian suit of black cashmere, matching gloves and bag, court shoes. She wanted to send a clear message to Dr Gandhi: if anything went wrong, she would most certainly sue. It was also one of those days when she instinctively decided to let her figure have its head. A waisted white blouse, therefore, and her most dynamic white brassière. These luxurious expanses of silk were not aimed at Dr Gandhi (they were aimed at someone else); but perhaps the components of the olive cleavage would be making a core assertion – the assertion of life, life . . .

Dr Gandhi had taken due note of Russia's appearance, and derived some doctorly stimulation from it (the relative size of the nipples was what chiefly intrigued him); but he wasn't enjoying this second interview as much as he had enjoyed the first. The correlation of forces had already changed, as was now pretty well invariably the case. How much better it had been, how much more appreciated he had felt, when nobody knew anything – in the time before the publicity of knowledge. Now, instead of the sweating mutes of yesterday, you faced erratically wised-up mountebanks with half-assimilated case-histories, prognoses, quackeries. Dr Gandhi believed that it would be fractionally harder, henceforward, to get doctors to be doctors, such was the drain on the job-satisfaction. Russia Meo was of course an educated, indeed a distinguished woman, and he had never expected to be able to radiate downwards at her, like a Saturn. But nowadays (he reflected) every flop and waster in London had some four-eyed cousin or nephew prepared to scour the Web for all it knew . . . So Russia pressed from question to question; and, head injuries being head injuries, with their labyrinthine sequelae, Dr Gandhi was soon reduced to a drone of equivocation. He felt a familiar frowsiness come over him, alleviated, for a moment, when Russia turned to the white sheet of the window: the tautening of her bust allowed him to conclude that the nipples would be correspondingly large. This prompted a sexual thought, one unmoderated by the simultaneous reminder that large nipples would facilitate the business – if not the actual process – of lactation.

Russia, for her part, had not at all enjoyed her many hours in front of the computer, boning up on the head-injured. After reading one particular sentence ('Approach your spouse as you would a completely new relationship'), she had even burst from the house and stridden to the Jeremy Bentham for cigarettes. She smoked seven of them while making herself mistress of sub-sections with titles like 'Your New Domestic Life' and 'Your New Social Life', and so on. What do they mean, *new?* she kept thinking. (And what do they mean, *your?*) It is better, we always assume, to be prepared than not to be prepared – but not much better; with some eventualities, being prepared isn't any good either . . . Among other recent gains and accomplishments, women have naturally made considerable advances in the largely male preserve of self-centredness. And alongside the conviction that she would try her very best, there ran another – specifically, that there were some (no, many) possible outcomes, amply described on her screen, that she couldn't and wouldn't endure. She was not being ruthless, merely modern: come *on.* But then Russia confronted another sentence, one that made her hate herself, and weep, and valorously insufflate. The sentence went, 'There is only one "miracle cure", and that is love.' And so now she said it a different way: come on. Come *on* . . .

As he stirred for the third or fourth time that morning, Xan Meo saw his wife, sitting, waiting, on the bedside chair. She said immediately,

'I was just reading about you. Well, not *you*, but people in your condition. Now, Xan, I want to say *this*: *don't* fall for the "two-year" myth. It's an old wives' tale that's caused a lot of unnecessary pain. They say that "after two years" you're not going to recover any further. It's *not true*, Xan. You can go on recovering for *much* longer than that. It can take five years! It can take ten! Ask around in your support group and you'll see that it's so!'

Xan needed more time than he would have liked to realise that all this was in itself an old wives' tale – or a first wife's tale, to put it another way. This wasn't Russia. This was Pearl. She went on:

'You know, something like this, it can make you grateful for what you already have. I know *I'm* grateful for what I already have: a lump sum, and not alimony. Because you do know, don't you, that only twenty-five per cent of head-injured patients are in full employment three months after their accidents?'

He straightened himself up and with both hands smoothed back his scattered hair; he supposed – and it was a supposition prompted or at least borne out by Pearl's smile – that he had never looked balder. Rather more generally, his cheeks and forehead seemed to be dotted with excrescences, asperities – as if, while he'd slept, someone had sliced and daubed a loaf of bread above his face, leaving it covered with crumbs and seeds held in place by coagulating butter. He was glad that Pearl couldn't see his knees: on the inner side of either patella, visible fluid waves, like fat worms.

'Where are the boys?' he said. 'They're here?'

'They're in the caff. They'll be along . . . One of the things you'll have to steel yourself for, my darling, is a net drop in your IQ. Studies show. Shouldn't affect the acting but it won't be too clever for the writing, will it? I don't know about the rhythm guitar. You know what really worries me?'

Xan waited.

'What really worries me is how it'll affect your relationship with Russia. Sitting there at dinner, you won't know what she's on about. Because that was always very important to you, in the past – her mind. You used to say so. It wouldn't matter that much if you were still with me. Not that I'd look at you now, in your state. We could just hang around staring at the wall. But with *her* . . .'

Over in the nook by the door several head-injured young men were sitting in front of the television, watching the only human pursuit dedicated to the infliction of head injuries: the two guys in the square ring, with the shiny shorts and the gumshields.

'You've gone very quiet, Xan. I expect it's a bit of a strain, putting a few simple words together.'

'Oh I can talk all right.'

'So you can. And don't worry about the longer ones – you know, the ones with two or more syllables: they'll come.'

In fairness to Pearl (and Xan, silently, within himself, had already made such a concession), it should be recorded that after reading about the attack she telephoned the hospital and screamed at various people, demanding, as the mother of Xan's sons, a full and detailed diagnosis, which she got; and this she had passed on to her boys with the gentlest and most hopeful construction. Pearl was a good mother. She was not, perhaps, everybody's automatic choice as an ex-wife. But she was a good mother.

'The worst thing, they say – they *say* . . . The worst thing, they say, is what it does to your sex life.'

A woman, it has been observed (by a woman, two hundred years ago), is fine only for herself. Man is indifferent to nuance; and the only things another woman will respond gratefully to are obvious signs of poverty or bad taste. Pearl didn't dress only for herself. She dressed for everyone – herself included. Today she

65

wore a black leather jacket that squeaked and glistened, a snow-white cashmere sweater, and a pink flowered skirt of startling brevity (plus witchy ankle-high boots, also black, and flouncy little socks, also white). There was one more thing: one more thing she was wearing.

He had known Pearl, on and off, since infancy; and the lost world of their marriage (he had come to feel) was regressive or animalistic or even prehistoric – a land of lizards. There were things that, even today, he would never dare tell Russia. For instance, the fact that after twelve years together (years qualified by month-long silences, trial separations, separate holidays, frequent fistfights, and ceaseless adultery) their erotic life continued to improve – if *improve* is quite the word we want. Everything else was bottomlessly horrible, by the end: they had reached a state (as one of their counsellors put it) of 'conjugal paranoia'. The two boys were long past going down on their knees and begging their parents to separate. It was not until Michael and David were well into their second and more serious hunger strike (eighty-four hours) that Xan and Pearl snapped out of it and called the lawyers. But throughout this period their erotic life continued to improve – or, to put it another way, continued to take up more and more of their time.

'It can go either way,' she said: 'your sex life. Either you're not interested – that's what usually happens. Or else you're interested in nothing else. Which d'you think it's going to be?'

Xan waited.

'Let's do a little test. Ready?'

He knew what was coming, and he knew where he'd look. To fix it: Pearl O'Daniel was tall and lean (and wore her auburn hair short and spiky); her hips were narrow, but her thighs were widely set, splaying upwards and outwards from the knee; and it was in the space between her legs, in this triangular absence (the shape of a capital y), that her gravity-centre lay . . . Now one of the predicates of Pearl's character was that she always went too far. Her greatest admirers would instantly admit it: she always went too far. Even in the company of those who themselves always went too far, she always went too far. And now, in St Mary's, Pearl went too far. Uncrossing her thighs and crossing her ankles, she revealed this space, and Xan, still defeatedly low in the bed, contemplated it. His ex-wife, of course, had not committed the sexual illiteracy of wearing nothing, underneath: she was wearing something, and not just anything. He was familiar with it – pearly white, and studded with stars. On the morning of the day the decree nisi came through, Xan had had the whole thing in his mouth, while Pearl looked approvingly on.

'Which is it?' she asked. 'All or nothing.'

'Of the two, I don't know, I'd have to say nothing.'

'Well *done*, Xan. A long word: nothing. Ah. Here are the boys.' She stood up and waved. Then from her fathomless tote-bag she removed a newspaper and stretched the page out at him: three photographs – Xan, Pearl, Russia. 'She's going to give you grief about this,' she said.

As his sons approached, Xan made another effort to straighten himself against the rails behind his back. Again, with trembling hands, he rearranged the trembling wefts of his hair. The bed, the whole stall here, felt like a display-case of age and ruin, in ashtray colours . . . Michael and David took up position on either side of him. They regarded their father, not with solemnity, alarm or disappointment, but with acceptance; and immediately he took comfort from it.

David, the younger, kissed his cheek and said, 'I'm sorry, Dad.'

Michael, the elder, kissed his cheek and said, 'Dad? Who were the fucking *bastards* who did this to you?'

'Michael,' said Pearl.

'Well that's it,' said Xan, who remembered, pretty much. 'You don't remember.'

But he couldn't remember the impact, nor the moments

leading up to it. Tilda Quant had told him that there was a fear-centre in the brain, a dense knot of neurons deep inside either hemisphere and normally associated with the sense of *smell*. Here was the control tower of your horrors and hauntings. Sometimes the brain could suppress the most painful memories (and military scientists, she said, were trying to duplicate the effect with a devil-pill that would quell all qualms). So now his brain was protecting him from his memory. But he wanted the memory and constantly sought it out. He wanted the smell of the memory.

'Never fear, boys. Soon I'm going to go out there', he said (in a voice, in an accent, that even Pearl found hard to recognise), 'and get them fucking dogs.'

Like somebody moving from one life to another, Russia walked along a tube of glass – one hundred feet above the road that separated the two sections of the hospital. She was leaving theory, now, and entering practice.

Her anxiety, her suspense, was currently devoted to a fit of slanderous detestation aimed at Natwar Gandhi – and at all doctors everywhere. As a student of twentieth-century history, she knew about the 'chemistry', as opposed to the 'physics', of the USSR's interrogation teams, the vivisectionists of Japan; when, in 1941, the German doctors were given a free hand in their treatment of the infirm and the supposedly insane, the following phase became known as 'wild euthanasia'. Doctoring talent – healing – danced closely with its opposite. Given the chance (it seemed), these pulse-taking, brow-fondling trundlers would be wrapping up children's heads in old newspapers, and strolling about, in a collegiate spirit, with the packages under their arms.

All of which they did do. But Russia, now, was hating Dr Gandhi (her chest swelled, her nostrils broadened) for his refusal to protect her from any of her fears. The prognosis was good; still, he would rule nothing out. And the glint that came into his face when he described negative outcomes: the glint of relished life-power. Yes, he must get a lot of that, in Intensive Care. While he talked, Russia found herself imagining what his senses had been trained to tolerate – unspeakable textures, fantastic stenches. Nor, as she took her leave, could she spurn the consolation that this doctor, like most other doctors, would drop down dead within a week of his retirement. It was to do with power, and when that went, they went.

She pressed the button. Something dropped in her. She sighed as the lift sighed.

'No, boys,' Pearl was saying, 'Dad'll be back on his feet before we know it. And up to his old tricks again. Won't you Xan.'

'. . . Course I will.'

'Of course he will. Whoo-pa. Here she comes. *Christ* she's fat. Russia! I've been admiring your picture in the newspaper!'

Explosive Anger and Irritability, Family Abuse, Grief and Depression, Lack of Insight and Awareness, Bladder and Bowel Incontinence, Anxiety and Panic, Sexual Problems, Loss of Love, Coping with Loss of Love, Letting Go . . . Russia walked on, making herself taller. The waisted blouse, the dynamic brassière, the olive cleavage: all this – just in case – had been for Pearl.

2. The high-IQ moron

What *used* to be funny? wondered Clint Smoker. What's funny now? And is it *still* funny?

A hushed conference room in the sick building. On the other side of the sealed window a tubercular pigeon silently flapped and thrashed. The Chief Publisher sat at his desk with his face in his palms.

For the *Morning Lark* was in crisis. Desmond Heaf (who made a habit of disappearing, of fading in and out of things) had returned, on a thirty-hour flight from the South Pacific, to rally his men.

He eventually said, 'I simply don't see how something as extreme as this could have actually . . . What were you *thinking* of?' Gingerly and evasively he looked down at the double-page spread flattened out in front of him. 'Sacred heart of Jesus. I mean, it's not in *nature* . . .'

'When I saw the first one,' said Clint, 'I thought it was an exposé on Battersea Dogs' Home.'

'Yeah,' said Jeff Strite, 'or a "shock issue" about Romanian mental homes.'

'And the actual damage, so far?'

'This whole thing is being taken very personally,' said Mackelyne. 'There's a lot of anger out there.'

'Are we losing them, Supermaniam?'

'Judging by my e's, they're all dying of heart attacks.'

'That's good, that is,' said Heaf. 'We're *killing* our own wankers.'

Supermaniam said, 'It's like Black Thursday.'

On the Wednesday before Black Thursday, the *Lark* had put together a playful piece about the *Guinness Book of Records* and the new category saluting the biggest ever, or longest ever, male member. On the same page (with more than a little twinkle in its eye) the *Lark* had reproduced a twelve-inch ruler and (tongue still firmly in cheek) challenged its readers to make an invidious comparison. As an obvious tease – or so the *Lark* believed – the twelve-inch ruler had been renumbered to make it look like a six-inch ruler. Soon after dawn it started coming in: word of the Black Thursday suicides.

Heaf said, 'Bill. You made up these pages. How did you physically bring yourself to do it?'

'When the first lot came in,' said Bill Woyno, 'I assumed they were taking the piss. When the next lot came in I must have thought, Well, this is . . . this is what it's like.'

'Let's face it, lads,' said Clint, 'we've gone and strafed ourselves in the metatarsus on this one. But there's a way out of it, Chief. May I essay a marxist analysis?'

'By all means, Clint,' said Heaf with a frown of intense respect.

'Right. The quality broadsheets are aimed at the establishment and the intelligentsia. The upmarket tabloids are aimed at the bourgeoisie. The downmarket tabloids are aimed at the proletariat. At the *Lark* our target wanker is *unemployed*.'

'Come to the point, Clint.'

'Well: who can you pull when you're on the dole? We've delivered an insult to all our wankers – a deserved insult, but an insult. We're saying, we're *proving*, that our readers' richards, if any, are straight out of the Black Lagoon.'

Four days earlier the *Morning Lark*, with considerable pomp, had launched its new feature, Readers' Richards. And the death threats had started coming in that morning.

'"Your ankles will be nice and warm"', Heaf incredulously quoted, '"as you feast your todger on another array of top-grade totty, submitted by our red-blooded . . ."' He sat back. 'Sweet mother of Christ, will you look at that – that *troll* in the top left-hand corner.'

'I'm getting e's from blokes who're stapling the pages together in case they see it by accident.'

'You should have a look at what we're *not* using. Every last one of them takes years off your life.'

'You got to brace yourself, and even then . . .'

'There's not that many to choose from. And we're already running out.'

'Three point seven million wankers,' said Heaf weightily. 'And this is the best they can do. Well then. What's our course of action?'

'Simple,' said Jeff Strite. 'Scrap it. Without comment.'

'No. See,' said Clint, 'that's *another* insult. And it's not what they're after.' He pointed at the four heaped stacks of printed protests. '*They* can't believe it either. They're not telling us to scrap it. They're telling us to say it isn't so.'

'And there's a road out of this, Clint?'

'Yeah, Chief. We can turn it around. Over a period of a few days we weed out the Wives and start replacing them with models.'

'What, our own girls? Bit obvious, isn't it?'

'Well, not the Donna Stranges of this world, obviously. Use more like the also-rans. And if a famous face does get in there now and then . . . See, it's not overly rational, is it, their response? We've kicked them in the arse. We've insulted them. Now let's flatter them.'

In the fight for the *Lark*'s ideological soul, Clint Smoker was always alertingly radical. He alone, it sometimes seemed, had a true estimation of their typical reader. He now went on to add,

'It'll go down okay. You could fill that spread with filmstars *and* have a strap saying *dream on, you stupid sods* and it would still go down okay. The other thing we need to do is improve the decor. Not these bleeding . . . coalholes. Look at the one on the middle right.'

Heaf rotated his head ninety degrees to the left, and then realigned it very slowly before jerking back from the page.

Clint said, 'That could illustrate a piece about white slavery or slum housing. The whole spread could. No. We want reasonable birds on three-piece suites. Or better. And if you had them in the driveways of stately homes, I assure you, our wankers would be none the wiser.'

There was a silence of about half a minute.

'Thank you for those words, Clint,' said Heaf. 'Make it so. Additional points . . . Now. All the other papers are going on about the NEO, the asteroid or whatever it is, and I'm sure our instinct was sound when we decided we'd completely ignore it.

72

But with all these earth-shaking events going on – aren't we short-changing the wanker on current affairs? I think we should at least *mention* the main wars and plagues and famines and what have you. Now I know our emphasis is essentially domestic, but with the world situation as it is I can't help thinking we're slacking off a bit on our foreign news.'

'I agree, Chief,' said Strite. 'I could do with another month in Bangkok.'

Everyone laughed tensely.

What's funny? thought Clint. Gentle reader. Reader, I married him. *T.S. Eliot: A Reader's Guide. Hypocrite lecteur! mon semblable, mon frere!*

> dear clint: your remarx about your
> childhood struck a chord. i 2 never
> felt th@ i was '1 of the "gang"'.
> some of us seem 2 have been
> singled out. We r, in some sense,
> 'special'. & i no th@ if i ever find
> some1 2 spend the rest of my days
> with, then he would have 2 b
> 'special' 2.

Clint had recently read a piece in a magazine which posited the emergence of a new human type: the high-IQ moron. Wised-up, affectless, and non-empathetic, high-IQ morons, according to the writer (a woman novelist), were also supercontemporary in their acceptance of all technological and cultural change – an acceptance both unflinching and unsmiling. So Clint was relieved, in a way, to find himself flinching and smiling, smiling and flinching, at the authorial style of his newfound penpal. In the text-messaging line, and so on, he had seen the King's English far more miserably disfigured. But never quite like this. Never, quite, in the service of mutual exploration and courtship – and with such good grammar. Clint knew about grammar. Mr and Mrs Smoker: both schoolteachers. And old hippies. Old – now dead – hippies. Dead hippies. Jesus: what happened?

Still, Clint wasn't about to be critical. Clint? Critical when it came to birds? Deprived for so long of female influence, he felt – well, these words of hers were like a lifeline to the guy. Like a lifeline.

He knew that the distance between himself and the world of women was getting greater. Each night, as he entered the Borgesian metropolis of electronic pornography – with its infinities, its immortalities – Clint was, in a sense, travelling towards women. But he was also travelling away from them. And the distance was getting greater all the time.

What happened? What was emanating from him, what was he giving off? He was, he thought, no uglier (and by now much richer) than the bloke you saw all over the place with his trusting female companion who was always ready to kiss his earring or stroke the nap of his fuzz or gaze into his dark glasses with a smile of roguish forgiveness.

Must be nice, he thought. Ring it up when you're walking down the street: so everybody knows. 'Hello, love, it's me. I'm walking down the street. What's for dinner?' Romantic evening. Table set for two. Slip it a Narcopam in its coffee: take the pressure off.

Must be nice. But it never had been nice. Even when things were bowling along all friendly, he always sensed the weight, the sinkage, the falling mercury inside his chest. Because he knew full well that they were just waiting – waiting for their chance. In bed, of course, the eternal battle was to *make them feel it*: to transform them with your strength. And that's what the books said women were after too, at one remove: the metamorphosis of impregnation by the strongest available male. So they were always waiting, calculating, comparing – always ready to belittle . . .

This, at any rate, was what Clint kept telling himself (wash your hands of them; they're all the same; and so on). But his unconscious mind suspected otherwise. He heard from his unconscious mind, sometimes. On Sunday afternoons as he lay abed licking his nasal handcuffs in the hopeless pit of his Foulness semi, he would sometimes hear it say: 'I don't know, mate. There's going to be grief. I don't know, mate. It's all going to end in tears.'

She was like a lifeline to the guy:

> my man of the moment (& i do
> mean moment) is of the 'macho'
> type. u no: down the gym all Sat,
> football on Sun morning & 10nis
> in the afternoon. borING! i like a
> fella who drinx beer in front of the
> tele – with me on his lap! in bed,
> while we r having 6, he moans at
> me 2 scream. i tell him: i'm not
> the kind that will per4m @ your
> beck & call! don't (me with TH@
> sort! i suppose he thinx th@
> screaming = abandon. but i don't
> WANT abandon. y o y, clint, do
> people use 6 2 infl8 their own
> gr&iosity?

Although the piece of paper he had in his hand was merely a printout of an e-mail, Clint held it to his cuffed nostrils, as if hoping for an intimation of her scent. And he had read it, oh, three or four dozen times. I'm not going to mess this one up, he thought: no way.

> the trouble is i've never been able
> 2 'sack' a man. 2 anger a man. i

wouldn't dare. offend a MAN? so i
have 2 go on mildly displeasing
him (and th@'s bad enough) till he
pax his bags & moves on. how? o
u no, clint – little things. i 4get 2
praise him as of10 as i used 2. i
refuse 2 wipe his p off the toilet
seat. i speak up 4 myself. wh@ i'm
really saying is: join the q, m8, 2
the back door! clint, i'm tired of it.
let me b clear: i h8 the 'new man'
2, so 'caring' in the bedroom. 'did
u finish?' 'was it good 4 u 2?' yes!
7th heaven! cloud 9! y can't
people just b themselves, clint? 2
much herd instinct, 2 much falsity,
2 much pre10ce.

    ps: 3 cheers 4 'readers' richards'.
a real tonic 4 the gentler 6: gr8
scott, there's hope 4 us all!

'Your messages are like a breath of fresh air,' mused Clint as
he precomposed his reply. 'Now you've seen my ugly mug often
enough in the *Lark*. I'm no looks snob – can't afford to be! But
it would be nice to put a face to your words of wisdom. And
maybe a name . . .' And she still hadn't said whether she thought
size mattered.

Only one thing troubled him. Market research had shown,
time and time again, that the *Morning Lark* had no women readers.
So the question remained: what sort of bird read the *Lark*?

He paused there, at his desk. Clint was about to begin a piece.
But he paused at his desk there.

'. . . Uh, is uh, is And around?'

'Who's this?'

'Uh, Pete.'

'No he ain't,' said a much smaller voice than the one he was used to. 'Harrison, careful, darling. They've got him down as missing. No, don't do that, sweetheart – there's a good boy. They've got him down as a missing person.'

Clint said he was sorry to bother. He thought: Jesus – don't say Joseph Andrews. Then: pop round and cheer her up. Then: no. Leave all that out. Or: the proverbial'll –

'– Ah Clint,' said Heaf. 'It's not as serious, but something else has just blown up in our faces.'

'And what's that, Chief?'

'Pervs Him Right.'

'Ah. The Walthamstow Wanker.'

'The same. But one crisis per day, eh? A couple of things, Clint. There's a word in your Video Review column that gave me a bit of a turn. Where are we.'

He flattened the page out on Clint's worksurface. The strapline said Blinkie Bob's Video Review. In the corner was a mugshot. Not Clint, but some portmanteau imaging creation: a face grotesquely wall-eyed, and bent at an angle, tongue lolling, with two hair-matted palms loosely raised.

Heaf said, 'Now where . . . ? Here we are. Uh, "and have your bogroll handy for when gueststar Dork Bogarde pumps his lovepiss over the heaving norks of our very own Donna Strange". What, may I ask, is *lovepiss*?'

'Semen, Chief.'

'Oh. Oh. I thought our house style was "manjuice". Oh. Well that's all right then. You know, it disgusts me, sometimes, what we do here. It does. How are things progressing with Ainsley Car?'

'Well the ice-boot's come off. Have to wait till he's playing again, for the visibility. But it's looking good, isn't it, with the new charges.'

Clint remembered that Heaf didn't follow football. He went on,

'They're nicking him for match-fixing now. Said he took half a mil from a Malaysian businessman to throw it for Rangers last season. Our wankers'll *hate* him for that: sacrilege, Chief. Maybe we can get Beryl done during the trial.'

'Proceed as you think fit, Clint. And you said you were following through with our royal coverage.'

'I'm on it, Chief.'

'It warms your heart, doesn't it, Clint. We always assumed that the royals were felt to be an irrelevance – an anachronism. And old Queen Pam, of course, was a rather forbidding figure. But now she's been gone for two years, and what with the Princess flowering into maturity, there's been a tremendous upsurge of affectionate interest – reflected in Mackelyne's figures – across the entire spectrum of our wankership.'

'Yeah well what it is is, now that Vicky needs a bra, it's reminded them that Henry's still on bread and water. They think it's time he started getting stuck in again.'

'You think?'

'Read Smoker on Saturday. Long think-piece.'

'Title?'

'"Is The King Normal?"'

3. Excalibur

He was in a ridiculous situation.

On the day of his birth the guns of the Royal Fleet all over the world boomed forth their joy. 'Our thoughts go out', said Churchill in the House of Commons (the Second World War was in memory yet green), 'to the mother and father and, in a special way, to the little Prince, now born into this world of strife and storm.' He was only a few hours old when he made headlines in every language and every alphabet. At school he discovered that his father's face was on the coins he presented at the tuckshop, and on the stamps he used to send his letters home. Before his visit, as a twelve-year-old, to Papua New Guinea, the island tom-toms sounded all night long. He was still a teenager when he represented his country at the funeral of Charles de Gaulle: he stood between Mrs Gandhi and Richard Nixon. Then came majority, marriage, murder – and the crown: the recognition, the oath, the anointing, the investiture, the enthronement, the homage.

All his personal dramas were national dramas. He was in a ridiculous situation. He was the King of England.

Henry IX was staying at the Greater House, his unheatable 300-room drum in Southern Hertfordshire. He had dined *à deux* with his little brother, Prince Alfred, Duke of Clarence, in the private room of a three-star restaurant on the Strand.

'The barman here, Felix, is absolutely marvellous,' he had said. 'He makes a truly splendid drink called a Scorpion. Ah, there you are. Two Scorpions! No: make that *four* Scorpions . . . Now tell me, dear boy. Are you going to *merry* this "Lyn" of yours?'

'You know, old thing, I don't see how I can marry *anyone*.'

'Why ever not, you ass?'

'Because I'm such a disgusting lech. We all are. Except you. Old chap.'

'. . . Now where are those Scorpions?'

The words stayed with him. And as he sat up, alone, at home (before the fire, under a heap of rugs and dogs), waiting for Bugger's call, Henry thought: yes, true enough. And why? Prince Alfred, at forty-nine, was still the hyperactive satyromaniac he had been from the age of thirteen (when he raped his first house-maid). His father, Richard IV, had gratified epic appetites, before his late marriage; and his grandfather, John II, was a notorious debauchee. And Henry IX?

By the time he reached his twentieth year, the Prince of Wales, as he then was, showed no more interest in sexual intercourse than he showed in polo or parachuting. He had a hectic and quite drunken social life, and many women friends. What, then, made him decline or ignore the countless importunities, ranging from the near-undetectable to the melodramatic, that tended to come a prince's way? It seemed to be nothing more complicated than fear of effort. A concerned Richard IV, abetted by the Queen Consort, arranged for the Prince to be visited by a lady-in-waiting – a young widow called Edith Beresford-Hale. Edith surprised Henry one night in the Kyle of Tongue. The Prince had retired after a damaging night with the forty or fifty 'guns' who had come up to scrag his wildlife. Of course, Henry himself never had anything to do with that. But he gamely went along with Edith Beresford-Hale. She bounced him around on top of her for a couple of minutes; then there was a smell of fire-tinged male changing-rooms, and Edith made a joke.

Then the Prince did what the King and Queen had by no means intended. He fell in love with Edith – or, at any rate, he confined himself to Edith. Though press and public assumed that he was sleeping with at least one or two of the young beauties he frequently squired, Henry was faithful for the next five years. He looked in on Edith about three times a month. She was thirty-one, and of comfortable figure and temperament. Not unlike his mother: the tweed skirt, the hardwearing shoes.

So Henry was in his mid-twenties when he began to be disquieted by a younger friend: the Honourable Pamela North. He gave Edith a house, a world cruise, and a pension, and started paying court to Pamela. On the day after the Royal Wedding (and a princely marriage, said Bagehot, was the most brilliant edition of a universal fact) Henry wrote to his brother, Prince Alfred: 'Everything was plain sailing, which was a relief. You saw when I kissed her on the balcony and the crowd went absolutely bonkers? Well, it was a bit like that in the bedroom. I felt the country's expectations on my shoulders, albeit in a rather agreeable way. I felt them urging me on. And everything was plain sailing. <u>You</u> know what I mean: I was very good!' And how could it have been otherwise, on that night, with his blood so thrilled and brimmed by the people's love?

The Prince had just turned twenty-seven when Richard was blown apart on a fishing-boat off the west coast of Ireland. Also on board was the King's cousin, who was the last Viceroy of India (and its first Governor-General); thus the murders had many claimants – Muslims, Sikhs, Hindus, and so on, as well as the more obvious and proximate suspects . . . Nevertheless, this period, with all its magnified emotion (emotion magnified by fifty million), saw Henry at his erotic apogee. England celebrated the Coronation in a mood of fierce defiance and euphoria; and the power-surge, for Henry IX, was carried over into the royal bed, with its gilt posts, its four boules bearing ducal crowns, its tester of purple satin embroidered with lilies, garters and portcullises, its valance of cloth of gold. During their second honeymoon, on the Royal Yacht, as the royal couple sat at table, serenaded by a romantic medley from a band of Royal Marines, Henry smiled sternly at Pamela when the hour of retirement drew near. Sexually, being king got him safely into his thirties (for a while, one of his many nicknames was Excalibur). But by now they were 'trying' for an heir . . .

After the birth of the Princess Victoria, Henry's lovelife no longer looked to the calendar and the lunar cycle: now it looked to the appointment-book. This duty-roster approach became a habit. It was, of course, a bad habit. Love was by royal appointment, just like everything else. And the male, even the royal male, the most brilliant edition, cannot do this. He cannot master it: expectation – the appointment with expectation. On top of all this, Pamela, as she got older, looked more and more unmistakably like a man.

One afternoon, at five past three, the Queen Consort said, with gruff puzzlement: 'What's the *matter* with it, Hotty? Oh come on, this is hopeless!' . . . And that was all it took. Not a single second of his waking life had a thing in common with anyone else's, but Henry's vulnerability, at least, was universal; here he came down from the mountain and took his chances among his fellow men. What *was* the matter with it? Good question. From this time forth, whenever the King saw a '3pm: Pammy' on his schedule, he felt a force settle on his chest, like a harness; and it wouldn't slacken until the rendezvous upstairs had somehow been survived. He searched his memory for a precursor of this apprehension, for he knew it to be there. Yes. The hours leading up to an earlier rendezvous, also by appointment: when he went to the housemaster's study to be thrashed.

But the negative epiphany – his life's cur moment – was waiting for him up in the Kyle of Tongue.

Brendan Urquhart-Gordon listened. The ringing stopped, and there were sounds of effort; and then – expressing no more than mildly hurt feelings – came a whimper of canine protest.

'Pepper, get *off*. Bee*na*. Is that you, Bugger? The bally – the bally phone got stuck under Beena and General Monck. And now there are hairs all over it, and some . . . disgusting flux or other. General! Get . . . Where are you, Bugger?'

'I am being driven north-east from the Cap to Nice airport, sir. Rather fast.'

To his right, beyond the forecourts of the supermarkets and hotels and petrol-stations, the modest lapping of the Mediterranean; to his left, not seen but sensed, the villa colours, the spotlights and crickets and sprinklers. Beside him sat compact, handsome, ageing Oughtred.

'Well, Bugger?'

'We have a crime-scene, sir. Much follows from this. We also have very compelling deductive evidence that the motive or the intention could not possibly –'

'Don't jabber your conclusions at me, Bugger. And stop

sounding so pleased with yourself. I'm *ill* with this, Bugger, and it's *not* funny.'

Brendan reproached himself: he had failed to dissimulate the pep of forensic success. He said, 'How insensitive of me, sir. Forgive me.'

'Forgiven. Now get on with it, Bugger. Oh a bottle of rather *good* red wine, if you would, Love? And one of your savoury snacks?'

'We're on the tarmac now, sir. Can you hear the plane? . . . We're begin break up.'

'Hello? Hello?'

'Sir, this is need to know. The motive, intention, not possibly pecuniary. Media nor blackmail. Talk to.'

After tapping it and shaking it, Henry slid the telephone back under General Monck; and, when Love returned, he asked him for a pack of cards.

Imagine: the kings and the queens. And what are we? Tens, twos?

Celibate himself, Brendan Urquhart-Gordon was an abnormally observant friend. And Henry, in any case, presented no challenge to the imaginative powers. He was legible; he was easy to read.

On a 'Pammy' day – or a day featuring 'another bally three-o'clocker', as Brendan had heard him put it – Henry would be quite useless all morning (incapable of consecutive thought), and would start yelling for brandy at about half past twelve. At five to three, up he trudged, returning at a quarter to four . . . If things had gone reasonably well, then Henry would assume a put-upon but stoical air (interestingly, there seemed to be no dividend of relief). If things had gone badly, then the King's parched face bore the skullshadow of mortality.

So one evening, in the library at the Greater House, Brendan looked up from a preselected report by the British Medical Association, and said casually,

'A giant step forward for mankind, wouldn't you say, sir? Potentium. The cause of so much male insecurity banished by the wand of physic. There will be no more wars.'

'. . . What *are* you banging on about, Bugger?'

'Sir, Potentium. A male-potency drug. Tested and patented and freely available. You take it on an *ad hoc* basis, sir. A single pill and Bob's your uncle. There will be no more wars.'

Henry stared into space for a good five minutes, blinking slowly and numbly, like an owl. Then he turned away and said, 'No no. One can't be doing with that *monkey*-glends business.'

And that would be that. And who was Brendan to carp? He used to tell himself that he thrived on his own inhibitions. But perhaps that was personal propaganda; and the obverse would never be tested. The fact remained that the bed he spent so much time trying not to think about had an occupant, and that occupant was a passive male. No, there never was a case more pusillanimous than his own. Given the choice between chastity and the reification of his schoolyard nickname, Bugger chose chastity. So it was all over very early: when he was eight.

'After four hours in the Château, sir, I was saying to myself, "Hello, this is a bit of a frost." We'd done all twenty-seven bathrooms. No shortage of white bathtubs, and no shortage of soap. But the alignments, the background colours, wouldn't match. Then I remembered the Yellow House, sir.'

'Indeed, Bugger.'

'Where the Princess often . . . bathed and changed after tennis before going on to the swimming-pool. And that, sir, was where the intrusion took place. A slat on the top section of the airing-cupboard facing the bath had been partly excised. On the shelf above the boiler we found a Vortex DigiCam 5000. The videodisc had of course been removed. Oughtred, who is still there, unsurprisingly reports that there are no prints and the registration numbers and so on have been scoured smooth.'

'So are we further for'ard, Bugger? I don't quite . . .'

The two men were in a security vehicle outside the Mansion House, where Henry was due to attend an anniversary dinner of the British Architectural Association (and where he would later 'say a few words': keep up the good work and whatnot). For a moment the King seemed to submit to the oppression of his surroundings: a mobile granny-flat littered with display screens, transmitters, earphones. Right in front of his chin there hovered a poised mike, with what seemed to be a leather condom clipped to its shaft. There was a jar of Bovril on the counter and, balanced on its lid, a smeared tablespoon.

'We have more, sir. But already we can make certain deductions. The unlikelihood of any pecuniary motive. At first I thought, well, the DigiCam 5 is worth about three thousand pounds – they got it in, why didn't they get it out? And this rather handily exonerates all the staff, as I realised when I was about to corral them for questioning.'

'I don't quite follow.'

'The servants simply can't have known about it or they'd have reported it or stolen it. This was rather spectacularly confirmed by Oughtred, not an hour ago. The DigiCam 5 is amazingly portable – but not this one. The camera, sir, is inlaid with *gold* . . .'

Henry eructed liverishly behind his hand. 'How perfectly vile all this makes me feel. My tummy's in ruins. I shall have to give my speech with my legs doublecrossed. What are they telling us, Bugger?'

'They're telling us that they're rich already and that they want something else. Not money.'

'What else have I got but money? I am a constitutional monarch and by definition I have no power. Glory, yes. But no power.'

'Is glory power?' asked Urquhart-Gordon. And he added to himself excitedly: is it negative power?

* * *

The next morning, as he cautiously overcame a cup of lemon tea (he would normally have a proper English breakfast: all the usual stuff plus lots of chops and pies), Henry IX received a communication from his private secretary:

FYI, sir. Copied out while hunched over the Château visitors' book. Please forgive informalities. Present during the Princess's stay (chronology of arrival):

Henry R; Bill and Joan Sussex; Brendan Urquhart-Gordon; Prince Alfred and Chicago Jones; Chippy and Catherine Edenderry; the Sultan and Sultana of Perak; Boy and Emma Robville; Juliet Ormonde; Lady Arabella Mont; John and Nicola Kimbolton; Joy Wilson; Prince Mohammad Faed (and wives); Hank Davis; the Emir of Qatar (and wives); He Zizhen. NB: at one point there were 47 minors at the Château, including 15 teenage boys.

Ah, He, He, He Zizhen . . . Just over a year after the Queen's accident, Henry found himself dining alone with Edith Beresford-Hale. However easily explained (and graciously excused), the straining, trembling, wheezing fiasco that followed was enough to convince the King: all that was all over. Edith was still a widow, or rather a widow once more, and there had been other changes. For example, she was sixty-three. But Henry made no allowances, and was quite prepared to tiptoe from the scene with his slippers in his hand. 'That was a *last*,' he said hurriedly to himself. 'What's the *matter* with it, Hotty?' the Queen had asked, giving Excalibur a rough tug or two before tossing it impatiently aside. 'Oh come on, this is hopeless!' Well indeed. What *was* the matter with it?

Then came He . . . 'May I tell you a secret?' she said in her accentless English, joining him as he smoked a cigar on a balcony of the Chinese Embassy in Paris. Henry turned (and noticed the sudden absence of his escort, Captain Mate). His universe was a gallery of strangers, and here was someone doubly other: the lavish black quiff, the fractional asymmetry of her lidless eyes (one eye happy, one eye sad), the strong teeth rather carelessly stacked into their prows. He inclined his sandy head at an avuncular angle . . . Now, to be clear: world-historical beauties (women perpetually dogged by tearful trillionaires) had come at him fairly steadily during the past twelve months. Many talented tongues had scoured – had practically drained – the royal ear. And the King might have flinched but he always leant willingly into it, hoping for an answer in himself, which never came . . . He Zizhen stood on tiptoe. Then there was contact. It seemed as if a butterfly had taken up residence in his tympanum – no, make that *two* butterflies; and they were mating. At once his collateral heart (so torpid, so workshy, so decidedly valetudinarian) felt like a length of towel-rack.

Subliminally, in his dreams, it worried him. The sexual coincidence: himself, in the Château, with the otherness of He in his arms; and, across the lawn, the Princess surprised in the Yellow House.

February 14 (11.20 a.m.): 101 Heavy

First Officer Nick Chopko: If it's designed to do it, it'll do it. God I'm tired. How about it, Cap?

Flight Engineer Hal Ward: Guy was telling me he was so tired coming into Honolulu it was like he was drunk. Not just drunk but totally smashed.

Captain John Macmanaman: I was reading in *AUN*, *both* pilots on a *commuter* fell asleep about two minutes after takeoff. Now with a sealed cockpit you don't want to . . .

Chopko: The attendants were screaming and banging on the door. They were practically in space when they came to.

Macmanaman: Not where you want to be today . . . You know what the Aztecs called comets? 'Smoking stars.' Because of the trail, I guess. You'll get your nap, Nick. But you'll have to excuse me for a second. I want to say hello to a passenger.

'Takeoff rough enough for you?' he said.

'Ah I trust you, John,' said Reynolds.

In the surplice of his uniform, hat in hand, he bent to kiss her. The man in 2A briefly ogled the Captain, but then kept wrenching his head around and staring back through the port-hole to monitor the performance of the wing.

'Welcome to widowworld. How are you bearing up, Rennie?'

'Good. No, I feel wonderful. There's a gap, and the end was horrible, but let's not kid ourselves. You knew him:'

In the hold, the corpse of Royce Traynor (full of wax and formaldehyde) was waiting with its teeth bared.

CHAPTER FOUR

1. The thing which is called world

'"So-called 'Renaissance Man' Xan Meo, attacked and hospitalised in late October,"' read Russia, '"may have been the victim of his own past, which is mired in criminality and violence."'

Xan listened, on this his first day home.

'"His father, Mick Meo, was a prosperous East End gangster who served numerous jail terms for armed robbery, theft, fraud, tax-evasion, extortion with menaces, and affray.

'"In 1978, while in his sixties, Mick Meo was sentenced to nine years' imprisonment for attempted murder, and died in jail. His victim was his own son-in-law, Damon Susan, the husband of his daughter Leda. Himself an ex-convict, Susan was confined to a wheelchair after the incident. He never recovered from injuries described at the time as 'unusually appalling', and is now in a hospice in West Sussex."'

'You know all that. There's nothing new here.'

Russia inhaled. She seemed to be sucking colour into her face . . .

'"Xan Meo's first wife, Pearl O'Daniel, a theatrical costumier" – oh, sure – "emerged from a similar background. Her father and all three of her brothers have served time for crimes of violence, and she herself has two convictions for possession of cocaine.

'"Keeping up the family tradition of injuring close relatives, Meo himself attracted the attention of the police after an incident with Angus O'Daniel, his wife's eldest brother, who declined to press charges. And in his youth Meo was convicted of a litany of minor offences, including Actual Bodily Harm." What's the difference between Actual and Grievous?'

'Uh, extent of injury. Grievous is worse. Actual's bullshit.'

'"While there is nothing to suggest, as yet, that the recent attack on Meo had any direct connection with his past, we do know that violence tends to double back on itself. Violence begets violence. However lucrative Meo's background may have been in shaping his portrayals of lowlife characters, on the screen and on the page, he may find that he is now paying for his past."'

'It's not a "past". It's a providence. I mean a provenance.'

'"Meo's marriage to O'Daniel was dissolved five years ago on grounds, among others, of physical abuse. Within months he married again. His second wife is dah dah dah . . ."'

'No, go on. Who's my second wife? Remind me.'

'"Dr Russia Tannenbaum, who teaches at King's College, London, and is the author of a university-press bestseller about the children of tyrants." Remarkable.'

'Remarkable how?'

'No errors of fact.'

Russia pushed the bulky, frazzled tabloid across the sofa towards him. Xan saw that the piece was illustrated to shore up its theme. The photograph of Pearl belonged to a set she had circulated during one of the more regrettable spasms of their divorce: her left cheekbone was bruised and the eye above it was swollen shut (and Xan, in the same desperate struggle, had received a broken nose). As for Russia, she'd been taken by surprise in the street somewhere, and looked as though she was about to be mugged. Xan was represented by a still from a TV movie called *99 Stitches*, in which he had played the part of 'Striper' McTavish: he had a broken bottle in one hand and a claw-hammer in the other.

'Well you can't say you wasn't . . .' said Xan. 'You can't say you weren't warned.'

She contemplated him. His face now seemed to wear a coating, a cladding – the hospitalic subtraction of vigour and

90

light. It was also, again, oddly leonine: something top-of-the-food-chain in the contented wreath of the mouth. This face feared no predator.

'I'll come back at them. In the press. I'll get on to Rory,' he said. 'I'll tell my side.'

Billie entered, without escort. In the last couple of months she had established her right to glide unaccompanied round the house – much to the profit of her inner life. Increasingly often you saw the eyes give a freshened bulge: new acquisitions, new annexations, in the forming brain.

'Get a book, darling,' said Russia, 'and Daddy will read.'

'Look at the size of this lousy rag,' said Xan as he let it slip from his lap to the floor. 'I'm on page eighty-six. That's one good thing about being in the papers these days. If you're on the news pages up front then they've got you. If not, you're okay. Because you can't fucking find it.'

Russia was certain: he had never done that before – sworn in front of Billie.

'Want it this one,' said the child.

And Xan turned his attention to a family of well-dressed elephants awaiting sustenance in a palatial dining-room.

'I'm that one,' said Billie. 'And Mummy's that one. And Baba's that one. And Lada's that one.'

Xan pointed to the head of the table, where the father sat. 'Who's *that* one?'

'. . . *No* one.'

That one wasn't anyone. It was just an elephant in a blue suit.

Deficit-denial, energy-debt, fatigue-management: they knew the kind of things to expect. And they went about it like sensible people.

Russia's maternity sabbatical was coming to an end (and there was that conference in Germany), and Imaculada's trip to Brazil was imminent and unpostponable; but Xan, in his condition, wasn't going anywhere: so it seemed obvious. He would spend his days lolling and idling with the girls, and would make himself useful, as lackadaisically as he liked, about the house.

Both projects proved beyond him.

Very soon it became clear that he could be trusted with nothing. The spacious kitchen, where Xan spent most of his suddenly limitless free time (he was keen to reassert his culinary skills), became a psycho's laboratory of molten frying-pans, blackened pots and blazing skillets; the waste-disposer would be chewing its way through one of his dropped tablespoons while the microwave juddered and seethed. Things slid through his fingers – spillages, sickening breakages. The toaster scorched him, the coffee-grinder finesprayed him. Even the fridge stood revealed as his foe.

Elsewhere he left traces of himself around the house, like messages sent from one animal to another. A sock, a vest, a pair of underpants, on the stairs, in the sitting-room – but also his wastes, his emanations. Whenever she went near it the bathtub always seemed to contain two feet of cold swill bearing a greenish mantle; there were flannels, scraps of tissue paper, wadded with mucus and earwax, and little middens of scurf and nail-clippings, leavings, peelings. Most signally, of course, no amount of asking could persuade him to flush the toilet: as you opened the front door you felt you were entering some coop in rustic Dorset, or the Zoo, or a men's room from the Third World. Now, at night, his armpits gave off a smell of meat.

They were at the table, with the teamugs and the newspapers. If asked to describe the atmosphere, Russia would have called it pseudo-normal. Then he said,

'Chicks like salad.'

'What?'

'Chicks like salad. That's a real difference between the sexes. Chicks like salad.'

'You eat salad.'

'Yeah but I don't *like* salad. No man likes salad. Chicks like salad. And I can prove it.'

She waited. 'How?'

'Chicks eat salad *when they're stoned*. A bloke would want his chocolate bar or his sugar sandwich. Not some bullshit tomato. A chick'll eat salad in the *morning*. From the fridge. Only a chick would do that. That's how sick chicks are. Christ, is that the phone?'

'It's the fridge.'

'The fridge?'

'It's new. Haven't you noticed? It makes a noise if you leave the door open. You left the door open.'

'Fuck off!' he called out to it. 'I wonder. Am I the first man on earth to tell his fridge to fuck off?'

It came again: a vicious chirrup.

'Oi you. Fuck off out of it!'

'Instead of telling it to fuck off, why don't you go and shut it?'

'*You* shut it. And I mean your mouth and all.'

'Don't talk to me like that.'

'Why not? Are you getting your period or something. Okay, I'll make allowances. Red Rag is running in the two-thirty. You've got the painters in.'

The words came out this way: 'Please try and remember yourself,' said Russia.

After a moment his head and his shoulders dropped and he said, 'That's exactly what I'm trying to do . . . I *am* trying. You can't imagine how hard I'm trying. You don't know this thing. I can tell you. It's a real *cunt*.'

The doorbell buzzed. Russia swung the fridge door shut on her way to the stairs.

My room, Xan thought . . . Outside is cold, but my room is warm, but my fridge is cold . . .

When Russia came back she saw that her husband was doing

93

two things at once. Such multitasking was now rare. Doing one thing at once was difficult enough. Still, there he sat on the sofa, where he slept and wept.

Meanwhile, the little girls handed down their judgements.

Both had at first seemed astonished but on the whole delighted to see him. Billie, in the front hall on the first day, had smiled so wide that he feared her face might break: the corners of her mouth almost disappeared into her hair. He didn't encounter Sophie until first thing the next morning: she was what he saw when he opened his eyes. Whereas Billie, in the same situation, would have inserted herself between her parents like the crossbar of a capital *h* (H for *home*, perhaps – but with the further suggestion of a thwarting wedge), Sophie kept to the side of her mother (with whom, again resonantly, she was making the beast with no backs). Sophie too smiled. And when he opened his eyes twenty minutes later she was still smiling, and he knew it was the same smile, held good as he slept. Sophie's smile lacked the unsustainable emphasis of Billie's. It was faithful, grateful, and above all proprietorial; she had written him off, and now he was home. He reached out and felt her arm. The warmth this event had created, his return, came back at him through her blue-veined wrist.

Billie changed slowly. She consented to be picked up and hugged, but after a couple of seconds she would wriggle for release with disconcerting vigour. Later on, when he crouched to receive her, she twirled away and then looked up at him through splayed fingers. And when he prevailed upon her to settle down to a book (come, read: the sky is falling!), and he bent down and kissed the parting of her hair, she would jerk back and rub her head and say, 'Oh *Dad*' – as if Dad was nothing more than the name he went by. She sidled up to him and asked in an embarrassed whisper if he had brought her a present; when he offered to bathe her she declined – but said he could watch. She had begun to treat him, he realised, like a moderately intriguing family friend. Billie was of that breed of little girl who, in certain lights, resembles a twenty-five-year-old emerging (with considerable advantage) from her second divorce. This formed, knowing, worldly face was the one she turned on him now. Seventh or eighth in line, he was the louche and ponderous suitor whom, against her better judgement, no doubt, she had decided to keep on file.

Sophie changed suddenly. Sophie turned, in an instant.

It was his third day home. Some logistical entanglement had forced Russia to leave him alone in the house with the baby: a configuration never repeated. Sophie was supposedly down for the night (it was about seven o'clock), and he hadn't thought much of it when he heard the cries from her room. She had now been on the planet for almost a year. These cries of hers were confident, almost businesslike (she knew the score). He had heard her in far greater confusion and disarray. Why was it so hard for them, sometimes, to go from one state to another? What were they separating themselves from, with such bitter difficulty? In sleep, it seemed, they lost their hold on love and life; and when they woke, sometimes, they couldn't shake off this dream of freefall.

He went in and decribbed her and took her back out into the light. She saw his face – and all the dogs of London must have snapped to attention. A scream is a blunt instrument; this was more like a whistle, piercingly focused, and focused on him . . . She twisted away, quietening, stiffening. Then by degrees she tracked back, infusing her lungs with short hot gasps of suspense: perhaps – obedient to the intensity of Sophie's wish – her father would now be transformed into Russia or Imaculada. On finding that this hadn't happened, she reestablished herself on the outer limit of distress. Then it went on getting gradually worse.

There came a crucial interval, in the garden under the apple tree. He had somehow juggled and manhandled her down the stairs, half the time on his rump, and drawing himself along on the lifeline of the banister, with the baby wedged in his knitted armpits.

They gained the kitchen; he tried all he knew, and nothing worked. So he pushed his way out of the back door – and the cooler air, and the pale-blue evening above, seemed to reposition her. After a while she was able to meet his gaze. Her eyes: to contemplate them was like floating in a pond or a slow-moving river. Competing currents and temperatures subtly coursed; one of these undertows looked like trust, and he tried to swim towards it; but it was soon lost, sluiced out, in other undertows. Then he abandoned his pleading whispers and just held her to him as he groaned and shuddered. It was like the last days of Pearl: twins joined at the chest and now under the knife, in inseparable pain. Nearly an hour later Russia returned with the fetched Billie. Within ten minutes Sophie was asleep, piteously but resignedly clutching her duck.

Thereafter he would sometimes look into Sophie's eyes, in search of that pulse of trust. He couldn't find it. And she cried, now, the moment he entered the room. At supper, when the baby was with them, her seat like a pair of medieval underpants bolted to the table, Xan ate with one hand in a fixed salute, shielding his face from her sight.

And Russia?

'You'll remember this in pain, boy.' Well, he remembered *that*. *'You went and* named *him!'* Named *who*?

He remembered the Dickheads, the dead duck upside down in the green canal. The sunset, like a firefighting operation. The paparazzo sparrow (*'Is that your "bird"?'*). *'Why'd you do it, son? You went and* named *him!'* Named who?

Xan had read in the books, in the literature of head injury, that an experience needs time to become a memory. Not long – maybe a second or two. And the blow had come so quickly, so hard upon. The significant name didn't have time to become a memory. And perhaps (the books suggested) that memory-pause was a cerebral reflex – of self-protection. The brain didn't want to remember the blow.

But he wanted to remember it. In epileptic longhand, with his pen shooting off, accelerating off in all directions, he retraced the steps of that October evening, saying *come on, come on* with an East End cadence (said in this way, *come on* rhymes with *German*; in the East End it was normally reserved for watching fights). Sometimes he could get as far back as the smell of the assailant's breath, the assailant's hormones, wrapped round his neck like a scarf. But no further. It was like an investigation into the very early universe, that infinitesimal fragment of time which was obscured by the violence of the initial conditions. You couldn't quite reach the Big Bang – no matter what you did.

At his desk he also worked on his diary, as instructed. Record *everything*, they told him. And he recorded everything:

> Woke at ten. Rose at eleven. Cold water on face. Went downstairs (lost balance twice). Baby there – cried. Ate cereal. Made tea, scalding hand. Had shit. Searched long time for address book. Phoned agent. Sat at desk. Wrote this.

He'd been in a state of combat-readiness, when he went down. And his body remembered that. But now he was a cripple: a cripple who was spoiling for war.

Outside was for healthy people, and he didn't go there. Even his visits to the mailbox at the end of the front garden (a distance of fifteen feet) took him to the brink of a chaotic immensity. It made his face flicker.

Outside was the thing which is called world.

'Do you mind if I use a tape recorder? You didn't last time, as I remember. Rory said you wanted to give this a definite emphasis.'

'Yeah well we'll come to that. But – yes. I mean to send a message.'

'Okay . . . When did you first realise that your father . . . ?'

'Was a villain. When I was little my mother used to tell me he was in the army. He'd go away for a year and Mum'd say he's in – I don't know – Vietnam. "But we're not in Vietnam, Mum." "Well your dad is, that's all I know." And then there were all these brown letters from Broadmoor and Strangeways, and he'd come back as pale as a polyp, so I had my doubts. And around then, see, the villains found a new toy: publicity. They all started doing what I'm doing now. Giving interviews.'

Xan had said much of this before – in interviews. And the sentences, even the paragraphs, were still there. But now something else was trying to ail his speech.

'Villains? It doesn't make a lot of sense.'

'No, it don't, and they all paid for it. They thought it was a great new way of winding up the oppo – you know, sticking it to the Old Bill. But you can't have it both ways. You don't want to be riling up a bloke who's getting good overtime. So I'd read him in the news, mouthing off about how they couldn't do him for this or that caper, and then he'd go away for another stretch. Where is it this time, Mum. Mozambique? Anyhow, you don't pick your dad, do you. Or your childhood.'

'Were you part of all that, growing up?'

'I was me mother's boy, and she was crooked too, but dead against the violence. I was a scrapper, mind. Don't ask me why but I loved a fight. I'd go into pubs outside the borough. The sort of places where the carpet sucked the shoes off your feet. You ordered a pint, drank it in one, and put the glass upside down on the bar. That meant: I'll have it with any man here. Someone went and put me in hospital for three months, just before my dad went away for the nine. Mum went absolutely spare. What with my sister already running wild. I went direct from Princess Beatrice to this fucking barracks of a boarding-school in Littlehampton on the south coast. Basically a crammer for posh dropouts. A couple of years of that and then Lit and Drama at Sussex. I changed. I was a hippie. But I could still fight. And a hippie who could fight was something to be.'

'At university you were quite a ladies' man . . .'

'Every bloke was quite a ladies' man in them . . . in those days. In those days, for a while, girls went to bed with you even when they didn't want to. Peer-group pressure, that is. If I was above average, it was because I could offer them . . . pacifism from a uh, from a position of strength. I was covered in beads and flower scarves, but when some fucking great rocker come stamping up I'd say, "I smell grease." Or go over to a gang of skinheads and call them a load of little fascist cunts. If you *can* fight, you don't *have* to fight. And you don't have to cower. And girls like that, whatever they say. Uh, look, mate – I'm fading. Sorry. It's, it's my condition.'

'If you like I can . . . Are you sure? Last question, then. Could you say something about your father and the attempted murder.'

'Okay. My sister Leda, rest her soul, she got roughed up by her husband. And me dad's done him. Give him a fucking good hiding. Said he'd gladly do ten years for him and that's what he got. And I'll tell you something else and all. The bloke who put me in hospital for the three months: it was him. Mick Meo. For why? I've gone into the yard, and there he is, having this fight to the death with some other mad prick. I dragged him off and he done me. Three months. One week later he's done me brother-in-law, who never walked again, and gone away for his nine. Then he's gone and done the Governor at Gartree and got hisself topped by the screws in the Strong Cell . . .

'No. Wait, wait . . . See, I split from the villain world, but things stay with you. One is complete contempt for the police. In America the police, they're working-class heroes. Here they're working-class dogs. They're scabs and traitors. They take the rich man's shilling to guard his gear in the property war. There's talk about honour among thieves. That's all bollocks. But there's rules. Now, whoever did me in October or had me done – I get the feeling they think I've been telling tales to the Old Bill. And that is something I would *never do*. When the police uh, questioned me about the attack I said I remembered nothing. And they can come round here again and I'll tell them I remember nothing. It ain't true, but that's what I'll tell them. They can stick red-hot pokers up me arse, and that's what I'll tell them. Understand? Me, I'm the nicest bloke in the world. You know, in the car. Come on, darling. No – after *you*. But if someone . . . Now I spit in the eyes of whoever did me or had me done. I tell him: you got business with me, then you fucking come down . . . you come down . . .'

Even in sleep his face held its distortion.

Then there was the kind of whispering behind half-shut doors that gets done around the sick and the unpredictable and the violent.

Pearl, when her ex-husband called, was dependably merciless.

'Would you like to talk to a boy? I'll find one in a minute. But first, Xan, I want to ask about your care-giver. I mean the – where is it? – "the non-head-injured party in your relationship". She'll be in mourning, Xan, for the person you once were. That's quite natural. It says here you both have to "let go" of the "old" Xan Meo – the one who could get about the place and earn a living. He's gone, Xan! And listen: don't be afraid to cry. It says here you should talk about all the good old times and get the old photos out and have a good old blub.'

Xan wasn't gone. He had to believe that he wasn't gone. Reality was like a weak dream, in early morning. You sense the weakness of the dream-authority and in velvet revolution you rise up, you rise up; you try to take control of the nonsensical narrative – to guide it towards pleasure, or away from fear. The dream was weak, but so was the dreamer. And another wave would come and he would go under.

'Mm,' said Billie, 'yummy water.'

Using both hands she placed the empty glass on the kitchen table and then drifted from the room.

'Yummy *water*?' said Xan. 'Well, a man condemned to die finds water delicious. Air delicious. Maybe it works the other way round.'

With the broadsheet on her lap Russia watched him. They both knew that talking made Xan manic, now. They had of course discussed it. And it made him manic.

'I can't believe you said all this. It was your intention, was it, to sound like an animal.'

'It's the dialect of the tribe. It will be understood.'

'By whom?'

'By the party concerned. Do I swear a lot?'

'Generally, or in the interview? . . . No. "Little fascist bastards". "Mad prick". No.'

'And how's me . . . how's my English?'

'Your English?' She shrugged and said, 'It parses.'

'Thought I could feel my English going. Bloke must have cleaned it up. Tea', he added, 'is bullshit. I want coffee. You're on your second cup of Colombian and I'm still on the bullshit. What's for dinner?'

'Fish.'

'Seafood is bullshit. I want meat.'

'You can't have meat. You can't have coffee. Not yet.'

'What have I got to look forward to? This evening, before my meal, I'll drink a couple of glasses of near-beer. And if *beer* is bullshit, which it is, what's *near*-beer? It's not even bullshit. It's bullshit bullshit. And then what? A plate of bullshit. And yummy water.'

Russia stood up. He followed her to the counter, saying,

'I should keep my mouth shut, shouldn't I. Because if a woman isn't liking you, she isn't going to like anything you *say*. It could be fit for Hamlet and she isn't going to like it.'

'You know what I'm thinking? It's not that you've become a brute. I'm thinking you were a brute all along.'

'Oh, nice, that is. I get smashed over the fucking head, and now nobody loves me any more. The girls don't. You don't.'

'You're doing it again. You're standing too close to me.'

'No I'm not.'

'Jesus, you are really freaking me out. Get *away*. And guess what.'

'What?'

'Your *zipper's* undone.'

Yes, that's right, that's right. The worst things of all were happening upstairs: in the master bedroom.

2. His Voluminousness

The first sentence almost made him roll over backwards:

> dear clint: r u as other men r?

But he was lying down at the time: on his humid sack in the Foulness semi.

> (i ask because <u>u</u> ask: about size
> m@tering.) well if u're not as
> other men r: don't worry. my
> current 'other', orl&o, wields a big
> 1, of which he is inordin8ely
> proud. but take my word 4 it,
> clint, u don't want a bloody
> great 21.

A bloody great . . . twenty-one? he thought. Oh: the 1's an *l*.

> they're overr8ed! l h8 them! & what
> an un4tun8 effect it has on the

ego: he thinks he's the b's knees. it's
not size th@ m@ters, clint. it's love
th@ m@ters.
u ask also 4 my name. i don't no y
i'm feeling quite so shy about it. it
suddenly seems so intim8. the 1st
act of commitment, if u will. u want
2 no my name. well it's . . . k8.
there. i've said it. 'k8.' '"k8 . . ."'
& u ask about my loox. 1st, my
figure. 1 swain was consider8
enough 2 tell me th@ my 'tits were
crap'. another ventured the opinion
th@ i had 'a crap arse'.

So she's taken her nox — fuck, her knocks — too, Clint noted.
Poor little thing.

(no young gentleman has yet proved
sufficiently gallant 2 aver th@ i
have 'a crap cunt'.) in fact i am
inordin8ly proud of my body as it
has developed over the years. i'm
not a c@walk cutout, nor a mega-
boobed 6-queen: just an honest
middle-w8. & @ 25, i'm bloomin'!

Age-difference: perfect, thought Clint.

as 4 my face. my i's r green (tho
not with n v!). my hair is s&y &
'flyaway'. men have a habit of saying
th@ i am blessed with a submissive
& yielding manner, in an old-fash-

ioned way: quintessentially femi9.
i'm 5' 7", and i no u r a taller man,
clint. which is as it should b. height
m@ters: th@'s an axiom@ic rule of
@traction.

And you're right. You're not wrong. You're right, thought
Clint. Know why? Birds want tall nippers: Darwin and that.

a while ago i did some c@alogue
modelling work. i was also a
bingo-caller & prize-presenter @
the Mirage in King's X, and u have
2 b pretty pretty be4 they let u do
th@. i even appeared in the pp. of
your aug. journal. not what u
think! (tell u 18er. just u w8 & c.)
must –. 2dle-oo! k8.

Not in Readers' Richards, surely to God, thought Clint. And
then his doorbell rang.

This event, in most households no great matter, invariably
represented the direst of emergencies at 24, The Grove, Foulness.
There was a time when he would have simply sprinted upstairs,
positioned a hand-mirror between the outer wall and the drain-
pipe, and eyed the front step from the porthole, treating each case
on its merits. But such free and easy dealings with the outside
world belonged to a happier time. Now Clint crawled across the
floor and locked himself in the bathroom, where he assumed the
fetal position on the damp tiles. The doorbell's morse: how he
writhed like a lab-rat to its jabs. Next came silence, increasingly
gorgeous, until the silence was itself silenced – by a sound that
would have taken him over the top at Passchendaele: the car alarm
of the Avenger.

In his untethered bathrobe and Y-fronts tinged grey as if with the smear of newsprint, Smoker pitched himself out into the morning.

'Oi, my *car* . . .'

It was one of those days when the ocean medium had leaked into the lower air, bodying forth a sopping mist and mast-high cloudlets that looked solid to the touch. There was the Avenger at the bottom of the dead front garden, longsufferingly honking; and there was the broad shape on the seaward side of it, leaning on it, waiting there.

'That's my *car* . . .'

Now the broad shape moved clear.

'Ah. Eh up,' said Clint, showing his palms. 'Now, mate. No. You ain't . . . you ain't about to dispense the proverbial I hope. I've been a good boy, mate. Utterly oyster. I never –'

Mal Bale raised a stocky index finger to his upper lip. His manner, Clint was pleased to see, was not concertedly threatening: not all hot and righteous, like it had been that time on the Thames, outside the Cocked Pinkie. Mal's manner was merely disaffected, inconvenienced . . . Clint thought for a moment. He was a newspaperman. Newspapering was in his veins. One day, at the office, he had typed out the forbidden name on a search-engine, which he never launched. For a moment he had felt like the science-fiction physicist who fears that he may obliterate the universe at the touch of a key.

'It ain't that,' said Mal.

'Then why are you here, mate?'

'I am here as a representative', said Mal, 'of Ebony Escorts.'

Jesus, not the escorts again. With some people you can never . . . Sheer spite on her part, thought Clint. Though – okay – maybe he'd overdone it a bit on the His Voluminousness.

The girl, Rehab, had humiliated him totally and, this being the case, had thoroughly deserved the lesson he'd taught her. She went and let him down at one of the *Lark*'s Sovereign Suppers (monthly occasions, held in the private rooms of prestigious Soho restaurants). Heaf was there of course, with his sheep, Mrs Heaf, and Mackelyne was there with his, Mrs Mackelyne, and Strite was there with some dolly or poppet, and Supermaniam was there with one of his many-armed subcontinental divinities . . .

Told, and paid, to pretend that she was Clint's girlfriend, Rehab explained to the assembled accompany that she was an escort girl told, and paid, to pretend that she was Clint's girl-friend.

'Ladies. Guys,' Clint had said. 'I'd like to introduce you to a certain someone who's become very special to me. Ladies. Guys. Say hi to Rehab.'

'Charmed,' said Heaf. 'Sit here, dear.'

'Dear' is right, thought Clint. You couldn't call them darling or sweetheart, but you could definitely call them dear.

'Now tell me, dear: how long have you and Clint known each other?'

Rehab looked at her watch and said, 'An hour and fifteen minutes.'

And then it all came out.

Apart from anything else it was a flagrant breach of contract. They'd done the budgeting earlier on: this much for every fondly shared reminiscence, this much for every stroke of Clint's hand, this much for every blown kiss and melting gaze, this much for every proffered spoonful of her *crème brûlée*.

Afterwards, on their optioned-for but uncosted return to the hotel, Clint, using all his charm and the promise, at least, of a significant fraction of his net worth, induced Rehab to take her clothes off and go and prepare herself in the bathroom. Which he then locked, and walked out with all her gear under his arm. And that was the extent of it. There had been no suggestion whatever of the hair-tugging and nipple-twisting that had so expensively marred his encounter with Scheherazade from Escorts De

Luxe. All Rehab'd had to do was screech down the fifteen floors until a passerby told the doorman.

On top of leaving himself alone for a couple of nights, Clint had prepared for his date with Rehab by taking three Potentium and five His Voluminousness. His Voluminousness was another webdrug Clint had started using. It was meant to increase the bulk of your ejaculations 'to porno proportions', according to the literature. And it did. You might have your doubts about the quality (the colour, the texture, the redolence, and so on), but you couldn't argue with the quantity.

In this lay Clint's error – and Rehab's grievance. First, drinks in the bar, and Clint with his pen poised over the paper napkin, sketching out the manifest (and keeping his eye on all the sundries). Then the rush of the elevator beneath your feet, the heavy moment as the key entered the lock, the azure carpet, the floral curtains . . . Now at these prices a bloke'll want fair dealing – and Rehab was gypping him left and right. So, when the moment came, Clint reckoned he'd do a Dork Bogarde to Rehab's Donna Strange. He had been aiming for her chest (not her lower abdomen, as negotiated), and hadn't meant to lash it all over her throat and neck and hair.

Then Rehab's hubbub, yelling down the phone for the drier and the extra shampoo. They were half an hour late for dinner, and he gave her a piece of his mind in the cab. She was a professional, wasn't she? Where was her pride? A girl like her, used to dealing with nutters and perverts and inadequates, and she raises Cain over a lad who happens to have a bit of man in him? He said it again and again: Where was her pride? And this too perhaps explained why a recently goosed Rehab, on arrival at the table, was so thoroughly out of sorts . . .

What would a baby look like, made of that stuff? thought Clint (and it was the second time in recent days that he had found himself thinking about babies). He hadn't even got it on her face – which, at the time, had been rigidly averted. For fifty-five minutes, with that one brief interruption, Clint thought about the farinaceous sports bra he had daubed on Rehab's persian breasts (before the thing whipped out of control like a rogue powerhose) as the Avenger bombed back to Foulness.

It was in the Avenger that they now sat, the two of them, Clint and Mal. The engine was whirring (like a sewing-machine), for the warmth and the muted radio; and Clint, now contritely dressed in chinos and polo-neck, had produced a thermos of coffee. Both men were smoking with dedication, perhaps because the Avenger smelt so powerfully of human feet. Clint couldn't understand why: the great tugs of his shoes, with their claws and cleats, featured moisture-wicking fleece lining and ozone-resistant sole-beds leavened for superior sweat-management; and the semi didn't smell of human feet, so far as he could tell. When Mal asked why they didn't go indoors Clint said that his live-in, Kate, who was insanely jealous, would murder him if she got wind of this one.

'You've got a nice bird at home. Why d'you want to be out there paying for it?'

'Yeah. Well.'

'And this ain't the first time there's been trouble, is it, mate. I don't understand people like you. Your live-in. You bat her about and all?'

Clint said, 'No way. Never do that.' But he was keeping his head down.

'Well you got to make good.'

For the second time in eighteen hours Clint had before him an itemised bill of sale. But this invoice did not consist of fancy favours, of costly caresses . . . 'A grand for the clothes?' he said, leaning back. 'I bunged them in a flowerpot in the passage. They be okay.'

'Never mind the clothes. It's the distress and the humiliation you're paying for, boy. You should be glad you're dealing with me and not with her two brothers. Izzat and Watban.'

'Okay, mate. Deal. Look uh, no hard feelings, all right? And I want you to know, Mal mate, that on the other matter . . .'

Clint trailed off, and they were silent. Then Mal said, 'Yeah – that. It don't . . . It ain't sitting well with me, that.'

The Avenger was so high off the ground that Mal chose to clamber down rear-forward. Clint, who had been within to fetch the cheque, wondered at the great natural sweep of Mal's backside, which seemed to rise up from the middle of his thighs and then proceed to the third or fourth notch of his spine. This gluteus maximus: it was the base of all Mal's operations; every decision would be referred to it. And Clint? Despite the man's size, his heavy-boned mass, there was just a vacuum, and an apologetic fold or flap, in the rump of his chinos (and not having a backside didn't mean that he didn't have spots all over it). In the mirror, when he looked: it was as if his buttocks belonged to a much smaller man who kept them emphatically clenched.

'What happened here, mate?'

'Uh, at Basildon I come off the A13 and cut through the Bends. This sheepdog shot out at me. I swerved . . .'

'A sheepdog? That ain't a dog. It's a sheep. Look.'

'No it was a dog. With curly white hair.'

'What, like a poodle. A poodle in the Bends?'

'I don't know. Not a sheep. Just a dog.'

'. . . So you'd rather kill a dog than a sheep.'

'Don't know about *rather*.' But, yeah, Clint found he had subliminally assumed that a dog was inferior to a sheep. Which didn't make a lot of sense. Analogously (perhaps) he noticed that he wasn't sure whether this or that woman was attractive or not-so-attractive. He could spot the difference between a centrefold and a Reader's Richard, but he was none too clever, he thought, on the gradations in between.

'Why, because a sheep is man's best friend?' pursued Mal. 'They have sheepdogs. They don't have dogsheep, do they. You got a sheep in there, have you, that fetches your slippers? Or guards the back door? Clint: you take care.'

Clint gestured farewell to the stern of Mal's elderly German saloon. I don't know, mate, he said to himself. I just don't know . . .

The mist had lifted; out to sea a wildhaired wave collapsed, not all in one piece but laterally, from left to right, like a trail of gunpowder under the torch.

Bet that sheep, thought Clint – bet that sheep . . . The sheep had been standing on the verge, like an old country personage wise (by now) to the ways of cars. On the verge in its drenched white woollie.

Bet that sheep felt it when I come up on it. *Boof.*

'The Walthamstow Wanker', said Desmond Heaf, 'has alas emerged from his coma, and we've had a pretty stiff letter from Tulkinghorn, Summerson and Nice, no less. In your report, Jeff, you said he was ogling a party of little girls in the public pool. Well, according to this, you can't even *see* the swimming-pool from the gallery in question. It's over some squash courts which were not in use at the time. I don't suppose you happened to check.'

'Check?' said Strite. 'Course I didn't check. I got it from my boy at the cop shop, Chief. Since when do we check?'

'Tulkinghorn, Summerson and Nice have also taken exception to our tone.' Heaf held up the clipping. '"So if you're passing 19 Floral Crescent, and you've got a spare brick on you, or a bottleful of petrol, then you know where to fling it." An incitement to violence against the family of an innocent man in Intensive Care.'

'Innocent? He was having a wank in public,' said Strite indignantly. 'What's innocent about that?'

'Says here he was massaging his sore hip when Mrs Mop burst in on him. And she's seventy-eight and half-blind.'

'Then why'd he do a runner? With his trousers round his ankles. If you'll excuse me Chief, I'll get back to my boy.'

Clint looked on judiciously as Strite left the conference room.

He also wanted to get out of there – and into Back Numbers. Arriving at his workstation, with his latte and his brioche, Clint had found a new message from Kate: 'well, u r an importun8 l, & no mistake! i appeared in the pp of your estimable sheet on the following d8.' Which she gave: well, month and year. 'it was in the "casebook" feature opposite the "ecstasy aunt". u'll no which l is my l: the 3 principals r called brett, ferdin& & sue. go & have a look c, & let me no if i'm "up 2 snuff".' Ah, *yes*: *Casebook*, thought Clint pitilessly. For there were few things that Clint relished more than a powerful Casebook. And now he would set eyes on the woman with whom, he increasingly felt, his destiny was somehow entwined. He said,

'No disrespect to Jeff, Chief, but I always thought we were baying up the bum bonsai on Pervs Him Right.'

'Please elaborate, Clint.'

Jeff Strite came back in. He looked vindicated, redeemed.

Clint shrugged and said, 'He's a wanker.'

'Who's a wanker?'

'The *Walthamstow* Wanker.'

'You mean he's a *reader*?'

'No, Chief. I mean he's a *wanker*.'

'And he *is* a wanker and all,' said Strite. 'My boy said they'd taken some "erotic material" off him. Got it stored down in the basement somewhere and he'll be looking it out.'

'There you are,' said Clint, folding his arms. 'Unless it was *Nonce Monthly* he had on his knees . . .'

Heaf said, 'I don't quite follow you, Clint.'

'He's not a paedophile. He's just a wanker. And wankers are the people the *Lark*'s on the side of. Wankers are what we're all about.'

The Chief had a cornered look. Most of Clint's really radical brilliancies, he found, took several days to sink in. 'So we should . . . *support* him? No, no, Clint, I think you do our . . . our *real* wankers a definite injustice here. There were certainly grounds for suspicion that he was a paedophile. You're forgetting the enormous groundswell of wanker response to our Nuke the Nonces campaign.'

'You keep saying that, Chief. But as Mackelyne has often pointed out, the response to Nuke the Nonces was virtually undetectable . . . It's Mrs Mop we should have gone after.'

'For putting him in a coma.'

'And for ruining his wank. Fling a brick through *her* front window.'

For a moment a bad-dream glaze descended on Desmond Heaf, and his brow was suddenly and minutely sequinned with sweat. After about ten seconds of steady recuperation he said, '. . . Royal comment. I think this is building quite well. Rather touchingly, the King's enforced chastity is awakening the most profound concerns of our – and uh, I'll be interested to hear your view, Clint, on the line we should take on the tragedy in Cold Blow Lane. So what's the King to do? By the way, Supermaniam, I thought you overstepped the bounds of good taste with your think-piece . . . "Quick Mate While She's Warm". I thought Clint's editorial the next day was far more sensitive and appropriate. Where is it? "Time To Pull The Plug On Pam".'

Clint stood with his arms akimbo in the anarchical locker-room of Back Numbers. Over nine hundred *Lark*s lay slumped in drunken stacks, in leaning heaps; and Clint's arms were charcoal to the elbow by the time he had assembled the thirty issues of the relevant June.

Like all the other yellow-mast tabloids, the *Morning Lark* ran a Casebook feature opposite its problem page. Its problem page did not resemble the other problem pages, with their typical integration of the commonplace (Our Loving Is Over Too Quickly) and the phenomenal (I Came Home To Find My Husband In Bed With My Dad: all this). The *Lark*'s problem page dealt not in problems but in outlandish gratifications; it was in-house pornography, much of it written by Clint Smoker. On the other hand, the *Lark*'s Casebook veered close to mainstream: in a dozen photographs with added bubbles for speech and thought, it dramatised the confusions of personable young people who tended to be dressed in their underwear.

Needing delay, needing equipoise, Clint dug out his mobile and called Ainsley Car.

'Right,' said the troubled striker, after a prompt. 'I do Donna, then I have Beryl.'

'Other way round, mate.'

'I have Beryl, then I do Donna.'

'Jesus. You have Donna, then you do Beryl . . . Doesn't have to be Donna, mind.'

'What about that "Amfea" . . .'

Clint remembered 'Anthea'. Cheesy little blonde who was, none the less, sixteen. Very popular: posing with her mum in matching thongs.

'Nah mate. "Anthea" fell pregnant and jacked it in. Her mum's a gran at thirty-two.'

'Okay then. Donna'll do. I'll do Donna.'

'*Have* Donna,' corrected Clint.

Ah, *yes* – this was it: Brett, Ferdinand and Sue. And for a moment Clint turned away . . . When you entered an escort agency for the first time and were received by the madamic co-ordinatrix: she gave you the 'brochure' and left you alone with it – and that was power. In that plump album each smile, each cleavage, each towering beehive represented different futures which, nevertheless, and on varying pay-scales, all promised the same outcome. Now, in contemplating Kate, Clint would be taking up a humbler post. It was more like a youthful blind date, when you peeked round the corner, then moved forward or walked away . . . Clint peeked, squinting. His eyes jolted down on her. Then with deliberate force he smacked his head back against the wall, groaned, laughed, sighed. No glamour queen or ballroom dancer, but prettily unassertive, and of the crowd, like a poster of a missing person. And could he see it? Could he see it? Yeah, mate, he could see it. Him and her, and hand in hand: 'Hey, I'd like you to meet a very special friend of mine. Ladies, guys. Say hi to . . .'

Clint went back to his workstation, where he deployed angle-lamp and magnifying glass. It was an exceptionally compelling Casebook in its own right: a triangular predicament, as so often, but one with universal reach. In its opening frames you saw Sue at home with live-in lover Brett. Sue scrubbing the kitchen lino in tears, tanktopped Brett standing over her with his fists clenched; Brett watching the football with a pair of Union Jack underpants over his head, while Sue does the ironing; then Brett, clutching cue and dufflebag, telling Sue he's off on a road trip playing pool for his pub. Enter Ferdinand. You looked at Ferdinand and you thought – you know: Shelley. Poet and dreamer, with his flyaway hair, his flowers and his flattery: your eyes are like stars . . . Sue had her clothes off twice. In the first shot she is being taken from behind by a Brett showing all his teeth – but her body was almost entirely eclipsed by the thought-bubble, 'Gaw, I wish Brett had ever heard of foreplay.' In the second, she lay on her back with her legs apart, but her modesty was preserved by Ferdinand's streaming locks, together with another bubble, saying: 'Mmm. Brett reckons only gays do this, but I think it's lovely.' The final frame showed Sue sitting alone on the blondwood bed, with elbow on knee and palm on cheek, eyes raised ceilingward: 'I know Brett has his faults, but Ferdinand seems too good to be true. How can I choose between them?'

Low self-image, that is, thought Clint. As an afterthought he skimmed the 'Words of Wisdom' with which every Casebook drew to a close. Sue was advised, by Donna Strange, to forget about Ferdinand and stick with Brett.

Plaintive little smile on its face. Of course, she was only acting. But with that roundness of eye, that philosophical underlip: you couldn't imagine her giving you grief, undermining you, belittling you . . . Don't fret: you're up to snuff, my darling. You're all right. Yeah, you'll do.

3. Cold Blow Lane

'We'll need the army for this one, sir.'

'The army? Don't talk rot, Bugger.'

'Just a light, calming presence, sir. It's a most . . . thankless situation. Forgive the gloom, sir, but I can't even imagine a positive outcome.'

'Nor can I. But don't ask me to reconsider. I can't refuse Loulou anything – as she well knows. That's the whole trouble. She's my cousin, after all, and she didn't get into this fix on purpose. We'll just have to get on with it.'

'Sir. I don't suppose *now* would be a good moment to discuss the ramifications of the Sino-Russian entente?'

'Ramification number one being that I shall have to give up He Zizhen, I suppose. And if the pair of them fall out, do you think I'll get her beck?'

'Just to remind Your Majesty that nothing affects the people's mood so much as the cost of filling their cars.'

'I'm well aware of that, thank you, Bugger. Ah.'

Love entered. The impressive wingspan of his ears was picked out by the low sun that lurked behind him. He gave an arthritic bow and said,

'If you're ready, sir?'

'Coming, Love: I'll follow. What is it today, Bugger? Brucellosis. No. Q-fever.'

'Venezuelan equine encephalomyelitis, sir.'

'Ouch. And what's that when it's at home?'

'Viral inflammation of the brain and spinal cord, sir.'

Henry IX rose and looked about himself. 'Not much of a boudoir, is it? Now Bugger: you won't get an attack of thrift, I hope. Have Blaise or Henri come and have a quick recce, and then spend money doing what they say. And get some decent furniture from the French Suite.' He looked round the room through the fine drizzle of his dislike for it. 'This place was good enough for my grandfather. But it's not good enough for me. And Bugger.'

'Yes, sir?'

'I hesitate to tell you this because it'll make you watch the pennies . . . I'll only be using this place *once*. Do you take my meaning, Bugger?'

'Very wise, sir.'

'It would be a catastrophe.'

'An absolute catastrophe.'

'But I won't be a swine and not say goodbye to her properly. Yes, properly, Bugger. That means I'll make the position clear the moment she walks through the door. If she spends only ten seconds in this room that's *all the more* reason to make it nice . . . Not many men have to subordinate their hearts to the price of petrol. I am one of them. And frankly it's a *bit much*.'

'I should look upon it, sir, as one of your many sacrifices.'

'He will give no trouble. She will give no trouble.'

And the King's private secretary agreed, on the whole. Brendan had of course run a check on He, months ago: daughter of the long-serving Chinese Ambassador in Paris; mistress for nine years to a Scandinavian head of state; probably in need of a nestegg. And she would get a nestegg, Brendan knew.

'Sorry to lumber you with all this, Bugger. It's not your job, but *do* make it comfy.'

Brendan was left alone, in the neglected gazebo. It wasn't his job – but what was his job? Scandal-management, scandal-control. Scandals were like periodic tidal waves of varying height and mass. This business with Loulou – Louisa, Duchess of

Ormonde: the wave did not tower or hover, but its innards might churn with surprising guile. Just now, the exposure of the King's affair with He Zizhen would hide the sun – and would not stop, would not stop till it had rolled through villages. And as for the wave that could be gathering for the Princess: it was the work of a thousand Krakatoas . . .

Leaning back on the striped sofa, Brendan was now warmed by a feeling of luxury quite unconnected to his immediate surroundings: John II's chintzy – and of course chilly – lovenest reminded him of the Royal Train before Henry belaboured it with his millions. The warmth of ease had been drawn out of him by the silence – as he realised when a truck-sized lawnmower blew past like a whale before fading into the silence of distance. And that silence, emphasised by weakly festive birdsong, had allowed him to listen to his own heart and take warmth from it.

When Victoria was four she went to bed without saying good-night, and Brendan had felt it – all the blood within him. When Victoria was fourteen . . . It was on the last leg of her California tour; diversion was at an end, and what awaited her now was boredom, royal boredom – boredom cloudless and entire. Halfway through the final afternoon it became clear to him that the Princess was no longer there, that she had sent out an emissary, a simulacrum, a lifesize photograph, leaving her soul to curl up in the dark somewhere while she smiled at strangers, smiled at strangers – as if being fourteen wasn't work enough, he had thought . . . Later, with an apologetic inclination of the head, Brendan asked her to choose between this or that logistical punc-tilio as she approached the next unveiling or investiture: who should nod, who should bow. The Princess let her tongue slide out of the corner of her mouth and raised her hands towards him with the thumbs and forefingers in the shape of two V's. 'W': 'Whatever'. And he had felt it again, all of it, all the blood within him. Girls of thirteen, fourteen, fifteen, they sometimes wear a look of panic: the eyes are trapped in the changing face.

Where am I heading? From childhood the presence of the Princess had always contained agitation, a tremor of electricity; but there was no dismay in it. For the time being she looked like a thrillingly ardent woodland creature in an animated cartoon. Still, there wasn't any doubt about the destination, which was womanhood.

He wanted to protect her, but for now he was passive, he was helpless. Well, one royal scandal at a time, he thought. Brendan felt like going for a twenty-mile hike. Instead, he took his laptop from his briefcase and started learning all he could about the prison riot in Cold Blow Lane.

Early that month the Duchess of Ormonde had swept south across the Thames to Millwall, there to cut the ribbon on a new shopping mall and fitness centre in the famously and stubbornly depressed manor of the Isle of Dogs. After the ceremony a peoplecarrier full of the Duchess's security men mounted the pavement at speed, accidentally ramming the moped of a certain Jimmy O'Nione who, at that point, had half a second to live. The Isle of Dogs was the Isle of Dogs, and so the crisis merely intensified when O'Nione stood revealed as a career criminal (much incarcerated, with a mesmerising record), who moreover, on that day (judging by the disposition of loot and tool in his saddlebag), was clearly on his way from one crime to another. Two days after the shopping mall and the fitness centre had been plundered and torched, the Duchess's office announced its intention to install a marble plaque in Cold Blow Lane, to honour O'Nione, which the Duchess would herself unveil ('In memory of the valued member of the community, James Patrick O'Nione, who died so tragically at this site'). In the meantime Cold Blow Prison had come out in florid riot; the inmates had now made their base on the chapel roof, which overlooked O'Nione's cenotaph.

The Cold Blow mutiny (Brendan now learnt) had nothing to

do with Jimmy O'Nione – though he had, inevitably, spent a year or two behind its walls . . . The cause lay in the broodings of Prisoner Dean Bull, who, during a visit from his teenage girl-friend, Diana, began to have doubts about her constancy. 'As a young offender prepares himself for a protracted sentence,' blogged one old lag on the quickly assembled Cold Blow website, 'you expect sentimental relationships to come under strain.' So Dean feared that Diana, on her next visit, would tell him that she couldn't wait twenty-three years. He was right. And he was ready. Brendan groaned, and sighed, and read on.

Preceded by his metal chair, Dean came through the plexi-glass partition and set about Diana's face with one of its shards. Now: every last prisoner in Cold Blow, not excluding Dean Bull, fully accepted that he would face a supplementary sentence and the loss of all remission. Dean, now twenty-one, would be released in his mid-fifties: this was fair enough. What rankled was the beating he'd taken from the guards. Because Dean, it was pointed out, had conducted himself, once his deed was done, with marked restraint, dropping his weapon and (after muttering, 'See how that goes down down the pub Friday') raising his hands in submission – before the first nightsticks chopped him to the ground. Some of the sterner romantics now sliding around the chapel roof (they had a seized laptop up there, and several mobile phones) argued that Dean had had no choice anyway, being a man truly in love, and what more precious token could he have offered than twelve years of his prime? More sober hands agreed that that wasn't the point. What had come to pass was 'a *personal matter*, strictly between Diana and Dean'. And then word came down from the hospital cells about the severity and duration of the stoving they'd given him . . .

By accompanying the Duchess to the shrine of Jimmy O'Nione, Henry IX was doing his favourite cousin a kindness: that was the thing to emphasise, thought Brendan. A nasty busi-ness (and a weird conjunction), made no easier by its timing:

Henry was going down to Cold Blow on the morning after his final assignation with He Zizhen.

And on that day Brendan would have an unexpected message to pass on to the King, concerning the matter of the Princess.

Barefoot, and led by Colonel Mate, He walked the length of the ha-ha in the midgey dusk, and then emerged alone between the hedgerows for the last stretch to the lovenest of John II. In that lovenest, a nestegg (two baldrics of fire opals), and a king whose hand was already at his lips, bidding adieu.

Henry shot up from his chair and listened: He's feet on the bare boards of the veranda . . . Once upon a time she had shown him the shoes worn by her greatgrandmother, the warlord's concubine, in Shandong, where the Yellow River meets the Yellow Sea: they resembled the party boots of a three-year-old. The woman's feet had been 'bound' in the traditional way – broken, crushed, then dressed and swaddled. This greatly increased her erotic worth (He explained to a horrified Henry): the crippled woman, when she walked, when she stood, evoked 'a willow wavering in the wind'. He Zizhen had then imitated her grand-mother's agonised and papery tread, and the King's arms had surged out towards her. Why? Why did he want to enfold that willow? The spectacle aroused him – but not as much as the sound of He's feet on the wooden slats, registering her shape, her soft mass, the grasshalms on her dewy soles, all coming closer.

Shoeless, she was smaller, now, and he was correspondingly augmented, when he took her in his arms. He whispered what he had to say, and He whispered back. And He said she understood.

It was with sound, with a whisper, that she had first enticed him; and although the faculties of touch, taste, smell and sight, He maintained, could be reasonably well served in erotic play, what of the sense of hearing? In her view, the use of *mots gros*, of verbal *cochoneries*, was a plausible but ultimately misguided attempt to redress the deficit. Dirty talk was sadomasochism without the sticks and stones; and the King, clearly, wasn't that kind of animal. He Zizhen, who moaned so musically among the pillows, additionally deployed the geisha device, *rin no tama*; Henry did not enquire too closely (it seemed to be a ball within a ball suspended in liquid), and he never sensed the slightest obstruction; he felt, however, that he was pacing or jogging or sprinting (this would depend on the gear she'd put him in) through the shallows of a tropical swamp. There was another office she performed noisily, even deafeningly – to the great joy of the King . . . Once, slumped in a deckchair on the Royal Yacht, he had awoken to this sound: it was the swimming-pool, slopping and gulping, smacking its lips, a storm within a storm on the Bay of Biscay. He had stared out, and the brawny herring-gulls looked like sparrows before the great carry of the waves.

Now in his grandfather's gazebo he lay back helplessly, like a child being changed. Soon (he thought) we will enter He, and she will sigh so prettily. And that is everything, everything: just to kiss and to say the name, whispering 'Her'. Which was how you said it. Which was the sound of who He was.

'I didn't think it my place', said Love, with a stretched look in his neck and forehead, 'to confront His Majesty with it, sir. And God knows we get enough eccentrics. But the tone of it, sir, I thought . . .'

'I'm quite sure you're doing the right thing, Love,' said Brendan Urquhart-Gordon, intrigued and encouraged by the timbre of Love's disquiet – troubled, wondering. 'As always.'

'I thank you, sir.'

Brendan and other aides were at the Greater House, and climbing into their cars. The King had gone on ahead in some sort of armoured dormobile with Colonel Forster and his men, to Cold Blow Lane.

'Chippy?' called Brendan. 'Have I got five minutes?'

'At the outside,' said Chippy Edenderry, exposing his watch.

He followed Love through the flapped door, decisively exchanging one atmosphere for another, darker, warmer, with the thick smell of sweat and soap and gravy dinners. Brendan inhaled it, and moved on, into the alternate world of belowstairs . . . It would have been far worse under Richard IV, of course, when domestic staff were paid the absolute minimum on principle (glory being power, and so on), but the House of England was always hedged by the smells and textures of vassalage – it was always waiting behind the flapped, floor-trailing door. Brendan knew that all servants hated their masters. Even Love, who was as loyal as they came, even Love would feel this hate. The hate smelt too: it was like the smell of mice. Brendan found unexpected relief in the contemplation of Love's left ear: a vortex of iron filings.

They entered a brownish parlour lined with straightbacked chairs. Ceremoniously Love now donned his white gloves, waggling his raised fingers into them, and Brendan gained the brief but comprehensive impression that he was about to be examined by a doctor of humble practice and increasingly uncertain skills. With a superstitious glance over his shoulder, Love indicated a low table which bore a telephone of recent design and an answering-machine of embarrassing antiquity and bulk.

'You're rather at the mercy of this contraption, sir. It's the final message, I'm afraid.'

The white finger quivered down on the Start button, and Love backed out of the room.

It was not possible to skip or hasten, so Brendan, feeling the growing weight of Chippy's impatience, had to sit through a series of yokellish instructions and enquiries from various caterers and vendors, plus three long and repetitive plaints from a bedridden relative, who hoped for Love's help in a move from sanatorium to hospice. Then, suddenly, this voice, so heavily deepened and distorted that Brendan took it to be the final incapacity – the death-drawl – of the old machine.

'For the attention of the King. On the last day of this month the material on the Princess joins that which is public and open to general observation. Note well: the Palace should insist, and should continue to insist, that the material is faked. *Faked, faked. Mere digital fabrication. Mere light and magic.'*

Brendan became aware of the petulant honking from the drive. He pried the twin spools from the machine, which gave its contents up to him, in all innocence, seemingly scandalised by what it had housed. Then he strode down the tepid passage. The flapped door opened, and let him out, and closed again.

Just before noon Henry England debouched from Chopper F1 of the King's Flight, hurrying low across the striped turf of Millwall Football Ground. He wore a silk cashmere overcoat, a dark lounge suit, and a black silk tie – in deference to the memory of Jimmy O'Nione (Henry's office had already lamented the death, in evasively universal terms: a life so full of energy, cut down even as it flowered – this, despite O'Nione's great age). On foot and under heavy plainclothes escort, he crossed Lovelynch Road, and joined the assembly on the broad forecourt of the Juno Estate. There he was greeted by the parliamentary member, the representatives of the local council, various trembling beadles and burghers, and a squad of shrunken, bemedalled regimental pensioners in their frayed crimson tunics, ready for one final war. The crowd, the press, the police, the light presence of soldiery in camouflage gear, the battlement of His Majesty's house of correction, which beetled over O'Nione's shrine: all this lay round the corner, waiting. But every other car coming down Cold Blow Lane gave the prisoners its toot of encouragement and support, and was answered by a ragged wail from the chapel roof.

Hearing this, Henry said vaguely, 'Why don't they just . . . get them down?'

'They were hoping the weather would do it for them, sir,' said the parliamentary member. 'Best policeman in the world, the weather. Best prison-guard too. But now of course, sir, it's unseasonably mild.'

The King might have remarked that the word 'unseasonable' had lost much of its force. The days didn't care what season it was. Above them now thrummed high-pressure blue; the sky was vibrating with it. Henry was accustomed to feelings of hallucinogenic expansion: the sense that he was the same size, the same thing, as the United Kingdom (and Canada and Australia and whatnot). Now – underslept and breakfastless, sexually wealthy but also bereft – he felt that the sky, too, was his colony, and that he was at the heart of its blue vibrations.

Louisa, Duchess of Ormonde, arrived in her hearse-like limousine. She wore a black suit and blouse and a black hat with pendant veil, which she lifted to kiss the King. They were standing apart, and Henry identified a sliver of moisture in the corner of his mouth; likewise her gloved fingers trailed meaningly across his palm. With a beseeching frown she told him how perfectly angelic he was being; and Henry felt the erotic component, the fractional overspill, in her gratitude. They had played doctors at the age of six; he had woken up thinking about her, for a while, during his years with Edith Beresford-Hale; and there had been an evening, not too long after the Queen's accident, when something glazed and reptilian had settled on him between the second and the third course of their closeted dinner. Now he looked down at her muscular ankles, her chunky black shoes. She was so securely rooted to the earth, like Pammy. And Henry thought of the shoes of the greatgrandmother of He Zizhen. No, he didn't want to see a woman wavering like a willow in the wind. But when they were so securely rooted . . . even in bed, with their feet off the ground: they just 'got on with it', in a mild kind of tizzy. They were never what He so often was; they were never lucid, never lost.

'Oh well,' she said. 'Best foot forward.'

'Indeed. *Prosequare.*'

Brendan Urquhart-Gordon and Chippy Edenderry joined the procession just as it turned into Cold Blow Lane. And so there it was: the crowd-flanked arroyo and, dead ahead, the curved wall of the prison like the stern of a ship – and the inmates all over the rigging. In the hope of increasing its impact, Henry IX's participation, on this day, had not been scheduled or canvassed, and there was, at first, a sudden caution in the burbly ruffle of the crowd, and brief desistance from the cat-calls and ear-hurting wolf-whistles of the prisoners – many of whom, after all, were technically dependent, for their release, on His Majesty's Pleasure. It didn't last. Brendan, as he paced behind Henry England and Louisa, Duchess of Ormonde, looked left and right and tried to individualise those gathered here: those whose hearts were hurting for Jimmy O'Nione. The dead man had had no family, no friends, and no known associates or even accomplices. It was the community itself that smouldered and smarted for him. Looking beyond the weary, gritty hatred of these faces, Brendan saw the terraced streets that curled and tapered off from Cold Blow: a corner shop, a barber's writhing pole, an encaged headline at an angle on the pavement. Here, he thought, the dust-devils, the little twisters of rubbish, would spin the other way, answering to the prison and its gravity. The air smelt of cheap ghosts – those that had died cheaply: street accidents, bludgeonings, mattress fires.

They halted. The Duchess moved forward and steadied herself in front of a black-draped table which bore a microphone and a wreath. Thirty feet beyond, O'Nione's stolen scooter, exceeding the speed limit when it was clipped by the swerving peoplecarrier, had slammed into the knee-high kerbstone at forty miles per hour; maintaining that velocity, its helmetless rider had torpedoed into the redbrick wall of Cold Blow Prison. It was here, at the plaque, that the Duchess would lay her wreath, in commemoration of the life of Jimmy O'Nione.

'Good-day to you and bless you one and all,' began Louisa,

Duchess of Ormonde, steering her way into the fragile hush. 'We are gathered here to bid farewell to a much-loved member of the community: Jimmy O'Nione . . . "He has outsoared the shadow of our night; Envy and calumny and hate and pain, And that unrest which men miscall delight, Can touch him not and torture not again . . . Mourn not for O'Nione . . . While burning through the inmost veil of Heaven, The soul of O'Nione, like a star, Beacons from the abode where the Eternal are." Thank you. I shall now lay the wreath. There will then be a minute's silence.'

Oh no there won't, thought Henry. You see: noise is all they have. Everything detachable from the chapel roof had long ago been hurled down into the courtyard; noise was all they had left; and they would use it . . . Even before the monkey-grunts began, the prisoners had reminded him of primates, more specifically the Barbary apes – tailless macaques – he had leerily eyed on the Rock of Gibraltar in the course of a recent cruise: the hopping and capering, the squatting and teeth-baring, the picking, the *scratching* . . . And these monkey-grunts, poundingly concerted, reminded him in their turn of an international football match he had attended five years ago: one hundred thousand voices had raised his hair and his flesh with the fanatic unanimity of their 'God Save the King'; but when play began, and the ball arrived at the feet of a black player on the other side? The noise made by the prisoners, now (like the vibration of a titanic double bass), was in connotation sexual merely, as the womanly Duchess bustled to the wall; her head was piously bowed anyway, of course, as she approached O'Nione's shrine, but she seemed also to be shrinking under it, the carnal thump of it, beaten, beaten down. Reflexively Henry stepped forward in his cashmere overcoat and stood with his hands on his hips and his elbows outturned.

Brendan found that he had crushed his arms to his sides, anti-akimbo, as he cringed for the King.

On the chapeltop there now followed a moment of hesitation, and of arrest. And in that moment Henry was confronted by the elementary fact that the prisoners were men, not chimps or baboons (no, nor the viciously jerked marionettes to which an alternative impulse had likened them). In their singlets and half-buttoned shirts, their scrawny flares of winded denim, they were men – men in power. It was a funny kind of power, but it was power: power enough to call forth the King. And have him stand to attention. Seeing their drunkenly childish delight in this, Henry smiled. Unreservedly and unforgettably he smiled – and was answered by a savage roar. But as soon as he composed himself and turned a priestly gaze on the Duchess, now curtseying before the cenotaph of Jimmy O'Nione, and the minute's silence began . . .

Despite the unsettling discoveries in the vacated bedsitting-room (the stolen property, the forged passports and pension-books, the fantastic cache of female underwear, and the carcass of her missing budgerigar), Jimmy O'Nione's landlady was among the crowd that had gathered that day at Cold Blow – largely, it was true, to see the Duchess (she had seen the King up close before, but what an unexpected bonus *that* was, him coming by . . .). And during the minute's silence: such a torrent of filth you never heard in all your life. It was as if those men up there had *rehearsed* it. The Duchess shrank back as if she couldn't believe her senses. *Suck my. Lick my. Drink my. Eat my.* And what did we get when the minute's silence was over, and they stopped? A minute's silence: we were all in pure shock. And then when she walked away, quaking on her heels:

Get *your arse out*, get *your arse out*, GET *your arse out* for the boys – oogh!

Well, I must say, that was a nice welcome they give her!

'You see them elsewhere,' said Brendan Urquhart-Gordon. 'Alien moral systems.'

'Yes, Bugger, but we did rather scrag one of their lot. As they'd see it. The chap who had the prang.'

'. . . I thought the *people* were more for you than agin you today, sir. But the prisoners . . .'

'Well, they're prisoners, Bugger.'

It was a monarchical trait: the inability to disapprove of any of his subjects. The urge to correct them, and if necessary by hard means, yes; but not the urge to disapprove of them. It would be like disapproving of yourself. And yet the King had been confusedly thinking, as he ran low under the battering blades of Chopper F1, that sex was the opposite of torture (thinking, in particular, that the sounds He made were the opposite of torture). Both were exquisitely intimate; and both relied on carnal knowledge. And then the prisoners and their chant, which was also sex and also torture. The prisoners, who were the champions of the deed of Dean Bull, and of Dean Bull's words . . .

'From a different *source* you say, Bugger.'

Henry and Urquhart-Gordon were briefly occupying a private apartment in a gentlemen's club off Pall Mall (where the King was due to host a luncheon). In the neighbouring room Oughtred was accepting delivery of a tape recorder from the BBC; only the national broadcasting corporation, it seemed, could be depended on for a sufficiently ancient machine. The second communication: Henry knew its gist. He had twice excused himself and tiptoed to the bathroom.

'Who can be sure, sir, but it may well be a positive development. Ah. Thank you, Oughtred. I'll be in touch.'

The two men left one room for another similarly appointed: an ambience of silver and crystal and deep-brown panelling, with an elderly rictus to it, like a mask of empire. Watched warily by Henry, Brendan approached the fat contraption and started poking at its buttons. They listened to the pleading farewells of Love's stricken relative, and then: '*For the attention of the King . . .*'

Brendan addressed himself to Henry's wondering frown: 'If this isn't a feint of some kind, sir, it may even be that we have a waverer, if not a friend, in the camp of the intruder.'

The tape spooled on. And they heard the metallic addendum: '*Prepare. Prepare the press. Prepare the Princess.*'

'Oh, Christ, Bugger. This is really going to happen.'

February 14 (12.01 p.m.): 101 Heavy

Flight Attendant Robynne Davis: Anybody home?

Captain John Macmanaman: Oh, hi, Robynne.

Davis: Here you go. Robynne's Fruitjuice Special.

First Officer Nick Chopko: Thank you.

Macmanaman: Mmm. What's in it?

Davis: Secret recipe. Guess.

Macmanaman: Well . . . Orange juice.

Davis: You got that from the colour, right?

Chopko: And, uh, cranberry?

Davis: And?

Chopko: Lilt?

Davis: Close. Ting. Diet Ting.

Flight Engineer Hal Ward: Be even better with some dark rum in it.

Davis: Yeah, right.

Ward: A little vodka.

Davis: Yeah, right.

Ward: Or a little gin, maybe.

Davis: Yeah, right.

Ward: Or some *light* rum in it . . .

Davis: Yeah right.

Ward: Excuse me.

Macmanaman: . . . Where's he gone, our wrench [Flight Engineer]?

Davis: To make a nuisance of himself with Conchita in Business.

Chopko: You can't blame the guy.

Macmanaman: You can blame the guy. The radar, Nick? See the weather coming? Get permission to climb. Uh, three nine zero. Robynne? Put them down back there. The girls too.

Davis: You got it.

Air Traffic Control: I hear you, one oh one heavy.

Chopko: Request permission to climb to three nine zero.

ATC: . . . That's a confirm. Three niner zero, one oh one heavy.

* * *

The plane revealed her silver breast to the sun. As she rose, a cross-wind jolted her fiercely to starboard: a beast of the upper air had tried to seize her, and then let her slip from his grasp like a bar of soap. The lateral motion was enough to free the coffin of Royce Traynor from the pair of mountain bikes that had lightly braced it. Royce fell flat on his face and was then shudderingly drawn towards the opening to Pallet No. 3. As the climb steepened another sideways lurch flipped him over the low partition. He rolled on his side and pitched up against a rank of canisters marked HAZMAT (Hazardous Material): Class B and Class C-3 dynamite propellants and rocket motors for fighter-aircraft ejection seats.

CHAPTER FIVE

1. In the master bedroom

'Pearl? It's me.' There must come a point (he thought) when you couldn't still say that – to your ex-wife: It's me. There must come a point when *me* turned into somebody else. You had to abdicate. 'Uh, is there a boy to hand?'

'Xan. Xan, I was just chuckling over a misprint in a book I'm reading,' she said warmly. 'I was dying to share it with you because I knew it would appeal to your sense of humour. Have you still got one, by the way? I mean a sense of humour, because it says here you can lose that too. The book's about crazy people and the misprint comes in the chapter called "Post-Traumatic Psychosis" under the subheading "Changes in Sexuality". Ready?'

Both his sons owned mobile phones, of course. For a while mobile phones had seemed to make them safer. The boys were like electronically tagged criminals: you could trace them, monitor them, when they went out. But when they went out they were always being attacked – by criminals who wanted their mobile phones. When *Xan* went out, which he now obliged himself to do, most days, he was very regularly unnerved by mobile phones – by the disembodied voices, moving up behind you or off to one side of you, testifying, with such iterative force, to the need of the human being for connection – or for self-dilution; these voices were the voices of the lonesome crowd, needing to come together . . . Never eager to face Pearl, Xan always tried his sons on their mobile phones. What you got was a beep for a message (rarely responded to), preceded by forty-eight bars of hate-crammed music inciting you to act like somebody crazy. As for people who talked to themselves and really were crazy, you should issue them with mobile phones; and then they could go around talking to themselves and no one would think they were crazy.

'"The sexuality of the head-injured male"', said Pearl, '– and most head-injured people *are* male, Xan, because men are generally more physical and impulsive . . . Yes: "The sexuality of the head-injured male may be affected by importence." Im-portence, with an *r*. Don't you think that's incredibly funny? It says it all really, doesn't it. I just *screamed*.'

'Yeah, well . . .'

'They're both out. I'll tell them you rang.'

He was the father of her boys, and Pearl was a good mother. She satirised his masculinity (he sometimes sensed) because she needed to know how much of it he had – and if he fell short, then so might her sons, which she wouldn't want. More specifically Pearl hoped to enrich his desire for vengeance. On all questions of reprisal she was unreflectingly fundamentalist. And so was he, apparently; he thought he wasn't, but he was. Pearl would understand – and Russia would not understand – that vengeance was something he had to have. All his senses wanted it, needed it. And even in his weakest moments, moments of flickering fragility, he was sure that vengeance would come. It could not be otherwise. And just by living, by lasting, by not dying, he was getting closer to it.

'Me?' he had once told Russia. 'I wouldn't hurt a fly.' This had perhaps been true, for a while. It was certainly true no longer. Now he spent at least an hour a day, with swat and spraycan, trying to hurt them, trying to kill them: flies. Wasps he left alone if the children were elsewhere; bees he respectfully spared; and spiders – fly-eaters – were his familiars, his enemies' enemies. Flies he hunted down: the fatter and hairier they were, the worse he needed to see them dead. Some seemed armoured: they looked like the attack aircraft of the twenty-second century. And when they rubbed their wrists together the way they did: was it in anticipation of it, or was it in satisfaction with the vengeance they had already exacted, the vengeance of ugliness? The ugliness spoke to him. When they rubbed their wrists together, they seemed to be sharpening their knives.

Such substantial creatures could not be dispatched with the brute physics of the swat; the disgust of it would travel up through your hand and along your arm and into your gorge. 'So Potent You'll Watch Them Drop', said the blurb on his spraycan. And he did watch. For a few seconds they buzzed about their business, as if the fatal blast was something they would at once shrug off. Then it was all over them, like age: every possible affliction. The wings sharply shrivelled; the taut rods of their legs became as crinkly as pubic hair. They were little old men – but not dying as we do. In the hospitals, even in the execution chambers, in the last rooms, human beings didn't hammer themselves against the windowpanes or the mirrors and then plop to the floor, enragedly buzzing, and spinning on their spines.

What were they doing here anyway, so late in the year? What atmospheric betrayal sustained them? They were living carrion – dead already, already dead.

At St George's Avenue there had been few visitors since the night of the accident. Three or four broad-shouldered, blue-chinned men in shiny suits came to sit with Xan for an hour or so; he kept asking them if he had 'upset' someone, if someone had a 'problem' with him that he didn't know about; the broad shoulders shrugged, the blue chins gravely shook. They stopped coming. He had actor friends, director friends, producer friends; such people (and Xan partly understood this, because he was partly one of them) cannot bring themselves to contemplate failure or distress or humiliation. His writer friends might have taken a different attitude, but he didn't have any; so the writers stayed away too. The crowd he used to play guitar with: they came, and kept coming, for a while. And the boys kept coming.

On the Tuesday of the third week Russia conducted an experiment. With not yet entirely humourless resignation she had read, in the books, that 'head-injured people often find it easier to relate to the elderly, who also cannot keep up the fast pace that the peers of a head-injured person expect.' All right, she thought: but what's in it for the elderly? Then, seated at her desk, with her head held still in her hands, Russia took her lower lip between her teeth, and alighted on the Richardsons: late seventies, and good old sports. She had a long chat with Margot on the telephone; and Margot was amenable, stressing her immunity to all extremes of boredom, embarrassment and alarm. It went ahead.

The four of them were in the upstairs sitting-room, the Meos, the Richardsons. Earlier, in nighties, their hair thickly coiled from the bath, Billie and Sophie had been presented, to considerable acclaim. Russia attended, now and then, to the drinks tray (a lone bottle of Chardonnay, plus all Xan's near-beers, his sodas, his juices and squashes and quashes), while the man himself sat facing their guests, his expression especially leonine that evening, his mouth curved downwards at the edges, grand, sleepy, all-tolerant. Margot Richardson, better known as Margot Drexler, Emeritus Professor of Modern History at UCL, was talking about the world situation with particular reference to Kashmir.

'It is incumbent upon the West', she said in her seminar style, 'to establish a cold-war culture in the subcontinent. Starting with the hotline. Plus arms-limitation talks, test-ban treaties, crisis-management channels, and the rest of the wherewithal. We waged such a war for forty years. We know how you do it. They don't. But then there's *religion*. In Gujarat some peanut-wallah refuses to say "Hail Ram" and the next thing you know there's two thousand dead. On one side of the border there's Hindu Nationalism, and on the other there's Islam. Think of it: nuclear jihad.'

'Pakistan', said Xan Meo, 'is bullshit.'

'. . . The clinical term for it is *perseveration*,' explained Russia, after a pause. 'You don't mind my saying this, do you, honey? When you have an accident like Xan's you can get hooked on certain words or ideas. We seem to have drawn "bullshit".' Yes, she thought: 'bullshit', and its not very numerous synonyms. 'There's also a touch of *Witzelsucht*, or inappropriate humour. My, how they love that word "inappropriate". It'll pass.'

'But Pakistan *is* bullshit. India is India but Pakistan is plain bullshit. They just cobbled it together on the map. "Pakistan" is a uh, an abbreviation. It could be Kapistan. Or Akpistan. Total bullshit.'

Margot said quickly, 'Xan's right in a way. "Pakistan" *is* an acronym. And if they lost Kashmir, they'd lose the *k*. It would have to be . . . Apistan.'

'Anyway it's Krapistan as it is. What I don't get about Partition is this. What I don't get about Pakistan is this. You take one country and turn it into two countries that are bound to go to war. And this was . . . two years after Hiroshima. Which is just round the corner. Geographically. Now you don't have to be . . . what's he called? Cosanostra . . .'

'Nostradamus.'

'Nostradamus . . .'

While Xan continued, Russia's eyes settled on Lewis Richardson. As was the case with many husbands of distinguished women, his project was the radiation of quietly relentless approval. The creases of his face, when Margot spoke, gave tiny flinches of encouragement and affection and pride. Russia was reminded that Xan had had something of that in him, once upon a time: silent but expressive approbation, directed at her. Silent respect – and it was gone.

'On the uh, woman question,' he was saying, 'they've gone *backwards*. In the north, guess what the punishment is if you get raped. You get raped. You know, kid,' he said to Russia, 'the books are wrong. It's not old people that make me relaxed. It's young people. Like the boys. Because they don't know who they are either.'

Russia blew her bangs off her brow and said, 'What a day *I've* had — beginning at five, when Sophie woke up for good. Then Billie went to school for around five minutes, and then I had both of them till two. Then three hours of teaching. And I still haven't touched my Munich lecture. I guess I'll work on it tonight until Sophie wakes up again.'

'Ah,' said Xan authoritatively. 'There goes my fuck.'

Into the silence that followed he said, 'So when's the comet due then?'

'I hate space,' said Russia evenly.

Xan said, 'The comet is the come of heaven.'

But maybe come here to unmake us.

Meanwhile, in the master bedroom . . . On the night of Xan's return from hospital Russia had been more or less pleasantly surprised when, with the dull glow of the linoleum still on him, he had clambered up on top of her. Afterwards, she praised him and calmed him, and there were avowals. She thought: what could be more — natural? The next night it happened again, and the next. And the next morning, and the next. Having subsided, he lay there trembling like an engine. Russia thought about this engine. It would be that of a large vehicle, stationary but locked in a high gear, and the stick would be flailing and juddering in its attempt not to stall.

'What do they say?' said Billie, in the kitchen, during a play-date. Her friend had just produced a pair of badges; and the badges said Just Say No.

'They say Just Say No.'

'Just Say No to what?'

'They don't say. They just say Just Say No.'

Russia had started just saying no. It worked — but only for half an hour. He had started following her around the house.

When she submitted, she often felt, as he shifted her body about, as he arranged it on the bottom sheet, that he had taken on the role of her personal trainer; at other times he was like a good trencherman settling down to the systematic completion of an enormous meal. And when, after an hour or so of that, he seemed quite certain to conclude, he would suddenly go as static and abstract as a stick insect; and then he'd resume, like someone doggedly trying to shoulder his way through a locked door. Russia remembered a phrase Xan had once used anecdotally: 'he gave her a right seeing-to'. Yes: that was what she was being given. The only time she ever considered herself aroused was when he deployed maximum animal force and she could say she was being ravished and it wasn't her fault. But this thought more or less instantly produced a counterthought, not quite political or even intellectual, but trained up: something like – did I take two degrees and study history so I could get raped in a cave? At first she had faked orgasms. Then she started faking migraines. And now the migraines were real.

'Can't we go to a hotel this afternoon', he kept asking, '– just for a couple of hours?'

She laughingly declined: work, children. When this response had at last proved itself incapable of changing the subject, Russia tried saying something weird. It was a thought she had had; Xan's return had proved to be far from rejuvenating. She said,

'Hotel bedrooms are all right. But I don't like hotel bathrooms. I don't like the mirrors in the bathrooms.'

Before changing the subject Xan said, '. . . But we needn't *go* in the bathroom.'

She had of course talked to Tilda Quant, among others. There was a name for it: Post-Traumatic Satyriasis. It had to do with the hypothalamus and the release of testosterone. Tilda said there was a drug you could give him (or put in his coffee): cyproterone acetate. The trademark was Androcur.

One afternoon he was breathing over her shoulder while she sat at her desk.

'What's that?' he asked.

'E-mails.'

'But what's this? And this?'

'Pornography,' she said.

Without another word he sloped off to his basement flat across the road – and sloped back again, two hours later, smelling of public swimming-pools and shorted electricity . . . But he still loomed up on her, later, five seconds after lights-out.

And the worst thing was that all this wasn't the worst thing. Not any more.

Xan wanted to go to bed with his wife all the time for two good reasons: she was his ideal, and she was there. But he wanted to go to bed with all other women all the time too. If he could persuade Russia to stop working and farm out the children and spend her spare time coating herself in unguents and underwear: this would have contained it. But Russia wasn't going to do that . . . When, fumblingly, feeling like *it* in a game of blindman's-bluff, he groped his way into the thick detail of the city and reached the casbah – the souk, the chowk – of Britannia Junction, he seldom saw a woman of any age whose bathwater he would have declined to drink. And they wanted him too, he realised. With subtle salacity they sent signals to him, with their mouths, their eyelashes, their tongues. They dressed for him, they even mortified their flesh for him – those nuts and bolts in their heads were cuneiform, telling him what to expect, when the time came. But the time wouldn't come, because he couldn't be sure (and this was a massive consideration) that these women, many of them young and strong, wouldn't hurt him. And he could be sure that Russia wouldn't hurt him.

Sometimes an itch (say in the septum of the upper lip) announces itself as far more baldly intolerable than any pain – perhaps because there is the power to quell it, in an instant, with the swipe of a finger. But Xan couldn't do that. His heart itched, his soul itched. It felt connected to the need for vengeance. Vengeance was the relief of unbearable humiliation. And so at night, when he invaded Russia, that's what he was doing: seeking relief from it. More distantly, he felt that some historic wrong had at last found redress, as if his god, so inexplicably crippled, was once again more powerful than the god of his enemies.

Climax.

Russia's day was assuming certain proportions. Awake all night anyway with Sophie (this now brought its comforts: Xan stood on the stairs for hours, waiting), she rose at six-thirty and breakfasted with the girls, at which stage she noted the first rumours of her menstrual cramps. Next, she went into college, and finished, corrected and then delivered her lecture. At three in the afternoon she would fly from Gatwick to Munich where she would sight-translate the same lecture into German at a conference on 'Geli Raubal and Eva Braun'. The only possible return flight got her into Manchester with a good chance of making the last express to London. She hoped to be home by about half past twelve.

Late in the afternoon of the same day her husband was struck by a thought. He realised that he owed himself two drinks: two drinks, four cigarettes (and half an hour of writhing reminiscence – if, that is, he could manage reminiscence). 'I never did have those Dickheads,' he said out loud. 'I was going to toast the boys but then . . .' And this was an important moment for him: a new memory, and one that took him close to the epicentre. It pushed him into attempting something he had long postponed: a reenactment of October 29 . . . He watched Imaculada bathe the girls. At six o'clock he put on his overcoat. 'I'm off out, me,' he said, and opened the front door. It was darker now, darker in the year, with the sun pitching a lower ball across the sky. The sky *is* falling, thought Xan Meo. Where's the king? Where's the fox?

He approached the main road: to his right, the garden (pram-like Primrose Hill), to his left – left field, and the city . . . So, the rink of Parkway and Camden Lock and Camden High Street, the black gallows of the traffic lights. At this time of day you saw guys in suits heading home with a briefcase in one hand and, in the other, a plastic bag containing provisions for one. Will this be me, myself? he thought. It wasn't only the women: he was looking at the men differently too, weighing them, grading them – fearing them. On the phone, with Pearl, he had felt as break-able as a lightbulb when she told him that her older brother, the enormous Angus, was thirsting for a rematch. And now when he saw them (and they're always there), the male figures in the street who disclosed the preparedness for violence (for continuation *by other means*), he knew he could find no answer to it; and he would have to find an answer, if there was to be vengeance . . . He bought his cigarettes at BestCost. Even the striplights seemed to be trying to hurt his head.

Xan glanced round the door of the High Street bookshop, and ascertained that *Lucoʒade* was no longer on the table marked Our Staff Recommends. He turned up Delancey Street and passed the café where he no longer played rhythm guitar every second Wednesday night. Then left down Mornington Crescent, under the busy trees, and a sinus whistle from the points and wires above the railtracks. '*Harrison! Move* your . . .' Sometimes an aeroplane can sound a note of warning. There were four of them in the sky, but far beyond earshot. Their contrails left chalkmarks on the firmament. They are chalking us up for some-thing, measuring us up for something . . . A thick and shaggy brown cloud had spread itself over the streetlamps, resembling the pelt of a bear or an ape, but with a punk colour in it (perhaps the result of chemical confusion), like the khaki of an old Elastoplast.

There was Hollywood, and he entered.

* * *

He said to the kid (a different kid), 'Uh, I'll have a . . . What happened to the Dickheads?'

'New menu.'

'Okay. I'll have a Shithead. No: *two* Shitheads. What's the difference between a Dickhead and a Shithead anyway?'

'Benedictine. In the Dickhead.'

'Well sling some Benedictine in the Shithead. Because what I really want is a Dickhead. Or two Dickheads.'

'Or you could have a Dickhead *and* a Shithead.'

'Well. Now we've come this far with the Dickheads . . .'

The paved terrace was once again deserted; more than deserted – disused. No dead duck upended in the turbid canal, no firefighting sunset. And where was his bird ('Is that your "bird"?'), his cockney sparrow? . . . Six weeks had passed, and, according to the books, he was supposed to be emerging from a period of false consciousness – though Incredulity, he thought, was a better word for it than Denial. He was currently scheduled to experience a deepening of melancholy as he grasped the true dimensions of his impoverishment. But Xan had considered himself pauperised right from the start; and he feared further demotion. What was stopping his family from abandoning him? Didn't they now see, as he now saw, the unsuspected weakness of all prohibitions? And why was he bullying Russia, why was he torturing her with the sex weapon? To bind her to him, so she had to stay – or just to get another one in, before she left? Or to punish himself, himself, and bring about his own ejection? The groan he suddenly uttered rose steadily in pitch, and a passerby, pausing to listen, might have thought that Xan Meo was about to throw up.

Minutes passed. His present condition, he realised, physiologically reminded him of his sister's death – and its attack on his own life-force. At the time (for about a year) he had thought: We'll never be immortal. Because it's the deaths of others that kill us . . . Suddenly he felt a vibration of troubled air on the back of his neck. There followed a moment of craven brittleness, then he turned . . . It was she, it was she (he was now sure it was *she*): the paparazza sparrow, with her chattering shutters. And as the bird bobbed and fussed about him, he said out loud,

'What happened, darling? You saw it. What happened?'

Unlike the grimly assimilated pigeons (for whom flight was simply a last resort), the paparazza remained a creature of the air, she remained haughtily other. Before she twittered off she fixed him for an instant with the neutral madness of her eyes. Xan felt a flow, or a change of temperature, in his mind. And he remembered: 'You'll remember this in pain, boy. You went and *named* him. In black and white.' *In black and white* . . .

'Bless you,' he said.

This was fresh information. It meant that he had named his enemy in something he had *written*. And so, with fluttering fingers, he wrote that down too, in the notebook they'd told him to keep about the details of his day: visits to the bathroom, food eaten, words exchanged with Billie, the whereabouts of his keys.

The significant name was in *Lucozade*.

He now switched to Shitheads, and for a little while he felt very happy and proud.

With its moodswings, its motor-failures (its slurrings and staggerings), its weepiness, its vaulting lechery, its encouragement of words and actions that sowed the seeds of regret, Xan's post-traumatic condition reminded him of something: drunkenness. So after a few more drinks in Hollywood it occurred to him, rather drunkenly perhaps, that drunkenness, in his new world, might give him a clear head. Intending to explore the hypothesis, he lit out for the savage pubs of Camden High Street and Kentish Town Road.

'Now in London it's the congestion, the congestion,' said the slender young Irishman crushed up against the bar in the Turk's

Head. 'Everywhere. Now back home: go a mile out of Dublin and you won't see a sinner all day.'

Wedging his whole forearm across his breast, Xan bent his head, and lowered his underjaw, to gain access to his third quart of London Pride. We all sin. What else do we all do? There were many sinners in the Turk's Head, many breathers, thinkers, dreamers. Not everyone can walk or talk or hear or see, but we are all of us drinkers, micturaters. Eaters, excreters, everywhere. Xan got another quart of Pride off the feeder behind the wooden slab.

He fell in with a group of fuckers round the pool-table. And it was good. The female gobblers didn't stir him, and the male platers didn't scare him. There was fellow feeling: they were all in this together. Some shitters left – but new pissers took their place. Every farter bought a drink. This went on for a long time. Then he bade farewell to the assembled wankers, and moved on.

Later, as he stood in the throbbing toilet of a jazz bar in Camden Road, Xan looked at his watch and was most surprised to see that it was two o'clock in the morning. But this did not undermine the spirit of squinting concentration he had entered into as he reloosened his trousers. His immediate objective? Having just consumed a very great deal of dun-coloured tapwater, Xan's immediate objective was to find out whether he was man enough to piss his own shit off the back of the porcelain bowl. He wasn't quite man enough to do that, but then this was very butch shit, this shit: mutton vindaloo, pork kebab, cajun pizza, jalapeñas relleñas. Coming out of his stall, and thinking with some focus about getting home – his luck turned. There was a machine on the wall which, on the insertion of a pound coin, dispensed a generous handful of rudimentary cologne: the very thing to kill the smell of pub. He had lots of pound coins and, why, he fairly soused himself in the sugary fragrance. His cigarettes had run out long ago but that didn't matter because he'd bought lots of cheap cigars.

After a long search he found the exit and the fresh air. Pausing only to leave a stack of sick in the gutter (and chewing all the more heartily on the soaked butt of his last perfecto), Xan went home with a clear plan (he'd just fling on the light and spin round): the detailed exaction of his connubial rights.

And all this wasn't the worst thing. The worst thing had to do with Billie.

2. Storm in a teacup

'Oh, before I go, sir. I was talking earlier today to some friends in Madrid. Do you remember a scandal of uh, five years ago or so, sir, involving King Bartolomé?'

'Would you very kindly remind me, Bugger.'

'Certainly, sir. There was in existence a video-recording, widely circulated at the time, of the King having some kind of session with the wife of the local polo pro.'

'The local *what*? . . . Oh. Oh. I thought you were talking in Spanish. Well?'

'There was a gagging order which the press pretty much obeyed, and the whole thing was forgotten in a year.'

'A year? Is this meant to cheer me up, Bugger? Besides, Tolo's not a real . . . He keeps up no kind of style at all. That business was just another . . . another suburban scandal.'

'True in a way, sir.'

'Victoria is the future Queen of England, Bugger. The eyes of all the world are on the Princess.'

'True, sir.'

'Oh God, Bugger, what am I going to *say*? No, don't tell me now or I'll toss and turn. And I take it you've chucked those mullahs for tomorrow morning.'

'Absolutely, sir. You're free until one. May I wish you a good night's rest?'

'A fond hope, but you may. And the same to you, Bugger.'

Henry IX sat slumped on the seat of easement. Every few seconds he drew his body up into a posture of acute enquiry, then slumped once more.

'Steady on there,' he said. 'Yes, most painful. Have a heart, old thing. *Oof*.'

Henry *VIII* employed a man called Sir Thomas Heneage, who, in his capacity of Groom of the Stool, had the dubious privilege of attending every royal evacuation (with a damp flannel ready in his hand). But Henry IX was all alone.

'Ow! Now I *say*. That was, that was . . .'

His tummy troubles had been complicated by an attack of 'stress eczema' in an optimally inconvenient site. The King hadn't needed this assurance from the ennobled surgeon: 'Secondary infection is of course unavoidable.' It was already clear to Henry that, generally speaking, the arse was a disaster waiting to happen. How could you keep something clean when it was pegged out in the cloaca maxima? And you couldn't *rest* the arse either, funnily enough; the arse was never idle, even when you were sitting on it. Walking was the worst: a frenzy of formication, right up the root of you. And to seek one's bed only fomented heat, and the ants' trail became a nest of hornets.

'Now that's just *not on*, do you hear? Out of court! Foul! Ah, here it –'

With a flinch that made his ears roar Henry ejected what might have been a medium-sized handgun; he then applied about a furlong of toilet paper, and made the exquisite switch from garderobe to bidet. The abominable tingle now subsided. It had at last been comprehensively scratched, from within. And it would be several minutes before he went back to wishing (not very constructively, true) that he was the prettiest prettyboy in an

Alabaman prison . . . The garderobe was a genuine museum piece: with its scales and weights and pinions, it looked like an orrery, or an instrument of recondite torture. The bidet was a squat marble trough with varicose veins, and would have been perfectly at home in any old hospital or madhouse.

Now into the tub for a thoroughly good soak. Henry was near-brahminical in his hygiene, and this was unusual for an England: luxury, in the royal houses, never extended to the bathrooms, which were cold and huge and littered with washing-machines and badminton nets and basketfuls of kittens. He was his own man in other ways too, of course. Among the toiletries lined up on the slab beneath the mirror, for example, one would not find the fierce little gadget, like a pewter knuckleduster, with which Richard IV had tormented his tubes of toothpaste. Henry was an enemy of thrift: he was one of nature's overtippers. Retiring domestics, after half a century of service, used to receive a monogrammed tea-towel, or a bathmat, or a free-visit coupon to the Rubens Room at Windsor. After Henry's accession they got twenty cases of vintage champagne, or a nice new car. He also doubled all salaries – and then shruggingly halved them again, after the public revelation of his astronomical overdraft. The treats and bonuses he still hurled about were now being financed by secret sales from the Englands' private Prado – a Titian here, a Delacroix there. Brendan Urquhart-Gordon could almost hear the creak of the tumbrels and the gnashing of the ringside knitting-needles when Henry said, with a pout, that 'Christmas wouldn't be Christmas' if his gift-budget was confined to six figures.

When the King was at stool, it could be argued, he was mingling with his people. He was coming down from his castle and doing what everyone else did. First he mingled. Now he slummed, applying Lord Fletcher's ferocious lotion by means of a disposable glove. As he did so he was ambushed by an unmanageable thought: he could hardly ask Victoria – his ministering angel, the faith-healer of every little scrape and scratch and ache and pain – to kiss it better.

The recent days had passed with fell velocity. Now he had three clear hours before they came for him – a stretch of time that suddenly seemed almost geologically vast. Seated at his desk, drinking China tea, he played patience, and solitaire. Eleven o'clock came and went without making the slightest impression on his complacency, and so did eleven-thirty and eleven-forty-five – though it was 'a slight blow', he had to admit, when the minute-hand gave its tic-like tick and dourly advanced beyond noon. Still, fifty-nine minutes: an eternity. At about ten to three Henry was beginning his twenty-seventh game of solo. Ten minutes – no, eleven! Donkey's years. The red queen, the black king, the red king, the black queen. Six minutes; five . . . He came close to protesting that he still had thirty seconds left when there was the knock on the door, and Love loomed.

Brendan was keeping his counsel. The Royal Rolls had barely taken its place in the convoy, and the King (after a curt good-day) emphatically produced from his side pocket a paperback booklet called *Pastime Puzzles – 24*. He was now immersed in a cryptic crossword . . . It always filled Brendan with affectionate amazement: the amount of time his employer was capable of devoting – around blue Caribbean poolsides, on Alpine terraces – to the same edition of *Pastime Puzzles*. Over the course of one long summer (New Zealand, Australia, Africa, Micronesia) Brendan had reread the complete works of Henry James while Henry frowned at, doodled in, and frequently gummed back together his copy of *Pastime Puzzles – 19*. An intensely ticklish moment had arisen from this, when, in some Kenyan treehouse, as they sipped their gimlets, Henry said,

'Quite a good joke in that book of mine . . . Uh, there's a young chap who goes to prison for a very long time. And he's a bit worried about how he's going to kill all that . . . time. Someone tells him there are jigsaws in the book trolley they wheel round. He gets a jigsaw. It's the sort of jigsaw Tori had when she was – hang on, I'm giving it away. You know, wooden, with about twelve pieces. He uh, he finishes the jigsaw and says to his cellmate, "I've finished!" And his cellmate says, "Yes, you ass, but it took you ten months." And our man says, "Ah, but it says on the packet 'Three to Five Years'."'

They both reached for their drinks at the same moment. They both looked down at the same moment: on the table between them, *Pastime Puzzles – 19*, next to the soft pigskin of *The Princess Casamassima*.

'What an extraordinary colour you've gone, Bugger.'

And there was Henry on the veranda the next day, flexing himself into a copy of *Pastime Puzzles – 20* . . .

Now Brendan attended to the two necks, glassed off like exhibits, in the front seat, one long and thin (Rhodes, the most senior chauffeur), the other short and fat (Captain Mate). Mate's neck was also tanned and pocked; barely a pore had escaped corruption – it looked like sand after rain.

'Oh I say, how fearfully *clever*,' crowed Henry, filling in a four-letter vertical answer in the bottom right-hand corner of the grid. He had been applying himself to his crossword for over an hour. After another ten minutes he put it aside. 'Can't seem to get going', he said, 'on these bally cryptics. Let's watch the news.'

Rhodes's neck and Mate's neck were now erased from sight, as the King, by the deft use of a dial, interposed a drape of black felt. He then took the clicker from the arm-rest and poked it towards the television screen while also skilfully engaging the power button – as if he was involved (thought Brendan) in a battle of wits. The screen fizzed, and awakened.

'There,' he said. 'Now I have a notion that I deserve a drink.'

Henry sat back with it, his brandy, raising the balloon in both palms like a woman with a cup of something hot. For outside, beyond the treated windows, the blue morning had collapsed utterly, and the southbound motorway was a seething, sizzling mess of drenched metal and rubber, under skies the colour of dogs' lips . . . When Henry came to the throne, about a quarter of the population still believed that he had been personally appointed by God; well, stress eczema, where he had it, surely exploded the Divine Right of Kings. It had first seized him, this condition, in the week after Pamela's accident. Lord Fletcher drew the obvious conclusion; but Henry, still writhing from his epiphanic cur moment ('Oh *no*, Pemmy. But at least this means . . . At least this means . . .'), suspected otherwise. It was not the accident so much as the inconceivably onerous task of breaking the news to the Princess. Henry, who could barely bring himself to be the author of the most trifling disappointment, who suffered for weeks if he denied her a final swim, a third lollipop, an eleventh bedtime story . . . There was a two-day hiatus (and news embargo) while she was spirited off a cruise ship in the Aleutians. Meanwhile, with tweezers and blowtorch, stress eczema was exposing the nerve ends of his nethermost fissures and faults. And when he told her, in the library at the Greater House, he additionally squirmed on his confidential nettlebed. Now welcoming the pain, now fully accepting it, he took her outside and walked her up and down the length of the stream for hours and hours and talked and talked and talked to her.

Brendan said: 'By Christ, did you see that?'

'He . . . disappeared.'

'Hoo! They won't be showing *that* again.'

'He disappeared.'

On the television: a street scene, a loose group of shoppers, hurriers. And then one of them disappeared, leaving a hole in the world, with death tearing out of it.

After some moments Brendan said, 'Horrorism. That's what we've just witnessed, sir. An act of horrorism.'

Henry looked at him promptingly. The Royal Rolls, with its

convoy of peoplecarriers, left the main road and entered the scalloped grounds of the Abbey.

'Angst, anxiety, concern, worry,' said Brendan, who recognised Henry's tactic, his voodoo of deferral: no talk of Victoria until the car was quenched of motion. 'You are being chased by a wild beast which you already *fear*,' he went on. 'That fear turns to terror as the chase begins. And that terror turns to horror when the chase ends. Horror is when it's upon you, when it's actually *there*.'

But they weren't there, and, ahead of them, the grounds swept on.

'Continue, Bugger,' said Henry tightly.

Almost floundering, Brendan said, 'The bomber . . . To the bomber, death is not death. And life isn't life, either, but illusion. There is something called the demographic bomb – the birth bomb. The bomb of birth, the bomb of death.'

They pulled up.

'A form of words, Bugger.'

'. . . Well, sir, I suggest you confine yourself to what we may reasonably suppose will soon be the stuff of common knowledge.'

'Spell it out, if you please.'

Brendan did so.

'Mm. Perfectly decent little place. I shall need you, Bugger, at ten to five.'

Between the Royal Rolls and the double doors of the Abbey lay a gauntlet of umbrellas.

Dear Princess Victoria,

Or how about, simply, 'Victoria'? I expect you must be fed up to the back teeth with all the endless pomp and circumstance in your life. There's none of that nonsense round here, and I cordially extend an open invitation for

you to pay us a visit any time you like. Don't stand on
ceremony! We don't subscribe to ceremony.

We usually dine at a reasonably early hour. Good
plain fare, such as has been enjoyed in England for
centuries. Our caravan contains two totally separate
rooms. Once Mother has gone to bed, privacy is virtually guaranteed.

We will then have the leisure to relax on the divan
and get to know each other over a few beers. I'll start
by kissing you oh so slowly. So gently. So tenderly. Oh
so lovingly. Then when you say the moment is right
and not a moment before (this is totally your 'call' as
they say) I'll haul out my

Brendan yawned, and stopped reading (there were many
pages yet to come). He was in the lounge, with his briefcase on
his knees, going through another batch of the Princess's
restricted mail: mail she never saw. To begin with he had thought
that the enemy might have shown its hand at some earlier point;
he no longer thought it had, and persevered merely to give
himself the feeling that he was getting somewhere. But of course
these letters to the Princess were not from the world of pro-
action. They came from the world of onanistic longing – and
coarse sentimentality, and impotent sadism. Even at their most
violent, and some were very violent indeed, they seemed to moan
with inertia: a humiliated stasis. Nor would such men be going
to France, bearing gold . . .

His wristwatch was cocked up on the table in front of him.
He was ready. As he crushed the letters into their file (Restrained
Correspondence) he asked himself why he had spent so long on
such an obvious waste of time. He admitted that he indulged in
fantasies of protection, of interposing himself between the
world and the Princess. Was that his job, just now: a fantasy of
protection?

* * *

With a show of capped teeth in his rubbery face, Captain Mate ushered him into the Oak Gallery – closed that afternoon, of course, for the King's use. Henry and Victoria were on a chesterfield at the far end of the room, some sixty feet away. The remains of a substantial tea were being removed by Love and his helpers. As Brendan approached, and as the scene cleared, he found himself thinking of earlier times: father and daughter would spend whole days, whole weekends, lolling on a sofa like this, watching television or merely dozing and mumbling and occasionally rousing themselves for a game of I Spy. The King hadn't changed; but she was older now, this autumn – more erect, and more inclined, it seemed to him, to maintain a distance between herself and her father.

'How lovely to see you, Brendan.'

'Always a delight, ma'am. I hope the Princess has had her fill of sticky buns?'

'Oh yes. I had masses.'

'And were they sufficiently "greedy"?'

'Oh yes. Very piggy indeed.'

Brendan thought: I'm always behind – not a year behind, but always half a season. He said, 'Forgive me. I've interrupted you.'

'My daughter was discoursing on *Islam*, if you please,' said Henry. Of course, the King was religious, in his way: strictly non-ecumenical Prayer Book Church of England. 'It's like talking to a bally mullah.'

'Oh poo. I was making Daddy cross by saying that Muslims seem to have much more feeling for each other than Christians. There's a real bond, and I think that's very attractive.'

'Is the Princess', asked Brendan lightly, 'feeling herself "drawn" to Mecca?'

'God no. I don't *think* I've got any faith in me. I just find it all very riveting.'

Henry was no longer dreaming of Alabaman prisons. He had hit upon a more aristocratic excoriation: the smoking poker administered to Richard II (for crimes of 'effeminacy'). And then the usurper Bolingbroke journeyed to the Holy Land to purge his guilt with fire and sword . . . Henry had at some point been informed by the Duchess of Ormonde that fifteen-year-olds were fifteen-year-olds, and that he should be pleased it was religion she was keen on, and not anorexia. Recalling this, he bafflingly volunteered,

'You'd be better off having another round of sticky buns, my darling – and never mind about *Mecca* . . .'

Brendan turned his frown on the Princess, who wagged her head with a look of contented inanity. Then the smile she gave him: how it decanted itself upwards, from the mouth and through the frame of the nose and into the eyes, where it lingered in the folds of the orbits . . . Brendan was devoted to Henry; and yet Henry sometimes made him feel as if he had kissed his life away for some evanescent frippery – for a monogrammed butter-pat, in a deadly dining-room full of the ghosts of sweating placemen. But with the Princess it was love. What kind of love he didn't know, but it was plainly love.

'The sands of time, sir,' he said, tapping his watch with a fingertip.

'Yes yes, Bugger. Sorry: Brendan. What about the women then, eh, sweetheart? I expect you'd go a bit blank, my precious, if I told you to wear a uh, a black *tepee* for the rest of your days.'

Victoria sat forward, rubbing her hands together as if in ablution, and said, 'But think of the agonies that Western women go through because of their looks. The constant worries and comparisons. It's forced on you too. This stupid vanity is forced on you. What bliss it would be not to have to think about it ever again. Oh, the privacy of it!'

'Well we can talk about that another time. My dearest, I have some rather unsettling news.'

Within a minute Brendan believed that the whole of terrestrial existence was just a breath away from cardiovascular collapse. He stared at the King, and thought: can you not feel it, man? Can you not *hear* it?

Though never as hurtfully as in the present case, Victoria's integrity had of course been pierced and breached many times before; and, since childhood, she had always reacted with the same robust indignation. There was nothing regal in it – on the contrary, there was something severely republican and every-woman in her steep frown, her straight neck. It was for a version of this that Brendan had more or less unthinkingly prepared himself. And now? While her father, gazing resolutely ceiling-ward as he writhed around on his cushion, delivered the agreed preamble ('it appears that the vultures are up to their old tricks'), Victoria did no more than sigh and stiffen. But as soon as Henry meandered in on the particular ('the Château', 'the Yellow House'), she bared the teeth that were still too broad for her face, and her head dropped, by degrees, like the resilient jolts of a second-hand. Now Brendan could feel the heartbeat of the Princess, pressing in on his exterior ear. And soon the sound of her pulse – the slow, gonging throb – was entirely subsumed by his own.

'Well it'll soon blow over, my dear,' said Henry, writhing around in earnest now, like a man playing footsie with a moving target. He was practically flat on his back.

'We'll just have to get on with it,' he managed to add. 'Storm in a teacup, all hands on deck.'

Brendan thought: she wants to disappear. She wouldn't want the nails and the bolts and the shrapnel. But that's what she wants to do. She wants to disappear.

'*Perfectly* decent little place,' said the King as he strode through the mountain tunnel of the Abbey archway – saying it as if Brendan, and Victoria, and everyone else, kept maintaining other-wise, in tireless error. 'I don't know about you, Bugger, but I thought she took that fairly well.'

He couldn't answer . . . During the last half-hour, in the Oak Gallery, the ambient air had made steady gains in clarity, as if a succession of blankets were being removed from an exalted skylight; and now the actors had stepped out into a blue thaw of dripping glitter. At the foot of the cliffside lay the town, waiting, palpating like a dog that has just shaken itself dry. There was an invitation to the spirit – rise up; and all this, he knew, all this was only mist and rain to the Princess . . .

She was standing with her back turned, and slightly apart, to one side of her own entourage (the forecourt was now a millpond of Security), on a strip of lawn between the path and a bed of pink flowers. Looking at her hunched shape, he knew again what it was like to be fifteen: when you suffered, your every cell suffered. She was wearing black jeans and a short leather jacket, and he wondered why, with the young and indivisibly wretched, it was the tensed buttocks that best expressed all this strength and pain.

Brendan marched forward. As he came round in front of her he was prepared to see tears but her eyes were their normal blue. Yet clogged with chemicals, as was her mouth, chemicals of distress, and giving off a sour breath.

So he did something for which there was no precedent. He embraced her, saying,

'He will forgive you anything and everything, you may be sure. Without a second thought. And so will I. He will always protect you. And so will I.'

'Forgive me?' she said. With the words evenly stressed, he thought, as he dropped her hand and backed away.

In the Royal Rolls the King, with a showily dexterous flick of the wrist, activated the television and sat back with a contented grunt to watch the snooker for the rest of the drive. 'Oh, perfect weight . . . They make it look so . . . Now. Has he got the angle on the yellow?'

After about an hour Brendan started to think logically, or at least consecutively. If one used one's imagination (he told himself), Victoria's reaction could probably be readily explained. What do we do in bathrooms? Nothing we're very proud of. A bodily function, perhaps. The use of a tampon, conceivably. Or something rather more intimate. Which woman friend had informed him that young girls referred to the hand-held shower as 'Rain Man'? And she was *fifteen*. Remember that: the outlandish disproportion of being fifteen, when you were waiting to find out who you were.

'*Shot.* Now he'll come down for the blue . . . Oh no, he's gone too *far* . . . Foul stroke!'

That embrace: a startling impropriety, never to be repeated, but none the less an unalterable fact. He recalled the tragic sourness of her breath. And the rigidity of her body – and the answering rigidity of his own ancillary heart. All the blood within him: all of it.

'Here we are. Well I'm pleased to have got that out of the way, Bugger. I won't pretend it hasn't been playing on my mind. In a week or two I expect this'll all be a thing of the past.'

Brendan spoke with only an instant's forethought. You fool, you fool, he said to himself. Didn't you see that her fear was waiting for it – for this day, for this hour? He said,

'I disagree, sir. In fact I suggest that I turn this car round and go straight back to St Bathsheba's. The Princess must be taken out of school at once and then secluded – I suggest Ewelme. If the illicit material is indeed made public on the thirty-first, then I suggest also that we take the advice of uh, our mole and insist from the outset that the material is faked. It's a ghastly gamble, I know, but the chance won't come again. Meanwhile we must work out a strategy of damage-limitation with Downing Street. Sir, this *isn't* going to be a storm in a teacup.'

'Steady on, Bugger. Do you know something I don't?'

'It's only a deduction, sir, but I think it's sound. The Princess was not alone in the bathroom of the Yellow House.'

This is going to be a storm in all the oceans of the thing which is called world.

And the thought: God how she needs her mother.

3. Car-sweat

The two-storeyed Avenger lay in wait under the Esso sign. Welcome Break. Stop and Shop. Smoker consistently drove out here and just sat in the car or did his e's on the laptop. You have 124 new messages. People coming and going: it's more cheerful. You fill her up, grab a bay by the cash machine. And stroll inside if you want, for a pizza or whatever. At the Esso you often also get carpools. And women on mobile phones, women waiting alone under the lights in the forecourt with that waiting posture – doing nothing but waiting; they stand like that in the parks and recs with a leather lead in their hand: waiting for the dog to do its business. You could lower your window, saying, 'Lost your lift then, love? Hop in.' But the age of the random ride was over. Mobile phones: increased backup. You can have a brief exchange, there on the kerbside. Pass the time. Feel the confinement lift a little bit. It's funny. They must think: I climb into that car, I pass through that glass, then I'm in his mirrorworld – he'll have power, with its warp and distortion. He can *turn*. Every man sits on an anti-man. And the weathered saloon, ticking over in the suburban sidestreet, has its oil and coolant, its dark engine, beneath the windshield's reflection of the leaves and the branches.

In Clint's evening paper there was an 'artist's impression' of the Princess in her bath. You know: like in a court case. The artist was not a very good artist; the impression was not a very good impression. Idealised (and, as it were, self-bowdlerised by the placement of her limbs), the image of the Princess might have graced the greetings cards sent by a suburban madam to selected members of her clientele. Reduced to an artist's impression, on account of the shielding order. Bit late now, thought Clint: a case of bolting the stable door after the graniverous quadruped has gone AWOL. Everyone on earth was gawping at the stills, on the Net, in the foreign press – and, of course, in the *Morning Lark*, which, that morning, had consisted of nothing else. The official line, from above, was that the material was all faked anyway: software, pseudofilm, 'without ontology'. Either that, or some snapper hides in the toilet for a month . . . What Clint couldn't work out was who benefited. *Cui bono?* – apart from the *Lark*, with its triple print-run . . . Clint: never gone that big on the younger bird. But virgins had their points. Bet they felt you more. And they couldn't tell you were crap at it, having nothing to compare.

You have 125 new messages. About 120 of them would be from commercial concerns: invitations to Clint to shower money on his genitalia – by various means and for various purposes. Three or four would be chat-room flirtations with indistinguishable career-girls, all of them apparently chasing the next leg-up or leg-over. Clint visualised a succession of fierce little hussies, with lips crimped in ceaseless calculation. But of course they could be anyone: these were rigged-up identities, summoned out of the ether. It was said of the Web that its contents were (on average) about 60 per cent true. And you, mate, he said to himself: can you swear any better? . . . And then it came, the voice that seemed to penetrate his solitude:

> clint: how r u, dear man? i
> detected a note of melancholy in
> your most recent e, so i thought
> i'd cheer u up with some verbal
> 4play. u have asked 4 my views
> on anal 6 & related ?s. well, i'm

all 4 it if it gets the job done
quicker. i said be4 th@ the best
prix r small & soft, & i'm aware
th@ anal 6 demands gr8er 10sion.
so it's 6 of 1 & 1/2 a dozen of
the other! i'm very happy to
per4m oral 6 @ any time. what's
my style? i no th@ some girls r
merely rather affection8 2 the
man's 2l. i consider this 'cock-i'd'!
u should go @ it 40ssimo. rule:
never kiss your man after fell8io –
by god, u'd be calling him a bum-
b&it! as 4 cunnilingus, th@'s
strictly verbo10.

Blimey: she's ideal. Talk about taking the pressure off. With this bird, expectation's reduced to nil . . . But that's all very well, that is. That's all very fine and large. Because the wound's in you, my son. There ain't anyone else who can sort this out: it's down to you, mate. You yourself.

Before driving back to his Foulness semi, Clint topped up the Avenger at the pumps. They talked their heads off about sex and cars, but look at this: look at the mechanised brothel of the forecourt. In every bay, in every trap, there was a man with a hulking nozzle in his mitt; you lifted the cover, and there was the sliding aperture; then you poured in the power while the digits flickered.

Fat splats of water fell unevenly from the ribbed roof. Not rain: just drops of car-sweat.

'So what was in this "dirty bomb"?'

'Radioactive medical waste, Chief, plus ringworm, West Nile virus, liquid gangrene, and a cladding of mad cow.'

'And what do this lot call themselves?'

'Uh, the Legion of the Pure.'

Clint thought: what's funny? Is it *still* funny? Was it *ever* funny?

'And they blew themselves up on purpose.'

'No, Chief. By accident. It went off in the airport carpark.'

'And who were they followers of?'

'Uh, you know: the bloke with no tackle.'

'Actually, Chief, he *has* got tackle,' said Clint. 'Records show. It's funny, that. Like Hitler's only got one ball.'

'Was he the one that went to the stripclub?'

'That wasn't true either.'

Heaf seemed disappointed. 'Well we certainly spent enough space on it. Did he go *near* the stripclub? . . . Anyway, we can only keep hammering on about racial profiling at airports. This is Clint in today's: "And at the security checkpoints, what do we see? Some gimp of a granny being fisted in half, while the dune-rat called Zui'zide al Bomba sails past with a J-cloth on his bonce and a flamethrower over his shoulder. And followed by his three best friends, Hijaq, Kydnap and Drugrun."' Heaf slapped the page with his fingernails. '*That's* what I call an editorial. Anyone who looks remotely Arab should have their lives made an absolute torment for the rest of the century.'

'What happened to "Bints in Burkas"?' said Donna Strange, who was sitting in. 'I did one and you never ran it.'

'Yes. Whatever happened to "Bints in Burkas"?'

'"Bints in Burkas"? We backed off on that one, Chief.'

Mackelyne read from the minutes: ' ". . . reached the decision not to go ahead, out of deference to the deepest personal convictions of our wankers."'

'And we thought they might dirty-bomb *us*.'

'Mm. And what about the royal angle? The list of demands. It didn't actually *reach* the King, did it?'

'No. They found it floating around in the carpark.'

'But the *tone* of it. Completely outrageous. How did it begin?'

'"Greetings, Slave. God, who controls the clouds, who —"'

'Yes yes. But "slave"! I mean, I find that quite unbelievable. Apart from the Vatican there's not an institution on earth that's older than the monarchy. And along comes some little snake-charmer, some casbah cutthroat . . .'

'Well this is it, Chief. That's what unbelievers are, in their eyes. According to them,' said Clint with a shrug, 'we're shit.'

'But to say the *King's* shit,' said Heaf, who seldom swore. 'I mean, if *he's* shit, if our *king's* shit, then what are *we*? We ought to . . . Ah, but religion's a very curious thing, you know, and that's why we've always steered clear of it. I'm Catholic myself, of course, though partly lapsed. I don't think we've ever pinned it down, have we, Mack? We know everything there is to know about our typical wanker, but what he *believes* remains a mystery.'

Clint said, 'A mystery wrapped in an enigma, Chief.'

'The sampling varies as in no other sphere,' Mackelyne went on. 'There's only one thing we know for sure.'

'Which is?'

'They all hate *nuns*.'

'. . . Well I'm glad we've joined the fray. The smell of cordite at last,' said Heaf. 'Now. Can we at least have a *filler* on Russia–China?'

Smoker sat smoking in Room 2011 of the Bostonian Hotel on Meagure Street. Darius, the seven-foot Seventh Day Adventist, lay shoeless on the sofa, reading the Gideon Bible: Book of Revelation . . . In Room 2013 Ainsley Car was supposedly in the process of having Donna, prior to doing Beryl.

'"Words",' keyed Clint, '"cannot convey the torment I am going through," said a sickened "Dodgem" Car last night in an exclusive interview with the *Morning Lark*. "The pressures on the pro footballer of today are something you wouldn't believe. And as the world knows, I've had a long and painful struggle with my 'demons'. Football isn't about winning. It isn't about losing. It's about glory. And yes, I've feasted on the recognition. Runner-up in the Premiership with Wanderers. A winner's medal in the Ivatex Data Systems Cup with United. That 'banana' consolation goal for Wales in the quarter-final at the Bernabéu.

"'And God knows I've had my share of grief. The endless months in hospital wards and prison yards. The tragic death of Sir Bobby Miles a scant ten days after my 'challenge from hell' and the crippling civil action that followed. Relegation with United. Tell me about it – the booze, the birds, the brawls. I've been there. And who's stood at my side through thick and thin, through the good, the bad, and the bubbly? My childhood sweetheart and now my bride. Little Beryl.'"

"'For the time is at hand,'" said Darius conversationally. 'Her in there: that's Jezebel. "And the ten horns which thou sawest upon the beast, these shall hate the whore, and shall make her desolate and naked, and shall eat her flesh, and burn her with fire."'

'Charming.'

'It's coming, man. The hour is at hand. "And, lo, there was a great earthquake; and the sun became black as sackcloth of hair, and the moon became as blood; and the stars of the heaven fell unto the earth . . ."'

'Oh. That. The comet. Your lot were a bit quick off the mark with the last one. Didn't they all top themselves in advance, your lot, over in California?'

'Not my lot. My lot won't even be here, man. It's all yours.' For a moment Darius laughed quietly. 'You think *America's* powerful. Taste the wrath of the big guy, bro. Coming to *getcha* . . .'

'Where's the meaning in it? Just blind natural forces.'

'No blind. The comet is like me, man. Muscle. Muscle of God.'

The room – the hotel – was postmodern, but darkly, unplayfully so. It seemed that the gunmetal furniture was trying to look like the refrigerator, the television, the safe. Among the gaunt gadgets on Clint's worksurface was an anomalously ovoid Babicom (supplied by the *Lark*'s lone parent, Desmond Heaf). He reached for the dial. You could hear Ainsley's slurred and labouring baritone, Donna's bold alto.

. . . for the both of them. The uh, the mongrel's Bena. The Alsatian's Mick. Know why I love dogs?

Tell me, love.

Dogs don't kick you when you're down.

That's true.

Dogs don't nag at you. Dogs don't rip you fucking off. Dogs don't give you bullshit.

They give you dogshit.

Yeah but . . . yeah but . . . Dogs don't —

'Jesus. Well at least they're in bed by the sound of it.'

'How long's he got?' asked Darius. 'You'd think he'd be making a pig of himself. Donna Strange?'

'"I always enjoy the *Lark*'s annual Top Titcrack Competition (pages 19–26)," typed Clint. "It's a chance to have a few drinks and a laugh and generally relax. After the lunch and the playoff, we sat around with the proud winner, Donna Strange, and had a few drinks. Spirits were high. And it was hard to take your eyes off Donna's cleavage. Talk about Silicone Valley! A bit later someone suggested that we move on to the bar for a few drinks. At this stage, the thought of any monkey business was the last thing on my mind. I'm a happily married man. And after all, little Beryl was due to join me at seven.

'"After a few drinks Donna suggested we move on to the restaurant for a snack and a few drinks. Call me naïve, but I thought little of it when Donna complained of hoarseness in the foyer and asked for a glass of water. We went up to my room on the twentieth floor. I don't know if she was having me on about the tickle in her pipe. But this was for certain. Five seconds after that door closed behind us, Donna Strange had a frog in her —"'

— I've nutmegged their number two and come haring into the box. The goalie's come out to close me down but I've gone and chipped him. Two-all. The crowd's going spare. In the eighty-sevemf minute, Gibbsy's played a long ball out to the left . . .

'The time is nigh.'

'Yeah, well. Donna knows what time it is.'

Clint now typed very fast for fifteen minutes. '"At last,"' he went on, '"she smiled up from beneath my sopping knackers. I needed no second invitation when she offered to start taking her clothes off. In all the excitement I clean forgot that . . ."'

'Five to,' said Darius.

. . . with a power header just before half-time. Shortly after the resumption I —

Where are we now, Dodge? Kestrel Juniors?

Kestrel Juniors? No, love, this is the Under Nines. Shortly after the —

Here, darling, we'd better get started.

. . . I'm uh, I'm not bothered.

Pardon?

I'm not bothered. With Beryl due. Bit embarrassing for a bloke, his wife seeing him with his arse in the air. No offence.

I don't mind, sweetheart, but it's not up to us, is it? Look . . . Undo your . . . If I . . . Just get your . . .

'He's not even got his clobber off!' cried Darius.

'She'll have him. Donna Strange? She'll jack him up. She'll be there.'

And now they could hear her, through the Babicom (its red light straining), through the matt wall: Donna, gathering it up from the depths.

Ainsley Car had impressed it upon Clint that Beryl was a woman of pathological punctuality – especially in her dealings with things like Central London, and public spaces, and Ainsley Car when he was putting himself about . . . Clint approached the door and opened it narrowly. The hand-mirror he held gave him a flickering view of the empty passage. He stuck his head out – his head, like the shaved hump of a camel. The Bostonian had recently been dragged into the twenty-first century, but it remained an old, sprawling, fire-haunted hotel: the corridor unreeled itself like an opium vision, as if to infinity. Clint waited. At 7.58 the specklike pixel of Beryl Car began to detach itself from the distance. So small; and already so strafed by fears. Funny: she's getting nearer – but no bigger. And *shit* nothing himself, he thought . . . Her want of inches was like an exertion of humility; and the stride, too, was just a series of starts and hesitations, buffeted by invisible fingerstabs of mockery or reproach.

Sternly Clint backed into Room 2011. 'Wait for it,' he whispered. 'First the waterworks. Then *boof*.'

With their heads dipped and their mouths stretched in grins of suspense, the two men listened to what they had heard many times before. But only on their television sets: the shuddering, self-righteous birthsong of Donna Strange – so operatically brought to bed.

He gave it half a minute longer, then stepped up and opened the door. He looked left, he looked right.

'You little bitch,' he said.

Clint entered the conference room, the next day, to a standing ovation. There was nothing triumphal in it. Rather, the applause expressed a grave and considered solidarity – a sense that, though much had been achieved, much abided their care; a sense that, however uncertain the outcome, the attempt itself had spoken, and not in a quiet voice, for professional intrepidity and *esprit*.

'Well thanks, lads, for the moral support. Thanks, Chief. Appreciated. It was never going to be easy out there last night, but I was . . . "Doing Beryl" was *my* baby, and I wasn't about to mess this one up. No danger.'

It was Desmond Heaf's practice, when the paper mounted

one of its *coups de théâtre*, to retire to the sidelines for a day or two. He now had the air of a fuddled corporal emerging from a foxhole. 'Would you care to take us through it, Clint?'

'Okay. Beryl's done a runner on us. Yup. Seems she approached the door, heard Donna belting it out – and she's done a runner.' Down the far end of the passage she was disappearing into the motes at the vista's end. 'So be it: plan B. I got Dodgem out from under Donna and hauled him next door. I said, "Dodge? You know what you got to do, boy? You got to go in there and do Donna."'

'I almost gave birth when I saw it,' said Heaf. That morning's edition rattled faintly in his grip: WHY I DID DONNA BY AINSLEY CAR * WORLD EXCLUSIVE * Dodgem Goes Apes**t After Hotel Sex Fest. 'Why I did *Donna*?'

'"Do Donna?" says Dodgem,' said Clint. '"Why do I do Donna?" I said, "You don't *do* Donna. What you do is you 'do' Donna: when I give the word, you make a racket and smash up the furniture, and we'll do the rest." He said, "But why, mate?" I said, "If it's motivation you're after, she's just cost you your marriage." Course I was rewriting it in my head: the piece. Like: "When I realised that those three hours of madness might mean the loss of little Beryl, my anger naturally turned on the rotten slag who'd led me astray." Et cetera. Then I rang Marge Fitzmaurice.'

Clint's colleagues were listening with unrelieved solemnity, their faces dry and grey. Even Supermaniam looked like Voltaire.

'I told Marge to get her vanity case and her fat arse over to the Bostonian instanter . . . It was a pleasure to watch her work. If you turn the page, Chief – the bruises on the inner thigh? And on the bosom? Then we slung in the black eye and the split lip. I told Dodge to get started. Give him a minute and I'll call Security. Well I heard a thud or two, nothing much, and I looked back in: Ainsley's on the floor, and there's Donna in her pants smashing his head in with a glass ashtray. Said he took a right swing at her, so she did him. After that it was just logistics.'

'Had Ainsley been drinking?'

'Drinking? He doesn't remember anything from about noon on. And guess what. He didn't do Donna – and he didn't have her either. Rather talk about his dogs and Kestrel Juniors. Donna straddled him and that, for Beryl, but it was strictly soft-core.'

'Well I never did,' said Heaf. 'Congratulations, Clint. You handled a difficult situation with considerable delicacy, and it all came out for the best. Jeff?'

'Tomorrow', said Strite, 'it's Donna's Story.'

'Angle?'

'Uh . . . She deeply respects the strength of Ainsley's feelings for Beryl. No way in this world will she press charges. Says the rough stuff shrinks to insignificance compared to the five-star porking he gave her earlier. You know: have you seen the size of him?'

There's a word for it. Don't you worry. Oh yeah, there's a word for it all right. Contempt.

The men in the locker-room will gasp with envy. Will gasp with envy.

You can take all the shrinks and minders and trickcyclists or whatever you want to call them . . . It's down to you, mate. It's down to you.

One told him he was crap in bed. One called him a crap fuck. At first he didn't understand, and responded in kind. He invited them to come back and try him again when they'd lost a couple of tons and had their arses fixed. Then understanding began to dawn. 'Oh. Is this as big as Clint gets?' – and this, by now, was a Clint preempurpled with Potentium. Raillery, is it? Later that night: payback. 'Gaw,' he'd said, as she took off her bra: 'when you have a baby, you'll have to get it pissed, you will, before it'll go near that little lot.' 'Oi. Take your ring off for God's sake,' she'd said, after a full minute of foreplay. 'Ring?

168

What ring? That's me watch.' But understanding was beginning to dawn. *Go on, laugh*, he was already muttering as he
unbuckled his belt. *Get your laughing done with*. They didn't
laugh. They said: 'I'm sorry, love, but I can't feel you.' They
said: 'I can't feel you, Clint. I'm trying, but you're not there.'
Not there! Those microscopic insects called no-see-ums: they
bite. And Clint? No-see-um – and no-feel-um. He's not there.
Where is he if he's not there?

The men in the locker-room will gasp with envy, gasp with
envy. There's a word for it: contempt.

You have 125 new messages: half of them offered riven virgins
and pregnant grannies; the other half offered penis-enlargement
strategies – and Clint had tried them all.

Meet the challenge of any woman . . . you will be in total
command . . . remain your secret . . . discovered by Dr Trofim
Frenkel, MD . . . why settle for . . . your maximum potential . . .
herbs found in Polynesia . . . 'I feel great about myself' (PL,
Germany) . . . natural scents that turn women into . . . 55 million
satisfied customers . . . piston assembly . . . non-removable spring-
loaded . . . pistol-trigger press pump . . . 'I am already 12 inches
but I'm going for 14' (RB, USA) . . .

Why stop there, mate? Why not 28? Why not 56? We'd be
like the men on the Esso forecourt, with the steel nozzles, the
flickering digits, the fat splats of car-sweat.

At home Clint had flexers and extenders, fancy philtres in
tubs and tubes, pulleys, lozenges, unguents, humidors, all over
the house, in trunks and suitcases and cardboard boxes and ten-
gallon bags. No African scarifier had subjected himself to more
thorough and various mortification; down there, Clint had under-
gone every possible metamorphosis – except growth. There had
been temporary, and terrifying, enlargements. But nothing you'd
want to keep . . .

Then of course there was the radical solution. And Clint
(while on assignment) had once got as far as the surgery waiting-

room of a Dr Christer Ekland in Stockholm; he filled in forms for ten minutes before he burst out through the door. And by now he had heard many sufficiently gruesome stories about Life after the Knife . . . How the shame – how the shame was predisposed to bring down more shame. Shame came from receiving, from sustaining, that other thing, contempt.

I don't know, mate, but it's down to you. They talk about the shrinks, the minders, the trickcyclists . . . And Clint had always feared such an investigation: he wondered what *else* they'd find . . . But you can't go any further, not down this road. You've got to open your head, and let them in.

'Absolutely glorious weather,' said Heaf. 'Today, London will be hotter than Dubai. What we'll have here is a café society. Like on the Continent.'

Clint said, 'The big news climatewise, they're saying, is the Ice Age. Which is coming up. After uh, ten thousand years of decent weather, muck out the igloo, boys, and hunker down for ninety millennia of frostbite.'

'. . . Then maybe global warming isn't such a bad thing after all!'

'Yeah, they're saying – yeah: but if you wet your pants at the beginning of a blizzard, it won't keep you warm for very long. You're obviously in a brilliant mood, Chief?'

'Well. Yes, well, it's true. I can't be unhappy today.'

Everyone turned to the masterscreen. This was showing the four-second loop of the Princess. Each man present had watched it a couple of hundred times; and the room fell silent as they watched it yet again. *The first second*: supine in the white bath, the Princess is rhythmically spooning water on to her throat with her left hand. *The second second*: she pauses, as if to listen; the splashing, the lapping of the water – this has ceased. *The third second*: she sits up suddenly. *The fourth second*: she turns her head to the right as her body rotates through ninety degrees, causing the water to slide and swirl across her cocked hip. Then black.

'For us, that's a licence to print money,' said Mackelyne. 'If the gagging order holds. They can download it themselves but it's not the same. Our wankers'll want something to keep – to cherish. And that's what we'll give them.'

'Hold your fire, Mack.' Heaf joined his hands behind the back of his neck and said conversationally, 'Donna Strange opened an abortion clinic in Belfast – today at noon . . . There were protestors, of course, and it was covered on local TV. Donna looked radiant.'

Supermaniam said, 'What about the black eye and the split lip?'

'No trace of either.' Heaf added brightly, 'We can always claim she put makeup on it.'

'What, makeup on the makeup?' said Clint. 'I can see why you're not bothered, Chief. After all, April Fool's Day is only three and a half months off. We can say we jumped the gun.'

Heaf guffawed with his head thrown back. He reached across the table for a tasselled folder, saying, 'From Tulkinghorn, Summerson and Nice, no less. It seems that we are now faced with the legal question of whether our photocaptions constitute a uh . . . "an incitement to masturbation".' He held up a clipping between finger and thumb. '"Does Steffi give you a stiffi? Roll your sleeve up, son, and get to work!" Or the following, from your Blinkie Bob Video Review, Clint. "You'll be needing a box of tissues for this one (make that a mansize!). And I *don't* mean it's a weepie."'

'Tulkinghorn, Summerson and Nice,' said Clint. 'Don't they represent the Walthamstow Wanker?'

'They do. You see, the "erotic material" being consulted at the public baths on that fateful day was nothing other than the *Morning Lark*. So the Walthamstow Wanker . . .'

'Is a wanker! You're doing my bonce in here, Chief. Tell you what. Can I have a month's holiday starting tomorrow?'

'Course you can, dear boy. The thing is, none of this matters, journalistically, because everyone pretends we're not a newspaper. Well all that is about to change.'

Heaf stood. They waited.

'I'm late, I'm late,' he sang, 'for a very important date . . .'

'Where at, Chief?'

'At Number Ten Downing Street. By order of the King.'

'. . . They'll gag you. They'll gag you, Chief.'

'Maybe they will, maybe they will. Uh, what did we have in mind for tomorrow?'

Supermaniam unfurled the mockup. It said: 'Souvenir Issue * The Little Princess Frame By Frame * FUTURE Q. OF E. GANGF**KED ON CAMERA??'

'Mm. Await my call. That may need some toning down.'

'If you feel strongly about it, Chief,' said Clint, 'we'll add another question mark.'

It came through when he was back at his workstation and talking to the travel people, Virtually There. It said:

fl@ e, 49 m@tock est8, n7

dear clint: @ last – the dex r
clearing! he's not a gr8 hint-taker,
orl&o, & he hasn't noticed i've
stopped talking 2 him. but he has
noticed i've stopped making his t.
'y don't u make my t any more?'
& i say, 'you can make your own
bloody t!' but he's as obstin8 as a
mule. th@'s the word 4 him: asi9.
he still wants 6 every nite, but i've
got a new str@agem: not washing.
let's c how long he can st& the
s10ch! . . . a whole new future is

opening up 4 me now. a new
2morrow, clint. my thoughts &
hopes r turning 2wards some1 else
– some1 not a 1,000 miles from
where u st&, my v dear friend. on
our first d8, whenever th@ may b,
if we feel like a cuddle, y the 1
not! but th@ doesn't have 2 lead
2 anything but sleep, & in the
morning i'll make the t! still, i
think it's a good thing 4 u 2 take
a journey 2 distant 1&s – 2
reflect, 2 ponder, 2 rumin8. i shall
be w8ing here 4 u – like a nun, a
noviti8, ready 2 become a bride of
X! well, dear 1, i kiss your h&s.
fare 4th, & find the lite! k8.

So on his last Sunday before jetting off, Clint drove to N7:
just to reconnoitre, and maybe catch a glimpse. Trapped in traffic
on Parkway, and gazing out, he noticed a smart-looking woman
whom he thought you'd call fanciable, despite the doublepram
she wielded. As he watched, she pulled up short, came round in
front of the two nippers – and crouched, in earnest interchange.
Shit: if he'd been in a normal car, instead of the Avenger, he'd
have been able to see right up her skirt. Clint moved on.

'Start again. He what?' said Russia Meo.

'He hugged me too hard,' said Billie.

'Start again. Where was Imaculada?'

'In the kitchen with Baba. I went out to the shed where Daddy
was and we saw the fox on the roof.'

'You saw the fox through the skylight? Through the glass?
And then?'

'I couldn't breathe. Daddy hugged me too hard.'

February 14 (12.25 p.m.): 101 Heavy

The man in 2A returned to his seat. The woman in 2B, Reynolds Traynor, said,

'Why do you keep doing that? Don't look so stricken. You're making me nervous.'

'It's just a precaution.'

'Relax. Have a drink. Flying's safe. It's safer than walking.'

'Depends how you figure it. Per passenger-mile – right. But if you figure it per journey, it's about the same as motorcycling.'

'. . . When you grope your way up and down the cabin – why do you keep doing that?'

'It's so I can get to the emergency doors with my eyes shut. In case of smoke. Only I'd be doing it on my knees. More oxygen. Avoid the flashover. Twenty-two per cent of aviation fatalities are caused by fire.'

'Really.'

'Second only to blunt trauma.'

Flight Engineer Hal Ward: Ah, that's better. I am a whole new hombre . . . If, as they say, you can judge the health of a carrier by the age of the flight attendants, then you're in okay shape.

First Officer Nick Chopko: That's because they're all dead by the time they're thirty-five. This is CigAir, pal.

Ward: Flew Air K last week and the broads could hardly walk . . . That one in Business, what is it, Conchita? Awesome bod. Oh, mercy, I could do her some harm.

Captain John Macmanaman: The hell with that kind of talk, Flight Engineer. Not in my cockpit, son.

Ward: Sorry, Cap.

Macmanaman: Forget it. Hey, Nick. Look at the power. Look at the speed. Oh sure. We're going to stall at maximum up here . . . Nick? Hal? See what I see? Thrust-reversers are engaged.

Chopko: Jesus Christ. It's fictitious, right?

Macmanaman: Damn right it's fictitious. Or we'd be in cartwheel.

If it's fictitious – what *else* is fictitious?

In Pallet No. 3 the corpse of Royce Traynor minutely rearranged itself. Its chin now rested on one of the canisters marked HAZMAT. Extreme turbulence would be needed before Royce could make his next move.

His mahogany coffin was hard and heavy. Like the past, he was dead and gone. But Royce was still hard and heavy with it: hard and heavy with the past.

PART II

PART II

CHAPTER SIX

1. The Decembrist

Wearing a black tracksuit as refulgent as perfect shoeshine, he stepped out into the afternoon. His storefresh white trainers, his dark glasses, his bronzed countenance, his backswept silver hair: in the pharmacy, from which he was now absenting himself, they called him the Professor or the Englishman. But he was the Decembrist: well advanced into the final month of his year. It was a distinguished face, its lines apparently connected to something ancient or the study of something ancient – Etruscan Pottery, Linear B.

But here he was, in a modern setting: video rental, liquor locker, radio shack. The Decembrist was of medium height (and was heading, by now, towards less than medium); he was not conspicuous in a country – America – where old men dressed like children. Watch an aeroplane climbing a blue sky for long enough and a globule of sunshine will eventually kiss it and coat it and drip from it. So, too, with the glossy garb of the Decembrist, which blackly glittered. Above the suit, his handsome, martyred face. Below it, the white dots of his gyms. Out in the lot the cars were waiting, all in line but all dissimilar, like a conscript army of machines.

There was caution in his stride but nothing frail or halt, which was just as well: a recreational vehicle weighing several tons jerked backwards out of its trap, and the Decembrist's hands flew from his pockets as he himself jerked clear, seeming to levitate, with an avian lightness. But the sound he made was equine – whinnying, rearing, longtoothed.

The driver drew level, a cellphone nestling in the cup of his jaw (and what beautiful golden hair he had, also busy in the light, with its bullion, its specie), and said, in answer to the Decembrist's disbelieving stare:

'Fuck *you*.'

Having manoeuvred itself into the clear, the great bus surged forward, and now the film rewound – with the Decembrist moving suddenly into its speed and the wheels yelping to a halt six inches from his knees. After some exasperated honking the driver reversed, swerved, and sped on his way, the word *asshole* included in the passing gulp of his rhythm and blues.

The Decembrist paused, his lips working, and then pushed on to his German saloon.

He sat, days later, on an upright chair by the swimming-pool – the swimming-pool and its motion jigsaw. The pool moved, always and helplessly, but the man was still, his head thrown back as if in agonised exhaustion. Around him the acres of grass, the couch grass, the bent grass, the cheat grass; and the squirt of the ceaseless sprinklers, hissing like a monstrous cicada . . . In one movement he stirred and stood. Cruise-wear, now: the swing top, the blue pantaloons, the white canvas deck-shoes. He also sported a dude-ranch cowboy belt, which he now straightened. The cartridge sockets were empty, but the holsters had been modified to contain two slender spraycans. One spraycan specialised in mosquitoes and other insects of the air; the other spraycan specialised in ants.

First, an hour with his accountant. Then an hour with his gardener. He was served lunch on the canopied deck. He wiped his mouth and got to his feet. The wasp came weaving towards him the way they do, like a punchy old southpaw, with its half-remembered moves, its ponderous fakes and feints. He drew with his left and caught it full in the face. And the wasp *rose up*, bristling in grief and femininity and youth. They meandered towards you so middle-aged, but they too had youth, and delicacy and clarity of colour. He didn't stay to watch its bouncings and wormings and coilings.

He moved on to the stables, and had words with a well-built young man called Rodney Vee.

'Rodney.' With a remind-me intonation and a lordly frown he asked, 'How long . . . ?'

'Since Monday, sir.'

'And where are we now?'

'Friday, sir.'

He nodded and made a further indication with a sideways movement of his head.

They went past the back of the imported barn and down some steps and into the anteroom of the disused garage. He again wagged his head before Rodney opened the inner door.

At first it sounded like a large animal trying to breathe, and then it sounded like a small animal trying to cry.

'That'll be all, Rodney,' he said.

He stepped forward. In the far corner a young man was strapped naked to a baronial dining-chair with a sack over his head. The young man's chest was shaking, lamenting, and his breath was fierce and nasal – eddy upon eddy.

The Decembrist pulled up a footstool. Grumblingly he sorted through the tray of implements at his feet: skewers, chisels.

Half an hour passed.

He stood up. He lifted the cowl of sacking. After a flustered glance round the room his head dropped and he reached for his spraycans, one in the left, one in the right.

The young man's golden hair was gone.

'Open your eyes! *Behold*. Fuck . . . *ME*?' said Joseph Andrews.

'You can take this *fucking little bumboy*, and stuff him in a *fucking mailbag*, and go and . . . and go and . . .' Andrews caught his breath. 'And go and sling him over the *fucking top* at Quaker Quarry!'

'It will be done, sir. It will be done,' said Rodney Vee, who then closed the inner door and added, 'Are you serious, Boss?'

'Well . . . Give him a few hours to compose his thoughts. Nah. Where's he live?'

'Vermilion Hills, Boss.'

'Yeah. You *tell* him it's the Quarry. But you take him to fucking Vermilion Hills and sling him out the fucking van. On the road. And not lightly. One . . . two . . . three. *Boof.* Eh up. Ruthie rings Queenie, right?'

Rodney nodded. They were coming up the steps and into the sun.

'She says, "Mum? You won't like it, but I'm marrying Ahmed." And Queenie's gone, "What? You marry that Ahmed and you never darken me door again." "But I love him!" All this. Six months go by. The phone rings and it's Ruthie. "Mum! Come and take me away! Aw, what he's been doing to me!" "So," says Queenie, "your sins've found you out." "Come on, Mum, don't fuck about." "Now calm down, love. I'll be over in a minicab. Where are you?"

'It's a fucking great mosque of a place on The Bishop's Avenue. Queenie's come through the gates and up the drive. She've rung the bell and the butler's led her through five reception rooms. Picassos. Rembrandts. Cézannes. Ruthie's on the couch, crying its little heart out. Queenie's give her a hug and gone, "Ruthie, what is it? Tell your mother. I'm sure you and Ahmed can sort this out."

'Ruthie's gone, "Mum? Aw, what he's been doing to me! When I come here, me arsehole was the size of a five-pee piece." "Yes, dear?" "Well now it's the size of a *fifty*-pee piece. Take me home." Queenie looks round the room and says, "Let's get it straight. You're giving up all this for forty-five pee?"

'Ah, here she comes. Here come them famous lils.'

2. Cora Susan

Here she comes: Cora Susan.

She had a hundred yards of lawn to cross. Seen from that distance, she looked like the platonic ideal of a young mother. But where were the children? Peering through the prisms of the sprinkler spray, you expected to make them out, the children, circling her, tumbling at her feet. That must be why she walked so slowly, with an air of dreamy purpose (always one step behind, one step beyond) – to keep pace with the children. But there were no children . . . As usual, she wore a dress of white cotton, and a broad straw hat. The straps of a straw bag depended from her left shoulder (is that where she kept the wipes and diapers, the rolled-up sock with spit on it – for emergency cleansings of childish mouths? No: there were no children). A slight arrhythmia in the clack of her sandals: time delay, diminishing as she neared. Cora Susan's hair was long and straight and fine, and a lucent grey, reminding you that grey was a colour – a colour like any other colour. She was thirty-six and five foot one.

'Have a chair, dear. Paquita's fetching you a nice glass of wine. I have unfortunate news.'

She took off her hat but remained standing on the lined deck. Unanswerably womanly, but not a mother. The spheres of her grey eyes were too shallow, and without the faults and nicks that they give you – that children give you. Her mouth contained something ungenerous, something resolutely unindulgent; it did not extend outwards into the world – it stayed within. And the secondary sexual characteristics, the breasts, the famous breasts. They were above all binocular: they were the eyes of a different creature, a different type of being, with qualities not necessarily shared by Cora Susan – candour, innocence, even purity. No child would maul them. There were reasons for all this.

Wine for Cora, one glass served by Paquita, and the bottle kept in an ice-bucket on the tray. For Joseph Andrews – Lucozade (couriered out from England by the gross). Every few seconds he slowly reached forward and touched her, rested a light palm on her, almost doctorly – on the elbow, the hand, the wrist.

'It's your father, dear. What can I say? He's gone. He's passed away . . . No great shock but he was your *father*, Cora. Now. You was – you was never told the truth, dear. Your gran's version, dear. How'd it go?'

'As it was handed down to me,' she said in her accentless and warmly civilised voice, 'Dad crippled himself falling off some mountain, and Mum converted and went to Israel. And I went to Canada with Old Ma Susan. That bit's true.'

'. . . Mick Meo did him, Cora. Your own grandfather did your dad.'

Audibly she breathed in, breathed out.

'Relations between the Susans and the Meos was never of the smoothest. And I don't just mean your mum and dad's marriage. I know what Mick Meo done to Damon Susan. He drew a nine for it: attempted murder. How much do you uh . . . ?'

'Oh, Jo, please. Tell me everything.'

'That's the spirit, Cora. That's my girl . . . Your mum and dad was chucking things at each other even before they was engaged. It was that kind of uh, relationship – a right old scrap. Then, as ill chance would have it, come the day when your mum calls Mick and tells him Damon's took a liberty with her. A right liberty.'

'Meaning?'

'Not to put uh, too fine a point on it, dear, he give her one up the khyber.'

With no change in her tone and modulation Cora said, 'He give me one up the khyber and all.'

'I *know* he did, dear.' Again, the hand on her wrist. 'And if *Mick* had known that then there's no chance Damon'd've lived. There'd have been none of this fucky *nattempted*. That I can assure you.

'There was no mobile phones in them days. Leda's left a message at the workshed. Mick's out nicking high-voltage cables – dangerous work, skilled work – but he was a very good thief was Mick. He calls back: "He *what*?" But Mick's out in Stoke and it's the fucking miners' strike and he . . . Anyway. He's gone in there at dawn.'

'Floral Grove. Stoke Newington.'

'He's gone in there at dawn. Your mum and dad's fast asleep. In the same bed. So, I don't know: must have patched it up. For the time being. Your granddad's gone and drawn the curtains back. You know: rise and shine. Now unfortunately Mick's still in his work clothes. Heavy boots with the shallow spikes. And the reinforced gauntlets – for them cables. Oh and his helmet. So he's on Damon now, straddling him like, and nutting him and that, and the roundarms with the big gloves. Then Leda's on *Mick*: seems she's had a change of heart if you please. So Mick's gone and locked her in the bathroom, and he give her a tap and all, unfortunately – but she was his own *daughter*, Cora . . .

'Damon's lying there weltering in his own blood. "Ah fuck. Ah Jesus." All this. Mick's gone, "How's your nose?" "How's me *nose*? I'm blind, mate!" Then he've started trying to uh, you know, "reason" with him. You know: "Uh, Mick mate. Look uh, no complaints. Fair's fair. I stepped out of line. You taught me a lesson. That's it. End of." And Mick's gone, "It's a crime of passion we got here, boy." Course he's been puzzling for a means of doing Damon for years. "This is *nothing*, son. This is *nothing*."

'Mick's dragged Damon on to the floor and got on the bed hisself. Then he's broke both his legs. Jumping like. Then, when you could do what you liked with them, Damon's pins is wedged sideways and your granddad's taking running kicks at his cods and his chopper. With the workboots, more's the pity. Damon's not making much noise any more but now Leda's come round and she's yelling her head off next door. But Mick didn't pay her no mind.

'When he's broke his arms and all his fingers, he picks him up by his hair and what's left of his bollocks and slings him out the window, sad to say.'

'And was the window open at the time?'

'Unfortunately not.'

'I'm trying to remember the house. They were on the second floor, weren't they?'

'Alas no. They was on the third.'

'There was a lawn there. It was just lawn in the back.'

'If only. That really *was* unfortunate. Just the previous week Damon's had a rockery put in. So he come down on that. And it was that what done for him, landing on his bonce as he did. He was in Intensive Care for nearly a year. And of course Mick went away for his nine. Course, he could have pleaded uh, mitigating circumstances. "Your Honour, I did him because he's give me daughter one up the khyber." But he didn't want to tar her with it, so he never. Then Old Ma Susan spirits you away to Vancouver. And you was lost to the Meos for ever.'

'And Mum?'

'You're not touching your wine, dear. As for your mum, she done the rounds a bit and then settled down with Tony Odgers. Then he's gone and got a seven for demanding with menaces. Teddy Ambrose come out at last and she's took up with him. Then Teddy's got cut to pieces in a ruck outside the World Upside Down. Your mum's played the field a bit, then she's pulled herself together and for a time she's made a go of it with Ian Thorogood. Then he gets himself choked in a headlock whilst in police custody. Things was going not bad between your mum and Frank Purdom. Then Nick Odgers come out, for about a week, but long enough to do Frank Purdom, and your mum's back to her old tricks. Keith Room was very good with her till he pulled a twelve, and then she've raised eyebrows by shacking up with Thelonius Curtly. And when he gets hisself topped she's let herself down, many thought, by throwing in her lot with Lon

Chang You. But she was on the drink and worse by then. To be perfectly frank with you, Cora, her reputation was beginning to suffer. They was calling her Khyber Kath by the end. Funny kind of name, that. I never did learn how she come by the "Kath" bit of it. How you feeling, dear?'

'Oh, tolerably well.'

'You're a hard girl, Cora. You've had to be. You frighten even me sometimes – what I seen in you. Now okay, your dad weren't the best of fathers, but he was your father. Your natural father, dear. Damon done what he done. Damon was Damon. He messed with you, and there ain't no excuse for that. But you was still a *family*. And Mick Meo, by his overly hasty behaviour . . . Now if I know my Cora Susan she's not going to bend over for that. She's going to want to *hurt* somebody. And there's only one of them left. Uncle Xan.'

'Uncle Xan.'

'I give him a smack meself the other day. About something nothing whatsoever to do with the Susans.'

'Oh?'

'He fucking grassed me up. Then he's gone to the papers saying he never! *And* he called me a mad prick . . .' Joseph Andrews shook his head and gave a smile of yokellish incredulity. On the table before them lay a green folder. He reached for it. 'Here: ". . . whoever did me in October or had me done . . . they think I've been telling tales to the Old Bill. And that is something I would *never do* . . . They can stick red-hot pokers up my arse . . . whoever did me I tell him, you come down and . . ." Now that's *game*, that is,' he added with unqualified admiration. 'No less than he should have said, of course. But these days that's *game*. There's Mick in him, Cora. And there's Mick in you and all.'

'And the money.'

'And the money. Hebe's money. Skinned you out of it. You're going back for the funeral, of course? . . . Have a read of that. And the other matter?'

'Beyond all expectation.'

'Gaw, I got to pinch meself with the price we're getting on this one. Talk about a thrust.' He brought his clawed hands together. 'The *double play*. I tell you, darling, if it all goes through all right you can *have* my end of it. I *give* it to you, dear. Jesus, the *satisfaction*. It's beautiful. Cora? We done them sweet.'

The green file went in the straw bag and Cora Susan kissed Joseph Andrews and walked away across the coarse sward. Moving with an air of dreamy purpose – always one step behind, one step beyond.

3. Denizen

About twenty miles to the north-east Clint Smoker was settling into his half of a cabana in the grounds of a Moorish mansion known locally as the Ponderosa. In Clint's quarters, as in everybody else's, there was a large and lavish reproduction of Michelangelo's 'The Creation' on the wall facing the picture window. Clint typed:

> Chief: Got here all right. The hotel's gorgeous. My companion, Kate, is particularly taken with the oiled dwarves who line the driveway day and night. Shop. You've got your gagging order and I hope you're happy.

Yeah, thought Clint. According to Jeff Strite, Heaf was summoned, not to Downing Street, but to a sweltering basement at the FPA – along with every other e-zine and nude-mag chancer in the British Isles. A man from the Palace with a double-barrelled name came on and told them that the material on the Princess was a fake and a fiction, and would they please shut up about it. Heaf returned to the *Lark* shedding tears of pride.

I think you're experiencing an accounting problem in the marble department, but that's me: cynical. Still, we can pursue related and parallel themes on little Vicky. I have an idea or two. Here as promised is the revisionist editorial on the Walthamstow Wanker:

Over the past month, a tragedy has unfolded in the heart of Essex.

For two days and two nights, an innocent and injured man — and we're proud to call him a *Lark* reader — languished without treatment in a Rotherhithe nick before being released on bail.

He now faces charges of public indecency.

And for what?

Health boffins have long agreed that a regular visit to Thumb Street is crucial to masculine well-being.

Every man-jack of us knows that a decent toss reduces tension, setting you up for the rest of the day.

And there's nothing better for a sound night's sleep.

Imagine.

In the seclusion of an unoccupied area of a public baths, this stainless individual was seeking relief over his daily edition of the paper you now hold in your hand.

But who should burst in on him but some old boiler with a bucket and mop.

Congratulations, darling!

You f**ked that one up!

In his confusion, and sadly impeded by his clothing, he slipped on the damp stone steps, incurring serious injury.

Little did he know that his tribulation — yes, his martyrdom — was yet to begin.

We say to this man that he has not been forgotten.

We say to this man that we are with him and will stay by his side.

We say: fist your mister for the Walthamstow One.

Clint had briefly admired his bathroom but had not yet used it. Now he lifted the ox-collar; he bestrid the bowl. After a few seconds, he found he was undergoing a sense of gradual depersonalisation, as if about to receive the introductory chords and colours of a life-changing illness. His stare moved to the left. The basin: how small it was. His stare moved to the right. The bogroll-holder, the actual gauge of the tissue: scaled down. And the can he straddled: like a potty. When you wiped yourself it looked . . . Yes, there was definitely a gain in contrast. And every little helped.

Strollingly he returned to his studio. Shower and change in a minute: off with the aeroplane-wear (the radiant trainers, the aerodynamic shell suit) and on with something smart. An inaugural drinks party was scheduled for half past five. Meet your fellow — clients? inmates? guests? What did the brochure call them: residents? No, *denizens*. Denizens of the San Sebastiano Academy for Men of Compact Intromission . . . The reproduction on the wall facing the picture window. Whew, the state of that Adam. Come on, you've got to fit him up a bit better than that. You can't send him out there with that *cashew* between his legs.

Was Michelangelo taking the piss — taking the michael? Was God?

4. At Ewelme

'*Qi?* Q, *i?* No no no. You can't have a q without a u. Now if you let that stand I shall most certainly challenge . . . Challenge! . . . Where are we. Q, i, indeed. What does it mean? Ah, do you see, all the q's have u's after them. Hello, that's very odd. "An individual person's life-force, the free flow of which within the body is believed to ensure physical and spiritual health." . . . Well God help us. What happens now? *I* get docked the points. Bother. And you've done it *twice*: two *qi*s and an *if*. On the triple word.'

'Sixty-nine.'

'Sixty-*nine*? I'm now minus thirteen. And I'm changing my letters. Where's the bag?'

'I'm sorry, Daddy, but please may I be excused?'

'Oh don't go up now, darling. We've barely started. Stay and have a lovely warm hot chocolate at least . . .'

A minute later Henry said, 'What would you, Bugger? I'm trying to keep her spirits up and it's exhausting her. And me. And when I try to draw her out . . .'

'Write to her, sir,' said Brendan. 'Write.'

The King stayed up late, listening to the Irish Sea. Ewelme stood on the north-western tip of the Welsh peninsula, at the end of a mile-long single-lane causeway. Its situation, together with the infallibly dreadful weather, deterred all intruders – and indeed all visitors: no one who had stayed at Ewelme ever willingly returned. Henry, at his desk, in his overcoat, felt his ears vibrate as the tower bell sounded the quarter-hour. The wind was committing murders in the night, sudden abductions, terrible smotherings . . .

My dearest sweetheart,

My soul hurts for you, it truly does. I have never seen you so deeply low. Even after Mummy's accident, the energy of your youth somehow seemed to carry you onward. Now you sleep sixteen hours a day and hardly eat anything. (And when you are awake you're curled up with the Koran, or the Upanishads or the Targum or God knows what.) I do wish you'd agree to have a <u>chat</u> with Sir Edward, if nothing more.

My darling, I don't know <u>exactly</u> what is troubling you. I know roughly what is troubling you. While you are in all things the chief sufferer, this ignorance is very heavy for your father. Rather than agonising about something in particular, I find I'm agonising about <u>everything</u>. I dare not close my eyes for fear of what I may see. I implore you to tell me what actually happened in the Yellow House, my dearest (who surprised you there?). And I earnestly do believe that you will feel the benefit. And if you had some sort of a romp with one of those pretty Arab boys, what of it?

The vultures. Our official position is that the material is faked. You and I are aware that the material, at least in part, is <u>not</u> faked. I was less confident than Brendan. None the less, there has been no rebuttal, let alone refutation, which is presumably in the enemies' power. This is very much to the good (it has quietened things down a bit). Brendan says their silence reflects a certain incapacity on their part. And there is another fairly encouraging likelihood, which I will tell you about if you will only talk to me.

I have just read this through, and it's such a curate's egg! 'Good in parts' – albeit thoroughly rotten. I yearn to express the unconditional love and sympathy I feel, but I just sound selfish and pompous. It's my poor character!

Sweetheart, my one, my only jewel, I beseech you: let us be in this together. I want to reach out and physically take some of the weight from your shoulders. Remember. It's we two now.

5. February 14 (1.10 p.m.): 101 Heavy

Captain John Macmanaman: How's our Flight Engineer?
First Officer Nick Chopko: Out cold.
Macmanaman: He can coax the computer along, I'll give him that. I'd have killed it and gone to direct law . . . You know the rooftiles they have in England? Sheets of grey slate?

Chopko: Like machetes.

Macmanaman: This one, you could see it coming. Rennie thought it was a dead bird. It just twirled into him. Here.

Chopko: Jesus.

Macmanaman: . . . Royce Traynor was only ever going to fly CigAir when he was in the condition he's in today.

Chopko: Dead.

Macmanaman: Dead. For him it was like a mission. Rennie said there was nothing – repeat, nothing – he liked more than telling someone to put a cigarette out. He'd get up in the middle of the night and call a cab if there was a good chance of telling someone to put a cigarette out. And get this. Rennie smoked a pack a day for forty-three years without him knowing. He would have killed her. *Killed* her. I think she did it to have something on him, to stick it to him. Why don't people leave, Nick? Why don't they just leave?

Chopko: I don't know either.

Macmanaman: Addictive personality . . . I don't like it up here. It's too thin up here. I don't like the physics of it up here. The difference between max and stall is just a couple of knots. It's like a slide on black ice. Ask for three seven oh. Wait. The windshear: feel it's moving around in back of us. It's like . . . Uh, put everybody down, Nick. And the girls when they've secured the carts. This is my third time and I can feel it coming. There's clear air [clear air turbulence] out there. I can feel it this time.

Four minutes later Flight 101 dropped a thousand yards at the speed of gravity: thirty-two feet per second per second. The coffin of Royce Traynor leapt from the floor of Pallet 3 and smashed into its ceiling. After a beat it smashed back down again. It landed corner-first on one of the canisters marked HAZMAT. There was an atrocious sneeze of thick pink liquid, then a steadier, seeping flow. After twenty-five minutes the dominant pool of thick pink liquid would begin to fume.

6. Apologia – 1

Joseph Andrews was in his office, upstairs. Two sloping sheets of glass formed an isosceles triangle with the floor. You could see every freckle, every nostril hair : . . He held a microphone in his hand: buxom, corded, the mike of a bygone crooner. The *pause* button gave a little *click* whenever he freed it or engaged it.

'[*Click.*] I want to tell you me story. Man to man. Let you be the judge. Let you be the judge . . . [*Click.*] . . . Gaw, where do I . . . ? Go on then. Go on. [*Click.*]

'I had such a reputation for enduring pain that when the prison dentist offered me an injection I felt pretty much duty-bound to chin him.

'So he've gone off to see *his* dentist. And then of course the screws done me in the Strong Cell. Par for the course. Me cheek was out here. When the dentist come back [*click*] with his fucking jaw in a sling [*click*] . . . Well. They took a right liberty. I was in a straitjacket with me head in a clamp and me mouth wedged open with a sawblade. Ooh and that dentist, he's give me abscess a right going over. Dear oh dear. They was watching to see if I'd flinch but I never. [*Click.*]

'[*Click.*] There ain't a form of punishment meted out in His Majesty's Prisons that I've not took. Bread and water, deprivation of mattress, Refractory Block, PCFO. In the hospital wing they've give me the Blinder and the Crapper. They slip it in your coffee. The Blinder ain't so bad – you just go all legless like. But the Crapper . . . you can kill a man in a week in that manner. I've had the Cat and the Birch. It's a fallacy that I used to whistle while they was giving me the corporal. But on the thirteenth stroke I used to do a lovely yawn, and he'd come in with a will on the final five. Trying to make you cry out. No chance. The Birch is worst. It's more uh, detrimental to a man's dignity, being as how it's on your arse. I mean you got some man on your shoulders, for the Cat. But it's just a baby, your arse is.

'Them's only the *official* punishments. They've pissed in me tea and flobbed on me grub. For five weeks they've kept me in the Box on the Strap Plank: another right liberty. But what it is is: the niggles. Like me mum come up to see me in Durham – a two-day journey in them days – and an hour before she's due they've gone and transferred me to Strangeways! That's how low they'll stoop. These are men who live to see other men confined. Like they take away your Association on a technicality – and there's that little smirk. You see that look on they face, and you know you'll have to do them. Just a question of when. And then of course they do you. Fact of life. [*Click.*]

'[*Click.*] I want to tell you me story, man to man. Right or wrong, let you be the judge.

'Like many a face I was, in me youth, an avid boxer. I won four of me first eleven fights at Bermondsey Baths. Which don't sound too clever. But I never lost one! In fact they was all knock-outs. See, I had an unfortunate tendency to get meself disqualified. Instead of standing there with me hand held high, as victor, while the other bloke got stretchered off, I'd still be kneeling on the canvas and giving him what for. It was a struggle to uh, channel me aggression. In the eleventh fight I've left the ref for dead and all. So they banned me. [*Click.*] And Mr Shackleton, the Director of the YBPA, never knew what hit him – I come up on him that nice. [*Click.*] After that decision I had no choice but to turn to a life of crime.

'Me first trouble with the Law was for possession of an offensive weapon. Not *def*ensive, oh no. *Off*ensive. The Old Bill gives you a spin and it's one of them uh, circular conversations. "Oi. What's this?" "What's it look like?" "Why you carrying a knife?" "I always do." "What for?" "I always carry a knife." "Yeah but why?" "Because I always do." Blah blah blah. I was eight. So then the social's upped and packed me off to Approved School. And then of course I did me Borstal. And even in me boxing days I've had a spell or two in Pentonville for Smash and Grab.

Smash and Grab: definition of a glass brassière, if you like. This'd be the late Thirties. Then the war come . . . Now don't get me wrong. We was patriotic and that. In their struggle against the spectre of Nazism, we wished the armed forces all the luck in the world. But you wasn't going to be donning togs for the powers-that-be. No chance. [*Click*.] And if a Tommy come your way on a dark night, the slag'd live to regret it. [*Click*.] So in the war years you was either inside or on your toes from the Conscription. In 1944, when I was finishing me three in Wormwood Scrubs, Sir Oswald Mosley, of Blackshirt fame, and his wife, Lady Diana, was interned there. There was a plan on to do him during Exercise, but he come over as a perfectly reasonable sort of bloke and we've left him be.

'Things opened up beautiful after the war, with all the austerity. We was forging ration-books and otherwise like billy-o. Then in the year of your birth I get me first decent thrust – and me first serious bird. Swings and roundabouts. [*Click. Click*.] Funny word that: *bird*. Comes from *birdlime*, rhyming with *time*. Birdlime was the sticky stuff they put on the branches of trees to kill the birds. Sticky fingers, see: thieving. But it's the birds that cop it, not the branches, so it don't quite work out. *Bird* also means "girl". A *richard* is a sort, Richard the Third rhyming with bird. [*Click*.] Rhyming-slang: load of bollocks. [*Click*.] But I'm told the word *bird* comes from *bride*, originally. Anyway.

'It was the Airport Job. Heath Row – two words – it was in them days. Also known as the Protective Assurance Robbery. An overnight cargo of diamonds plus £160,000 in hard cash – millions in today's money. The guards was supposed to be drugged: barbitone in they coffee. But when I give one a nudge [*click*] with me fucking iron bar [*click*] the others have jumped up and steamed in. They was Ghost Squad! Well, I don't know, they must have expected schoolboys. They hadn't reckoned on me, Ginger, Dodger, Gimlet, Whippo, Chick and Yocker, and we did them something gruesome. When we come out the coppers is there mob-handed and we've had another almighty mill. I reckoned I was well away. I've slipped under a police van and clung on to the exhaust. You know: first traffic-light and I'd be away. But they've only put the sirens on and roared off to Battersea nick – fifteen mile away. By then me chest and forearms was welded to the pipe. They had to cut me free before they banged me up, and I still bear them scars. One of the Ghost Squad boys was on the critical list, and offing a copper was a topping offence in them days. I even got me mum to send him a bunch of grapes – to a copper. But that's one of them uh [click] them uh [click] them strange paradoxes you've stuck youself with when you gone and played the game I've played.

'I served every hour of me fourteen. In them days, if you was flogged, you never lost no remission for subsequent misdemeanours. So me first week in Winson Green I thought: let's do the Governor, and get the Cat. I done the Governor: spun the legs out from under him in the vegetable garden and come down on his face with me shovel. The screws've give me a right sticking – win some, lose some – but when me flogging come up, there's questions from the Home Secretary in the House of Commons! And God stone me if they don't go chucko. I've had some black hours on the in, but nothing compares to that morning when they've gone and cancelled me Cat. I had so many run-ins, thereafter, they was always trying to have me declared mental!

'When I come out after me fourteen – that was 1949, so this'd be 1963 – I find meself in an awkward situation. That's what so often happens after you come out: like as not, you're straight back in. Me sister Polly was at that period the common-law wife of Pongo Droy. A while ago Pongo've cut Noel Shortly – who's nicked him! That's to say: *Noel's reported Pongo to the Law*. Which, for me . . . Well Pongo's not having that, is he? He's pulled three months, which is a bit stiff, because in them days you could go berserk with a blade and expect no more than a ten-bob fine. While Pongo's away his brother Hughie's done Duncan Shortly,

Noel's dad. So Duncan's nephew, Cecil O'Rourke, puts Hughie's lights out in the World Upside Down. Pongo's fucking come out, he's [*click*] *fuck* . . . Ah, fuck it [*click*] he's glassed Cecil, and now he's gone looking for Noel. Who was waiting for him, with a sawn-off. Pongo's lost both legs from the knee down and Polly's come running to me. I've only been out a week. I wasn't interested till she told me Noel'd nicked Pongo for the stabbing. That got me off me arse. The result was I drew an eight for Aggravated Manslaughter.

'It was 1975 when I come out – I served an extra three for me part in the so-called "mangle riot" at Winson Green. And by now I'm going: enough's enough. As you yourself know, a man has to adapt and change with the times. A further two-year term for Grievous give me more leisure to think. I hadn't been out for long when I was fancied for a murder [*click*] which I fucking done [*click*], the case being dismissed in the absence of any evidence whatsoever. And Life was eighteen years in them days. No, son, I said to meself. Time to turn over a new leaf. Strike out on a different path. I've gone and emigrated to the Costa del Sol. And thus began me long and, in the end, tragic association with Keith the Snake. [*Click*.]

'Get this in here. [*Click*.] You don't know of me personally, but me name might ring a bell. I don't know – are you a reading man? Me, I never was a reader. Didn't seem to have the time. Nah: wasn't that. See, in prison, it's just another way they can hurt you. "Where's your book gone, Jo? Bookworms must have eaten it." And then the little smirk. And then of course you'd do them and they'd do you. Goes with the territory. I never held with reading in the nick. Don't believe in it. You hear about blokes getting degrees from fucking Oxford while they're banged up. I never held with that because as soon as they start the reading they get religious and all. Nutters who've sliced up families of six going round with they hands clasped behind they back. Praying and that. Don't hold with it. If I see a con with a Bible they was due a bash. I know what loss of freedom is, what confinement is, but me thoughts are me own. It's like the Kray Twins, from *their* book: "Flowers are God smiling at us." And if that don't send you to the bog then I don't know what will.

'But one day the book trolley come round. As it's gone past I see the spines and one of them's only called *Joseph Andrews*! Me first thought was: someone's gone and taken a right raging liberty. Someone's gone and done me uh, me life story with no permission whatsoever. I give the screw a shout – and the slag's name is Henry Fielding. But of course after a while I've calmed meself down. *Joseph Andrews* was one of the first English novels, published as early as 1742. I got me TV glasses for a read of it and I've not made head or tail of the language they use in them days. But there's something very near the beginning, about a good man being more . . . influential than a bad. And them's wise words . . .

'Years later I've come across another book, in three volumes, entitled *Tom Jones*. Must be the life story of the singer, I've thought, him of "It's Not Unusual" fame. But no: it was only by the same fella – Henry Fielding. I always was an avid Tom Jones fan, and to this day I'll get on a plane to attend one of his concerts. "It's Not Unusual" was his greatest hit, but me own favourite's got to be "The Green, Green Grass of Home".

'I want you to think about that. If you would: the green, green grass of home.'

Click. Joseph Andrews now summoned his amanuensis, Manfred Curbishley: braces, a horseshoe of hair going round the back of his head, mouth and eyes as moist as oysters. He looked as though he'd never left London – never left the bookies' office in the Mile End Road. And a drinker's face, with its pattern of heat: its oxbow of oxblood.

With a wag of the head: 'There's more, but you can start turning this into English. And take out all the language . . . Where's Rodney?'

'Accompanying Miss Susan to the airport, Boss.'

'Course he is, course he is.'

The frowning gaze of Joseph Andrews (every mote of age visible in the carbonated air) settled on the green file, which lay open on his desk. Cora, he now saw, had underlined a name in one of the clippings. He adjusted his glasses: Pearl O'Daniel. With an inner murmur he pictured her father: Ossie O'Daniel. A good man, a sound man, a man of principle: never took any fucking rubbish from the screws. Remember once he came into Association in the middle of the day with his privates hanging out. This was at Strangeways. There'd just been an off – someone kicking up. No one said anything about Ossie and his privates, not even the screws. He'd just had twenty-four of the Birch that morning, so you made allowances, and tactfully turned the other way.

7. We two

Brendan Urquhart-Gordon lay in bed with his laptop. The imagery being fed through to him was from Oughtred; it attempted to duplicate, by the use of 'isosurfaces and volumetric rendering', the material on the Princess. Emboldeningly, the counterfeits of the first stills could not be distinguished from the originals – or at least not by the unassisted eye; and the four-second loop, where the Princess swivelled in the bath, was an apparently perfect simulacrum, down to the very eddies of the water. But the attempt to morph the enemy's latest offering, the attempt to carve it out of light and magic, was a clear failure. Here the technology came up against its structural limits. Brendan could feel his body temperature climb: the inner casuist was acknowledging the first great wound in his defence. He thought (again): if the enemy so much as gave the time and place – the Château, the Yellow House . . . A chimerical mischief would at once become something actual, something to be investigated, and the media . . .

The new image, anonymously remailed on to the Net that morning, showed the Princess in three-quarter profile. It was an enlargement, and the quality – the definition – seemed relatively weak. Yet this much became clear: she was not alone. It wasn't a shadow, louring above her. It was an implicit presence, demanded by the demeanour of the Princess. Her crossed hands resting on her shoulders, the angle of her torso minutely averted from the hypothetical entity, her expression . . . This was what the technology couldn't capture: it couldn't capture the complexity of the Princess's expression. She looked surprised, and shocked too, but not quite startled or fearful; she looked intensely anxious; she looked slightly sick. But it was the eyes and their pitiful attempt at comity, at courtesy, at *good manners*: this could not be duplicated.

Retaining his pyjamas, and adding all his sweaters, Brendan got dressed and went to the King. He found him in his dressing-room, sitting before the empty grate with his face in his hands. Without looking up Henry pointed at something on the low table. Was it a golf ball? No, it was a crumpled sheet of paper. Brendan didn't find it pleasant to watch the King flatten and straighten this out, his lower lip pendulous with reluctant concentration, and then pass it on with a sigh that closed his eyes. Brendan asked for and was given permission to activate the one-bar electric fire. Don't like that colon, he thought, as he settled down to it:

Dear Daddy:
    So it's 'we two' now, is it? Mummy will be delighted when she hears. But she won't hear. Perhaps I could have told <u>Mummy</u> what happened in the Yellow House, even though she would have been much more horrified than you. But I can't do that, can I? Because it's just 'we two'.

I'm so sad to learn that you're suffering. On the other hand I am absolutely fine. It's *nice* to know that everyone on earth is leering at you. I don't dare look at any of it, but I've talked to my friends, until I stopped daring to do that too. The very air seems full of me; even the wind seems to say my name. But the air and the wind are polluted. When I'm not sleeping, or sitting there with you, not eating, I'm bathing. And even bathing, now, deeply reinfects me. Even the clear water feels like sewage.

I want to get farther and farther away from the thing which is called World.

May I close with a few quotations from your letter? 'Thoroughly rotten . . . It's my poor character . . . Sweetheart . . . let us be in this together.'

Uh-huh?

'I dare not close my eyes for fear of what I may see.'

Oh go on and close them. It's nothing you haven't seen before.

I didn't ask to be born. I didn't ask to be –

V.

'I am blind, like a kitten,' said Henry in a slurred voice. 'I see nothing. Do you think it possible, Bugger, to do something truly dreadful in your sleep and not remember it?'

Brendan moved closer. He hoped to dredge up words of comfort for his liege lord. Henry had settled on a certain eventuality: 'What of it, if she had some sort of romp with one of those pretty Arab boys?' There would be a better time to tell him that the visitor to the Yellow House was an adult, and not just another child.

8. Use Your Head

Chief: Tonight I'll e you the pilot piece for the column. I suggest the byline 'Yellow Dog' (photo of snarling pariah). Then, if anyone asks, we can say it's satire and comes from Jonathan Swift (the cases I'll use will be all generic, so nobody can sue). You know like the Modest Proposal where he told the starving Irish to eat their own nippers. Look, there's a big Vicky story brewing in LA which we can develop without stepping out of line. A flesh video called 'Princess Lolita'. Humungous hit – what with the timing. Can't buy that kind of publicity. More later. Weather here still superb high pressure. Saw that three people fucking *drowned* in the rain in SE England. That's what I like to hear. Clint.

'Hey asshole. What's five times eight?'

Rich said, '. . . Fifty.'

'Oh yeah? And what's five times ten?'

Rich said, '. . . Forty-seven.'

There was laughter, in which Clint joined. He was attending class at the Academy, along with nine other denizens. Rich stood naked on a dais at the far end of the room. He was ridiculously endowed, endowed beyond all utility (his head and torso seemed mere afterthoughts: a howdah and canopy tacked on to the trunk), and he was supposed to be a genuine retard. In fact he was a would-be porno star acting under instructions. The Director of the Academy, John Working, had used genuine retards in earlier days, but it was hard to get hold of the right kind, and they were always injuring themselves or molesting the help. At the nightly poolside cookouts, Working also employed a nonorchid headmaster from Central LA who, strolling naked from table to table, knowledgeably answered questions on everything under the sun; the would-be porno star had to stand there too, stupidly eating hamburger after hot dog, while the Academy denizens sat back with their smoked trout and their ewe-cheese salads.

'Hey shithead. In the Bible. Adam and . . . ?'

Rich said, '. . . Ivy.'

'Hey dorkbrain. How many Commandments are there?'

Rich said, '. . . Nine.'

Clint was not to be left out: 'Hey. Who shall inherit the earth, cunt?'

> dear clint: so! u have been sent to
> cali4nia 2 cover the *princess lolita*
> phenomenon 4 the *lark*! it's just
> come out here 2, but u can only get
> it in the 6 shops, and they're so c-d:
> i'll have 2 get my brother (well, 1/2-
> brother) 2 get 1 4 me. every1's
> talking about it: they say the actress
> is the absolute twin of our vicky
> (she's barely 17) & per4ms the usual
> r&y stunts with stableboys &
> diplom@s, not 2 mention some 69
> with a lady-in-w8ing! that's what i
> am, clint: a lady in w8ing . . . so! k
> pasa? i've never been stateside, but
> i've read some boox. indian
> reservations with t-p's & heap big
> totem poles? or all very spanish with
> k-n pepper & "iladas? e me all, dear
> 1. i can't tell u how much happier i
> am without orl&o. i o u 1 4 th@.
> 2nite i'm @ home with my father.
> so deliciously sed8! hurry back 2
> engl&. i think it's time, don't u? k8.

Most birds you meet in the chat-rooms, thought Clint, as he relaxed in his cabana: they're virtual. They ain't there, not really:

a bootstrap botchjob of mannerisms and affectations. But this one? A real character, a bubbly personality with a smashing sense of humour. And a good family girl, too, who knew her place, unlike some . . .

Cracking his knuckles, Clint moved to the table and the waiting laptop. He inhaled richly. He felt an unfamiliar afflatus: what was the phrase – taking dictation from heaven?

Yellow Dog's Diary

- So some nun took a knock from a stolen car and was left bleeding on a zebra crossing.

   Now, before we put our boxer pants into the tumble drier, let's have a look at the other side of it.

   The coppers openly admitted that the lad had had a few.

   In actual fact he was *four times over the limit*.

   It would have been a miracle if he'd *noticed* giving her a tap.

   So much for 'hit and run'.

   As for her?

   Thirty years old and she's 'a bride of Christ'.

   In other words she's crossed her legs forever to concentrate on her 'good works'.

   Pass the sickbag someone.

   Word from the hospital is on the grim side, so at least *she'll* be off the streets for a year or two.

   But what about the others?

   We're the ones that have got to look at you, darlings.

   Never had the strength of a man in you and it shows.

   So when you go out in public, get your hair done and put some powder on that ugly old boat, for f**k's sake.

- So a so-called 'referee's assistant' ('linesman' was good enough in my day) got kicked to death by players, management and crowd after a disputed decision at the North-East derby at the Stadium of Light, where they really care about their football.

  Yes, care.

  That's C-A-R-E, alright?

  True, video replays leave little doubt that a red card was in order, and that, given the career-ending injury that resulted, a yellow would not have sufficed.

  But they don't f**k about up Tyneside way.

  If you so much as

Clint worked on. Then, having filed, he sat down on the sofa and empowered the TV and the VCR. He was looking forward to seeing *Princess Lolita*. But normal porno was forbidden at the Academy: you had to watch the stuff they provided as part of your kit. Academy porno, true, had much in common with normal porno: the acting, for example, was free of all conviction. So you had to wonder, when the bloke stripped down, at the bird's gasp of gratitude and awe. There she was now: swooning at the sight of another no-see-um – another inverted exclamation-mark (in, what, fourteen-point?). And the next bit, there, look. What was she doing – picking her teeth? Clint was supposed to pay special attention to the thirty-minute cunnilingus sequence that followed, but he found himself reaching for the remote. And you had to suspend the old disbelief entirely when at last he plunged into her: the way she twists and judders and starts singing Wagner. To be fair, the women in Academy porno were among the smallest he had ever seen. Not kids or midgets – just incredibly small. Real throwabouts . . .

'Use Your Head' was the Academy motto. Much of the class activity was overseen by a retired porno star called Dimity Qwest, now a respected activist and therapist, who showed you how to work the fake quim they doled out to you on arrival. In time, they all became slobberingly proficient at the art of oral love. Clint had found it a low moment, to be sure, when Dimity told him to regard his organ as a middle finger without the nail; but then she cheered him up by touting the likelihood of anal bliss, increased access to the tradesmen's entrance being something the smaller bloke could legitimately expect. You were meant to practise in your cabana. The thing had a 'pleasure meter' on it, about halfway to the hypothetical navel, which showed you when you were getting warm.

If asked, Clint would have said that he was responding to the treatment. Definitely. After all, nobody's perfect and everything's relative. And the lads at the pool, during the nude brunch: a good few of them put a spring in his stride. Several denizens, moreover, during workshop, tearfully lamented the shaming meagreness of their ejaculations. Clint chipped in, saying that this was a department in which he happened to shine, and going on to describe his heroics with Rehab.

Now he cleaned his teeth in the scaled-down bathroom: the basin was no bigger than an ashtray. His artificial smile briefly quickened with sincerity as he thought about the porno interviews he'd lined up in Lovetown. Looking forward to *Princess Lolita*: see some decent todgers for once in his life. The absolute twin of our Vicky. Looking forward to Kate: lady in waiting.

* * *

9. Epithalamium

By now there were torn creases in the sheet of paper which winked at him whenever he picked the thing up. Through them you could see the other world – or so it seemed. The letter was now a week old; and there had since been the incident with the fox.

* * *

My dear Xan,

It would not be true to say that you raped me last night, but it would be true to say that you tried. I know this is a question you must in general be tired of hearing. Still, I must ask it. What do you remember?

It was about 2.20 when you put on the light. Then you crashed down on me and forced your tongue into my mouth and your hand between my legs. As well as being an amazing stinkbomb of cigars, beer, curry, vomit, and shit, you 'reeked of cheap ponce', to use your own phrase (you had just helped me out of a minicab – this was, or seems, years ago). I hit you on the head with closed fists about eight or nine times as hard as I could. I'm sorry. Your poor, poor head. Then I got out and ran upstairs and locked myself in with Baba. You followed, and battered on the door. Baba, incredibly, slept through it, but Billie woke up and sat down crying outside Imaculada's door, and she woke up too. She said that if she'd had a phone in her room she would certainly have called the police.

You were shouting your head off about your 'conjugal rights'. I think it's a rule, don't you, that whenever the 'rights' of marriage are invoked, by either one, then that's the end of that marriage. I don't know, this may only be true of the bedroom. In the last five years we have done a million things for each other that perhaps felt like duties or obligations or sacraments, but I never felt that either of us was asserting a right.

Our marriage is not over. But Xan, my dearest – you are scaring the shit out of me. And to think that there are supposed to be women who love to live in fear; no woman worth anything would put up with it for an instant. Shall I tell you what it's like? It's the desire, more intense than any you've ever felt, for something to be away from you. It's the tearing desire for something to be over.

Our marriage is not over. It is not over. Last night was an utter disaster for us, and it will take an incredible effort to recover from it. I know – who wants an incredible effort, in matters of the heart or anywhere else. But that's what lies ahead of you, beginning with hours and hours of Tilda Quant.

This is what I think has happened. Your past is your past, and you escaped it or evolved out of it. Over the years you wore down your prejudices and developed a set of rational contemporary attitudes – remember my saying that you were more feminist than I was? You were a little bit pious, if anything. Then, after you were hit, I thought at first you'd slipped back a generation or two. I now think it's more basic, more atavistic than that. Your attitudes and opinions aren't attitudes and opinions any more. They're beliefs, and primitive beliefs at that. If, today, you were to show me around your past, as you once did five years ago, you wouldn't be showing me Kropotkin's clubhouse on Worship Street, or Mother Woolf's spieler, or the pub called the World Upside Down. You'd be showing me your cave – or your treetop.

Two more things. You have started being different with Billie. And I don't mean all the incomprehensible rules and regimens you tried to impose on her (no one could work out what she was supposed to <u>do</u> with that apple every day: give it to her teacher? give it to you? eat it?). No, it's more serious than that. Remember, before, when she used to do her 'exercises', or when she did them for too long or too often, you'd get embarrassed or irritated and say 'Oh stop that, Billie' or 'Go and do that in your room'. Now you're transfixed by it. You practically pull up a chair. This is a qualitative change in you. What can I say? You give me the creeps, man. You give me the fucking creeps. See it from my side. If I started giving *you* the creeps they would be woman creeps, not man creeps. Women (I read) very rarely show a sexual interest in their children (and very rarely try to rape their husbands). You are a man and you always have that at your disposal – male heaviness.

Change back. Please change back. Oh please, please. Please become again the big, calm, slow-moving, encouraging, approving, protective, affectionate man you were before. Until you do that, and it <u>is</u> what you're going to do, you and I can have only one kind of intimacy. Remember that word we loved: epithalamium. (I've just looked it up and burst into tears.) I was faithful to you and you were faithful to me. Fidelity is all we've got. Take that away, now, and there's nothing. Fidelity is epithalamium. Epithalamium.

The last paragraph concerned itself with such matters as his packed case, the keys to the flat across the road, the fact that Imaculada had prepared the bed and lightly stocked the fridge, and so on. When he first read the letter (it was half past one the day after) Xan's first impulse was to do about fifty thousand pounds' worth of damage to the house. Fifty thousand pounds would be about right. The presence, in the kitchen, of Billie, Sophie and Imaculada was just enough to restrain him. Instead, he asked Imaculada, 'How can a man *rape* his wife? She's his *wife*. And *you* were going to *nick* me. Where is Russia? *Where, where, where?*' And he stood there with his fists raised and tensed . . .

He made an effort to reconstruct the night before, and achieved some tinkertoy success with a credit-card receipt from a nearby Indian restaurant, a temporary tattoo on his forearm (presumably allowing his reentry into some joint or dive), a beermat from the Turk's Head, and a coupon for an inexpensive cologne. Also, in his notebook, he had written: 'In black and white!! (a little bird told me).' Apart from a four-day hangover, this was all the evidence he had, and it meant nothing to him . . . The head-injured person cannot remember the moments leading up to the head injury; and this is perhaps a strategy of the mind, sparing you the pain of reliving it. Xan wondered whether the amnesia of inebriation was also self-protective: if strong and pure enough, the memory of how you were last night would kill you instantly. Why remember the time you lost everything you had?

The flat he now occupied was a garden flat – a basement flat. Even in summer it was sepulchral. And it wasn't summer. Xan stood up, now, and went into the kitchen, where it was brighter (and also colder). For a moment he thought he saw a human figure stir on the stone steps leading up to the neglected, the unloved back garden. It was not a human figure. It was a black rubbish-bag, in the process of shifting its weight: a very low thing, really, in the scale of existence – and keeling over further now like a tramp in his oilskins to be quietly sick after the usual incorrigible reverse.

Xan was obliging himself to reread Russia's letter at least twice a day. Its penultimate paragraph (oh please, please) he reread almost hourly. He was in treacherous psychological territory, but this he fully assented to. It *was* intimate, it was exclusively intimate: the thought that Russia, whatever else she was doing, was being faithful to him. Denied Russia, he himself wanted infidelity – he craved infidelity more ecstatically than ever. But he did accept that what she said was true. Fidelity was his lifeline, and without it he would be a man in water, without connection.

She called on the eighth day.

'Hello?'

'Xan?'

'Yes?'

'Well I'm here,' said a comfortable voice – educated, accentless. 'And I've kept my promise. I'm lying on the sofa in a rather grand and rather warm hotel room, and I'm all dressed up as a little girl. What that means is that everything I'm wearing is *much* too small. These panties, in particular, are *rid*iculous. So when would be good for you?'

'And you are?'

'And I am? I'm Karla. Idiot.'

'Do I know you?'

'Oh *come on*,' said Cora Susan.

CHAPTER SEVEN

1. We will go quietly

After a couple of days on his own, batching it in the basement down the road, Xan Meo slowly realised something. Before, he had lived in a house full of girls: two that were women, two that would be women thereafter. And now? Now he was living with a man – himself: he felt denuded, and hideously revealed. Xan didn't know the lines (and, in his present disposition, would have rejected them as unmanly), but he was sharing Adam's agony, after the Fall: '. . . cover me, ye pines, Ye cedars with innumerable boughs, Hide me . . .' He had fallen. He was a Septembrist, not a Decembrist, but he found it very ageing, his exclusion from the house with its women a hundred yards away – a minute's walk; yet Russia had sent him on a much longer journey through time.

Standing with one foot up on the toilet seat, Xan clipped his toenails – so kippered and curled. The nail of the big toe cleaved with a crackle; its immediate juniors each gave a defiant tick as he lopped them. But the nail of the little toe made no sound at all. How tactful, how very discreet. The nail of the little toe came quietly.

Reading the instructions on the packet of a store-bought meat pie, he noticed that an ampersand of eye-dreck jumped from word to word – like the bouncing ball above the nursery rhyme on the television, there to help the children sing along.

Passing the mirror, naked, he seemed to see a Rubens in the glass. That thickened, tightened feeling around the gut and saddle, making him feel that he was, to say the least of it, a couple of hundred bowel-movements behind the game. There was nothing wrong with Xan that a year in the lavatory wouldn't cure. But where would he find that year? Did he have that year?

Waking, and rubbing his face, he felt a pillow-crease like a duelling-scar on his cheek. He had just shoved himself out of a dream of kitchen chaos – buckets and coffee-grounds and upended rubbish-bags. No need to tidy up, not after dreams, he thought; no need to leave dreams as you'd expect to find them. But *this* was a dream about a man alone. So don't allow *that* room to let itself go: you'll be back. The duelling-scar was still on his cheek as he stood by the fridge and ate lunch. He caught himself in the glass of the garden door. Like a Junker: brainwashed, paranoid, talentless.

Climbing from the straightbacked chair, he gave voice to a groan. Sitting back down again, he gave voice to another. Anything and everything made him groan: bending, turning, wiping his brow. And the very old – *they* didn't groan all the time. They trained themselves not to; and so would he. We will come quietly, like the little toenail. We will go quietly. We won't make a sound.

On the fourth day he was allowed home for a probationary half-hour with the girls. Russia greeted him with a cousinly hug and then withdrew, but only tactically: she would look in, pass by, she would clump about on the stairs and on the floor above. This was meant to fortify Imaculada, whose sickened glances suggested (to Xan at least) that domestic disharmony was quite unknown in the slums of São Paulo . . . Billie was the kindest to him, consenting, after a while, to be lifted on to his lap for a book; then Russia appeared and loudly and brightly suggested that they sit on the sofa (side by side). Although Sophie burst into tears the instant she saw him, she recovered surprisingly well. Thereafter she cried only when he coughed. And Xan's cough had come on a bit in recent days. He coughed not in helpless reflex but with purpose and method, hacking the ragged edges off the soggy presence in his throat.

With Russia he tried to look the very picture of contrition, which was the best he could hope for, because contrition was not what he felt. He was perhaps open to intellectual persuasion about the solecism, the regrettable typo, of raping your wife. But a persuasion is not a conviction; and it would in the end be countered by the argument, or the unadorned encyclical, that your wife is your *wife*. Besides: everyone knew that a special indulgence should always be extended to men who, through no real fault of their own, happened to be unusually drunk. Yet Xan was making the effort. He was making the effort to be or at least seem reasonable, to bow to reason, as hereabouts interpreted. For instance, with Russia, he never succumbed to the ever-present temptation to ask (or order) her into the bedroom. The work of controlling or dissimulating these urges and grievances caused him to tremble, sometimes for a minute on end. During one of those minutes Russia looked at him and fleetingly imagined that he was trying not to laugh.

But nothing openly terrible happened, and his visits became longer, looser, laxer. Russia's patrols further receded; Imaculada would sometimes leave him briefly alone with Billie; and he was soon permitted to look in on them as they bathed . . . Observing the girls was now part of Xan's schedule, like his morning hour with Tilda Quant, and his first cautious sessions at Parkway Gym; but there was nothing routine about it – about observing the girls. Indeed, the experience was hallucinogenic, uncannily vivid and unstable: he never knew what it was going to do next. Why was it such a savage pleasure to watch them eat? Why was it of desperate importance to him – the volume of water they displaced in the bath? And why did they so often remind him of pornography: the lewd contortions, the self-fingerings, the slurping ingestions with chin and cheek dripping with milk or vanilla icecream? Why did he always expect them to die, every day, every night?

There was one time when Sophie fell apart early on, having been deprived of her afternoon nap, and was asleep in her room by a quarter to six. On his way out, Xan asked Russia if he might take a last look at her, and in he went. The blanketed figure seemed quite inert as he reached down and placed the flat of his hand on her spine. There elapsed an evanescent eternity before he felt the soft push of her breathing; and then he heard his own quiet retch of deliverance.

'She's down,' he said. He stood in his overcoat at the door of the small half-landing sitting-room, where Russia was watching the news. 'Dead to the world,' he added.

'Oh well. She'll wake at five.'

Russia continued to look up at him from her chair. The aero-dynamics of her face: its angled gauntness, in the present light, made him think of hunger, of famine.

'Answer me something,' she said. 'Why do you think Billie has stopped "exercising" when you're in the room? She mastur-bates in front of Imaculada and me – still. Why not you?'

'Maybe because I'm a man.'

'She didn't mind before. You've made her self-conscious about it. And then the fox.'

'I told you about the fox. The vixen. It was nothing. I just hugged her too hard.'

Xan was in the shed, stowing the garden hose, when Billie joined him. They heard the scrape on the skylight – and there above them was the weight of the fox, its underside, its crusty rump, its coat with its spines and quills. Billie cried out ('Look!'), and Xan snatched her into his arms as the animal tensely swivelled and stared. He had expected a moment of feral severity – a snarl, a show of teeth – and not the entreating frown with its depths of anxiety. An anxiety that no human could have borne for an instant. Then it fled, its nails scratching the glass, and Billie was strug-gling and cuffing his hands.

'I just hugged her too hard. I hurt my knee too.'

'Yes, she said. "Daddy hurt his knee too."'

He swayed backwards a couple of inches and said, 'With the girls, I don't know, I'm just generally het up about them. As though they've just come in from being lost. After dark. It's part of it. I'm trying. I'm trying.'

'This last week. It's gone okay.'

'Has it? I'm glad you think that. I know I've got a long way to go. My guidance systems . . . Anyway. Goodnight.'

Her eyes had flicked back to the television screen. His eyes followed. He was subliminally prepared for some footage of the modern world: the scorched chassis of a bus or truck, a bandaged shape being wheeled at speed down a hospital corridor, a woman wailing, with subtitles . . . What he saw seemed simpler: a phalanx of American soldiers – grunts, jarheads – crunching across a sandswept airstrip, each of them fantastically overequipped, like a one-man band. He thought: the jihads of the jarheads. He said, sounding surprised,

'*Semper fi*. Yes. *Semper fidelis*.'

'You know,' she began, staring full ahead, 'you're a lot more uh, gamesome than you used to be. In your speech. You used to be much more step-by-step. I liked it.' She looked up at him. 'I miss it. Still, yes: *semper fidelis*. At all times faithful.'

'Epithalamium.'

'. . . Epithalamium.'

But it was when he was alone in the flat at night that he really did his work with the little girls. He lay there twisting, arching, squirming, seeing them hurt, harmed, taken, their flesh pierced, their bones snapped, the shells of their skulls meeting concrete or steel. What he saw when he closed his eyes had the power to lift him off the sheet and flip him over, to double him up, to flip him back again. He thought: something's coming for them and I can't protect them, I can't protect them. And there were their faces showing fear, then terror, then horror, forcing more convulsions on him, causing him to writhe and thrash and seethe . . .

He had read about a woman who said she felt 'a profound calm' as her daughter was attacked and knifed before her eyes. Similarly, sleep appeared only when the thing had already happened in his mind, and their ruined bodies lay before him; he was afloat on a glazed lake of detachment, drenched with the chemicals that come at such a time – that come to take you to the other side. I can't protect them. They're mine, and I can't protect them. So why not rend them? Why not rape them?

You can live as an animal lives, and he thought he knew, now, why an animal would eat its young. To protect them – to put them back inside.

That little girl I see, walking past the window. Is that her, or is it just the ghost of my child?

2. Weird sister

It was on the eighth day that she called.

'So when would be good for you?'

'And you are?'

'And I am? I'm Karla. Idiot.'

'Do I know you?'

'Oh *come on*,' said Cora Susan. 'Wait. There's someone at the door. It's open! . . . Just put it there, please . . . Thank you. Thank you . . . Champagne. To celebrate my arrival. There's a half-bottle in the fridge but I don't like the brand and it's never quite enough, don't you find? Now look. I was under the *impression* that we had an understanding.'

'I'm sorry. "Karla"?'

'Yes, Karla. Christ. With a *k*.'

'Uh, wait. The thing is I had an accident about a month ago. And I –'

'An accident? What kind of accident?'

'A head injury. My memory's not what it was.'

'You have no memory of a woman called Karla? This is a grave disappointment. You seemed perfect for me. Poor you and all that, but you're probably no longer suitable.'

'Suitable for what?'

She sighed and said, 'I'll start at the beginning then. I'm a wonderfully rich, young, sane and pretty businesswoman who adores loveless sex. All right, I'm petite, but I have a superb body and I'm marvellously fit and brown. I pass through London twice a year. You were supposed to come to my hotel one afternoon and do whatever you liked to me. Then I get on a plane and put five thousand miles between us. Till next time. Now I suppose I'll have to keep an eye out for someone else. I've just seen the bill for the champagne. I love spending money but this is madness.'

'I uh, I really don't think I was ever on for that.'

'Oh? You seemed awfully pleased with the idea at the time.'

'When was that time?'

'In the summer at Pearl's . . . Well you can come and say hello at least. And Xan: hadn't you better defuse a very awkward situation? What if I get hysterical and call the house?'

'Where are you?'

She told him. He said,

'I think we'd better meet on neutral ground.'

'All right. We can meet in the *lobby* if you like. I'm busy till Friday so you'll have time to mull it over.'

'Friday's . . . Yes. Tomorrow I'm taking my boys away for the night.'

'Fascinating. Do you *really* not remember? Don't you remember what you said about my breasts? . . . Don't you remember *them*? That *is* alarming. You know, Xan, this may do you a lot of good. I'm sure that the moment you set eyes on me it'll all come flooding back.'

* * *

Cora wore black, tights, skirt, blouse, but she had not yet put on the black shoes, the black suit-top, the black hat with its pendant black veil. Now she faced the irksome task of achieving a French twist: the hair swept up and over to the side, secured by an armoury of pins. She began work in the bathroom but soon moved the whole operation next door. The hectic profusion of mirrors, at odd angles and elevations, made her feel watched – that mirror especially, with its inner eye.

She knew the literature. Victims of incest grow up thinking they have magical powers. For they do. All infants, all babies, believe they wield magic: one-year-olds, if you have particularly displeased them, can look up from their cots in astonishment that you have physically survived their anathemas, their callings-down. They grow out of it. But victims of incest, these girls, these weird sisters, never lose that faith. Because power is theirs: they can say a sentence, and make a family disappear.

Women whom Cora had earlier come across in support-groups and recovery programmes persisted with another notion: that they could seduce any male. And it was true, in their case, so long as the male was violent or inadequate; so long as the male was a rapist or an addict or a pimp or a bum . . . Cora believed she could seduce any male too, and she had not yet been proved wrong. But she had more in mind for Xan Meo than mere seduction – and the graphic disabusing of his wife. She didn't yet know what. It would come to her.

Five minutes before her car was due she picked up the phone and dialled and said, 'Hello, may I speak to Pearl, please? . . . Pearl! You don't know me but I'm an old flame of your ex-husband's . . . About eight years ago. Yes that's right: when you two were still married.' Cora held the phone at arm's length. 'Wait, wait. He was ghastly to me too, if that's any comfort . . . So – so I thought we might bury the hatchet and have a good natter,' she went on, 'over a few grams of cocaine.'

Soon afterwards Cora was in her overcoat. She instructed her gorge to stay where it was when she encountered the traditional flower-arrangements for the antinomian dead.

3. King Bastard

'So how's it go again?' he asked his sons.

'Your middle name plus the name of your street is your film-star name,' said Michael.

'And your pet's name plus the name of your street is your porn-star name,' said David.

Xan said, 'I haven't got a pet.'

'What was the last pet you had?'

'A dog. Called Softy.'

'Well then. Softy St George.'

Xan went on, 'Softy wasn't soft. Far from it. Salt-and-pepper Alsatian, and a real hardnut. When I was growing up I thought that was why Softy was in a rage all the time. Because of his name.'

They returned to what they were reading. Michael and David were reading the sports pages of the mainstream yellowtops. And Xan was reading himself: *Lucozade* . . . The three of them sat in a fast-food joint on Paradise Pier, among nursery colours. And the colours of the clientele? The colours of the English, their pinks and greys, would eventually be subsumed by the colours of the ultramundane. And how they needed these new colours, he thought. At the next table, a baby-bottle full of Pepsi was being offered by a white man to a brown child; his pallid hand, with its bruised tattoo, seemed to make great gains from the transaction. The smile of his black wife – this also greatly distinguished him.

'"Of his Kestrel Juniors Chivalric Medallion",' said David, '"shamed love-rat Ainsley Car has been sensationally stripped . . ." They reckon here he's going to Charlton. After prison.'

'Charlton? They're crap.'

'Car's crap. So's Charlton. He's crap and they're crap.'

'*Car's* crap. But Charlton aren't *that* crap.'

'Bullshit. They're less crap than he is but they're still crap.'

'Boys, boys: you've got to learn some new swearwords. Take crap, say. I mean, bullshit actually means something. Something fairly complicated. Something like: rubbish intended to deceive. But crap? Crap just means crap. As a word, crap is *so* crap.'

'That's the whole point of it. Crap's wicked.'

'Yeah. Crap's cool.'

'I'll tell you what *is* crap,' he said, flicking his book on to the table, 'and it's *this* shit.'

'. . . How d'you mean, Dad?'

'Don't worry about it. I'll tell you when you're older.'

They came out into the last of England. The rock, the winkles; the pigeon with a petrol prism on its neck, the dry-heaving gulls; and the sea, in its storm aftermath, all confused and distraught, not knowing its proper place. Everything on the pier, the slot arcades, the caffs and bars with their short change and short measure, the dodgems, the ghost train: the whole narrative painting was organised by a vast – and, in secret, vastly prosperous – slum family. This was all that was left of his childhood culture.

Thursday morning was bright and blue. He gave the boys about a hundred quid each and then sat alone on the rocks between the two piers, the Opera and the Paradise. Mariners talk about a twice-daily occurrence – when the waves 'reconsider'. Something of the kind appeared to be happening in front of him, though the sea was more orderly now; morale, *esprit de corps*, had been returned to it. The waves crashed and dragged; they flopped and trawled.

Xan wondered about the reasons for the sense of alleviation he was feeling. His memories of the place were piquant and pellucid and above all plentiful; and his engagement with *Lucozade* (he was about halfway through) seemed sure to be enlightening, whatever else it might cost him. But, no, it must be the boys, the boys. Was it merely their maleness, the laxity of their talk, the companionable squalor they had instantly brought to the set of rooms at the Crown? No, it was their un-examined acceptance of his altered state – and the fact that they couldn't possibly judge him. They too were in the process of abandoning a self and acceding to another. Like their father, they couldn't fully remember what they had been, and couldn't predict what they would become. They didn't know who they were either.

Michael and David spotted him from the corniche. The distant clouds were like continents; there goes Africa, there goes America. The sea was equal to the task (all in a day's work) of turning the rock he sat on into shingle. The waves flopped and dragged, and crashed and trawled. The foamline wore a sneer, then a grin, then a sneer, then a grin: phantoms of the opera, phantoms of the paradise.

'Is uh, Vicky back at school yet?' Xan asked.

They were in a taxi, on the way to the station; and as the car turned off the Parade they were given a clear view of St Bathsheba's on its crumbling clifftop – apparently no more than a year or two from the sea.

Michael said, 'No, they've got her salted away in the country somewhere. And why? The bloke who did it – he knocked her up.'

David said, 'She's four months gone. She's out here.'

'And there's worse to come,' said the elderly driver. 'The bloke who did it: one of our coloured brethren. And he give her a disease.'

Michael said, '. . . If it's a boy it'll be one of those bastard pretenders.'

'Bastard the First.'

'King Bastard.'

On the train Xan dozed, and his heart and mind loosened into shapeless candour. What he wanted, what he had to have, apart from revenge, was familial reinstatement with honour. It would be done. It would be made so. And he considered he'd performed pretty well with Russia, playing the man he used to be. On the other hand, as his head snapped up from sleep and then dipped back down into it, like the shifting height of the parallel wires on the telegraph poles beyond, on the other hand . . . His nodding thoughts kept going back, kept going forward, to the woman in the hotel room. The joys of fame: the cyclostyled circular from the teenage autograph-hound; the plea for funds from the Bulgarian theatre group; and, every now and then (and not for a long time now), a woman, coming at you from out of the ether. They were far from being forces for good, for stability, these women, he knew. But they *were* women. And it was nice to feel wanted, even by a wrecking-ball . . . Much would depend, of course, on her looks. He was determined to be faithful – at all times faithful; he wouldn't touch. Still, he might have to go up there for a little while and watch her swan around in her pants. And then slip quietly away.

4. Cora's call on Pearl

'Well I'll say this much for Xan Meo: he could pull. Enter and welcome. It was the television. His standard went soaring the minute he was on the television. Oh, just put it anywhere. Lovely tits, darling. And I bet they're yours, too. And the waist. *And* the arse . . . Jesus wept, he must have thought all his birthdays had come at once. Even your *stomach*'s a turn-on. And when was it? You'd have been even more of a little miracle then, at – what? –

twenty-nine, thirty? No. I bet you're better now. Sorry about the mess. You should see the boys' rooms. They come home from school and try on all their clothes. That's very kind of you. I could fancy some of that.'

Cora made room on the large kitchen table for the ritzy shopping-bag with the magnum of champagne in it, and then produced the snuffbox with its packed white powder.

'Ooh, go on then.'

A glance at the sitting-room, with its shawls and scarves showered over the furniture, and the multilayered clutter deposited as if by flashflood, told Cora that Pearl was no keeper of secrets. The house-presents she had brought were *de trop* – not unwelcome, but almost certainly otiose. Pearl's appearance was similarly informative: the livid cheeks and forehead, the irregular auburn spikes of her hair, the costume jewellery, the ash-smudged jacket, the short skirt. It was on the short skirt that Cora concentrated. She saw that this was Pearl's gravitational centre – the bandy thighs, the framed void. With a thrill of mortality Cora decided that the day Pearl finally stopped wearing short skirts would be the worst of her life. On the way to this rendezvous Cora's cab had encountered an old lady in the street (and Cora wasn't used to seeing old ladies in the street) bent almost triple in her search for purchase. The old lady was waiting at the zebra-crossing; the driver slowed and stopped; and, before starting off like a sick crab, she stared at him with a sneer of suspicion for at least twenty seconds, as if London taxis were well known to like ploughing into old ladies on zebra-crossings. Cora thought: try doing all that in a short skirt.

Pearl had both feet on the table, and had just rocked back from her seventh line of cocaine, when Cora introduced the subject of male sexuality, with particular reference to Xan Meo.

'It's too fizzy, isn't it,' said Pearl. 'Wiggle your finger in it. Like this. It makes the bubbles go away and you can drink it faster.

Whew. I haven't scarfed up as much . . . Uh, he uh, *wasn't* a fetishist. Like some. I knew a bloke who ricked his neck every time he heard a toilet flush. Another bloke could only do it wearing a mask and I had to pretend to be someone else — you know, a different person each time. I said, Ah come on for once. He said, It's like being gay — I can't do it otherwise. *Xan.* Xan liked frilly knickers and the rest of the bollocks but name me one that doesn't. With him it was a power thing. He'd want to *master* you. So, you know, you'd resist that and pretend it isn't doing anything for you. You're not in the mood and you're just letting him get on with it. Until you . . . That's what he liked. Well. What can you do with them? Either they're lording it or they've locked themselves in the bathroom. For a weep or a wank. Wiggle your finger in it.'

Cora now raised the question of Xan's current circumstances, and was pleased to see Pearl's shiver of flustered highmindedness: still greater indiscretion was on its way.

'Of course it's all off now, since he copped that smack on the head.' Her voice had a faint buzz to it, imparted by the furled tenner in her nose. 'He was always pretty keen, actually, but now he's all screwed up and can't think about anything else. Russia — I've got quite pally with Russia, on the phone at least. Russia had to kick him out after he came in and leapt on her in the middle of the night. She was that close to having him nicked. Said he'd become like a retarded child when they turn fourteen. They don't know what to do with it all. And here's something worse.'

Cora leant forward. With a look of righteous panic Pearl went on,

'Russia asked me whether . . . When I was divorcing him I told my lawyer Xan was messing with the boys. Total rubbish, but any port in a storm. And Russia asked me whether it was true. Because she thinks he might have been messing with Billie — that's their four-year-old and a sexy little minx according to the boys. Nothing definite, mind. It's the way he eyes her. Whoop. I wasn't supposed to tell anyone that, but you know what it's like with this stuff. Out it pops.'

'Oh it's safe with me,' said Cora. 'Mm, your garden looks awfully nice. Would you give me a tour before I go?'

Pearl stood swaying at the front door. She said,

'Oof: that fresh air's really done me in. And look at her. Like a daisy. We never did talk about you and your time with Xan . . . Yeah, *what* time, right? Aren't you clever . . . Ooh, you're going to start stirring it now, aren't you. Going to start mixing it. I'd say he's going to be a very lucky boy. For about half an hour. His head's on the block with her – one slip and it's all over. Let me know how you get on. I'll call Russia and feed her the dirt. Or do you do that bit too?'

5. It's Not Unusual

On Friday Xan rose at seven. He breakfasted with the girls, and with Imaculada, to compensate or atone for his absence later on – if, for some reason, he got held up at the hotel. And he did his hour with Tilda Quant. Next, at the gym, he worked much harder and longer than usual; his class-leader, Dominic, commended the extra rasping and straining with the benchpress. Back at the flat, as he was about to unpeel his stinking singlet, he said to himself: Don't wash. Go like this. That'll keep you honest . . . As a compromise (and this was by no means habitual) he stood under a cold shower for fifteen minutes. Tilda Quant might have said that the mechanism at play here was self-flagellatory: purgation in advance. Hell isn't just hot; it's cold, too.

No doubt it was in the same spirit that he surrendered to a much-postponed ordeal: he tried to write something. Just a couple of paragraphs (he told himself), a couple of hundred words describing the confusions that had beset him since his accident. He stopped after forty-five minutes and read what he'd put down. As he feared, it did not evoke so much as leadenly dramatise his condition. Indeed, it was just another symptom: *expressive dysphasia*. His concentration, he realised, was additionally impaired by the fact that he kept thinking about sex: sex in the afternoon. By now his imagination had long exhausted all known acts, stunts, positions, variations. By now it was unalloyed *nostalgie* – pure love of the mud. Xan sat there sinking, in his brown study.

With a smile of pain he picked up *Lucozade*, intending to finish it – or to finish 'Lucozade', the last and longest story.

Twelve pages in he got to his feet and said, 'Joseph Andrews?'

At that moment Mal Bale was two hundred yards away and heading straight for him. Well, not quite: he had a bit of business to get done *en route*. Only take a minute. Mal, this day, was on a dual mission. He didn't like the first thing he was going to do and he didn't like the second thing he was going to do. But he was going to do them. In his worn leather overcoat (the broad belt was like the metal strap on a barrel), Mal approached a hot-dog stand on the west pavement of Prince Albert Road.

'Go on then. How much? . . . Jesus, you don't take no prisoners, do you mate. Onions? Nah. Just the uh, the doings . . .'

The hot-dog man, a middle-aged rasta with every other tooth missing and a face wreathed and sallowed by half a century of keef, said coaxingly, 'You got to eat you onions, man. Put lead in you pencil.'

'I've got lead in me pencil, mate. Look at the state of that sausage: that's bioterror, that is. Do you know who I am? Do you know why I'm here?' Why *am* I here? he thought. At my time of life, and I'm frightening hot-dog stands. It's not even a stand. It's a fucking trolley . . . 'The cousins aren't having it.'

'But they's icecream!'

'Icecream, hot dogs: same difference.'

The hot-dog man stood fixed, with his dishcloth, his spatula.

'Look, you don't want your face on that grill, do you, you don't want this trolley down on you and them onions in your hair. And a squirt of ketchup up one ear. And a squirt of mustard up the fucking other.'

'I got youths, man.'

'Yeah well we've all got them. Sorry and that. But I'll be back in a bit and if you're still here it'll happen.'

Mal strode on, past St Mark's Church, to St George's Avenue.

He rang the bell and waited. Just as the door opened he heard a fierce shout from the street: '*Oi!*' He looked round, looked back again; then he shifted his feet, raised his outturned hands to shoulder height, and bowed his head. A passerby might have thought that Mal was hoping to settle an argument – hoping to find common ground – between husband and wife. Either that, or he was just trying to keep them apart.

'The punishment never fit the crime. It hasn't sat well with me, that. The punishment never fit the crime. Ah, lovely,' said Mal, accepting the mug of tea he'd apologetically asked for. The two of them were in the kitchen at the flat, round the table, Mal with his coat still on and a cigarette in his fist. 'He's told me: "Smash his fucking jawbone for him. See how he likes that. I want him eating through a straw for a spell. See then if he'll say my fucking name." The way he was going on, I thought you'd shopped him – I thought you'd tried a citizen's *arrest*. And all you did was put his name in a – in a *story*. Are you all right, mate?'

'Yeah, mate . . .'

Xan stood over the table. He could feel the violence hormones still squirrelling around in him: voluptuous killers of pain and reality. He had seen the stranger approach his house; and then he had recognised him. Xan came up the steps and into the street, ready for absolutely anything . . . Mal had a way, as he talked, of compressing his lips and raising his eyebrows and tipping his head, now to the left, now to the right: on the one hand this, on the one hand that. Xan now watched him with clogged calm, almost lovelike, and a sense of getting nearer to something. He said,

'I didn't even do that.'

'No. Come on. There it is in black and white.' He held up the magazine he'd brought with him. 'In *Punch*. And in the book and all. Joseph Andrews.'

Xan Meo was not a literary writer, but he had, in 'Lucozade', allowed himself an unwonted flourish. The story told of a middle-aged bodyguard who, at some earlier period in his career, had plied his trade on the American entertainment circuit. 'He had spent a year in Las Vegas, working for Joseph Andrews,' it said. And 'Lucozade' later mentioned that Joseph Andrews had retired to Los Angeles. And that was all.

'I didn't really mean Joseph Andrews,' said Xan, trying to explain. 'I meant Tom Jones.'

'Tom Jones?'

'The singer. You know: "It's Not Unusual". I meant Tom Jones.'

'. . . Well *that's* fucking unusual. Why didn't you *say* Tom Jones?'

'It's just uh, it's just a kind of joke. *Tom Jones*, *Joseph Andrews*: they're both novels by Henry Fielding . . . You can't say Tom Jones.'

'. . . Well you can't fucking say Joseph Andrews neither! Either. Jesus.' Mal, evidently appalled by such frivolity, took a moment to collect himself. Then he frowned and murmured, '"It's not unusual to be loved by anyone."' Mal frowned deeper, adding: '"Each day I touch the green, green grass of home" . . . I see the film *Tom Jones* when I was fourteen. It was me first X. I thought: here we go. Non-stop orgies and swearing. But it was just a load of pubs, and birds with their – with it all pushed up up here.'

Xan waited. It had been made clear at the outset that there were things Mal could tell him and things Mal couldn't.

'He's not called that now, Joseph Andrews. And he's sensitive about it. As well he might be.' Mal was now looking round about himself. 'You've paid, haven't you mate? You've paid. And the punishment never fit the crime. Tell you what. How about this: doing Snort.'

'Doing snort?'

'Doing Snort. The bloke who gave you two on the back of the head. *I'll* do him.'

Wait, thought Xan: I may need the practice. You weren't supposed to ask questions, but he said, 'I've got a feeling he isn't finished with me. Andrews.'

'A feeling? Well I hope you're wrong. But you have given him the right flaming hump, my friend. A very unpleasant man, Joseph Andrews. My father worked for him for thirty years till he got himself crippled by the oppo – the Plutarco Brothers. Me dad's a pitiful sight when he goes to Jo. Dragging one leg, his arm still twisted over, and his neck all bent to one side. And Jo's gone, "All right, the Plutarcos took a bit of a liberty with you. We'll have a whip." Give him sixty quid – and a kick in the arse as he limped from the room.' Again, the sway of the head, the arch of the eyebrow. 'All I can think of is it might go back to *Mick* Meo. I heard they was never on the best of terms. How's your health?'

'I'm all right physically. But not what I was.'

'And uh, at home?'

'I'm on probation.'

'Well you . . . you stick with it. Because that's the most important thing. You don't need me to tell you. At our age, boy, you're a joke without your wife. Your kids and that.'

Xan sat up and said suddenly, 'I've got to meet this girl in this hotel.'

'Ah. Right.'

Mal was a while getting to his feet. Face to face, with a strictly pragmatic air, he said, 'Then you know the possible consequences.'

6. Size zero – 1

Come and see me, she'd told him (inter alia), in my fat hotel. And Xan was now feeling the pull of a very heavy planet. The crystal moons, the mirrorballs, the space-squandering distances, the golden dome above the circling staircase – a *brochure vivante* for Atlantes. And down below, the marble streets of hairdressers, masseurs, of manicure and pedicure, of perfume and jewellery and *haute couture*. None of this was aimed at the *mind*, now was it? You felt it – the high pressure to live deliciously. And that was before you got to the food and the wine, the soft towels, the fresh white sheets.

He asked at the desk and was directed to a rank of telephones – telephones that might have been used by the courtiers of Louis Quatorze. 'Karla?' he said. 'It's me.'

'I have a suite with a wet bar,' she said. 'Ride up.'

'No – as we said. Ride down, if you would.'

'What, wearing *this*? . . . only kidding. I'll be one minute.'

She was longer than that. As he took up position by the fountain, some distance from the bronze traps of the elevators, and as he survived each new half-carload of assorted maquillage, Xan had time to imagine her, upstairs, slipping or stepping out of one thing and slipping or stepping into another. Of course, he had been perfunctorily 'hoping' that she would be unattractive. But by now he couldn't be certain whether the way she looked, let alone the way she dressed, would make any difference. Tilda Quant was not attractive (she must have stood back in simple dismay when all the gifts were being handed out); and Xan found her very attractive indeed. And earlier still that morning he had found himself gazing entranced at the underslept Aztec obstinacy of Imaculada . . .

Down came another car (he was watching the crimson glints of the shaft diagrams), and another squaredance surged out of it, losing shape quickly in an atmosphere of hurry that had to do with the time of day and the coming of evening. She did not share in this hurry. The other passengers dispersed and she moved slowly through their fading speedlines. She walked as if impeded by the presence of small children – and you looked beyond her, beneath her, for these children; but they weren't there . . . Xan did what he had seen Billie do: he tipped back so fractionally that he could steady himself by the weakest elevation of his toes. She did not share in the hurry, nor in the confectionery, of the hotel. The sandals, the straw bag, the plain white dress. There was of course her figure to be assimilated; and only the most vicious corset, he thought at first, could so constrain the isthmus of her waist; but her body moved forward with the regular beat of that which is unsupported. When she was still some yards away he saw that she wearing no makeup, and this felt like an intimacy you could do nothing about. He couldn't place her. But the thing was that his body knew he had seen her before.

He inclined his head. She stood on tiptoe and kissed him on the corner of the mouth.

Xan had rehearsed the line uneasily, and now he delivered it uneasily: 'This is my first blind date for thirty years.'

'Blind? Well in one eye only. I know you. Do you know me?'

And he said, 'You, I don't know, you're . . . already-seen.'

She said, 'There's a surprisingly good cave of a bar back here.' And she took him by the arm.

He was, again, 'hoping' that the bar would be well lit and reasonably populous: that would be 'better', because she would then have less chance to do anything he might not 'like'. The way it went, he ducked into the Rose Room as if from an equatorial strand; and it took him a full minute to establish that there were no other customers. A blind date, and a deaf date too: the cottony darkness seemed to be pressing its paws against his eardrums as he followed the little white ghost to a distant booth: an opulent brothel of red velvet. Their faceless waiter appeared at once and lit the candle with a flourish before disappearing again. Now their faces were unsteadily illumined – but nothing else was. In these surroundings, he felt, languid and methodical fornication would not seem particularly daring. And a dumb date: a dumb date. She said,

'Now. *Déjà vu* in the proper sense, or in the vulgar? In the vulgar sense, already-seen just means already-seen. "It is with a distinct sense of *déjà vu* that we watch the Saints bear off the trophy for the second year running." In the proper sense it would mean that you *haven't* seen me before. You just get the feeling you have. Which is it?'

'The latter. I think. As I said, there are things wrong with my memory.'

'Of course it could be already-seen in a *really* vulgar sense. Supervulgar, in fact. We'll come to that. Ah.'

To Xan's dark-adapting eye the faceless waiter now looked implausibly young: he seemed about to recommend a glass of milk.

'I'll have what you have,' she said.

All the more reason, then, to order an ocean of blue ruin. To tell the truth, he would have given anything for a drink. He would have given anything – but not everything. For the time being he could see the line in the sand: on one side of it, all he had; on the other, all he'd lose. Milk, yes, or water, still water – liquid parched of all life. He asked if they served fresh orange juice, and was told that they did.

'Orange juice?' she said. 'I'm not having that. A large gin Martini, please, with a twist. Oh don't have orange juice. Have an espresso at least.'

'Okay, I'll have an espresso.'

'A double . . . I read your book. It's . . .'

He was gratified – but it was all too urgent in his mind and he could think of no other way of putting it. He said, 'It's up-your-arse, isn't it? Sorry. That sounds terrible. But you know what I mean.'

'You mean you toady to the reader. Well, there is a feeling of ingratiation. A kind of pan-inoffensiveness. And you seem to subscribe to various polite fictions about men and women. In my view. As if all enmity is over and we both now drink the milk of concord. And there's another thing. What's the one where the title is a girl's name? "Evie". Yes. After a thirty-page chase the narrator finally gets Evie into bed, and then, in my view, rather congratulates himself for not describing it. "No, I'm not going to tell you who put what where", and so on. What's that? Gallant? Evolved? Is that what the writer should do – shirk the task and strike an attitude? I'm being rather unfair here, because it's not just you. Good sex seems to be something that writing can't manage. Maybe the only thing. No: there's dreams. But why should that be? Mm. Excuse me while I get stuck into this lovely drink.'

'They say,' said Xan, 'they say that the writer stops speaking for anyone but himself. The quirks come out. It's no longer uh, universal.'

'Can't the quirks be universal? Aren't there things we *all* like?'

'It's funny. I don't often describe sex, but it's the first question I ask myself about a character: what they're like in bed.'

'Do you? Sorry: "what they're like" or "what they like"?'

'I suppose both. Or is it the same thing?'

'So if you were going to fictionalise me, which I don't recommend, you'd start how?'

'Why wouldn't you recommend it?'

'Because nobody believes in women like me. Or no woman does. Unless she was a victim too. Victims believe.'

'Victims of what?'

'Wait. I see you've evaded the question. Anyway. Good sex, as a subject, has to have a place to go. So a whole other form, a whole other industry, devotes itself to nothing else.'

'Pornography.'

'Pornography . . . *Porn* is a disgusting little word, isn't it? It's the most disgusting single thing in the whole phenomenon. *Porno*'s nothing like so bad. In the industry, we call it the industry. That's what you call it when you're in it. I'm in it . . . I said before that you may have already-seen me, in the supervulgar sense. It's been a while now, and there were reasons for it at the time, but I uh, "starred" in over a hundred movies. Blue movies. Karla White. For three years the only sex I had was the sex I had on camera. Porno-people aren't like non-porno-people. When we *watch* porno, we fast-forward through the sex to get to the acting. Now that's true perversity.'

'. . . What were the reasons?'

'I told you. Do you really not remember?'

'When? Where?'

'It was at Pearl's summer party: August thirty-first. Pretty chaotic, as usual. And, of course, no Russia. Remember? We talked for two hours and then went into the garden and did what we did.'

'What did we do?'

'We'll come to that. And I told you the reason. It was once a cliché, and is now a fallacy – but why do girls make blue movies? Because they were raped by their fathers. Between the age of six and nine, inclusive, my father raped me once a day . . . Now that's strange. That's *very* strange. Then you *do* remember.'

'Why d'you say that?'

'When I told you the first time you were hugely indignant on my behalf. Now look at you. You just blinked once. Slowly.'

'It's not that I remember you telling me. It's . . .'

'You don't think it's so shocking any more? Boy, you really *did* get a knock on the head, didn't you. Well all right. Let's consider. Is it so shocking? Some fathers, and not just mass-murdering yokels but stockbrokers and politicians – some fathers really do believe that incest is "natural". I made you so I can touch you, your first child should be your dad's: all that. It's an atavism. Because getting rid of incest, outgrowing incest, was part of the evolutionary advance, like outgrowing oestrus.'

'What?'

'Oestrus. Heat in women. There has never been a human society that doesn't observe incest taboos. But the one to do with fathers and daughters has always been the weakest. In the Bible there's every kind of prohibition. "Thou shalt not uncover the nakedness of thy father's sister; she is thine aunt; it is wickedness." But there's nothing specific about fathers and daughters.'

'Patriarchy.'

'Well yes. No. Masculinity. Mother–son incest barely exists. There are about twenty cases in the entire literature. And all the biblical restrictions are addressed to men. Men do it, and it's the same with the higher animals. Size. Masculine bulk. Men do it because men are big . . . If you were trying to dream up a justi-fication, then don't look at the past.'

She leant forward and sipped, parting her bright grey hair with her hands. Clearly these were strange words he was hearing. Then why didn't he find them strange?

'Look at the future. Us, us victims, we're not so frightened and repelled by the way the world is now: the end of normalcy. We always knew there was no moral order. So sleep with Billie, and introduce her to the void.'

'That's what it is, is it. It's a void.'

'It's very simplifying.' She smiled – the bright teeth shallow, feline – and said, 'Where I live there are all these treatment centres for vices and inadequacies and addictions. Incestuous fathers are taught how to sublimate. They make their poor wives dress up as little girls.'

He thought of Billie, of Sophie. 'School uniforms. Rompers and nappies.'

'Not quite that literal. It's something a lot of men like. Believe me. All you do is you wear things that are many many sizes too small. When I rang you and said I was dressed up as a little girl: I said it because that's a, that's a non-deuniversaliser. I don't know, it takes the stress out of it. Consider the notion of the baby-doll look. It's not only sublimation, it's comic relief. How serious can anything be when your dress hardly covers your waist?'

'You find? Uh, Karla, let me concentrate for a moment and . . . Yeah. I have seen you before. And it wouldn't have been on film.'

'How do you know?'

'I don't watch pornography.'

'You mean you *say* you don't watch pornography. Ooh. Then you're not the good modern person who wrote *Lucozade* . . . Unfair. You're just a generation out – you're still obliged to disapprove of it. It'll take a while, but pornography is heading for the mainstream. The industry, now, is always saying how respectable it is. Every time Dimity Qwest or Tori Fate opens a supermarket, the industry says how respectable it is. To say that, you have to say that masturbation has become respectable. And that's what they're saying. "Wanking's cool," I read the other day. "Handjobs are brilliant."'

'Handjobs are bullshit. But wait.'

He did watch pornography, now, in the status quo after. Previously he quite liked it when he saw it but also disapproved of it; now, he liked it a lot and approved of it, assented to it, blessed it. And yet it was no help to him, in his altered state. Because even pornography needed your memory; and there were things wrong with his memory. The streams and currents, the different pressures and temperatures: if these do not flow as they used to, if the memory cannot ride them . . . The physiological reaction occurred, but nothing was eased by it. As if his erotic past was lost, and his desires, undiluted and unballasted, were all pushed out in front of him, into the present and the actual.

'Oh don't be too hard on handjobs.' She spread her arms at shoulder height on the black velvet. 'It's not flattering, to be forgotten. It makes you feel forgettable.'

'That's not how it works. Three weeks before I got hit on the head it was Billie's fourth birthday.' He checked himself; then he pressed on. 'When I picked her up at lunchtime, which I don't usually do, she was very happy and excited. She said to the teacher, "And here comes my *lovely* daddy to take me home from school." You know: as if to cap it all. I said at the time that I'd remember that for the rest of my life, but I had to be reminded of it. Like my younger daughter's birth. Sophie's birth. I'd forgotten it. I've forgotten it. It's not there. I'd say you were pretty unforgettable. But I still might have forgotten you.'

'Then I'll have to remind you properly. Will you excuse me for a moment? You'll find me in a rather different mood when I return . . . All you do is – you wear things that are many many sizes too small. Many many sizes too small. Size zero. Don't watch me walk away. I'll feel self-conscious if you watch me walk away.'

So he watched her walk away and then sat there with his face in his hands.

7. Size zero – 2

Bent over marble in the Ladies, and watched by mirrors, Cora Susan applied light makeup.

Recently, in the industry, there was an actor, Randy Rivers, who kept faking his HIV-clearance – in industry terms his work permit; and he infected five actresses. As this unfolded, various violent people went looking for Randy. They all found him and they all let him be. The explanation she heard was that Randy's condition and circumstances could in no way be worsened: there was nothing to fuck up.

Cora hadn't quite put Xan in this category, but she had thought of Randy Rivers, over at Pearl's. Over at Pearl's: that was a good name for her. Pearl would have revealed everything – without the good alcohol, without the good cocaine. Similarly, Xan sounded like an ignoble candidate for the rhino horn and the Spanish fly: Xan, the shambling flasher and dirty-raincoat merchant of Pearl's adumbration. But it wasn't turning out that way. She knew about such things, and the resistance she felt from him was unexpectedly dogged: erratic and confused, but dogged. Seducing him, therefore, was now a matter of her self-respect and even her self-belief; it was vital to her private culture – to her inner suns and moons. And the other, more terrible punishment, if it had to come, could come later.

She approached from behind and placed her hands on his shoulders, saying, 'I'm going to have the same again. And I'll briefly hate you if you do likewise.'

'Then I'll have what you're having . . . You've put on makeup.'

'What's the difference?'

'You look a bit younger. No, older. No, more artificial. Like this place. And less familiar. I don't remember you at all now.'

'That's all right. You know, two cocktails is about my limit. It's funny that men are so starchy about drunk women – except in the bedroom. They don't want them sloppy. Except in the bedroom. Men do love a legless woman. I suppose it's the diminished responsibility. But you've got to time it right.'

Their drinks came, and she started to touch him. A hand on the arm, a hand on the hand: hand touching hand.

'You're a bit starchy, about the industry, aren't you? When I started out it seemed to me that I was *made* for the industry. Made.'

'Because of you and your father.'

'Well yes, but I meant physically made.' She took her hand from his and started counting off the fingers. 'One. Okay: father. Two. I can be candid with you, can't I? Two. My uh, netherhair is naturally minimalist, as they all are now. As *everyone* is now. Is that evolution too? Like men stopping having beards? Three. I wasn't born with a kiss-tattoo on my coccyx, but I do have a birthmark on my hip that's shaped like a valentine greeting. All I needed, for the complete look, was some great *rock* bolted into my navel. Or my tongue. Four. The bust. They seem fake. They seem fake because there's no asymmetry. They don't move fake but they *feel* fake. Feel.'

Up till now he hadn't stared at her breasts. On the contrary: they had been staring at him. But now he stared at them, and they stared back. 'Feel.' What could he say – that he'd 'prefer' not to? Instead, to postpone it a second or two, he said, 'I don't know what fake breasts feel like.'

'Yes you do. You've felt mine.'

'Have I? But yours aren't fake.'

'But they feel fake. Feel.'

He felt. She held his hand in place with her wrist and powerfully inhaled.

'If you put your cupped palm out of a car window and feel the air going past . . . Some breasts are thirty miles an hour. Some are fifty. I'd say mine are about seventy. Speed-limit breasts,' she said, and let his hand drop. 'Where was I? Yes. Five. I'm little.'

'What?'

'It's pretty obvious, isn't it? I measure five foot and a credit card. I weigh eight stone sopping wet. I magnify the man. I'm a cock-puppet . . . Now that last point has a bearing on what happened at Pearl's. I'm going to describe it to you, and then perhaps we'll know where we are. And I think I *will* have that third Martini. You may have to help me to my suite.'

On screen, actors blink only when they mean to; and when

Xan decided he wanted to be an actor he had spent a lot of time practising not blinking. 'Stop staring!' his mother used to say. 'I'm *not* staring. I'm practising not blinking!' Now, in the fat hotel, Xan was trying not to blink. Because whenever he did, he saw the two of them naked on the carwash of her bed . . . Yes, the world was going, was seeping away. He could feel bits of it closing down; they made a sound like a computer's final sigh – a faint ricochet, a distant *miaow* . . .

'It was about one o'clock in the morning. There was a hard core still at it in the sitting-room, but it was thinning out, and everyone was pretty far gone – except you, funnily enough. You weren't drinking, but there was other stuff going around and maybe you'd had a puff or a toot, I don't know. We agreed to meet in the garden. You know at the far end, through the arched trellis, there's a hut or Wendy house that's not actually on the property but you can get to it through the gap in the hedge?'

'We called it the Monkey House,' he said thickly. 'It belonged to the little girls next door. But they grew up.'

'Well, in we sneaked. It felt childish, and we were laughing quite a bit at first. You know: playing Doctors in the parkie's shed. Then it happened. Oh, nothing very serious. This came down, and this came up, and you caressed me fairly thoroughly. Listen, at one point . . . I was getting rather tired, standing on tiptoe, and I said it wasn't fair, your being so much bigger than me. And you lifted me up with one hand, so I was on your level. You used your other hand to steady me. But you lifted me up with one hand.'

'How?'

'How? It was the hand that was between my legs.'

There were too many monkeys jumping on the bed. One fell down and broke his head. They went to the doctor and the doctor said: No more monkeys jumping on the bed . . . Xan tensed himself, below. It was still there: like a section of solid cartilage.

'A reconstruction, a reenactment of that moment,' she was

saying, 'up in my suite, might bring it all back . . . Xan, I feel I may have alarmed you slightly, with all this talk of incest and pornography. Unstable things. Alien things. But as you see I'm in perfect physical and mental health. And I'm *little*. I know that after accidents people feel very fragile. But I won't hurt you. How could this' – she shrugged – 'hurt anyone? And you deserve it, Xan. You've had a very hard time and you *deserve* it. You don't have to touch if you don't want to. You can just watch me glide around in my underwear for a while. Size zero. And then slip quietly away.'

His memory had got him into this; and now maybe his memory was going to get him out. The first instant, in the lobby, had been for Xan a sexual *coup de foudre*; yet he still believed that he could muster some kind of counterforce to it – could avoid the occasion of sin. Thereafter a reptilian ponderousness had slowly spread itself over his body, coagulating into one purpose, one meaning. He was the slow-eyed crocodile who has watched and waited, who has watched and waited long enough. Simultaneously, for minutes on end, he felt like a heavenly body in space, urged towards another heavenly body of far greater gravity; he felt celestial attraction. Others, other things, the world: all of it was about to disappear . . . Then a memory came. A memory came, like a flare, bringing with it a series of forced deductions.

He remembered that on the evening of his injury, when he was on his way out of the house, on his way to Hollywood, to hospital, he had said to his wife: I have no secrets from you. And he remembered that he had meant it: he remembered the un-designing light of his own veracity. Every man has secrets from his wife, those letters, that photograph, the guest-appearances and thought-experiments that come as ghosts to the master bedroom. But Karla, with her dress around her waist: that qualified as a *secret*. In the last few minutes Xan had been hoping that what she said was true: that he had indeed lifted her off her feet. Because it was something well worth doing, and if you'd done it once, what was the point in not doing it again?

'And, in the morning, I get on a plane and fly five thousand miles.'

He said abruptly, 'If you're not a friend, what are you? Do you know the name of Joseph Andrews?'

She seemed to take it like a tiny blow from a tiny enemy. But her voice was firm and cool: 'Yes. It's in your book. I assumed it was just a joke about Henry Fielding. "Lucozade". Easily the best.'

'Thank you. I think so too. And you're *not* my enemy?'

'Oh I'm your enemy all right. Come *on*. What do you think? That I've got . . . that I've got a motion-sensitive camera up there? And tomorrow morning, a liveried courier delivers the cassette to your wife? It would start in the lift: we'd wait for an empty one. Look at this place. You can feel it on top of you, tons and tons of it saying that the body should have it good. I'm offering you a modern temptation: one with no consequences. Come on up. It's no more than what you deserve.'

The temptation, he considered, was implausibly extreme, and it would be ridiculous not to succumb to it. She was right. The fat hotel wanted it to happen. Before him, on the table, the two cocktail glasses were a pair of female thighs, and the two shots of unfinished booze, the slowly seething gin, were their hosiery . . . Against this luxury he could array only the luxury of uxoriousness – a luxury of the mind, merely. And Russia was far, very far, perhaps unrecapturably distant; and Karla was near.

Xan shook his head and at once she called for the bill.

'In the dictionary,' she said evenly, removing her key from her bag, 'the third meaning of *tempt* is to risk provoking a deity or abstract force. That's what *you've* just done. As a sexual temptation this was *nothing*. And now you're going to have to watch me walk away.'

'Wait. How do I –'

'Do what I did and call your agent. Now you're going to have to watch me walk away. And it's already too late to change your mind: this time. I'm going to leave you with a visual paradox. My mother was very feminine, but so was my father. And I'm a doublegirl. How does it go? Haunch touching haunch, breast touching breast, each touching each. Look at me walk away in my doubleskin. And you're going to think: that's my cock, walking away.'

She was on her feet in front of him: the sheer white dress with its pools and hollows. Now she swivelled, with the straw strap on her shoulder. She laughed harmonically and said, 'It's so sweet. Fathers have the ridiculous idea that . . .'

Over her shoulder she looked at him. He expected to find dislike in it, but her face seemed about to crumble and collapse, as Billie's might.

'You know, if you wanted to sexualise your relationship with your daughter – she'd go along with it. What else can she do? She can't do otherwise. When it comes to Daddy, little girls are certainties. Fathers have the idea that if they made a move their daughters would rear back and slap them across the face. And say: I'm not that kind of little girl. What kind of little girl do you take me for?'

And then she walked away.

That's what a good caveman is meant to do, isn't it? When he hears the snap of a twig, the breath of an animal or enemy, then he disappears – even if oestrus is spreadeagled before him. The desire to reproduce meets its counterforce, which is the desire to go on being alive.

Something very ancient but much less primitive also constrained him. She was familiar, intimately familiar; in both senses she was already-seen. He didn't know it, of course, but the face behind her face was that of his *mother*. And his sister, and himself. He had seen her in the past all right: when he was twenty and she was ten, when he was sixteen and she was six, when he was twelve and she was two, when he was ten and she was a baby.

Thou shalt not uncover the nakedness of thy sister's daughter; she is thy niece; it is wickedness.

8. Not knowing again

'Will you get me a drink?'

'Yeah, sure. What would you like?'

'Chocolate Mix.'

'Coming up.'

'I read this book but I fell asleep before I could finish the end. Now I started the beginning and I don't know it again.'

She often said that: 'don't know again' instead of 'don't remember'. He understood what she meant.

'Well let's sit down and read it properly.'

He was alone with Billie in the kitchen. Sophie was being aired by Imaculada on Primrose Hill. And Russia was a presence, somewhere above. Billie, now, was treating him not like a father, quite, but like a reasonably reliable uncle . . . Xan was doing what his father had done, many times: he was being genially, even cloyingly considerate to a child while also entertaining murderous thoughts about a fellow male.

'Will you die before me?'

'I'm afraid so, darling.'

'Will Mummy die before me?'

'I'm afraid so.'

'Will Sophie die before me?'

'I hope not.'

'Will I die before her?'

'I don't know, darling. Now let's read the book.'

Xan had spent the morning on the trail of his enemy. The search – equally unreal and prosaic – began in the True Crime section of the High Street bookshop. A surprising number of the gangland exposés and ghosted memoirs (of various blaggers and bruisers) ended with an index; and a surprising number of these indexes contained references to Andrews, Joseph: the Airport Job, the two long sentences, the suspected murder, and, some time later, a massive tax fraud. It disconcerted Xan, and also disappointed him, to learn that Andrews went back at least half a generation beyond his father: he would now be over eighty. When he returned to the flat Xan typed the forbidden name into a search-engine. After a while he had before him a loose and jangling biography, and even a press photograph. It showed a headmasterly figure, with his wet grey hair combed back and a glass of champagne defiantly raised, poolside, on a plastic chair; a teenage creole sat perched on his lap, wearing a bikini bottom and a wet T-shirt. This was Brazil, twenty years ago; and nothing else followed.

'Can we do the horses?'

'Come on then. Up you get. This is the way the children ride . . . They walk . . . they walk . . . they walk. This is the way the ladies ride. To trot, to trot, to trot, to trot. This is the way the –'

'I need to do a pooh-pooch.'

'Do you? Come on then.'

'Quick. I'm desperate.'

Unthinkingly at first, he followed the old protocol. He helped her with the metal buttons of her jeans, and placed her on the toilet seat; then he withdrew, to await her call when she was ready to be wiped. In earlier days Xan had not exactly relished this routine: after four and a half decades, wiping his own backside had lost much of its magic, and wiping Billie's just seemed like more of the same. But now he admitted to himself that he would rather do it than not. The admission entrained another thought:

he knew, he understood, why some animals licked their young clean.

'Daddy?' he heard her say. 'When people move, they don't move they houses. They move everything else. They move they *carpets* . . . they *beds* . . . they *tables* . . . they *toys* . . . they *blankets* . . .'

He stood in the passage, by the stairs, in front of the forward-leaning gilt mirror. To this mirror he idly directed the remains of his tortured vanity: the thickening excrescences beneath the eyes; the looming lagoons of his hairline (the shampoo was getting colder every year, every month). Yes, he was thinking, it was a pity, it was a tragedy, that Joseph Andrews was eighty-five years old. There was so little of his life left to ruin; on the other hand, how much more easily, and how much more loudly, might he snap.

'. . . they *pencils* . . . they *fridge* . . . they *books* . . . they *television* . . . Ready, Daddy.'

He entered. The pleasure the smell gave him – the smell of shit lite . . . Not dizziness but a sense of general physical insecurity retarded him as he leant over her, and wiped, and activated the flush.

'My ploompah's sore.'

'I'm not surprised. The treatment you give it. Stand on here.'

He placed her on the basin shelf. In recent months Billie had gained weight uniformly, like a coating. He could now see the preliminary form of her breasts through her shirt; then the stomach still infantilely outthrust; and then the vulva, like a longhand *w*, but all abraded and enflamed – written in pink and red. Xan registered an impulse to weep, but it wasn't straightforward, this impulse; some of it had to do with his futile twistings and writhings in the night; and some of it felt coarsely and unworthily tender, like crinkling your nose over a Christmas card.

'You want some cream on that,' he said.

He went into the passage and called Russia's name. He went

halfway up the flight of stairs and called a second time. 'Russia! We need you!' Then he made out the heavy clatter of the shower a floor and a half above; she would be in there under the thick jet, naked behind the panel of glass.

'I'm not going to hurt you,' he said.

He washed and dried his hands . . . Her subtle eyes pleadingly appraised him, then widened; then freshened and refreshened in what he took to be an accession of trust. And so his daubed fingertip sought the intima.

Billie gave a gasp of relief: it was a thing of the past. But she was staring beyond him now, and when he looked round he saw that Russia, her hair swept up in a turban and her dressing-gowned figure inanimately still, was watching from the stairs.

9. To Otherville

Rory McShane had quite enjoyed his dealings with Xan Meo, in the past. He had had him over to the house a few times, first with Pearl, then with Russia. But now that Xan's career was evidently shot, Rory had transferred him to a different part of his mind: he belonged with all those who had to be humoured. Presumably there would be no good news to give him, ever again.

'How's Russia.'

Xan stopped scowling and said, as if to himself, 'I go round there and she calls the uh, the authorities. Can you credit it. You go round to your own house, and your own wife calls the fucking filth. Can you credit it.' And he started scowling again.

Rory wondered whether Xan was drunk: there was a kind of cruising hostility in him, and the promise of untoward personality change. But he decided that these emanations, plus the unvarying gaze and the embittered slur, were probably what you ended up with when you were smashed on the head. Still, Rory was being uncharacteristically careful not to give offence.

'There are funds coming in,' said Rory. 'I'm checking, and there's a few bob coming in.'

'I've got a few bob. That's not the point. I got a few bob, mate.'

'Yes. That's right. If you don't mind my asking – and do tell me to fuck off if you like – where did it come from, your few bob?'

Xan stopped scowling and said, 'Me mum. My mother. She died in a single room in a terraced house in Effley Road, E4. She was the sort of old woman who used the same teabag five times. But we knew she had a fair bit in the bank. When she died' – and here he frowned, recalling Pearl's third audit – 'it turned out she didn't just own the house. She owned the street. Nineteen houses, full of nineteen hundred Patels, which is what the police call them. Bangladeshis. Slum landlady. But when we'd made it right, and we was . . . we were slinging money about in uh, reparations and that, there was still a tidy whack left over. She was a monster, my mum, but I adored her.' He closed his eyes as he said it: 'Fantastic businesswoman. It's not the money, mate. It's the employment. I can't write and I can't . . . perform. Act. I'm gone. But I'll hump scenery, I don't care. Give me employment.'

And he started scowling again.

'You look uh, buffed up.'

'I do the gym. Up down, up down. In out, in out. Go on then: Karla White.'

'Oh yes. Karla White. I hesitated to impugn you with it. But yes. Karla White.'

'Tell me.'

'You've had a so-called offer from Fucktown . . . From Lovetown. Sextown.'

'. . . Didn't they have a sniper there?'

'They still do. The Sextown Sniper. And she's still at large.'

'She?' Then Xan remembered that this was one of Rory's

party-turns. To Rory (fiftyish, long-haired, much-divorced) all
malefactors were playfully assumed to be female. Somebody'd
say: We had a burglar last night. And he'd say: How did she get
in? Somebody'd say: I was mugged on my way here. And he'd
say: Was she armed?

'And they'll never catch her either. They can't. You know
about Lovetown? The porno people . . . When the Washington
believers started cracking down on them, the porno people found
a zoning loophole and moved the whole shebang to the San
Sebastiano Valley, Little Hollywood, Southern California. It's a
state within a state. So the uh, SSPD, which consists of about
one guy, can't get federal help. And who cares if it's just porno
people who're getting shot at? Who cares if – I don't know –
Casey Cunt gets winged in the arm? It's God's way.'

'All porno.'

'All porno. Pornotown. Othertown. Now your so-called offer
. . . They've been madly Anglophile for some time – long before
the Princess business. A lot of the girls are English. English Rose,
Brit Isles. Greta Britain, Unity Kingdom. And the men give themselves English stage-names. And knighthoods. Sir Phallic
Guinness. Sir Bony Hopkins. Sir Dork Bogarde. What they like
to do now is hire mainstream British actors to play so-called
character parts. Some of my younger clients have done it.'

And here he named a few actors whom Xan was more or less
aware of.

'It has a kind of grunge cachet. Like with minor rockstars.
It's considered a blinding coup for a rockstar to have a porno
girlfriend.'

'What would be the work?'

'Well you won't be doing any fucking, and you certainly won't
be doing any acting. You'll have to do a bit of watching, I suppose.
You know: you learn your so-called lines in the cab to some
Moorish villa consisting entirely of dens. They'll have worked it
into the so-called storyline that you happen to be present while

uh, Brit and Bony have sex.' He leant into his computer screen. 'Mm. Usually it's like a parody of a Hollywood offer: Prestige Economy, BudgetBower, three-figure fee. But this looks pretty reasonable. More than reasonable for one day's work. Well it is Karla White. She owns *Princess Lolita* ∴. It's called *Crown Sugar* and you're Rameses the Great. Know what I think you should do?' said Rory dutifully. 'Sit in on some workshops. Do some classes. Go easy. Get back to where you were before.'

Like the dark-clad others, those drawn into the city and then released from it at seven p.m., he returned to his flat with a plastic shopping-bag: provisions for one. He warmed and ate some savoury mess or other; and he drank the red wine – but not all of it. For nearly a week his afternoons, his evenings, had been journeys to non-consciousness; he woke up in a flat where (it seemed) thirteen or fourteen people had caroused the night before. Then, one morning, while he roiled in his own gases and acids on the benchpress, he thought: being drunk was a way of saying that, in your opinion, the universe was bullshit. No, more: it was a way of saying that you thought the universe was crap. And he didn't think he did think that. So tonight he was sober as he sat there staring at the wall. He was sober when he went into the bedroom and looked out of the window at the house across the street: that was the status quo ante; that was where he was before.

'Hello?'

'Xan? Mal Bale. How are you, boy?'

'Oh, you know. Mustn't weaken.'

'Uh, listen. About doing Snort. We can't now. He's just gone away for twelve years.'

'I'm sorry to hear that. Still, that'll learn him. What was it?'

'Malicious wounding. Though by the sound of it Snort got as good as he give. We can have him done inside of course, but where's the satisfaction?'

'Yeah. No. So I'm still owed.'

'You're still owed.'

'I've been going over something you said about — about our friend. You said I placed him. You said I "put him there". Put him where? Put him on the page? Or put him in Los Angeles.'

'No comment.'

'Is he in Los Angeles?'

'Uh — no comment. If you get my meaning. Uh, you *fancy* it, do you mate?'

'Well it's not up to me, is it? If I don't do something, I'll feel like shit for the rest of my life. Who's Karla White?'

'Karla White? . . . Nah, mate. So how's your probation? You survived that, did you: the bird in the hotel?'

'Well I did and I didn't.'

He finished the bottle of wine, that night. He needed a bottle of wine to get him through it: that is to say, he needed a bottle of wine to get him through an evening with only a bottle of wine to get him through it.

In the silent argument he was always having in his head with Russia, and in his far noisier exchanges with her surrogate, Tilda Quant, Xan maintained that he had acted as any father would — but he knew that his heart had not been quite right, there in the bathroom, with Billie. 'If you wanted to sexualise your relationship with your daughter — she'd go along with it. What else can she do?' This had proved to be a terrible transmission: de-enlightenment. He wished he could forget this; he wished, in Billie's phrase, that he didn't know again. Her power, her rights (which depended on what? Civilisation?) had seemed to disappear; and his power, his rights — they had corrosively burgeoned. To be alone with somebody who *had no choice*: it was the extent of her helplessness that had made him want to weep. Because all this was tied up with his fear of her being hurt, cut, pierced, split, stuck. And over and above it, and under and beneath it, was his sense of his own entitlements and deserts, his privileges, warrants, beliefs, all of them apparently non-negotiable: his sense of what he was due.

There was also inside him somewhere a baby of pristine misery; every day he felt for it and held it and fed it, and every night he put it to bed. But things were clearer now, as he squirmed and twisted. All the signs pointed the same way.

He had been to hospital. He was going to go to Hollywood.

CHAPTER EIGHT

1. February 14 (1.15 p.m.): 101 Heavy

'Ladies and gentlemen,' said Nick Chopko: 'what we just experienced is known as CAT, or Clear Air Turbulence. It was quite a drop but uh, I'm pleased to report that we're in okay shape, thanks to the . . . the skill and foresight of our Captain, whose last flight this is, now that all four girls are through college, one of whom I'm proud to call my fiancée: Amy Macmanaman. Give it up for the Captain . . . We encountered a very powerful following wind resulting in pressure-differential loss on the wings, otherwise known as a stall. It seems that everyone was belted down except for Flight Attendant Conchita Martinez in Business, who remained attached to her secured cart but suffered a jarred shoulder. We suspect she'll pull through. Fortunately all the overhead lockers held but three. These did not contain the dumbbells and bowling-balls some of you like to stow up there. Just some pillows and blankets and a bunch of cartons of cigarettes. CAT is a potential emergency and a very rare event. It was my first time. It was almost certainly your first time. It wasn't the Captain's first time. We expect no further problems, but as a precaution we do ask that you keep your seatbelts securely fastened. Thank you.'

'Do you know', asked the man in 2A, 'the proportion of passengers, on average, that survive a plane crash?'

'No I don't,' said Reynolds. 'Three per cent?'

'Actually it's more like forty. There can be one survivor, and there can be one fatality. And everything in between.'

'Is that a fact.'

'. . . I don't even know what I'm doing here.'

'Excuse me?'

'I don't even smoke. This seat. This cabin. Right in the crumple zone. I always sit right at the back. In among the toilets. Then the rest of the plane's your buffer. I was booked on IA but they did my miles in Frankfurt and offered me the upgrade. It's crazy. I don't even smoke. The secondary inhalation's killing me.'

'Remember that nice breakfast you had. And think about your slippers. Concentrate on them.'

Not inordinately, not egregiously loud so much as very clear, very pure: the explosive failure, the rending crack, of the starboard engine; the grisly physics of its catapulting fan blades and rotor spokes; the clacking strafe of metal-piercing shrapnel.

Flight Engineer Hal Ward: Shit Christ Jesus.
First Officer Nick Chopko: Which is the which is the?
Ward: What the hell these guys have done.
Chopko: Pull back the power back.
Captain John Macmanaman: Come on now. Let's get ahold of the airplane. Come on now. Let's fly the airplane.

CigAir 101 started to pitch; and then, to the inestimable advantage of Royce Traynor, it started to yaw.

2. The face has holes in it

The slightly longer and (by all accounts) very much dirtier version of *Princess Lolita* arrived at Ewelme by courier. Brendan Urquhart-Gordon was committing a crime by taking delivery of it; but Oughtred had told him that the UK was already awash with the American original together with every variety of piratical counterfeit (and a marginally abbreviated edition, with all the non-sexual material excised, could be found by means of a dark and costly visit to the Net). In any case Brendan's sense of transgression could hardly have been livelier as he signed for the package and hurried to his room to hide it. That night they retired at ten. And Brendan's anticipation of the small-hour screening was quick to satisfy the greed of his insomnia. He rose at a quarter to three. Captain Mate had been spoken to; and, remarkably, all three doors to the library were equipped with functioning locks and keys ... At Ewelme, the rudimentary heating-system wound down long before midnight. In pyjamas, then, in dressing-gown and greatcoat, and socks and hiking-boots, Brendan activated the paraffin stove, slipped the cartridge into the machine and sat there with his breath smoking. He turned the light off. He turned the light on. He turned the light off. He reached for the remote control.

No man on earth, Brendan considered, would watch *Princess Lolita* with the curiosity that he himself would bring to it. For example, who else had a sane claim to being in love with Princess Victoria, the real princess, as he did? More generally the experience would give him essential information. As he put it to himself, a little frantically: was he a 'joseph', one of nature's neuters, bowing his head as God put the horns on him? Alas, poor Joseph. Hard to keep your chin up, and to go on looking so wise and true. And, yes: nice try with the beard ... Brendan consulted the worn memory of his embrace with the Princess, how all the blood within him ...

Princess Lolita began with a still of Tori Fate's birth certificate, followed by a datelined clapperboard introducing footage from the first day of principal photography. Brendan made the calculation: the actress had been barely a week past her seventeenth birthday when filming began. An establishing-shot of a castle tower; then Tori Fate under a sheet in a four-poster. Yes, like, like, very like. Yet without complexity, as if the actress herself had been morphed. And even the surface resemblance proved specious, or cosmetic, the moment she opened her mouth, turning to her attendant and asking her (not in an accent from Brooklyn or Mississippi, but in English, dubbed, clipped, elocuted English

– the voice, Brendan felt sure, of a woman of the King's vintage) about the arts of love . . . Lolita's lady-in-waiting, a glistening Amazon with occult tattoos on her muscular breasts, then undertook a demonstration. The enjoyment of such a spectacle, Brendan soon decided, was a test of male heterosexuality that he just didn't pass. Outer tongue against inner tongue, upper against under – but now came a jolt. When the strap-on phallus was conspiratorially produced, and handed to Tori Fate, who buckled it about herself and stood there with a hand on its base, Brendan felt an abject stirring, a sick twitch, between his legs.

He slithered around in his chair and made a noise intended to drown something out – my God: pornography turned the world upside down. You gave your head away, and what your mind liked no longer mattered; now the animal parts were in the driving-seat – and tall in the saddle. As Lolita took her Amazon from the rear, Brendan attended to the ordeal of his own arousal. You'd better hope that this doesn't happen, he thought, when you're watching the one about the oversexed undertaker, the coprophagic pigfarmer, the ladykilling ladykiller . . .

By this stage Brendan expected to be twitching and twisting for the full ninety minutes. Yet only one more revelation awaited him, and this was insidious or cumulative, like the reluctant awareness of footsteps behind you, at night, on a lonesome road. Quite soon, exposure to Lolita's sentimental education was reminding him of his only bullfight, in Barcelona: after the third kill, fascination and disquiet remained, but these feelings were quietly joined by boredom. As the heroine sedulously dallied – now with a jodhpured Spanish grandee, now with a rude young groom, now with a spangled diplomat, now with a rugged derelict plucked off the street – it seemed to Brendan that the performers, with more haste than lust, were working their way through a checklist or duty-roster: some of this, then some of that, and then this and then that, including some of this, not forgetting that, and then maybe this, and then *always* that. Always that – at the end.

Grinning, and grinning gratefully, on her knees, Princess Lolita, awaiting anointment.

When it was over he went through it again, availing himself of the remote control. Watching pornography, watching the sex of others (this was already clear to him), you were constantly saying, No don't do that – do this, stop, don't stop, proceed, desist. The viewer was helpless before the spatial dimensions, but the remote control gave him power over time. Deploying this power, Brendan concentrated on freeze-framed close-ups of the actress's face. From certain angles, yes, remarkably like, remarkably like. But older. And not just a year older . . . If *Princess Lolita* had shape or form, then power was its pattern. The exertion of that power remained symbolic, and counterintuitive: it was the handsome derelict who pinioned the Princess with a pair of paper handcuffs; it was the sleek grandee who followed her about on all fours, led by a gossamer leash. Yet always this moment at the end, when power was no longer held in balance. The face, smiling, with male seed dripping from it, hanging from it. Brendan didn't like this spectacle. But his blood did.

It was with a sense of himself revised dramatically downward that he stood, and pressed the *eject*. For a moment he entertained the informed certainty that the machine would now seize (trapping its contents for later delectation – Henry's, Victoria's), and he would have to wrench it apart with his teeth and fingernails. But here it came, disgustedly expectorated on to the tiled floor . . . On the way to his room he came round a corner and almost fell over her: the Princess. He flung out both hands in her direction, to catch or steady her, and so released what was lodged beneath his armpit: and in clear contravention of all life's laws (which demand that every dropped object lands the wrong way up), *Princess Lolita* came to rest face-down, and in near silence, on the tussocky pelt of the carpet. Even so he had time to think that his greatcoat and dressing-gown would now fly open, to reveal not the full complement of his pyamas but a pair diligently savaged by scissors, with the trousers, secured by elastic bands, ending just above the knee.

'I'm so sorry, ma'am. I do apologise.'

Victoria hugged her robe to her. Plainly she was heading for the cavernous bathroom which the three of them shared (along with the rabbits and the archery sets). He expected, as he focused, to find her poetically pale, as pale as the weak dawn that was now almost upon them. But she wore an uneven flush and a roseate brocade on her upper lip and septum – she had not been well, was not well, was of course not well, this Christmas, this long January . . .

'Oh never *mind*,' she said, and stepped round him. At the corner she bent and turned, saying, 'Brendan – you know there's only one thing he can do.'

'I'm sorry, ma'am?'

She flipped a hand in his direction, and was gone.

An hour later Brendan was still muttering into his pillow . . . How did it go again? Oh yes: work. That's all you were doing. Making 'headway', was it? And rousing yourself from the enforced torpor of Ewelme . . . Working is what *they're* doing and that's why they look so old: old in the eyes. Is pornography just filmed prostitution or is it something more gladiatorial? Those hospitalic condoms: they don't keep them on at the end. And the face has holes in it . . . Gladiators: were slaves. But could win their freedom. What exactly has happened to you? he asked himself. Slave, thou hast slain me. Villain, take my purse. If ever thou wilt thrive, bury my body . . . Tori Fate turned seventeen on January 3. *Princess Lolita* was begun on January 12 and released on January 19, the day after the Victoria story metastasised. So hard upon – it followed hard upon. And thus the phenomenon explained. At the back of the common mind, for reasons fair or foul, was a virgin princess. A fifteen-year-old girl – but the most brilliant edition.

3. Apologia – 2: Keith the Snake

'Did you dear? Did you dear? Ah. I trust me wreath was in its proper place? Ah. Did you dear? Did you dear? Ah. He's coming is he? *Hand*some. Yes dear. God bless.'

Joseph Andrews put down one instrument and picked up another. *Click.*

'Going through what I done so far, I think I could've give the wrong impression. You must think I'm a stubborn sort of so-and-so – a bit too stubborn, sometimes, for me own good! And it could be you ain't that far wrong. On the *last* day of me eighteen months for [*click*] Jesus. Oh yeah [*click*] for uh, for Affray, some bloke come up to me and says, "Fancy a run at the wall, mate?" They had a uh, refectory table in the yard – must have been fifteen feet, we've reckoned, on its end. So I said I'd be absolutely delighted. I fancied it the more as they'd already give me me civvies. In a pillowslip. Lob it over – up and away. As it was we was only gone half an hour. And of course, when they've dragged you back in, they lay about you with a will. Course *that*: does the bear do its business in the woods? They've stuck me with the eighteen months again plus another six for the break, plus another year for what we done to the couple whose car we've took. Now I've said at the time that having a run at the wall was the right thing to do and I'd do it again. You got to keep on having a go at them. You got to keep – kicking up, we call it. But then it comes over you that . . . that prison is like the sea. You can be the strongest swimmer there ever was and you can keep kicking up, and kicking up, and kicking up, like grim death with all you got till your very last gasp. But the sea is the sea. It'll stay where it is and it'll never tire. [*Click . . . Click.*]

'So when I come out from doing me eight I threw in me lot with Tony Eist and Keith the Snake. Import–export business on the Costa del Sol. Me and Tony've gone back a way, through Wormwood Scrubs, Borstal, Detention Centre and Approved

School. But this Keith the Snake was a new one on me. And you know what? Don't ask me why, but there was something about Keith the Snake that I didn't quite . . . Call it a sixth sense, if you like. I couldn't put me finger on it, but there was something about Keith the Snake that come over a bit offo. Lovely dresser, Keith the Snake. Not flash. Smart. Always beautifully turned out.

'What we was doing was we was . . . Now I liked a drink, in them days, but I've personally never held with drugs. Offer me an aspirin and I dash it from your hand. And drugs – they pose a danger to the young. Then again, you got to adapt and move with the times, as you yourself know fully well, and you can't keep clinging to the past. We had eighteen powerboats shifting two ton of heroin through Puerto Banus per month. What we was doing was we was making runs, twice a night, to Algiers, where the gear come in from the Pakis and the Afghans. We had it going up the coast and flooding into Europe through Marseille. It was a highly lucrative trade – but then there's always the human element . . .

'Now we was none of us model citizens, but Tony Eist . . . he just wasn't normal. In the old days, he'd have himself committing crimes even in his *alibis*. He'd go: "I was never in on the Brink-Mats lark. I was busy flogging this condemned Argie beef." Or: "How could I have been in on the Waterloo jewellers? I was up West, demanding with menaces." A very dishonest man, Tony Eist. So one day Keith the Snake come up to see me in me villa. He's said he's done his sums – and Tony's been hiving off millions for hisself! Well I wasn't having that now was I.

'I've gone over there and we've had it out. And I've done him. Then, not content with that, he's got hisself mangled up in his lawnmower. Diesel. Two-seater. And his wife, she hasn't done the sensible thing and said she've run him down by accident. She's gone and shopped me to the Spaniards! [*Click.*] Go on then. [*Click.*] See, there was complicating factors. I'm not about to go banging on about the Other or the Urge or whatever you want to call it. For me, there's too much of that kind of thing as it is. But we're talking man to man, and, well, I've been giving Tony's wife Angie one. If I did have a regrettable habit, back then, it was that: giving me mates' wives one. [*Click*.] And they daughters and all, in them days. Little Debbie. And she's gone and grassed me up to Angie! [*Click*.] So a bit of malice there, I'd reckon. Oh yes, a little bit of spite. The Spanish coppers was all bent as arseholes of course, but what could they do, with that bloody great swamp on the front lawn and no Tony? Me and Keith the Snake've grabbed what we could and roared round to Alicante, flogged the boat, and hopped on a tanker to Belfast.

'[*Click*.] Go on then. He's no different. Him? . . . *Goo* on. [*Click*.] Regarding the matter of uh, giving your mates' wives one. Now in them days that's considered not on. Something you don't do. See, you can only do it if you . . . if you fear no man. Because all right, it's naughty – but what's the blokes going to do? Come round and have it with me about it? No. They gives their wife a biff and otherwise, and that's it. End of story. Which they thoroughly deserve. That's a female weakness, that is. Weakness for power. Weakness for strength . . . I never was married but I got engaged the twice. By an unfortunate coincidence, both of them've gone and took they own lives, for reasons best known to theirselves.

'During our time in the uh, "Emerald Isle", Keith the Snake and me've come to London the once. I had a bone to pick with a bloke who'd taken a liberty with me, years back, in Strangeways. Fella name of Mick. I should've just done him, shouldn't I. [*Click*] Should've just taken a chopper to the cunt . . . [*Click*.] But no. Fancy a fair fight instead. I've gone over to his yard [*click*] with me lapels lined with razorblades [*click*] and called him out. Told him a home truth or two and all. What a ruck *that* was. I don't know who've come off worst. Still, I've remained active even from me hospital bed. And that was the only crime I committed on British soil that I never paid me debt to society for. I mean the matter of the gold bullion and the VAT. Me and Keith the Snake was convinced we've found a genuine loophole, as there's no VAT on the coins we melted down and sold back to the Bullion House. Customs and Excise begged to differ. That would be about seventeen million in today's money. And to that I'll come back to.

'So Keith the Snake and me've transferred our endeavour to Dublin, and made a totally fresh start. I asserted meself and encountered no difficulty whatsoever. Them Irish in the south, I don't know what they think they're thinking of half the time. Too much of the Danny Boy, I don't know. They couldn't *believe* Keith the Snake and me, and the measures we was prepared to take. All in all we had seven very happy years in Eire. Then we come to this business with the IRA, and the extremely unfortunate parting of the ways with Keith the Snake.

'Now me I never wanted no publicity. People prominent in the underworld, they've got this terrible weakness for it. I seen publicity do for face after face. You know, you got power, you want it noticed. We all want to be top dog, mister big, king bastard. But it can't work like that down here, see, where everything moves the other way . . . What happened was, I was driving along in me Merc and lost me concentration. Next thing I know, I've gone and injured a young woman, who unfortunately soon died. Pregnant and all. Well there was no end of a song and dance about that – though it's perfectly legal to give someone a spill if you're sober, and me lawyer said there's definitely something a bit iffy in me breathalyser report. And then it's come out who I am and what I'm worth. And the IRA think: eye-eye.

'I'm still on bail and I heard there's a kidnapping planned. Which is a joke. As a Cat-A prisoner I've marged me bread with all their top boys, and there's no way in this world they'd've fancied me for a nab. But by then Scotland Yard's sticking its nose in, and I've reckoned it's time to move on. I've said to Keith the Snake, "Keith mate? It's time to move on." And he's gone,

"I never ploughed into no pregnant sort. *You* move on." Fair enough. "Fine by me, mate. You go your way, I'll go mine." [*Click.*] And that — and *that's* his idea of loyalty . . . [*Click.*] So I've started making me arrangements to emigrate across the water.

'Come the very sad conclusion of me friendship with Keith the Snake. It started off foolish really: just one of them things, I suppose. I've had a drink and I've gone and done him. I go in to visit and I've said, "Keith mate. I sincerely apologise. I bitterly regret what's occurred, and can you find it in your heart to overlook it." So we shake and that. I know it's going to take time for the rift to heal. Then of course he's barely out of hospital and I've gone and done him again. Carved up all his suits and all. Lovely materials. Only the best . . . That was me weakness in them days. I'd get uh, argumentative in me drink. And he kept getting on me nerves. Same stupid talk. I says, "Why you always off with them brasses? Why don't you have a proper bird?" "What, so's you can stuff her? Why d'you stuff your mates' birds?" "Well I always do that." "Yeah but why?" "I always stuff me mates' birds." "Yeah but why?" "Because I always do." [*Click.*] "Hey Jo. You want to stuff my bird so you can pretend you're me?" "Oi!" "Hey Jo. You want to stuff my bird so you can pretend you're *her*?" . . . Well it was all off then. [*Click.*] One of them uh, circular arguments. Blah blah blah.

'So now I've done him the twice. And here's what we done. I've let him strap me to the paddock wall (this is in me farm near Balbriggan). First thing he's done, he's told me it was never Tony Eist who skanked me off in Spain. It was Keith the Snake all along! So I've gone, "That's water under the bridge, that is. Now do your worst, mate. But no tools. Done?" And Keith the Snake's gone, "Done." And what's he gone and done? He's gone and done me with the fucking *scythe*. There he is in his underpants, screaming his head off. And left me wallowing in me own blood. I've had more than two hundred stitches in me chest alone. One stripe come down from me ear, across me cheek, under me nose, over me mouth, along me jaw and into me neck. [*Click.*] He's had a go at me privates and all. That's how low he's stooped. Ah, Keith mate . . . What happened, boy? [*Click.*] Well, after a liberty like that, why he never finished the job I'll never know. Was he barmy or what?

'After a short uh, sojourn in Paraguay, Argentina and Brazil, I've pitched up in Southern California. And if me name rings a bell from the newspapers it's because you're thinking of an old geezer sitting round a swimming-pool in Rio with a glass of champagne and a halfcaste brass on his lap. That's me brother Fred, and no icecream's ever had it easier, with the pension I give him. Me record here in Southern California is absolutely stainless, and I've uh, amassed another fortune in the home-video industry. Totally legitimately. [*Click.*] And if you want to see a beauty-queen with her head up a giraffe's arse, or otherwise, I'd be delighted to oblige. [*Click.*] I've done uh, extensive fundraising work for charity, and I hold the post of Treasurer at the local Citizens' Community Association.

'See, I'm not such a bad bloke really, when all is said and done. Me, I'm the nicest fella in the world – in the car like, you know, after you, darling. In the shops: "Morning all" and "God bless". I've lived me life by me own rules – and, yes, and *woe betide* anyone that breaks them. I am who I am. Jo is Jo. It's just the road I went down. It's just the game I played. It's just the game I played.

'Now to business.'

A musclebound horsefly materialised on the spotted knuckle of his right hand. He reached slowly for the holster with his left.

'You didn't like that, did you mate . . .'

He leant forward to drink in the full fragrance of the propellant. Like a cut-price air-freshener – the negative essence of all the smells it was meant to conceal. His eyes moistened: takes you back.

It was like the choking sweetness of some new cell they've

just flung you in. Scented detergent, fighting a lost battle against another man's fluids, another man's fear.

4. Yellow Tongue

Clint Smoker sat, for now, in a milk bar on Ignacio Boulevard. He typed: 'So some so-called 15-year-old is crying "rape" after a bit of fun in a ditch with an older lad.' He deleted this: got to pace yourself . . . Clint was expected, ninety minutes from now, at Karla White Productions on Innocencio Drive . . . No, it had to be admitted: he was having the time of his jounalistic life, was Clint Smoker. That morning he had interviewed a pimp named DeRoger Monroe in the Lovetown Greyhound Station, and filed an admiring profile. Emptying sachet after sachet of sugar into his Coca-Cola, DeRoger had told him how it worked: you tell them to go out there and be superstars, while, in the meantime, you do hard drugs with other pimps. Then when the birds are down to their last tooth, you 'take them to Florida': give them a final pasting and then boot them out the door . . . Soon, Clint would be meeting with Karla White. And, later, there was the mouthwatering prospect of an hour with Dork Bogarde.

Nor was it merely Clint's reportage. What about the editorials, the think-pieces, the 'virtual cult' (as Strite had put it), back home, of Yellow Dog. He typed:

- So some grasping icequeen is seeking compensation for 'sexual harassment', having left her job after a bit of harmless horseplay round the water cooler.

  She's already had a few quid for her ripped clothes and the dental work.

  And now it's for 'emotional distress' that she's taking those nine lads to court.

Well she's not going to come clean, is she?

She's not going to say: I f**king loved it!

All the girls Yellow Dog's worked around go batty at the thought of a proper goose.

And don't tell me there's one of them, when you're alone in the lift, that doesn't like her nip being given a healthy twist.

Hallo, here comes old Marge, grunting and sighing with her mop and her pails.

She's down on those shiny red knees, moaning and groaning, with her great fat arse in the air.

Look lively lads – where's the office cattleprod?

Clint paused, and mused. Karla White: best norks in Lovetown. It's well known. Dark glasses? Check. He mused, and paused, and worked on:

• So some old boiler in Hammersmith got smacked about a bit by a couple of lads while they were relieving her of her pension.

Now that's well naughty, boys, and *don't* do it again.

But spare us the violin, okay.

Spare us the clock-stopping photos of the biddy with the black eyes.

She's only 77 – a child in this day and age – and she can f**king well take her chances like anybody else.

Besides, she's been stinking up the place for long enough, hasn't she?

When they get like that they're better off dead.

So get well soon Gran – if you must.

But leave out the f**king whinge this time. Alright?

A little light told Clint that he had an e in, which he now shared:

dear 1: o, it all went 1derfully,
1derfully – with dad. i was always
his favourite, u c. when i was a
child he worshipped the very
ground i walked on; 4 him, the
sun shone out of my * . . . he was
as punctual as ever, & as gallant,
with the bouquet of 4sythia and
the creamy chocol8s. always the
perfect gent 2 me, full of amusing
stories about his girlfriends. i
prepared his favourite dinner (tripe
& brains), with 40fied wine, in the
candlelite. Then the bombshell, the
utter c@astrophe: my father has
been diagnosed with : cancer. i am
absolutely devast8ed. k8.

Poor little *thing*, thought Clint. Still, that can work to a man's advantage. You get credit for not being dead.

For once in your life.

'Fucktown,' began Karla White, 'in its current phase, which could be ending around now with the *Princess Lolita* phenomenon, might as well be called Hatefucktown. That's the dominant form: Hatefuck. But let's go back a bit.'

'I'll just see if this . . .' said Clint, giving his tape recorder a malevolent stare.

'. . . Porno was self-policing until the second term of the last administration, when, as you know, all of a sudden we had a porno president. Porno, under this porno presidency, stopped policing itself and entered its Salo period.'

'Sorry, Karla. Salo?'

Karla considered her interlocutor, and wondered if there'd

be any point in telling him about Mussolini and the Republic of Filth. She was enough of an American to grant interviews more or less automatically, but she had run a light check on Clint; she knew about his recent stay at John Working's joint in the San Sebastiano Valley; she knew the circulation figures of the *Morning Lark*, and had some idea of its contents.

'An embrace of dirt,' she said. 'Immediately there was an overwhelming emphasis on male–female sodomy. The rallying cry was Pussies Are Bullshit. They'd sign off with it on the phone: "Pussies Are Bullshit!" One director said, "With anal, the actress's personality comes out." Oh sure: her personality. They talked about female virility, female testosterone. Which is strange considering the next phase, post-Pussies Are Bullshit.'

Clint steadied his dark glasses and resumed his attempt to stare out Karla's breasts. They stared back, irreproachably inno-cent and unblinking; and they awakened humility in him. He thought it was beautifully generous of her not to hide them, to allow them to be warmly present. It also occurred to him that at any moment they might count down from three and he'd do exactly as they said.

'The essential self-policing had to do with two areas, male–female violence and paedophilia. Male–female violence was called Black Eye, and began with the notorious "line", *Male Dawn*. They'd tell the girls: Don't be too proud to cry while we do this. Basically they roughed them up, and roughed them up for real. The paedophiliac tendency was unofficially known as Short Eye, where the girls wore kiddie clothes and talked in squeaky voices and played with dolls while granddads peed in their mouths. And worse. I'm serious. The nymphets *weren't* nymphets, of course. Along with your HIV-clearance, your birth certificate is your work permit. You have to produce it, even in geronto-porno, or White Hair. Even eighty-five-year-olds have always had to prove that they're over seventeen. That's porno.'

Clint thought: codger-todger. Good riff.

'All this came to an end when the new administration started their holy war on porno. Black Eye and Short Eye disappeared right away. Pussies Are Bullshit staggered on for a while, because male–female sodomy is not illegal in every state. But then some busybody – some spoilsport or killjoy, Clint – would buy a sodomy tape in Arkansas, where it isn't illegal, and take it to Alabama, where it is, and you'd be indicted in Montgomery. And so on. But porno people are believers too. It's the contrarian nature of the form. And they wouldn't give it up. Dozens of production companies were wiped out and some of the very top guys went to jail. And in an Alabaman correctional facility, I can assure you, they don't need to be told that pussies are bullshit. Then the zoning loophole, and the founding of Lovetown. And the dominant genre, these days, is unquestionably Hatefuck.'

They talked on – about Hatefuck, about Cockout, about Boxback, about Red Face, about Yellow Tongue . . . After an hour with Karla, Clint was becoming vaguely aware of his surroundings – glass, mirrors, tubular furniture. It might have been any old ad-firm except for the posters: porno girls, in porno colours, with porno pouts . . . *Throne Together*, *Royal Flesh*, *Pump and Circumstance*, *Anne of a Thousand Lays*, *Mary Queen of Sluts*, *Falstiff*, *King Rear*, and *Princess Lolita 2*, *Princess Lolita 3*, *Princess Lolita 4* . . .

Feeling something lift from her, Karla followed Clint's gaze. She said,

'They go together, don't they – porno and puns? It couldn't be otherwise. Because humourlessness is the lifeblood of porno. One genuine smile, and everything would disappear.'

'It's finished, though, this, isn't it: video. Now it's the Web.'

'Rentals *are* dying. Despite *Princess Lolita*. See the girls. They have a flared-pants look. A beehive look. The future's in inter-active. What they call "self-tailoring". And the viewer will direct.'

Clint slid off his sunglasses, and smiled, deciding to exercise his new confidence: the confidence he enjoyed as a Laureate of the San Sebastiano Academy for Men of Compact Intromission. He said,

'Do you miss it? Performing?'

'No,' said Karla, who had answered this question, and all others, many times before.

'You were an abused child, weren't you. Were they all that, the actresses?'

'There's something in it. It's the . . . creation myth of porno. But porno's just an industry now. Times change, Clint. I know a girl who goes to the Mature Video Awards with her *parents*. Her father came out brandishing her statuette for Best Anal.'

'Is there anything you wouldn't do? As an actress. Fisting and pissing and that?'

'. . . I stopped before it went that way. I stopped before Pussies Are Bullshit.'

'Uh, fancy a drink later?'

'With a view to what?'

'You tell me. You're the pro. Another day, another cock. You tell me.'

He noticed that she was staring at him with unchecked fascination – with entirely undissimulated fascination. Clint started to feel twenty-seven thousand dollars poorer – and Karla hadn't yet said what Karla said next.

'That's right. And the men I'm used to', she said, and suddenly seized the tumbler of water on her desk, 'are like *this*.'

Clint followed instructions: faced with noncompliance, construct the counterfactual. 'Well. Wouldn't have worked out anyway. Off to Hawaii in an hour or two.'

'I thought you were seeing Dork Bogarde.'

'He's uh, he's out of town himself.'

'No he's not,' said Karla, standing. 'I'm expecting him at Dolorosa Drive tomorrow morning. He's doing a scene with Charisma Trixxx. Day one of *Crown Sugar*.'

'Hold up. Got me days confused.' Clint added ruefully, 'Kate, she's always going on at me about it. So maybe I uh, I'll look in. Fly on the wall.'

With an illegible shudder she said, 'This set will most definitely be *closed*.'

That evening, after three hours of Black Eye and Cockout in his hotel, Clint attained a sense of belonging: a sense of belonging, in Lovetown.

Sir Dork Bogarde lived in a porno pad with a porno pal, Hick Johnsonson, in Lovetown's Fulgencio Falls. When Clint arrived, and was made welcome, they were out on the porno patio . . . In the small garden enchained porno parrots swore and shat around the porno pool. Dork lolled on a porno pouffe, his head supported by additional porno pillows; Hick poured the porno wine. It seemed that Dork had only one thing he wanted to talk about, however: porno pay.

'I mean there am I,' he said, with a certain finicky jauntiness embedded in his indignation, 'naked as I am. I'm out there, with sweat pouring off my person, cocking out . . . some little rube who's just climbed off the Dog – and I get three hundred dollars? Excuse me. Excuse me. While the guy *watching*, in an easy chair, some . . . asshole from Ye Olde England, gets ten grand? They do me that indignithy? I don't think so. I don't think so.'

Sincerely puzzled, and yet with the rosiness of genuine admiration (indignithy: he made other slips like that – but you had to hand it to the guy, with his porno pectorals, his porno ponytail, his monstrous porno penis, familiar to all Dork's fans), Clint said,

'Yeah but you're the one getting it wet, aren't you mate.'

Sir Dork implored Clint to consider something: porno pressure.

'Did it get here yet?' Dork asked Hick. 'It', Dork had told Clint earlier, was 'the tape of the test-fuck of Charisma Trixxx', to whom Dork was to be introduced the following day, on the set of *Crown Sugar*. 'Clint? Could you perform with three breaks for coffee and one for lunch? The lights? The people?'

'Yeah but there's a way round that now, isn't there.' Clint thought resentfully of Karla White, and what she had told him about porno and Potentium: 'They all use it and they all say they don't.'

'I never use it,' said Dork.

Clint recalled her words. Potentium, said Karla, had turned out to be a Midas curse for the porno male. Pre-Potentium, a *flop* meant a skipped day and a net loss. Post-Potentium, it meant that the man was ready fifteen minutes late, and had splotchy cheeks (hence Red Face) and a porno headache. But there were fewer suicides and crackups, and they all started using it. 'The change sparked controversy,' as Clint would later write; and we must remember, along with Dork Bogarde, that 'this was at the heighth of Pussies Are Bullshit' . . . Some said that Potentium was bullshit too: it affronted the market forces having to do with the reality of arousal. People who argued that way turned out to be purists – because the customer didn't care. 'Being able, or likely, to perform in public', Karla said, 'was once a marketable skill. Now anyone can do it. The men – the grunts, the stiffs – never were a draw. And now they're just life-support systems for a tab of Potentium.' Karla said she was surprised. She said she had always thought that the customer was a lot gayer than that . . .

Dork now confronted Clint with a porno paradox. 'See, Clint,' he said, 'we get pressure coming the other way: Cockout. How can a man fulfil his fanthasy when, hanging over him at all times, he faces the spectre of Cockout?'

After a while Dork returned to the subject of porno pay, and porno percentages, until Hick confirmed the arrival of the tape of the test-fuck of Charisma Trixxx.

'Look at that,' said Dork, gesturing at the screen. 'Suave ass. Sincere bush. I don't just mean the mohawk. I mean the presentation. I'm talking the whole box.'

'She chugs good,' allowed Hick.

'Good neck-work on the back-take.'

'And I like the tongue-slide on the feed-draw.'

Fifteen minutes later Hick said, 'Here we go. Gracious address for the facial.'

'. . . Wow,' said Dork. 'See that? Right in the *eye*.' Dork turned to Hick (it was established earlier that Hick had been known to do Gay). 'Does that hurt? I mean, does it kind of burn?'

'Burn? It's like fucking fire. And she didn't even flinch.'

'I won't have any kind of problem tomorrow. Flinch? She didn't even *blink*. Clint, hadn't you . . . ?'

'Yeah well thanks, lads,' said Clint. 'Dork mate. I happen to know one of your uh, conquests.' And he felt luxury as he pronounced her name: 'Donna Strange . . .'

'Excuse me?'

'Donna Strange . . .'

'Excuse me?'

'Uh – big English brunette with a silver streak in her hair and a crinkly mouth . . . She sucked you off underneath a pyramid and then you had her up the arse in a helium balloon. Then you landed on Everest and shot all over her tits.'

'. . . I spent on her breatsts? That's so – *passé*. You'd think I'd remember that.'

On his way back to the hotel Clint pulled in at another video store. And there it all was, yet again, laid out in categories, like a dramatisation of the words of Karla White. Not Hatefuck, because everything was Hatefuck unless labelled otherwise. But Cockout, and Bullshit Cockout, and Boxback, and Red Face, and White Hair, and Yellow Tongue ('Yellow Tongue', she said, 'is for those who miss the motel room, the handheld video cam, the ghoulish lighting, and the plain cast ill on drugs'), and, of course, the category called Princess Lolita.

He worked into the small hours on his starry-eyed profile of

Dork Bogarde. Then, to release tension, he pounded out some Yellow Dog. At about noon, London time, he received the following message:

> my only 1: thank u so much 4
> your e of consol8ion. i don't no y,
> but things r clearer now. it feels as
> if a gr8 w8 has been lifted from
> me. Even as my father lies in st
> &rew's, f8ally unwell . . . u no
> what i'm thinking? i think i'm
> 4lling in love with u, clint. yes u,
> and no 1 else. u, clint! u, u, u! r u
> o fait with the poetry of ezra £? as
> i transmitted this, i thought of the
> lines: '& now i bring the boy in,
> on his knees, & send this 1,000
> miles, thinking.' i'm mad 4 u, clint.
> come 2 me on your return. only
> when u & i r 1 will i feel truly @
> peace. 10derly, k8.
> ps: i vener8 yellow dog. i lite c&les
> to yellow dog. i make a god of
> yellow dog.

Yellow Dog wiped away his tears and settled down to an hour or two of Yellow Tongue.

5. Cur moment

The third (and final) message from their mole, their enemy's enemy, took the form of a no-fingerprints communication directed at Brendan's laptop. Earlier that day a similarly anon-dot service-provider released six new stills of the Princess, one of which, sensationally, showed her daunted face half-dimmed by the shadow of the intruder . . . The message Brendan received ran as follows: 'Ultimatum will be presented on February 10. Strongly advise immediate compliance. Please to reemphasise: the material on the Princess is all light and magic. All light and magic.' Feeling sick to his stomach, but also wonderfully lightheaded, Brendan issued a contemptuous press-release from Ewelme. Then he had his worst talk ever with the King.

'Here's a turn-up, sir,' he began. 'Captain Mate has resigned. Effective immediately.'

'I'm very pleased to hear it, Bugger.'

'It's a bit rum, though, sir. We can –'

'I've been meaning to chuck him for years.'

'Sir?'

'Yes, Bugger. On account of his physical appearance. But I could never be fagged. Now never mind him, and get on with it. You've got that glint in your eye, Bugger. Yes you have. You're preparing me for something horrid, I can tell.'

Henry looked out of the window of the Royal Train; but there was nothing to see. To be heading *north*, north from Ewelme with its mists and brown spume, and at the very worst time of year . . . He thought: the cur moment. I shall have to revisit it, relive it. The cur moment.

'That'll be all, Love.' Henry waited. He said, 'Do you believe in life after death?'

'You're changing the subject.'

'I'm not changing the subject. It's practically the only subject there is. With you. These days, darling.'

'Well yes I do. Do you?'

'. . . No.'

'See? What you have, it isn't faith. It's just habit.'

'Faith . . . faith is a power. It gets weaker as you age. Like all powers.'

'You *have* changed the subject. And the *subject*,' said the Princess, 'the *subject* is this. To distract attention from my uh, imbroglio in the Yellow House –'

'Whatever that was.'

'Whatever that was. To distract attention, and to win some sympathy from the media and the million,' she said, 'we're going to Scotland to kill Mummy.'

'Don't. Be. Silly . . . Darling.'

After a while he said, 'Bugger told me that you told him that there was something I could do. Uh, Brendan, rather. He took you to mean that there was something I could do – that would make it all right.'

'One thing I will tell you is that this isn't it. Murdering Mummy isn't it. Oh I'm not going to spring to your rescue. You'll have to get there on your own.'

Dusk was coming nearer. They rushed to meet it. He sat back, and looked for what comfort he could find in thoughts of He Zizhen.

In his bedroom at Tongue he was woken by the draughts at half past five. He kicked Love out of his army cot and then drank the tea with great gouts of brandy in it until his teeth stopped chattering. A bath of blood heat; a cold-water shave. He put on his black suit, and his hardiest overcoat – inherited from his father, Richard IV, and still a sober tribute to the protective power of cashmere and silk. He stepped out into the morning twilight and the cock-crow.

Unlike his numerical predecessor, who would habitually exhaust a dozen stallions in the space of an afternoon, Henry IX loathed anything that involved horses (with the single exception of Royal Ascot); but Pamela, of course, had been a lifelong equestrienne. Times beyond number he had shaken his head, from a seated position, and watched her trot off, seemingly about thirty feet from the ground . . . That September, at Tongue, the Queen Consort did not return from her second ride of the afternoon. Her mare, Godiva, returned; but Pamela did not return. The King seized a bicycle in the courtyard and, with much wobbling and wiggling . . . But now, on foot, in his overcoat, Henry moved from gravel to lawn, beginning to retrace these steps.

He remembered the way the colour of the day changed. At first he was merely very frightened, mostly for himself (the bicycle), and also rather bored (he could already hear the exasperating halloos of normality regained). On the cinder path he pedalled to the shoulder of the slope, and turned: Godiva, riderless in the stableyard. And then the colour of the day changed.

It was he who found her . . . Pamela had told him about the softened thump of the horse's hooves as you approached the chalk quarry, and thither he rode – until, with a horrified lurch, he skidded to a halt and assessed the obscenity in his path. A fat snake, already dead, already putrescent: fat, moist, yellow, like the voided boil of some tutelary troll or Friar Rush . . . Yes, he thought: Godiva could be forgiven for rearing at such a sight. And there, down the brambly slope, Pamela lay, in her boots, her jodhpurs, her tweed jacket, her velvet helmet, arched backwards over a boulder with her eyes wide open. The bike fell with a clatter and a brief purr of spokes. He moved through the snowscape, the moonscape, of the winter chalk.

'Oh no, Pemmy.' But he stressed it on the second and fourth syllables: he said it as he had said it many times before, when being reminded of some recurrent social chore, when interdicting a loud headscarf, or when she brought off a forceful roll at ludo or backgammon.

Then, rhythmically gathering air for his moment, his cur moment, Henry said, 'At least, at least, at least – at least there won't be any more bally . . .'; and it was then that his shoulders began to shudder: '. . . any more bally three-a-*clockers*.' And the words enveloped him like an unrecognisable fart, saying: yes, oh yes, this is you, this is you.

Aboard the helicopter they found a faint pulse in her groin, and an hour later she was on the machine at the Royal Inverness.

That was two years ago. In his black suit, his black coat, Henry stood in the white land of the chalk field. It was time to awaken the Princess.

The patient looked like an enormous and ancient squaw, with the warpaint of death on her, but regally breathing.

Henry passed his hand down through the air.

'Mummy's . . .' said Victoria.

'But she breathes.'

Victoria pointed to the parallel lines on the screen.

'But she breathes.'

And she breathed greedily, lustily. Could she still reach up and hold him and draw him in? And he smelt himself all over again – the smouldering smell of the male secret, like a fire doused in rivers of sweat.

'That's just the machine,' said Victoria. 'It's the machine that's breathing.'

'Turn it off,' he cried. 'Turn it off. Turn it off.'

6. February 14 (1.25 p.m.): 101 Heavy

System Aircraft Maintenance: One oh one heavy, please repeat.

Captain John Macmanaman: Confirm engine number-two explosive failure. Number-two accessory drive system is blown. Secondary debris hit the horizontal stabiliser and severed number-one line and number-three line. These hydraulic systems are *down*. Copy?

SAM: Copy, one oh one heavy. You lost number two.

Macmanaman: No. We lost all three.

SAM: One oh one heavy. You lost number three?

Macmanaman: We lost all of them.

SAM: One oh one heavy. You still have number one, right?

Macmanaman: All three are gone. Repeat. All three are gone.

SAM: One oh one heavy. Copy, copy. You have emergency hydraulics.

Macmanaman: Affirmative. But the goddamned auto won't disengage. It thinks one through three is fictitious. Extreme yaw. Extreme pitch.

Flight Engineer Hal Ward: Try it.

First Officer Nick Chopko: Yeah but . . .

Ward: *Try* it.

Chopko: . . . Auto disengaged!

Macmanaman: I feel it. I feel it. Auto disengaged. Hydraulic quantity returning. Now flying by direct law. Nose is coming up. Steadying. Steadying. Still yawing but no pitch. It won't give us flaps.

SAM: One oh one heavy. I'll clear frequency and give you Detroit.

Chopko: The backup hydraulics – where *are* they anyway?

Ward: Where they used to be, in the old days. Under the cabin floor.

Macmanaman: Come in!

Flight Attendant Robynne Davis: Is it over? Are we okay?

Macmanaman: We're coming out of it, Robynne. What's it like back there?

Davis: Like a vomitorium in ancient Rome. They can take a yaw but they hate a pitch.

Chopko: We got the pitch. We'll get the yaw. Now what?

Flight Attendant Conchita Martinez: Lucy says the floor's hot. The passengers are saying the cabin floor's hot. Left side. Between the wings.

Chopko: *Christ.* Any smoke?

Martinez: How could they tell?

Macmanaman: You know what we need? What we need is an airport.

No, you couldn't tell — about the smoke. A lavish bonfire of wet leaves would have made little difference to the pall. In Economy, 314 people had cigarettes in their mouths (they weren't giving up *now*), including the occupants of rows twenty-five to thirty, seats H and I and J, who, in addition, had their feet off the floor and tucked in underneath them.

There was smoke in the hold, too, under the port wing. But this was smoke of a different kind. With this kind of smoke (hot, thick, black), you wouldn't be breathing it: you'd be eating it. And it would be eating you . . . Just discernible in the pallet facing the cargo door, Royce Traynor, mantled in ebony, stood upright, slowly steadying on his base as if to regather his strength. When the plane yawed to starboard, he sank back, waiting, against a column of stacked bags. Next, the port wing began its sharp drop, and Royce, after bristling for an instant like a wave before it breaks, dived forward to butt the diagonal handle of the cargo door . . . This door was not a plug door, opening inwards, and kept slammed shut by air-pressure. It opened outwards, to increase holdspace and revenue . . . He's up again now, with the yaw to the right, and leaning back, in weary but determined contemplation. Then the tottering vertical and the piledrive into the handle of the cargo door, with all his weight. Which was the weight of what? Which was the weight of the past.

You could see why Royce had to do this. When the sprinklers came on, you could see why Royce had to do this. He couldn't trust to fire. It was now his aim to go for the very throat of the aircraft. Decompression, explosive decompression, was what he wanted to bring about, and the collapse, the catastrophic strangulation, of the cabin floor, with all its tubes and veins and arteries. Most proximately, the blown door would mean his own escape (he would be the first to go), his martyrdom, after death.

With no blood in him any more, just wax and formaldehyde, Royce sways. The front teeth, perhaps, are bared: the teeth of a sunbelt golf pro. Royce sways, but not drunkenly. He rests, catching his breath, unappeasably preparing himself for fresh assault.

PART III

CHAPTER NINE

1. The syrups of the sky

Xan Meo hit Fucktown at four p.m. on February 2, when the Fucktown Shuttle landed at Fucktown's Felixio International Skyport . . . All the signs, of course, said Lovetown, as in Welcome to Lovetown. But people very often accidentally called Lovetown Fucktown. It was clearly something Lovetown had had to get used to.

First, at LAX, he was required to pick up his suitcase and clear it through Immigration. This wait at the luggage carousel, he realised, was an interlude of enforced, of mandated ennui. It wasn't like standing at a bus-stop with nothing to read: the bus, when it came, would announce itself; and there were other things to look at. No, you had to go on watching, staring; you had to go on performing humble mental tasks involving the differentiation of shape; you had to go on dully imagining dull complication, dull delay. A lanky Englishman was talking fearfully to his mobile phone: 'It's going round . . . It's going round . . . It's not on it . . . It's stopped going round . . . It's going round . . . It's not on it . . . It's not on it . . . It's going round . . . It's not on it . . . It's not on it . . .' And, to Xan, this poem of boredom was like a douche of self-discovery. He couldn't remember when he'd last been bored, and this was what it was like. It was like civilisation. Because you're never *bored*, are you, when you're always raring to fuck or fight.

A courtesy car transferred him to the second airfield. Here the little toytown terminal contained a busy, frisky, jittery throng: multicoloured lovebirds massing ecstatically for the long flight south. Xan felt further depersonalised by the open and unsmiling use, hereabouts, of the byname Fucktown – as in 'LA–San Diego with a stopover in Fucktown', 'What takes you to Fucktown?' and (from a man in uniform) 'And is Fucktown your final destination?' For an instant, as he stood beneath the blatting, clacking information-board, he saw, or thought he saw, the directive '14:05: FUCKTOWN 5D LAST CALL. The twirling cubes quickly corrected themselves, with a paparazzo flutter. Lovetown's other cognomen seemed to be used only in reference to the Sextown Sniper . . .

In the plane his consciousness of anomaly, of regrettable innovation, persisted and ramified. It took him several minutes to identify an important absence – that of children. *All* planes have children on them. But not the shuttle to Lovetown: no babies, bassinets, no hefted bundles. Well Lovetown was a babyless place, he supposed. It was Adult. There were teenage passengers on board, male and female, who couldn't possibly be destined for erotic employment; but Lovetown needed its hatcheck girls, its busboys and carboys, just like anywhere else. And some of the older people maintained a patina of childishness – the cartoon, the picture book. As he returned from the toilet he noticed that some men and women got younger, or older, fast, as you walked towards them: about five years for every row of seats.

Surrounded by tans of butterscotch and eggyolk, by sculpted puppyfat in tanktop T-shirts, with noses too small or hair too big or mouths too wide, too full, and engaged in ceaseless laughter, as if the passengers were the unified audience of a coruscating comedy . . . The stewardesses in their blue suits looked more normal, less stylised in mien and gesture, than the intransigent titterers they tended. The Captain put them down in Lovetown, and the tube of canned sex emptied itself in relays of tits and pits and zits.

Again by courtesy car he was driven to the U Hotel, past suburban gardens of brown grass and haggard cacti. Xan read about it in the complimentary *Lovetown Journal*, fished from the pouch of the seat in front: the U Hotel belonged to a chain whose owner had earned 78 billion dollars for realising that *w* was the only non-monosyllable in the English alphabet. Scrapping the supposed abbreviation, which had human beings gabbling out nine syllables, and replacing it with three other syllables chosen at random (or, indeed, with the unabbreviated phrase 'world wide web') would save global businesstime half a decade per day . . .

As he climbed from the car a boobjob of a raindrop gutflopped on his baldspot. Lovetown: a sprung-rhythm land of earthquake, brushfire and mudslide, of stripmall, freeway and gridlock, of hatefuck, cockout and boxback, of blackeye, of whitehair, of yellowtongue.

'Hatefuck evolved very naturally in a way,' said the voice of Karla White, *'because there had never been . . . any love lost between the actors and the actresses. The girls earn five or six times more than the men, and the gap goes on widening. As you can imagine, the scenarios for Hatefuck are extremely monotonous. "So this is the big guy, huh?" "You'd better believe it, bitch." "Have you taken your pill like a good little boy?" And so on. And she'll ask him about the car he drives, if any, and the square-footage of his shitbox in Fulgencio Falls. Then came Cockout.'*

'Cockout,' said a man's voice.

'Cockout,' said Karla White.

Xan went on to the balcony and smoked a cigarette. Down at the desk they had told him about the English journalist who was recently arrested and jailed for smoking a cigarette in his room. They had also given him Karla's package: the script of *Crown Sugar*, the audiotape ('Background'), and his docket for the courtesy car which, the following morning, would take him to Dolorosa Drive . . .

'Cockout is a sub-genre, or an anti-genre, within Hatefuck. Much prized for its rarity, Cockout occurs when the man actually succeeds in arousing the woman – to such a point where she stops calling him

a piece of shit and starts offering encouragement or even praise. The father of Cockout, Lover, Trash My Ass, was an uncontrollable hit. Nothing like Princess Lolita, but very considerable business.

'*Very soon, "I cocked her out" became the pet boast of the porno male, "He cocked me out" the pet peeve of the porno female. But its rarity created pressure, giving rise to a further sub-genre, Bullshit Cockout. Bullshit Cockout is when the — usually very minor — porno female pretends, after grim resistance, to get herself cocked out. And a lot of ten-year-old porno started being recycled as, in effect, Bullshit Cockout, suggesting that that was what porno was, all along: Bullshit Cockout.*'

Below, Xan abruptly noticed, in about half of the thirty or forty plotlike gardens he could see, pornography was being made: little brown bodies around little blue pools.

'*True Cockout seemed to throw a lifeline to the porno male — to begin with, anyway. Every morning, as he thumbed his way to work, there was always the sustaining dream of getting hold of a head-lining actress and cocking her out. The grunts, the poor stiffs, started rating each other by their cockouts. You know, stats and averages — like baseball. There was even an actor called Cockout. Kirk Cockout. He sure didn't last long . . . Because Cockout was another poisoned chalice for the porno male. After a while no girl would even consider working with a guy who had cocked her out — or cocked out any of her friends. Porno men with any kind of rep for cockout stopped getting phonecalls. Then they started fearing cockout. A further humiliation was on its way in the form of Boxback.*'

'*Boxback.*'

'*Boxback.*'

The sun was dropping down over the shoulder of the building. He leafed through the twelve-page script of *Crown Sugar*. In his only scene, Xan was supposed to exchange some words with Charisma Trixxx and then watch her perform with Sir Dork Bogarde (as follows: 'Blow. Doggy. Cowgirl. Reverse Cowgirl. Facial'). His lines were not difficult or numerous but he was

surprised by the ease with which he got them by heart. He paused
. . . Something is happening to me, he thought. He paused, he
listened; there was inside him a great hope that he didn't dare
reach for; with it, or instead of it, might come pain and grief of
the same size. The bright sky was torn by contrails in various
stages of dissolution, some, way up, as solid-looking as
pipecleaners, others like white stockings, discarded, flung in the
air, or light bedding after beautysleep, others like breakers on an
inconceivably distant shore. He went through his lines again, in
his head. They were there.

'*Which brings us to the heart of it. This is just my view, of course,
but I hold it for reasons less obvious than they may appear. Boxback.
Ill-named, I think. And containing a serious structural flaw . . . Classic
Boxback is simply premature ejaculation – inflicted by the woman.
The more premature the better. Now it's certainly very humiliating
for the man, because he has to go again, much diminished. So: the
shower, the pill, the wait, the headache, the hatefuck. But this new
footage will precede the earlier ejaculation. Unlike Cockout, Boxback
leaves no filmed evidence of its own achievement. And then there's
the question of the Facial.*'

'*The Facial.*'

'*The Facial. Even the most rigorous Hatefuck demands the Facial.
Market force number one demands the Facial. And Boxback never
even tried to do without it. So what kind of victory is that? Sending
the grunt on his way with a sneer and a taunt when you've got his
come all over your chin? The Facial is there, always, because the
customer wants it to be there. What do men want? They want the
Facial. And it's the one sexual act that barely exists outside porno.
A prostitute might do it, but a free woman, on her knees? That's
another good reason for calling the Facial what they call it: the Money
Shot.*

'*You know . . . They sometimes call it the Popshot. They don't
call it the Momshot. Because, at one remove or other, you get the
feeling: it's how Daddy would have liked it. Beauty and the Beast,*

innocence and its opposite. And the woman looks up, from her knees,
at someone far more powerful than any lover . . .'

He drank half a bottle of wine, out on the balcony, with his early dinner. His equanimity now tired and wavered, and the evening clouds looked like wigs – toupees, perukes, the tawdry syrups of the sky. But then came Venus, with a pale aura, like a set of silver eyelashes, and simpering down at him. And then came the quarter-moon, seen at an unfamiliar angle, as if from somewhere behind, like a platonically perfect breast.

At nine o'clock there was a knock on the door.

'Who is it?'

It was the hoary bellboy, who offered him a bouquet of the most hideous flowers he had ever seen: redface and yellowtongue. Who is it? Joseph Andrews.

Xan checked: yes: it was still what he wanted.

2. Sickout at Dolorosa Drive

During thirty months of activity the Sextown Sniper seemed to have evolved a set of rules, or restraints: no high-velocity bullets, no headshots or heartshots, no freeway hits causing extra traffic backups, no incursions into Tuxedo Terrace or Dolorosa Drive where core property values might be undermined, no sarcastic notes beginning 'Grieve, blind worm' or 'I am God' for the mayor and the SSVPD, no targeting of Meso-Americans, no targeting of help of any kind, no targeting of the very young, the very old. And if a pointy-bearded Director of Photography got grazed across the ankle, if a towel-boy or a makeup-girl lost a finger or two, if Charity Divine had her hairstyle scorched or Schlong Gielgud stopped one in the rump – who cared? Porno people cared, but no one cared about porno people and what porno people cared about.

Facing the U Hotel, at ten-fifteen the next morning, the sights of the sniper, moving, ranging, from face to face: this one, that one. The circular frame holding a rounded simulacrum, like a miniature kept in a locket – the faces of those that are loved and lost. In its crosshairs the face of a porter, the face of an arriving porno star, the face of Xan Meo, the face of the delivery-man with the potplant over his shoulder.

'Sire, I crave a boon.'

'Name it, plaything.'

But before all that he needed to be delivered to Dolorosa Drive, and he needed to climb out of the courtesy car, and enter the mansion (there was a different porno crew, from some earlier shift, coming the other way), and kiss Karla White, which proved difficult to do, with the telephonic mouthpiece round her neck like a chinguard . . . She wore a two-piece black business suit, which faintly sparkled as if with motes of coaldust, and black heels.

'You're fine,' she said, in her warm, deep, accentless voice. 'You don't have to change. You're fine. I was hoping you'd have lunch with me tomorrow at my house on the beach. I'll send a car.'

'So I don't have to wear a crown or anything.'

'You're Rameses the Great,' she said, 'but you're on a time-travel vacation from BC to LA. With some of your entourage. You're fine . . . I apologise. Charisma Trixxx is keeping us waiting.'

'They *all* do that,' said the man in the white dressing-gown. 'Ninety-nine point nine per cent out of a hundred of them do that. How come I don't have one single *line*?'

'Xan, say hello to Dork Bogarde. You don't have any lines, Dork, because you're a mute.'

'Ah. Hence why . . .'

To Xan she went on, 'In narrative terms this is what's known as a side-fuck. It gives the seventeen-year-old a breather.' Karla's head registered a slight jolt and she walked away with a hand raised to her earphone, saying, 'Charisma? Charisma . . . Am I? . . . Now why's that? . . .'

Xan walked around the room. Such a scene was not unfamiliar to him: the half-dozen technicians and handymen and general noisemakers, the girl with the clipboard, the coffee-urn, the pretzel-bowl. On a white sofa beneath a window sat a young black man of impressive, even heroic appearance: representatively heroic. He stood up and introduced himself as Burl Rhody: Karla's bodyguard.

'Charisma's a noshow,' she now said.

'A first-*timer no*shows?' said Dork. 'What nextly? They noshow their fuck-tests?'

'The girls are calling it a herpes sickout,' said Karla, 'but what it amounts to is a three-day strike.'

'Charisma! Hello?' said Dork loudly into the air. 'There are other people on the planet, Charisma! Hello? Hello?'

'Who can we get?' asked the girl with the clipboard.

Karla said, 'It doesn't matter. I'll do it.'

For a moment Dork's face was a mask of dental work. Then he assumed a solemn, almost liturgical expression, and rose to his feet, saying,

'In all my many years I have served in the industry . . . never has it been bestowed upon me such an honour like this. A legend such as Karla White. I can assure you, dear lady, that I will master you with uh, with true sincerithy . . . and respecth.'

He shrugged off his robe and stood there . . . It wasn't a bodybuilder's pose, not quite. But the face was now nobly half averted; the right knee was bent inwards; the toes were flexed; the thumb and forefinger of each hand were joined in tight circles.

Matter-of-factly unbuttoning her jacket, Karla said, 'I'm sorry, Dork. You'll get your two-fifty or whatever it is and there's a car outside.' She turned on her heel. As she climbed the stairs she said, 'Burl. Would you mind taking a quick shower?'

'Sire, I crave a boon.'

'Name it, plaything. But know that I could have you blinded for addressing me with your eyes, trinket, because I am as the Sun.'

'True, O King . . . This youth who stands before you is not as other men are. He cannot speak and though his manly parts, as you see, are right and comely, he cannot spend. Do you understand me, Sire?'

'Perfectly, fraction.'

'So he must to the eunuchs. The milk of propagation is denied him.'

'To the eunuchs he goes then, instrument. *Him*, pawn, no dynasty awaits.'

'As the most skilled of all the whores in the slave harem, as the most schooled in all the nauseous arts, haply I can yet bring him to blossom.'

'Do so, toy.'

'Yet I have a further design, great sire.'

'Speak it, bauble.'

'As I serve this youth, so I would fain serve thee.'

'Puppet, begin.'

Karla swung down not to her knees but her haunches, in a catsuit made of coins.

3. The principle of lullabies

The next morning it was all over the *Journal*, pushed down the front page only by a further strike from the Sextown Sniper (a middle-aged porno star called Hick Johnsonson had been shot in the foot while reclining poolside at his home in Fulgencio Falls):

'Reports Of Major Cockout On Dolorosa Drive'.

Xan sat in the hotel restaurant with the *Journal* propped up against his coffee-pot. Two tables away a young couple, damply agleam under a coating of man-tan, were acrimoniously negotiating a full-scale dinner (with two kinds of wine), watched by a camera and a klieg light. He read on:

It was at first believed that the surprise Cockout was the handiwork of Sir Dork Bogarde, who has claimed several Cockouts in recent years, and that the Cockout was sustained by Charisma Trixxx, a first-timer, and so theoretically vulnerable to Cockout.

But sources have revealed that the attractive newcomer was not present yesterday on Dolorosa Drive. 'I think I got my wires crossed,' explains Trixxx. 'I was expecting the work but my agent said the shoot had been postponed.' Trixxx denies all knowledge of the herpes sickout called by Comptroller Dimity Qwest of the LUWA (see page 2). Dork Bogarde was unavailable for comment.

It appears, however, that the artists involved were Burl Rhody, an industry jouneyman who quit the business some years ago, and legend Karla White, now of Karla White Productions. 'I swear on my mother,' said a crewmember who prefers not to be named, 'it was classic Cockout. Beyond hot. He totally cocked her out.'

page 5: Dolorosa Drive: A Community Comes To Terms With Cockout
Editorial: Suspicion Of Bullshit In Karla White Cockout

He had the chauffeur drop him off a short distance from the house. As he turned into the drive he saw that Burl Rhody (non-coincidentally, Xan would later decide) was halfway down it, at the wheel of a blue convertible. Burl pulled up.

'She's given me the day off. And the night.'

These words were spoken with apparently effortless neutrality. Xan noticed a copy of the *Lovetown Journal* on Burl's passenger-seat.

Burl said, 'It was Bullshit.' He sank back for a moment.

Whether Burl was happier than usual Xan couldn't tell. But now he smiled with torpid nonchalance and said,

'You know what I was thinking, at the end? I thought, God I'm old. Porno . . . it's not for lazy people. Dork Bogarde is a celebrated asshole, but in general they aren't such a bad crowd. They look out for each other. Karla,' he said, 'Karla spends half her life on the girls' rights and the health shit. That's how fucked-up she is.'

Xan said, 'He's not here, is he? Andrews – Joseph Andrews.'

Burl didn't answer, but his frown told Xan no. His rather too affronted frown – no, not here, not now, not yet. He slowly engaged first gear, an almost hectic act, it seemed, and said,

'I've lived in the apartment over Karla White's garage for five years. And yesterday was our first time. Not our first attempt. Our first time. You know what she does when she gets aroused? She weeps.'

'She weeps?'

'Hot tears. Then everything stops. She stops. Then you stop.'

She wore her usual white dress, her usual shallow sandals. The trouble was that he thought he loved her.

On the upper balcony she poured him another glass of the skull-chilling wine and said, 'Don't you think we're all being incredibly cool about the comet?'

'Cool?'

'All women hate space. *I* hate space. I suppose you've taken an interest in it, the comet.'

He shrugged, in the affirmative. Before them lay the great beast of the Pacific Ocean.

'Then the first thing you'll have learnt is that comets aren't like asteroids, and you can't chart them. Because they're subject to non-gravitational forces like explosions and sublimations. They *say* it's going to miss.'

'Or shear.'

'Or shear. It's the size of Los Angeles. And it's going five times faster than a bullet. And the latest is that it's going to miss by fifty miles. Fifty miles.'

'It won't hit. They wouldn't have told us anything about it if they thought it was going to hit. They've done studies. Telling us about it would just add to the social cost. It won't hit.'

'If it does, the sky would ignite and then turn pitch black.'

'. . . And you'd be pleased.'

'What do you mean by that?' she said in a wronged voice.

'I'm sorry.'

'Oh you mean the void and nothing mattering and everything being allowed. I don't think nothing matters.'

Did he? Did the comet matter? Watching her shape move around from room to room made him think that it had already happened: the end of the thing which is called world. Every few seconds he thought about reaching for her, but his arms, his hands felt loth and cold.

'Nobody cares about the comet because it's not our fault.' After a while she said, 'I wish I hadn't been quite so rough on that sap Dork Bogarde. Are you hungry? Nor am I. Say if you are.'

The trouble was that he thought he loved her. And love had not guided him well in recent weeks and months, with his wife, his daughter. What kind of love was it? It seemed to have its life somewhere between what he felt for Russia and what he felt for Billie. The thing that further distinguished his love for Karla was that it persistently presented him with the cathartic emotions, those of pity and terror. In her presence, he was afraid and he was sorry. He wanted to protect her from all things – including things like himself. And his senses ached . . . The waves were for now holding good order, each one bristling up for sudden and ruthless and thrillingly opportune assault, and then pouncing, coming down hard, gnashing and frothing and enveloping with its teeth. And how bloodymindedly they came steaming into the boulders: the orgasmic impact, and then they shouldered their way into rockpool after rockpool, making waves that then had to be made again, after regrapplings, reslitherings.

Something was happening to him. It felt like a flow in the brain: rearrangements of currents and temperatures . . . Suddenly the sky went an olive colour, and the sea turned white.

'*Tormenta*,' she said.

'I want to lie down. I'm sorry, I'm not feeling well. I'll be all right if I lie down.'

She took him to her bedroom and left him alone to shed some clothes. He was already half asleep when she returned.

'I'll put this on you. The principle of lullabies – it's not the song. It's not that the song soothes and dopes you. The point is that you know the singer's still there. I can't sing, but I'll go on patting this shawl so you know I'm still there.'

While he slept and turned he kept remembering the final minutes of the sex-act he had witnessed on Dolorosa Drive.

Karla was on her knees. She was about to complete a presumably ancient human activity. But it didn't look ancient. It looked as though it had been invented earlier that day – or was now, in fact, in the process of coming into being. For the forward thrust the arms were clasped about Burl Rhody's waist; his phallus, ideally black, seemed to constitute an obstacle: she couldn't go past it, she couldn't go round it. No, she had to go through it, as if her real goal lay somewhere within his loins. On the reverse thrust, her hands were placed flatpalmed on his hipbones, to achieve greater traction, and each withdrawal ended with a tremendous smack of the lips before Rhody was as vociferously reengulfed. Then all was speed; and after a while he found himself thinking of a child with a party-whistle. And then she was Billie, or even Sophie, with yoghurt or vanilla icecream all over her face.

Consciousness was upon him. Before he opened his eyes he heard the sound of breathing. More than this, he heard sleep – the economical downdraughts which were the sound that sleep made . . . He found he was some way down the bed, under the sheet and the shawl; and the thing between his legs was a harsh concentration of gristle. He turned over: there was Karla's apparently headless body, and the sleepless and incorruptible interrogation of her breasts. He moved towards them.

Soon he heard her somnolent sigh of approval and felt her hands on his neck and hair as he squeezed and kissed. Time passed.

'I *love* you, I *love* you,' she said.

And when she started to weep, he paused, expecting her to stop (then *he'd* stop). But she didn't stop. Like Billie when she wept (faintly incredulous, naïvely eloquent), he thought. Her thighs were apart, and now his hand loomed. But then he reached out to her face and found that her cheeks were dry. Their eyes met. All was subtracted from him; and he turned away.

After several beats of his heart Xan said, 'See? . . . Love doesn't like fear. Size zero.'

'Oh, I suppose you mean it should be tucked in nicely while you sprint for your life down the beach . . . That's what they never say in the books or anywhere else. With a little girl you're big, even when you're little. You ought to go ahead with Billie. We get over it.'

'No you don't.'

'No we don't,' she said. '*Ob*viously.' And with a whip of the sheet she was gone.

When he was woken again, this time by the storm, he got out of bed and reached for his clothes as if they were items of body-armour. The thunder was escalatory: fusillade, cannonade, heavy artillery, the fundamentally egregious cataract of tactical nuclear strike. He opened the bedroom door. There was a figure on the balcony, smoking.

She said, 'God has got the movers in. There will be breakages. No, we don't. We don't get over it. *Ob*viously. In bed we don't know our rights.'

And he thought: obviously. Because that is what you do, Daddy, when you do that, when you play that game, when you go down that road. You place them in another dimension where they're always one step behind, one step beyond.

'Do you want to see Jo now?' she asked. 'You still want that?'

He said yes, but with a reluctance, and a sadness, that he took to be a failure of courage. 'Are you my enemy?'

'I used to be your enemy.' And she told him who she was.

'. . . Jesus Christ, Cora.'

Beyond, arthritic feelers of lightning were lancing out, sideways, upwards, forming coastlines with many fjords. There was a repeated jumpcut effect, and shifting blocks of nightscape.

Cora Susan waited with the keys.

4. Anger of the just

'Come in, dear. Come in out of the wet. Xan . . . They're waiting for you, dear, through there. Paquita'll get you anything you need. Bit of business.'

Joseph Andrews pushed open a red-leather swing door with a porthole in its brow. Around a cardtable you could see a fat hot man in braces, a small natty figure in a borsalino and a chalk-striped suit, a Chinese woman with a pair of sunglasses lodged in her quiff, and the set of a pair of unknowable shoulders. Cora went inside and the door swung shut behind her.

'*You've* got some arsehole coming here, haven't you mate? Are you daft or what? This way: follow me. Follow me.'

Xan was led into a long low room: its recreation of an English pub was not entirely literal, but there were damp beermats and glistening black plastic ashtrays on the round tables, as well as a dartboard, and horsebrass and horsehair and prints of racing scenes. A log fire drew noisily in the hearth, like emphysema, with additional sputters and spatters.

'First, the past,' he said, and lengthily exhaled. 'I'll say this for Mick Meo: you'd have to *hurt* him. I'll say this: you knew you was in a row when you was in a row with Mick Meo. You'd have to *hurt* him. A wall. A drop. We had it out the once back in them days, before he come on board. And it went on a bit but I done him. Six months later, when he's up and about again, he come on board and there was no hard feelings whatsoever. Him and me, we'd have a drink. On several occasions he invited me to his home. Consistently. I'd have little Leda on me knee. This was before your time, son.

'Then come the liberty. We was both in Strangeways. He'd pulled a three for grand larceny, whilst I was serving me six for uh . . . for malicious wounding. Now. Our mate Tony Odgers has lost remission for doing the two screws who've burnt a letter from his wife – in his face. I've said to Mick, "I'm not having that. I'll do the Governor." And Mick's gone, "*I'll* do him." And I've gone, "No *I'll* do him." And Mick's gone, "I'm not having that. No *I'll* do him." Deadlock.'

Said with a lingering stress on the last consonant, like the beginning of a cough, and joining all the other coughs in the log fire.

'So we've had a word with the Chaplain. It's arranged. A straightener, with gloves, in the main quad. It sometimes happened in them days. You sort it out, with the uh, permission of the Governor. The Governor didn't know what it's *about*, of course . . .'

Xan said, 'What *was* it about?'

'. . . About who'd do the Governor.'

'Yeah but *who'd* do the Governor? The winner or the loser?'

'Are you all right mate? . . . Well in the end they've had to drag us off ourselves. We was in the same ward in the hospital, but I've had it the worst because I've done one of the screws who've truncheoned us apart. Mick come out in the morning – and then come back that afternoon. In an appalling condition. I could tell by the state of him what he's done: he's done the Governor! Well I'm not having that. In the middle of the night I've slid out of me bed and crawled across the floor on me hands and knees and started giving him a whacking. Then they've shipped me off to Gartree. And after that, it's a funny thing: Mick and me was never on the out at the same time. And never in the same prison. And for them twenty years the liberty's festered . . .

'Then I'm over to London from Dublin: bit of business. I've heard he's come home and I've gone to the yard and I've called him out. He's said, "What's all this?" "What's all this? You done the Governor, you cunt." Then he reckons that he's worked that one off: "Me in me hospital bed and you clawing me fucking stitches apart." So I've gone, "All right. You want a liberty. Here's a liberty. Are you married to a fucking elephant?"'

Andrews paused. The log fire gobbed and hawked and retched. It, too, was like England: bus shelters, station waiting-rooms, the pub Gents on a Friday night.

'When's your birthday, cock?'

Xan told him.

'No it ain't. "*Your wife a fucky nelephant needs thirteen months to have a fucking baby?*" And I've took the piece of paper from me pocket,' said Andrews, taking the piece of paper from his pocket – the zippered pouch of his oilblack tracksuit. 'Registration of birth. And I've wiggled it in his face. "Where was you, nine months back from this? You was in fucking Winson Green, that's where. I've stuffed your wife and I've knocked her up and all. Your boy, he ain't your boy. He's fucking mine."

'Now that was me mistake . . . I overplayed me hand, you might say. Because he's like grim fucking death then he is, so that nothing . . . nothing . . . So he's giving me what for on the bare boards of the shed. And as he's putting me lights out I'm thinking, Well it's not your day, mate. Should have stayed in bed. But, you know, fair's fair. See, stuffing other villains' wives, it's like a statement. The right of señor you could call it. It says to the bloke: let's have you. And if he does you he does you. And Mick must have still had the hump because five days later he crippled Damon Susan and went away for his nine, out of me reach.

'. . . So I'm lying there, taking me medicine, as you got to do, and who should enter upon the scene, sticking his fucking oar in, but *you*, you cunt. Now I know Mick give you punishment. But that was *my* punishment, *not yourn*. And I'm *not having that*. Me own son, and all. Me own boy. Did that to his own father . . . You're very quiet over there.'

'Yeah that's right.'

'Ooh. May I enquire why?'

It had not been a failure of courage. It had been a failure of inclination – or of appetite. Xan said,

'Why? Because I'm trying not to corpse, mate. You're a fucking old *joke*, you are, boy. Look at you, you fucking old joke.'

'. . . Last time your mum come to see him in the nick she was eight months gone. She's bound herself up. And broke four ribs. "I've had him," she said. He's said, "Then where is he?" "They're doing his jaundice at Princess Beatrice." Ten weeks later she've took you to the Green, and Mick said you was a bit little but of course she's blamed it on the doctors . . . Dead dirty, your mum. Like your sister. Loved me muck on her face. Still in your chair are you?'

Joseph Andrews got to his feet – and the terrible moonbright dots of the trainers began to dance their dance, barely skimming off the stone floor. 'I still love a row,' he said. 'Ah I still love a good mill. Don't worry, mate. The hospital's nice and near.'

'I don't see why you uh –'

'Yeah *well I'm turning nasty in me old age* . . . Look at you. All I've took from you.'

'How old *are* you, Jo? Yeah, and look at the state of him. Gaw, *that's* a liberty, eh? That's a right kick in the arse, what anno domini's gone and done to you. And there's no vengeance for it. Why aren't you not having *that*? But no. He just bends over and waits for more of the same.'

Joseph Andrews took up position by the door. He seemed to be weighing something in his hands as he intoned, 'A man fights . . . with his arsehole. Power comes . . . in the form of anger, up through the arsehole,' he said heavily, breathing out. 'The righteous anger of the *just*. Up . . . it comes . . . up though the arsehole . . . and into the lining of a man. Come on. Where is it. Let's *see* it. Let's *have* it.'

Xan observed that Andrews was the sort of man who, in preparation, exhibits not the upper teeth but the lower. He got to his feet and walked towards him, saying,

'I'm not fighting that. I'm not *touching* that. You got . . . you got fucking drool all over your chin. Out of the road, you old joke. You old poof.'

And there seemed to be no question of the upshot till he felt a piercing, a timestopping stab to his forehead. But even if the blow had taken his head clean off there could be no question about the dynamics of the immediate future: the rules governing the motion of bodies under the action of forces. He clattered on and over, and Joseph Andrews buckled beneath him. There came a crack as his coccyx hit the stone, and then a faint whinnying sound, not human, not even organic, like a squawk of stressed metal. The logs and their maggots expectorated and regurgitated, hoiked and phthooked.

'Me ip,' he said consideringly. 'Me replacement's slid out. And me back and all. Yeah. Here it is.' And he let out a soft low roar, like a man come in from the cold and at last feeling the warmth of the fire . . . 'No, Simon. Rodney, let the man pass. Let him pass. *It's not over, boy. It's not over.*'

Within half an hour Xan was inspecting himself in his brutalist bathroom mirror: the one with the light inside it. There were two curved lesions, like bloodcoloured brackets, half an inch north-west of his eyes.

5. The Sextown Sniper

'Cora, is this wise? Aren't we throwing down a challenge to the Sextown Sniper?'

'The Sextown Sniper never works at night. And never takes headshots. I don't understand why some people go around in crash-helmets like they do . . . No one close to me has ever been hit – it's more like at one remove. Hick Johnsonson, the guy who lost all those toes? He shares a shitbox with Dork Bogarde. I'll put the roof up now for the freeway. Look at this. We should have taken the surface roads.'

Up ahead, the slowmoving river of crimson. And, to their left, the slowmoving river of yellow, flowing into Lovetown.

'How gay is Dork? How gay is Jo, in your view? How gay is porno, in your view?'

'Uh, *porno*'s quite gay. And we mean unacknowledged-gay, don't we. Not straight gay. Cryptogay. For instance, you'd have to be a *bit* gay to do a double anal, don't you think? Two men with a girl? Seriously. And triple anal. And a lot of them do gay porno anyway. They get more money because in gay the boys are the girls. No. In gay everyone's a girl. They call it "gay for pay". And once something rhymes in America, or alliterates, then it's a social norm. Jo . . .'

'He wants to have them so he does them. And has their wives.'

'Mm. Hence the love of pain: he's correcting himself for it. He had plenty of pain this morning. His op. They plugged his hip back in. He's in raging agony now and he won't touch his morphine. Hey. Your forehead.'

'Tried to blind me. His own son.'

'So you're not upset?'

'I don't see what difference it makes. In the newspaper I described Jo as "another mad prick". Another – like Mick Meo. I don't see what difference it makes.'

'It makes a difference to me. It more or less cancels my reason for going after you in the first place.'

'That's true. It also dilutes the incest – if we had. We still share Hebe Meo. Christ: my mum. Oh well. You've got to let it be. You can't go to your death-bed still . . . still obsessed by your kiddie cot. Easy for me to say. You're all right I hope?'

'Yeah. You know, you've undermined my magical thinking. The universal seductress – she won't fly any more. Maybe it'll be a relief. I'm quitting the vengeance business. And I'm considering quitting the industry. Now that I'm so rich. You know what's really wrong with porno? Getting older, two of you, sexually, that's the hardest thing, right? And the best thing, maybe. And porno's the sworn enemy of that.'

'. . . Cora, is Jo done with me?'

'Well he's the type, isn't he. They come back at you. Unless they're dead they come back at you.'

'Last night . . . I called him a poof.'

'What? Then he'll come back at you. Listen, I'll speak to him. He owes me.'

'Don't get out. You know, I loved your mother. She was wild, but she was a great sis to me. It killed me for a year when she died. And I love you. But in the right way.'

'Thanks. And me too. Here's a secret about the Sextown Sniper. It hasn't been made public because it's too sensitive politically. All the chicks would go on strike. The Sextown Sniper's a woman.'

'How can they tell?'

'Oh, it's just the things she leaves in her hides. Eyeline pencils. Knitting-patterns. Recipes. And why else would she never kill anyone?'

So he left Lovetown, home of the gentle, the tender, the loving Sextown Sniper. The commuter flight took him up over Fucktown, which stayed there like a circuit diagram, and towards Los Angeles, arrayed like the stagecape of some old crooner the size of a comet.

6. Men in power

He wrote it over Greenland:

> Dear Russia,
>
> I hesitate to set this down, because I am greatly afraid of recurrence – I am very greatly afraid of the misery of recurrence. But I feel like a man who wearily consults an old wound or grievance, and finds it isn't there.
>
> Over the last few days I think I've worked out what my accident did to me. I used to suspect that it had shorn me of certain values – the values of civilisation, more or less. Well it did do that. But it did something else too: it fucked up my talent for love. It fucked it up. Love was still there, but it was love of the wrong kind. There was a terrible agitation in it. An impotent agitation. And now that agitation seems to have gone, retreated, lifted.
>
> General thoughts are not my strength, but here's a general thought. Men were in power for five million

years. Now (where we live) they share it with women. That past has a weight, though we behave as if it doesn't. We behave as if the transition has been seamlessly achieved. Of <u>course</u> there's no going back. I went back. As if through a trapdoor I dropped into the past, and we shared that disaster. Still, we should acknowledge the weight of it, the past. Unconsciously, and not for long at a time, men miss women being tractable, and women miss men being decisive; but we can't <u>say</u> that. All I'm suggesting, perhaps, is that there's a deficiency of candour (and that's the thing that's wrong with what I write – or with what I wrote). It would be surprising if women weren't a little crazed by their gains in power, and if men weren't a little crazed by their losses. We will argue about this, I hope, and you will win and I won't mind. No, strike that out. You will win, and I will mind, but I'll probably pretend not to. What I'm saying is that it will take a century to work off those five billennia and consolidate the change. We pretend it is, but the change isn't yet intact and entire.

My memory is filling out – I can remember Billie saying 'here comes my lovely daddy to take me home from school' (she rose on her toes as she said it). And that's the kind of daddy I am going to go back to being, if you give me the chance. I wasn't quite right, in the head or the heart. Not right, not right. Memory. The only major gap now seems to be Sophie's birth; it's still gone, but I'm hoping it will reappear one day. I don't know why this absence oppresses me so much. Of course I can remember very clearly <u>declining</u> to watch Billie's caesarian. But I've forgotten Sophie's birth – and I don't want to be a man who has never watched a woman being born. Naturally I wish I could forget the creature I became, but I can't and I won't.

I may have done too much damage. I may have frightened and disgusted you too deeply and lastingly. And there's one other thing you're going to have to forgive me for – a strange kind of family entanglement. You'd think it premature (and alarming) if I were to write here about love. So I'll just say that my profound hope has to do with your generosity. You are too generous not to <u>try</u> to forgive me.

Much has happened. I will tell you everything. I can't understand why I want to tell you this now, but I do. In the past, when I thought about my father, I used to fantasise that he was allowed occasional glimpses of my life. Now of course he died when I was still married to Pearl. But I used to think: he would work it out, he would put two and two together, and see that I had married you now, and that we had these two girls, Billie and Sophie. I don't <u>believe</u> he can do that. But it would be good and right if he was allowed to, every now and then – the privilege expiring after a couple of generations, the story discreetly fading from view when the children are about sixty-five. And when we're dead, I should be allowed to watch the boys, and you and I should be allowed to watch the girls.

Epithalamium.

CHAPTER TEN

1. February 14 (2.19 p.m.): 101 Heavy

With furious precision the maddened corpse of Royce Traynor delivered its final, smashing blow, and he was gone, away, spinning end over end through the plane-shaking clouds . . .

The pressurised air in 101 Heavy now fled it too: a squall of dust and grit. The mid-section of the cabin floor instantly collapsed, severing all remaining hydraulic lines.

Reynolds felt the bang, the howl like a ricochet, the stinging wind, the harsh vibration. In ragged unison the oxygen-masks dropped and hovered. After a few seconds all the cigarette smoke was replaced by a thin white mist.

Captain John Macmanaman: . . . Feel it, Nick.
First Officer Nick Chopko: No . . .
Macmanaman: No quantity. None.
Flight Engineer Hal Ward: . . . You know the 'feel' they put into it's bullshit. It's just the computer. The yoke's bullshit.
Macmanaman: Engineer, we're flying by direct law.
Chopko: And if we reengage?
Macmanaman: We'd get fictitious feel, if anything. Gentlemen, we have no hydraulic control over this aircraft. She's banking. She's banking. The throttle, Nick. If you . . . She's coming back. She's coming back . . . We're just blundering around up here. We have no flaps and no spoilers. If we can get her down we're going to land at 300 knots with no reverse thrust and no brakes. We don't need an airport. We need an interstate. Three miles of good road. And one on our present setting. Nick. Brief SAM [System Aircraft Maintenance].

Hal? I'm going to be asking you to line up every kind of rescue and emergency we can get. She's banking. Come on back . . .

System Aircraft Maintenance: Copy your situation, one oh one heavy.

Macmanaman: We're just making grand clockwise circles up here . . .

SAM: I don't want to add to your cares, sir. But we'd better start thinking about the NEO window.

Macmanaman: Hey. Come on back. Come on back. Come on back to me.

2. Clint prepares

'So some so-called 14-year-old', he typed, 'has been crying "rape" after a bit of fun in a ditch with an older lad.'

> Have you *seen* this bird *(see photo)*?
> She looks 16 if she's a day.
> And how was he supposed to tell?
> The bloke'd had a few, as he freely admits.
> He's getting on a bit and his eyes aren't as sharp as they
>   were.
> And they say in that part of the woods it was so dark you
>   couldn't even —

Clint paused. He thought: got to be careful with the medication. Overdo it with the Narcopam and what happens? You're checking into the hotel with the bird slung over your shoulder.

> And who does the judge think he's kidding?
> He's got the gall to tell us there was 'no provocation'.

When the bird was wearing *a school uniform*.

What are we, c**ts?

He was sixty-six hours away from the date with Kate: Valentine's Day (nice touch). He could see himself parking the Avenger and crossing the road. In a kind of saunter. Hands in hip pockets. Just . . . looning over the road to her door. Well he was like the boyscouts, wasn't he: always prepared. The Potentium, the His Voluminousness (supplemented by a booster called Volume Control), the Valium, the Hellcat (Legally Not To Be Used Without Partner's Permission), the Narcopam (ditto), the Diploma from the Academy. The guy was oozing confidence.

3. Waking in the cold

Joseph Andrews sat before the tape recorder. He looked as if he had just climbed out of the swimming-pool; but his clothes were dry.

'*Come* on, Boss. Have half a Nurofen.'

In a strained and trembling voice he said, 'Fuck off out of it.'

'You had the local.'

'Against me will. Ready? And Manfred. You transcribe this now, all right?

'[*Click*.] Is it a crime to want to die in me own country? [*Click*.] Apart from a personal family matter and four or five blokes who know fucking well who they are [*click*] I pose no threat to society whatsoever. And the fact is, I've got you over a barrel, mate.

'Uh. Take out the "mate" and put in uh . . .'

He intended to add an evocation of his love of England. But the essence of what he really missed about it was waking in the cold, and feeling the rust in his hipbones, all wired up and saddled to a faint need to shit.

'Where's Simon? I need me *Simon*.'

4. Leather on willow

Brendan was reading it out loud and had come to the last page.

'"And the fact is, I've got you over a barrel, Your Majesty. I'm a confirmed royalist, and of course we all worshipped your mother and father. And it would break my heart if I was obliged to make the enclosed material public. I'm just an old man who wants to lay down his bones in the land of his fathers. I want to hear the chimes of Big Ben, I want to hear the sound of leather on willow at the village green, I want to walk down Worship Street and in through the doors of the World Upside Down. I'm coming into Heathrow on the afternoon of February 13, under my own name, and will take to my farmhouse in rural Essex. And that's the last you'll hear of me. But if I'm nicked on my way in, then you know the consequences. Respectfully, Joseph Andrews, Esquire. PS. If you don't mind me saying, you had some front, didn't you, claiming it was all a fake? I had half a mind to go public then and there, to get some respect. But wiser voices prevailed. Now you can stick to your guns and hopefully it'll all pass over quickly for the Princess. What with her mum and all. PPS. I see your cousin offed poor old Jimmy O'Nione down Cold Blow way. I knew Jimmy at Knavesmire, where we did an Inspector together. Jimmy O'Nione was one of the best."'

Brendan dropped his hands to his lap.

Henry uncrossed and recrossed his legs.

He said, 'And what is that, Bugger, may I ask?'

'A DVD, sir . . . A digital videodisc.'

'Well I suppose we'd better . . .'

The two men were in Brendan's rooms in St James's — not otherwise would such a viewing be possible. Not in any of the wintry palaces, the lashed castles . . . Brendan said,

'I'm wondering whether you have to expose yourself to this, sir. I could simply tell you what you needed to know.'

'Stop babying me, Bugger. Call Love and then lock the door.'

5. February 14 (3.44 p.m.): 101 Heavy

Captain John Macmanaman: Come on back to me. Come on back to me. No no no *no*. Wait. Now . . . Got to stay ahead of her, got to stay ahead of her. Got to lead her. Can't get behind her.

System Aircraft Maintenance: Captain, say souls on board and fuel remaining.

First Officer Nick Chopko: Three nine nine. Thirty-six seven, and dumping.

SAM: Only differential power. You're manoeuvring with the throttles . . . Slats are out?

Macmanaman: Slats? We don't have any slats. If we can get ourselves down while we're still horizontal, we're going to ditch. We're descending. Ah, now the nose is coming up. Easy. Easy.

Columbia [South Carolina] Approach: Copy your setting, one oh one heavy. The runway is ten thousand feet long.

Macmanaman: Can't use it. And we're not going to make Columbia. Find me a place to ditch on that setting. Nick, put the [landing] gear down.

Chopko: What?

Macmanaman: Throw it down.

Reynolds turned to the man in 2A, and she screamed. 'What's *that*?' she said. 'What? . . . I can't hear! Take it off!'

'A smoke-hood. Cost me two-thirty.'

'Ladies and gentleman,' said the exalted voice of Robynne Davis. 'As in all emergency landings we will be evacuating as soon as the aircraft is at rest. Passengers close to the exit doors, those in seats . . .'

A uniformed man came out of the cockpit. He leant over 2B and whispered something.

'Ma'am,' said Hal Ward, in the galley, 'would you please go to the bathroom and then quietly return to 22D. Business. Captain's orders.'

The inter-cabin curtains were open, and by straining his neck the man in 2A saw that Mrs Traynor's new seat was unlike his own. It was slightly narrower, and it faced the other way.

Chopko: Look at our *speed*.

Flight Engineer Hal Ward: The heavies aren't designed for this. We could just come apart up here.

SAM: Captain, on your present setting you're going to be coming in right under it.

Macmanaman: What are they saying? Thirty-three, thirty-four?

SAM: Their latest and best is an NEO altitude of twenty-one point four. Repeat, at 17.43. If you're not yet on the ground you're going to feel it. Heat and blast.

Macmanaman: And another thing. Watch the nose, Nick. No no no. Pull back, pull back, pull back.

6. What do princesses want?

On screen, the bathroom of the Yellow House: the passageway, the circular concavity of the tub, the mirrors, the towels on their pegs. Brendan flinched as a subtitle gave date and place. He turned. On the sofa the King stared levelly.

The Princess entered, in her tennis whites. She approached, smiling with amusement or satisfaction, and then vanished to the right. The sound of a sigh, the brisk drilling of micturation, the soft percussion of the toilet paper as it ripped. She reappeared with her shirt half-up and her skirt half-down, and limping as she kicked off her shoes. She threw on the taps. She paused for a full minute, examining a blemish on her forearm. Then she undressed carelessly, and in she climbed.

It hadn't wavered, the watching eye, stupidly imperturbable, like a security monitor. After a while you understood that it had now begun a painfully gradual zoom.

Here came the change of the Princess's expression – a listening face. The sound of a door opening and closing, and the audible rumour of advent. Then the white shape, still halved by shadow.

The quality of the sound, throughout, had been ticklishly distinct. And now the sudden surge of a human voice.

'I come from your father's bed. He sent me here to help you bathe.' It was He, it was He . . . He removed her robe, and held out a hand in such a way that the Princess must rise to receive it. He stepped in . . . The kissed neck and throat, the sponged breasts. The two bodies, one brown and full of gravity, one pale and light. And the two faces: one with its young astonishment and horror, the other with its ancient inclemency.

Brendan turned again. Henry had his arms up on the sofa's shoulders and his head was bent to one side. Moisture had had time to sink in around his closed eyes.

Some minutes later Brendan said, 'Sir? I think you . . .'

Henry sat up and stared. A different scene, now, gloom, luxury, a half-dressed He Zizhen attending to his own naked body, which looked utterly helpless, like a baby waiting to be changed.

'If it's any comfort to you, sir, I think we can say this of Miss Zizhen. She was our Enemy's Enemy.'

'It is *some* comfort, surprisingly enough, Bugger. This is over now. Oughtred at one end and the PM at the other. What remains is for us, or for me, to divine what the Princess wants. What do princesses want?'

7. Simon Finger

His crutch was of the sort that went all the way up the arm. Joseph Andrews leant it against the side of his desk and, after some bitter tottering, crashed down into his swivel chair.

'Sime,' he said when he was able.

He addressed a small middle-aged man in a chalkstriped suit and with foul eyes, pale round the poster-blue pupil: Simon Finger.

'Sime, mate. It's all bollocks, that: me threat. I'm a monarchist, mate. Always have been. And what I got on that lot'd make the royal family *disappear*. And I couldn't live with meself with that on me conscience. Knowing I'd done that, I couldn't rest easy in me grave. They nick me tomorrow, then I'll take me secret with me. Though Cora always have it, lest need be.'

In his ripe drawl – posher than the King – Simon Finger said, 'I couldn't agree more, Jo. It's a fine institution.'

'Where are we? Yeah, we'll be obliging Tony Tobin, Yocker Fitzmaurice, Kev Had and Nolberto Drago. You can do what you want with them other slags, but I want to be there for Nobby Drago.'

For a while Joseph Andrews unsystematically sifted through the papers on his desk. He held up a clipping.

'Calls me a mad prick. In print. Names me. Places me. As for what he said here the other night: no respect whatsoever. *And* he would've walked away if I'd've let him! Wouldn't stand. He wouldn't stand. Called me a . . . Me own son. Well I'm not having that. Her,' he said.

'Her? Isn't that rather . . . ?'

'Yeah. See. Cora've made me promise I won't hurt him. So I want you to hurt her, Simon. The wife. Because it's not gone away. And I'm owed. I want you to mark her, Simon. I want you to cut her face.'

'No. That's uh, incommensurate. I think that would undoubtedly be *un peu trop*.'

'. . . I don't understand you, Simon Finger. You got arsehole to spare. If a raging bull come at you, you'd stand. You'd stick your head in a fucking cement-mixer, you would. If you considered it the correct thing to do. I've just asked you to top four villains and you've barely shrugged. And you won't even . . . Uh all right. All right. Will you knock her about – will you do that at least?'

'What are we talking about here, Jo? A bloody nose and a black eye? . . . A handful of hair or two and a couple of teeth?'

He leant forward and spread his hands all-solvingly. 'Exactly. Just like any normal husband'd give her.'

Then Simon Finger helped Joseph Andrews down the stairs to join their friends for the little going-away party, Manfred, Rodney and Dominic, Cora Susan and Burl Rhody, Tori Fate, Captain Mate, and He Zizhen.

8. The vestal follow

They were all there for the midday meeting: Clint, Supermaniam, Strite, Mackelyne, Woyno, Donna Strange. Clint had just had a conversation with Donna Strange about Dork Bogarde. It was remarkably similar to the conversation he had had with Dork Bogarde about Donna Strange: she couldn't remember him either. Chemistry not quite right, thought Clint. Nevertheless he took this sophisticated exchange as a good omen for his rendezvous with Kate, now only hours away. He could see himself parking the Avenger and strolling across the road. Having a quiet wander across the road . . .

Supermaniam said, 'Ainsley Car reckons Durham's the best dryout centre he's ever been to. Course he's treated like a god in there. And Ainsley and Beryl are going to get married for the third time in the prison chapel. Could do a piece on that.'

Crinkling his nose, Desmond Heaf said, 'So you see some things turn out for the best.'

'Yeah. You know,' said Clint: '"The faded and disgraced football legend gave a wry smile as he added his own slops to the bucket of filth outside his cell. His wedding day had begun."'

'Oh I imagined something a bit softer in tone. Though point taken: football is the religion of our . . . Now,' said Heaf with a glance at his watch. 'It doesn't happen often – oh no – but every now and then, every now and then, in a publishing lifetime, you encounter an instance of the journalist's craft that simply takes your breath away . . . Yesterday morning I said to Clint here, "Clint? I've had a personal communication from the Palace via the FPA."' Heaf briefly waved a flyer-like sheet of paper in the air. 'It says that the tacit embargo on the Princess is now officially lapsed, but that they do respectfully ask that we maintain a certain tact and distance at this very sensitive time, following the demise of Queen Pamela. Explaining this, I said, "Clint? How about a little piece on Vicky? Something for the op-ed page. And not Yellow Dog, mind! More like your earlier light-hearted style. Now that all the scandal's blown over, and with her sixteenth birthday not that far off. To go with this nice new photograph. Lovely to see her laughing again, isn't it? . . . A turning of the page – the start of a fresh chapter." This morning I happened to open my *Lark* at the breakfast table, in the company of my wife and six daughters. Would you all now turn to page thirty-three. "Vicky With Nobs On".

'"Hi, *men*!"' Heaf recited. '"With these words Princess Vicky kissed goodbye to her catflap – and nun too soon says the *Lark*. Gore blimey, it was virgin on the ridiculous. These days British minge is spreading the butcher's apron aged 12 or 13. So high time Vicky had herself deflowered (what in carnation did you expect?) and jumped aboard the cherrygoround. We've *had* a Virgin Queen – Liz I. So loosen your belts for the Goer Princess.

'"Who's the (p)lucky boy then? Porking the Heir Suggestive is still a topping offence so this must have come from on high. Did she do a Blessed Mary and let the Lord God giveth her one? Or was it an inside job in at least two senses? We all knew that Vick's first pash would have to be posh. And it's well known that her Pop hasn't popped for more than two year. Maybe she said, 'Dad? I need a nob. Let's keep it in the (royal) family.' And he said, 'What the Hal?'

'"So out with the crown jewels, lads, and start dreaming. Now that one bloke's got his leg over, the vestal surely follow. After all those years of Queen Pam, known to every motorist as the Buckingham Turnoff (RIP), here's a royal to tauten the todge. Look across the page, lads, and raise your rifles. Ready, aim – and let Britannia drool the waves!"'

'. . . I never thought I'd ever hear myself say this, Clint. But you're fired.'

Mattock Estate, NW2. Homeless John and And New were sitting on the pavement.

'It ain't a bad patch, this,' said Homeless John. 'You can help people with their cars. Say, "Eh up, mate. You got a ticket. Tried to stop her but the cow give you one."'

'How's that help?' asked And.

'Well, prepare them. Warn them. Where you been then?'

'On an oil-rig. In the fucking North Sea.'

'Eh. Mega money.'

'If you're a driller, yeah. Not if you're licking out the fucking pie-warmer it ain't.'

The black Avenger crept up, with Clint's head in it like the hump of a camel.

Still seated, Homeless John made a series of unreadable gestures till Clint lowered the passenger window.

'Not there, mate. It's Residents' up to ten-thirty. Back up a bit and it's Pay and Display. Just beyond the yellow line. Beyond the yellow.'

Clint backed up, then climbed down, holding the two bottles of champagne by their necks in his left hand and the pigskin hamper in his right. 'Yeah cheers lads,' he said.

'Eh up then,' said Homeless John. 'I'm off home.'

And Clint started across the road. Nice to get going early: love in the afternoon. Roaming across the road, ambling, sort of happy-go-lucky. A loon, a wander. Pressure? There was no pressure, not with Kate. And he was prepared for every contingency: when shaken, his pockets sounded like a pair of maracas. Conversation? Okay: the new royal sensation, breaking as we speak. (Well out of that. Let them other mugs do it.) Or amuse her with the story of the two nights he had served in a Lovetown jail for smoking in his room. Every sprinkler in the whole hotel . . .

He admitted to himself that she had her little mannerisms. Like her paltry ingenuities on the keyboard. Some of her abbreviations saved her but one touch, and none at all when they included the use of the tab. And punctuation as visual pun: 'i must –'; 'orl&o's, of red hair'; and, of course, 'a 2nd 9-hour operation on his:'. And 6 for *sex* kept making him think she came from bleeding New Zealand. Unconsciously, too, of course, Clint was suffering from a proliferation of doubts in new areas: innovatory uncertainties. He had the sense that he was missing something – and not a detail. And he had already suspected, many times, and not just unconsciously, that she wasn't quite right in the head.

He pushed the button marked *k8*. Time passed. I bet that lamb felt it, he thought insensately, when I come up on it. The house opened out with a soft laugh and the smell of hot greens, and closed again.

9. February 14 (4.37 p.m.): 101 Heavy

Captain John Macmanaman: I've got a little more feel here. I don't know. Maybe the gear is giving us just a little bit of rudder, or maybe the air – it's lower, it's thicker.
Flight Engineer Hal Ward: What you got you got.
Macmanaman: How are you doing there, Nick?
First Officer Nick Chopko: . . . The numbers say drop the nose.

Reynolds knew why the Captain wanted her in a seat facing aft. You quickly intuited that you had a large piece of fixed furniture to cushion you, rather than the slender section of strapping enjoyed, for example, by the man in 2A. On the other hand there were unfamiliar sensations to be accommodated. When the plane met with resistance, in the shuddering clouds, it felt to her spine like acceleration. And the obverse: when the nose went down and they started to dive, it felt to her spine like reverse thrust.

But they didn't have reverse thrust.

Four hundred people gulped, as the plane jerked wildly to the left. So sudden, so sharp. She thought of the scrap of tissue paper in the steel toilet bowl, an hour or more ago, sucked sideways with the sound of a sneeze. As sharp as that.

People were no longer wailing, even at the most terrible drops and lurches. Except for some of the couples, people were no longer touching or talking but staring straight ahead. People had stopped saying that word, which they nearly all said and which was *fuck*. People travelling alone were no longer saying goodbye to their loved ones on their mobile phones. People were no longer saying goodbye to their loved ones, in their heads. People were saying goodbye to themselves.

LAST CHAPTER

1. Courtly love

Earlier in the morning of Valentine's Day, Brendan had break-fasted with the Princess, and they had had words.

'What do you want, ma'am?'

'. . . I want to be a part of the *umma*.'

'The *umma*, ma'am?'

'The body of Islam. That's why they pray five times a day. *Shorooq*, sunrise, *zhur*, noon, *asr*, mid-afternoon, *maghreb*, sunset, and *isha*, night. To recommit themselves to the body of Islam. For the act of prostration, the knees first, and then the hands. Brow, nose, both hands, both knees, and the underside of all your toes must touch the ground, and the fingers and toes must point towards Mecca. The conformity is an expression of the oneness of Islam. The *umma*.'

'. . . If you'll excuse me, ma'am.'

'You're off on your hike. Daddy doesn't have hikes. Or even walks.'

Her tone, he noted, was softer than it had been. More fond – or at least more proprietorial.

'Daddy takes strolls. No. Daddy takes *turns*.'

'Yes, ma'am,' he said, clutching his gloves, 'I hope to reach Gelding's Mere.'

Brendan headed north from the Greater House. He was surprised, in a way, by the devoutness of his secularism. Because he feared that his love could not survive it – a truly pious Princess. He could imagine his increasingly formal and detached response. He could imagine falling out of it: falling out of love. Love isn't blind, then, he thought. Or mine isn't. And what next, when love was gone? . . . Brendan sought to calm himself by looking at it practically. He didn't care which faith it was she turned to; but the immediate task, for political puposes, would be to steer her off towards (say) Buddhism.

The unbroken cloud was thick and grey and low, like underfelt. And he felt beneath, below, under – under the underfelt.

Hal Nine – he found out what *this* princess wanted.

They were taking a turn, arm in arm, along the trout stream (Henry was a great subliminal believer in the curative power of flowing water). Victoria was in any case much improved – after his epic abjections concerning He Zizhen.

'If I found out what you wanted and gave it to you, how would you change?'

'Well I'd stop all this religious stuff for a start.'

He looked at her eagerly, not because the possible outcome was attractive but because this voice, with its forthright calculation, was the voice he knew.

'Then I must find it out.'

'You won't. And even if you do, you won't do it. Knowing you.'

'Oh, if I find it out I will most certainly do it. Because then you'll have to come back to me.'

In the lull before lunch they took to the low table in the library for a couple of rubbers of Vanishing Whist.

'This is another thing you'll have to give up,' he said. 'No more piggy for breakfast either . . . Oof. Three. No, four. At least.' And he fanned them out, the court cards, the kings and the queens.

'None,' she said.

And abruptly he folded his hand, and slipped from the stool to his knees, and came round to her saying, 'Yes of course. Yes of course, yes of course, my dearest.'

* * *

When Brendan returned, at seven, he heard voices in the dining-room. He knocked and entered. And it seemed to him that they were unusually slow to acknowledge his presence: well, a game – or another game – of Scrabble was about to begin. An empty bottle of champagne stood between them on the table, and there was a cocktail-shaker suspiciously close to the King's brimming glass.

'Aha, the X,' she was saying. 'Which I fully intend to keep.'

'And I've got a Y. Rats. I don't even go first. You'll adore this, Bugger. I mean Brendan.'

'Oh call him Bugger for God's sake.'

'You'll adore this, Bugger.'

'Sir?'

'I can see you going all rosy. Procure for me the Instrument of Abdication, if you will! No. Make that *two* such instruments. One for her and one for me. Yes, Bugger, we're packing it in. A bit feeble, you could say, but there it is. I sent Boy to the Press Centre and Chippy to Number Ten. It's accomplished fact. What this princess wants is to stop being a princess.'

'You needn't absolutely do it, Daddy, if it's too horrible for you.'

'No no. All or nothing. All for love and the world well lost. Look. Look! He's all rosy . . . But no, when you stop to think for a minute, it's about time we all grew up, wouldn't you say? The people will have to grow up. I'll have to grow up. And if I can grow up, *they* can grow up. And then *she* can grow up. Uh! And the boredom. Uh! *Night*mare . . . And you know what's absolutely impossible about the monarchy, Bugger? It's such a . . . Darling, go and find Love and ask him for another one of these. The impossible thing is that it's such a . . .' He held up a hand until his daughter was perhaps a kilometre distant, and said in a fading whisper, 'It's such a . . .'

'Such a what, sir?'

'Such a . . .'

'I'm sorry, sir, such a . . . ?'

'Such a . . .'

Brendan said desperately, 'Such a belly *wink*, sir?'

'*No*, Bugger! Such a bally *wenk*!'

Then her musical laugh in the doorway, and Henry coughing and turning aside.

'And did you reach Gelding's Mere, Brendan?' she asked.

'I did not, Victoria. The mind was willing . . .'

He contemplated Victoria England and formed a rough plan for the rest of his life. She would actually need him more now – and Henry would need him less. He would love, and she would never know. So then: twenty or thirty winters without a kiss, a touch, a considering glance. And this love of his would be a hundred, no, a thousand times more than he deserved.

2. k8

'well, clint, how's trix?' asked k8. 'it's so nice 2 actually c u in the flesh. now u just relax & make yourself completely @ home . . .'

'Little house-present,' said Clint coolly. 'Moisten the piccolo so to speak.'

'how giving u r, clint. & this ruddy gr8 cr8 of goodies! now. u get the top off th@. & i'll b mother.'

His first thought was: Shelley. The undulant frizz of hair, the daunted orbits of the eyes, the sharp lips. She wore a black tanktop T-shirt and a Union Jack miniskirt – but then of course she had already mirthfully warned him about the girth of her thighs.

'How's your father, love?'

'decim8ed. all the way from caecum 2 rectum.'

'It never rains . . . Precipitation, then lovely weather for ducks.'

'bottoms up! here's mud in your i.'

It was around now that Clint started to feel really tragically ill. As they moved from the sink to the armchairs, and as she smoothed down her skirt with her sizable feelers, another gangrenous lunge passed slowly through him.

'1st, the $64,000?, clint: 6. u needn't worry. it'll b a relief 4 u 2 no this: i've never had a . , clint.'

'A what? . . . Period?'

'i've never had a . , clint. that's y i was so tickled th@ u seemed 2 want 2 initi8 a deb8 about children. as if *i* want a br@!'

'And I'm relieved, am I?'

'4 you're not th@ way inclined, r u, clint.'

'Why do you say that?'

'y? in scribendo veritas, yellow dog. it's all in h&, clint. i've been under the nife. but not 2 destroy – 2 cre8! i've got tits & a 21, clint. they do an operation where they w.'

'What did I hear you say to me?'

'They w, clint . . . clint, what r u *thinking*?' said k8. 'i kill it now? i kill it now?'

When he came out into the street (he hadn't touched her: just edged by with his arms shieldingly raised) he found that a grimy white van was doubleparked on the Avenger. 'How Am I Driving?' said its sticker. 'Like A Cunt,' someone had written in the dust. After a lot of parping and yelling and twisting about, Clint mounted the gutter, taking a left from a lamppost and a right from a railing, and ploughed through a hill of black rubbish-bags and on to the street. With his leg stretched straight over the pedal, in a yowl of revs, he shot through Mattock Estate and skidded into Britannia Junction, where he joined the ten-mile traffic jam that would, eventually, deliver him to the Bends and the open road he craved. He kept tearing off up sidestreets, kept buzzing round culs-de-sac like a hornet in a jamjar – like a particle in a cyclotron; then back to the bumper-to-bumper, where he hogged and jockeyed and lane-hopped. Down came the window for many a white-lipped slagging -- the evil eye, the crackling fist; at one point, in hopeless gridlock, he jumped down and briefly chased a young couple on an old scooter – and was of course easily outstripped, the man turning to give the tosser sign with a gauntleted hand. Weeping, twisting, brutally honking, he flanked and tacked through Thamesmead, Hornchurch, Noak Hill.

Then the open road. At this time Clint Smoker weighed four and a half tons. He had a top speed of a hundred and sixty miles per hour. The great blare of his voice (audible for miles), the great blaze of his eyes, tunnelling through the late afternoon. Even his backside carbuncles were now eight inches square.

3. The edge of the earth

There was a little reception committee for him, of course, and Joseph Andrews hadn't travelled alone. His people were unloading the Range Rover that Manfred had hired, and there were two other cars, blocking the road for now, outside the villa in rural Essex, near Gravesend, just where you come off the Bends.

'A fine fucking welcome this is,' he said. 'A fine fucking home-coming.'

Joseph Andrews stood at the gate, half slumped over his Zimmer frame. His eyes were clenched shut and his lower teeth bared, after the long journey.

'I come back to me own country,' he said to no one in particular, 'after twenty-five year. And what's the first thing I see in me *Evening Standard*? Plans for the uh, the fucking renounciation of the monarchy. I reckon they done it to spite me. Got half a mind to . . .' His closed eyes saw a swimming-pool: a motion jigsaw of crimson blood.

'That's down to you, that is, Boss,' said a passing figure. 'Pressures on the Princess.'

'. . . You're due a chinning for that, you are, Manfred Curbishley. And when you least expect it and all. No Scotch for you tonight. Face like a fucking chicken tandoori as it is. Where's Simon? Simon! Hadn't you better be getting along, son? . . . Gaw, now who's *this* doing his fucking nut.'

He thought it was an insect at first, and even reached feebly for his holster – which of course he would not be needing, in England, in February: a buzzing whine, with hysteria in it. Joseph Andrews raised his trembling head; but the eyes wouldn't open.

'Someone – someone go and . . .'

Brisk footsteps clicked past him. He heard the car change gear, down from third to second, then, with insane protest, from second to first; then a sterling cry of 'Halt!'; then a boost, then an atrocious concussion, then a faint *miaow* in the air, then a sound that opened the eyes of Joseph Andrews. It was a sound he had heard once before, in Strangeways, when a prison guard threw himself naked from the tower into the courtyard. An explosion, then something like a flurry of rain.

He threw aside his Zimmer frame and stepped forward. And he thought he had never seen anyone walking towards him as fast as this – walking to the edge of the earth, and intending to get there.

Mal Bale was within (he had been there half the day: turn on the heat and otherwise), coming out of a light nap on the chair in the hall. He heard it. He looked into the kitchen and told Manfred and Rodney to stay inside.

You couldn't see anything from the front path: just the lights of the cars and the garage lantern. Mal kept moving forward. And now other sounds, the squelch, the sob, the squelch, the sob.

There was a pink mist. And his own car, the elderly BM, was lavishly besplattered with flesh and plasma; on the bonnet was a brown brogue shoe with an ankle in it.

To the left, where the noises were coming from, you were blinded by the brights of the black jeep. Mal ducked out of the beam and edged round the garage doors.

Joseph Andrews lay dead on the road. Above him, his assailant, by now with painful weariness, delivered a few last blows with his tool – his spanner, his wrench. Then he threw it aside and seemed to be trying to weep. But he couldn't weep; and Mal saw why.

'Come on, son. You've done him now. It's over. Easy. Easy . . . Christ: *Clint* mate . . . Up. Up you come. We're going to help you now. We're going to help you, help you.'

Mal Bale thought: So that was Jo's last act on earth. With his prehensile right hand. The blinding of Clint Smoker.

4. February 14 (6.27 p.m.): 101 Heavy

Captain John Macmanaman: Come on back. Come on back! . . . Come on back to me. Level up the turn. No no no. Straighten out, straighten out.

System Aircraft Maintenance: Well I'm here, John, with my circular sliderule.

Macmanaman: Take me through it, Betty.

SAM: NEO will be twenty-one point three nine miles from you when it sheers. There'll be fireworks and some heat and you'll feel that instantly. We don't think that'll be important. But there'll be downwinds, John.

Flight Engineer Hal Ward: Well that's it.

SAM: I'm sorry. Now the heat'll come at the speed of light. The wind will come at the speed of sound. So after the flash you'll have one minute . . . nine seconds. Good luck. We're all rooting for you. *Really* rooting for you.

Macmanaman: Thanks, honey.

First Officer Nick Chopko: And here we have our so-called runway, gentlemen. See it?

Macmanaman: Hal?

'Three minutes,' said the voice of Hal Ward, and nothing else. Reynolds knew that John Macmanaman had been in a crash before – as a young man, and as a passenger. He'd told her about it a couple of times. He said it was like a silent movie: no sound at all, and black-and-white. Even the gust of fire was silent and black-and-white. And the dying, those slipping away but also those actually *in flames* had the same expression. One of wonder.

She eased her neck, and searched for better thoughts . . . John said he suddenly became a hundred different *me*s. All around him were wives, husbands, brothers, sisters, mothers, fathers, children. And then, later, the question of survival. It was like winning a squalid lottery, he said . . . Oh I get it, she said to herself. After nearly half a century Royce dies and then, three days later, I die too. Moral: don't marry at seventeen.

The passengers facing the prow were in the *brace* position, bent forward with their hands clasped over their heads. Reynolds, facing aft, sat normally, just hugging her neck, hugging her neck: Captain's orders.

And she knew – stone knew – that if they got through this alive she was going to make him marry her.

There was a yellow flash and she felt sweat form on her upper lip.

Ward: How long?

Macmanaman: Sixteen seconds. And God, right now, it's so *still*.

SAM: This isn't my field, but if the wind comes down, it's got to come back up, right? If you can just stay out there . . .

Macmanaman: Here it comes. Ride it. Ride it.

Ward: . . . Fucking *Christ*, the wing's coming down!

Macmanaman: Wait!

Ward: We're coming down on the wing!

Chopko: I love you, Amy!

There were rescue-and-emergency teams, at a distance, all along the cleared six miles of Interstate 95 – just south of the city of Florence, Florence County, South Carolina.

This is what the people saw and this is what they heard.

They saw the crucifix of Flight 101 coming out of the early afternoon above the red plateau. At first in perfect silence – until they heard the mournful chord of the stricken machine. Then its drunken slides and drifts, and its final circling, chest up, arms outflung: counterclockwise. As it steadied, as it bore down, there came the heavy flash from above, and, within a second, the comet's hair was a silver river from horizon to horizon . . .

The plane was perhaps five hundred feet from the ground when the downwind took it. It seemed to give a roar of pain and rage as it rocked and plunged. The left wing dropped and hit: a streak of sparks along the hard shoulder. Then the updraught: and Flight 101 violently levelled. One scorching ricochet, one hurt, wounded rearing-up with slats and panels flying off it, then touchdown, the resilient gathering of its rigidity, and on it powered beyond the cauldron of its wake.

And the mad hair, the silver tresses, streamed on above their heads, following the comet to Jupiter.

5. Yellow dog

It was six o'clock in London, and Xan was alone in the house with his younger daughter Sophie.

Earlier, as he ate his lunch standing by the fridge in the flat across the road, Russia had called and said (he was going to dinner there anyway), 'Can you come early and have Sophie for an hour?'

'I'd love to. But will she wear it?'

'I think so. Let's try it and see.'

'She's so flash now, Baba. And if she's not having it . . . What came up? Tell me, tell me.'

She talked about Billie's sleepover, Imaculada's night off. Then she said, 'A small man with a sort of Foreign Office accent approached me after my lecture on Tuesday. He told me he had some stuff on the Gaddafi boys and offered to bring it over. I'm meeting him in the Close at half past six. Disgusting name. Semen Something. Disgusting eyes: frothy blue. I'll be back around seven, seven-fifteen. Thanks for this.'

He went over to the house at five o'clock. Sophie looked upon him leniently. At six he poured himself a glass of beer, reminded himself to watch for the comet, and went back to reading the kind of books that featured one word per page.

Relations with the girls were pretty well renormalised. Sophie, now, was occasionally bashful or demure. He was not yet free to pick her up and hold her – she squirmed and simpered, and wouldn't quite collude. But with Billie he was fully reinstated. Once, to dramatise a point brought up by her bedside literature, he made a supposedly frightening face, and, having briefly faltered, Billie said, '*You* can't scare me. You're just my silly old daddy.' He had also done himself a power of good the other day, when Billie, using the arm of a chair, had embarked on what were known, hereabouts, as her exercises, and he had said, with mild vexation, 'Oh Billie' – and turned away (what was it that mildly vexed him: the sense of thwarted energy?). Then he met the eyes of his wife, and their frown of hope.

Xan, too, had hope. He even believed that he would be spending the night with Russia on this day: the day of the martyr Valentine. His wife, with her aerodynamic bone-structure: she used to put her tongue to the side and push, when she wanted a kiss – to draw attention to the cheek but also to make it *nearer*. And she had started doing that again, about twenty-four hours ago. If she asked him to stay, and to stay in her bed, he still wouldn't press his case. And what he was thinking about now, as he said things like 'car' and 'pig' and 'fork', were the nights when your wife sits near you after dinner, reading, motionless, like an artefact, like an Old Master, and all you're aware of is the texture of the paint.

He watched his daughter, crawling, and often getting to her feet and moving from handhold to handhold . . . On a certain level, Xan was aware, he entertained ridiculous expectations of Sophie Meo. She was his fourth child, and his second girl. *I've* got the idea by now, he sometimes found himself thinking. Why hasn't she? Is she really going to cough and shriek and shit everywhere, just like the other three, and fall over all the time, and spend a year saying *you* when she meant *me* ('help you! help you!'), and half a decade asking *why*, *why*, *why*? Well, he was ready for *why*, this time around. Instead of 'because . . .' he'd say 'guess'. Epiphenomenally, he wished that the laws of motion could be redrafted more indulgently with infants in mind, so that the smack of the face on the floor, when the arms failed, would be softer and quieter, and the weeping softer and quieter and also briefer, and the bump shallower-sided and a quieter red. Sophie moved from handhold to handhold.

Xan continued to wonder how much he was going to tell Russia about Cora Susan. In his letter he had promised her some sort of confession, and so he couldn't altogether avoid it. He knew one thing: he'd tell her about it *after*. And not soon after, either. But this confidence, this intimacy, would eventually be expected of him. He felt entitled to blur it slightly. Could you actually say, 'I kissed my niece's breasts'? Shouldn't you contain it – what was essentially a family embarrassment? And conceivably Russia might find out about it anyway, via Pearl. He could say: You have the right to retaliate. But with proportionality. You'll have to get your Uncle Mordecai to . . .

In Russia's eyes, naturally enough, Cora wore the taint of

pornography (and Xan himself had not escaped it, for all his careful editing of the footage from Dolorosa Drive). Russia's objections were mainly aesthetic objections – though not for that reason superficial; and the moral objections she saved for the end: 'She's both pimp and prostitute.' 'True,' he said, 'but there are reasons for that. Think.' 'Okay,' she said – 'but when I think about pornography, all I see is a man with a remote control in one hand and his cock in the other.' Well, yes; and, yes, the obscenification of everyday life was hesitantly entrained. He went on considering it. It could be that women wouldn't mind pornography if reproduction took place by some other means: by sneezing, say, or telepathy. Nobody bothered to object to the gay end of it, supposedly because of the absence of the other: the exploited. But maybe it wasn't that. Maybe women just couldn't bear to see it travestied, the act of love that peopled the world.

He intended to phone Cora – though maybe he should wait a while, he thought, before delivering the avuncular advice he had in mind. This advice was not particularly tasteful, but it was advice he could give her, because consanguinity had rendered him chaste. His erotic thoughts about Cora were now barely a memory. Which showed that the taboo was strong, was efficacious; it worked. He'd say: 'It sounds soft, and trite – but have a baby. When I look at you I always look for your children. That's what your breasts are looking for too: they're looking for your children. So get Burl Rhody to knock you up, and then spend all your money on help.' Or something like that. Xan now wondered, warily, whether Russia would go back to wanting another. He could take another child, he reckoned; and he wouldn't refuse if she insisted. But could he take another pregnancy? Pearl and Russia had not much differed here: pretty wonderful, the first time round; and then, the second time round, the self-righteous sumo wrestler, with her doomy naps behind curtained noons, her looming trudge, and every other breath a sigh from the depths. And mad with power.

His hopes, he realised, his ambitions, were gaining in strength and complacency and even . . . Yes, he was back – back in his life. And what did it look like now, through these quietly different eyes? Good. But he was also back in the thing which is called world. Two days earlier he had gone to collect Billie from school. The playground, as he approached it, was making the sound that playgrounds make: that of unserious panic. And he thought – what if that panic were not unserious? How precious it all is and how fragile it all is. The bare trees above his head were furred with snow. Their claws had become paws. But the snow would soon melt.

But I go to Hollywood but you go to . . .

Sophie passed by. She steadied herself with a hand on his knee. The dimples at the base of each finger looked like pluses and minuses. The plus and minus signs of babies. She would soon be walking – the faulty wiring and the hairtrigger readjustments, the involuntary three-yard sprints, the upward-shooting arms.

He made a call on the house line, and reached Pearl, who treated him gently (persisting in some obscure cycle of penitence), and gave him a boy. As he hung up, his mobile phone sounded in his jacket.

'Hello?'

'Xan? Mal Bale. He's dead.'

'Who is?'

'Joseph Andrews.'

'How?'

'Road accident. And another old bastard copped it and all. Simon Finger. *Smashed* to pieces he was. All over me BM. Thought you'd like to know. You all right?'

'Yeah mate . . .'

He hung up and sat still for a moment and closed his eyes.

He closed his eyes and saw the yellow dog.

Into the yard Xan had come, and heard a sound seemingly designed for his unease. The sound had a rhythm, like a murderous act of love: a grunt, then a muffled, slushy impact or convergence, then an answering moan. And over and above it the crying, the choric wail of the yellow dog. He moved past the stake where the animal was chained.

The yard – with its stacks of planks, its sinks and toilet bowls, its black entanglement of tyres – was the place where his sentimental understanding had so far been formed. He had trailed his sister Leda when she took her boyfriends there on summer nights, and watched her on her knees behind the disused cement-mixer, or up against the wheelless van with her skirt round her waist. The sometimes pouting, sometimes snarling pinups and calendar-girls tacked or gummed to the workshop wall; the dogs (earlier dogs) stoically stuck together in coition and awaiting the deliverance of the bucket; and – even further back – the hectic hen coming running to the screeching cock.

He tipped open the shed door and saw his father seated on another man's chest, straddling the flattened shoulders with his knees: Mick Meo over Joseph Andrews. How he kept raising his bleeding fist and letting it drop with a grunted *oom*, the wet slap of the blow, and the countering retch from beneath. And how weary it was, how sick and tired. For this, that. For that, this. 'Hey *Dad*,' he had said, coming forward to rush and quell. And how the man's greased and distorted face had filled with fresh fury as he rose up to envelop his boy.

While it happened (and he didn't remember much: at one point he was in mid-air, and taking an intense interest in the nature and texture of his destination) you could hear the yellow dog. Whining, weeping, and rolling its head as if to ease an aching neck, working its shoulders, trying to free itself of this thing – this thing on its back.

6. When they were small

Just after seven he opened the door to the garden and watched the comet with the child in his arms. 'Yook!' she said, pointing, but pointing as infants do: the bisection-point of thumb and fore-finger was the direction intended. The comet bustled east across the sky – a white light – with futile industry, like a terrible old man on a terrible old errand. Mustn't stop, mustn't stop. And utterly committed, suicidally committed, to Jupiter and its gravity. He imagined for a moment that he could hear it: a weak hiss of execration. Then came the affronted honk of a car in the street, and another honk sounding in defiant response, and he shook his head and smiled, returning to the small and the local concerns.

He was fetching some water for Sophie when he saw his wife coming past the front of the house. She was slightly hunched over, with an air of conscious remissness – as if, having been out too long, she was now stealing back, but confident of exoneration, and of frictionless readmittance. He heard her enter upstairs; he heard her throw her keys on to the hall table, and give the indignantly aspirated hoot she gave when something or other, in the exterior world, just hadn't worked out. 'Down in a minute,' she called. And he heard her running up the stairs; and, after a while, the clatter of the shower on the tub floor.

He turned. And there was someone else in the room: a new kind of person. Sophie was standing beside the heap of toys, not walking, just standing, unsupported – unconnected except by her feet to the floor. She was delighted, but she was delighted about something else (the scrap of paper in her hand), and didn't yet see that she had changed.

Xan moved forwards, saying, 'Baba, you're –'

It came to her. She was up: now how to get down? Her arms sprang skyward, her legs dipped at the knee – and she flipped herself backwards into the rubble of the building-blocks and Sticklebricks . . . When he reached for her she took his whole arm in both of hers, and when he hoisted her up he felt her hot wet snorting in his ear – but it wasn't serious, wasn't serious, wasn't serious at all.

As, nevertheless, he sat comforting her on the sofa, he looked at the lashes of her eyes, their tear-freshened zigzag – and he remembered her birth, and the zigzag, the frantic scribble of the heart-monitor as Sophie toiled within. He was already crying when she came (as he had cried when the boys came): not because of what they faced but because of what they had already suffered, all alone and at their very smallest. And minutes later, when Sophie came, for the first time in his life he was contemplating the human vulva with a sanity that knew no blindspots . . . She slipped away from him now and started moving round the room, from handhold to handhold. And he thought, with numb tautology: in this project of their protection, the hopelessly painful thing, when they were small, was their size, their small size, their very small size.

This is a work of unalloyed fiction, but several of the areas it touches on involved me in some light research. The following books proved especially helpful, and I should like to thank their authors (and/or editors).

Robert Lacey's *Royal* (Little, Brown) and Alison Weir's *Henry VIII: King and Court* (Jonathan Cape).

Tony Parker's *Life After Life* (Secker & Warburg) and the 'Mad Frank' Trilogy by Frankie Fraser (as told to James Morton) – *Mad Frank* (Little, Brown), *Mad Frank and Friends* (Little, Brown) and *Mad Frank's Diary* (Virgin).

Andrew Weir's *The Tombstone Imperative: The Truth About Air Safety* (Simon & Schuster) and *The Black Box*, edited by Malcolm MacPherson (HarperCollins).

Judith Lewis Herman's *Father–Daughter Incest* (Harvard University Press) and *Head Injury: The Facts* by Dorothy Gronwall, Philip Wrightson and Peter Waddel (Oxford University Press).